STORMING FREEDOM:
Thunder Strike

Konrad Karl Gatien &
Sreescanda

IRP NOVELS
u.s.a.

For information, contact: irpnovels@gmail.com

2015 EDITION PUBLISHED BY IRPNovels (USA)

ISBN 978-0-9838188-7-8   EAN 978-0-983818878
FICTION
1st Edition/1st Printing

w w w . i r p n o v e l s . c o m

Library of Congress Cataloging-in-Publication Data

Gatien, Konrad Karl & Sreescanda
Storming Freedom: Thunder Strike: a novel / Konrad Karl Gatien & Sreescanda.
Summary: "Two rival families who have masterminded every Presidency in US history are
locked in their greatest struggle yet over control of the most devastating WMD."
ISBN 978-0-9838188-7-8

1. Crime--Mystery--Fiction. 2. Crime--Police Procedural--Fiction.
3. Crime--Thriller--Fiction. Konrad Gatien & Sreescanda. II. Title.

For my father,
Who is always storming through life

Konrad

PROLOGUE

"I will not negotiate with a gun to my head," declared President Avery Walker, the first bachelor to occupy the Oval Office since James Buchanan.

He was reacting angrily to the stunning and rapid developments that began before dawn this morning when a KH-15, the world's most sophisticated electronic intelligence gathering satellite, made its routine pass over Cuba. Digital imaging sensors clicked off pictures that were relayed to a Tracking and Data Relay Satellite, one of a three-satellite constellation interlinking all American military reconnaissance in the sky. The TDRS transmitted to the Defense Communications Electronics Evaluation and Testing Activity Center at Fort Belvoir, Virginia, twenty miles south of Washington DC. The signal was recreated into a photograph and directed to Building No. 213 in the Washington Navy Yard on the corner of First and M Streets, otherwise known as the National Photographic Interpretation Center.

This whole process took mere seconds.

The NPIC was a windowless building eight blocks from Capitol Hill. Here, photo interpreters in front of computer terminals conducted Threat Analysis. The interpreter at the Cuba Station, a fifteen-year veteran, instantly recognized the sixty-foot long canisters being unloaded from a huge barge. He used to be at the North Korea and Iran stations. He knew the protocol. He summoned his supervisor, who confirmed his observation.

Shock waves rippled through the NPIC.

The supervisor immediately limited TALENT-KEYHOLE clearances, which referred to access to the KH-15 photographs. BYEMAN clearances, or operational information of the satellite, were withdrawn. All data gathered over Cuba came to be designated TOP SECRET NO FOREIGN. From here on out, only a handful of personnel would be privy to the surveillance pictures from Cuba. The supervisor returned to his office and placed a person-to-person call to the CIA, triggering a chain reaction that ended at the director's home fifteen minutes later.

He had been going through his morning ritual. Eating breakfast. Reading the stack of overnight intelligence reports for the president's daily National Security briefing at nine A.M. None even remotely hinted at this shocker from Cuba. The CIA director immediately called a teleconference of COMIREX, the Committee on Overhead Imagery Requirements and Exploitations. Participating were Defense Secretary Baron Hawke, Chairman of the Joint Chiefs of Staff, Jack Knight, the National Security Advisor, Secretary of State, Director of the Treasury, and nonvoting representatives from the Air Force, Army, and Navy intelligence services. The elaborate bureaucracy prevented a single agency from controlling spy satellites.

They unanimously approved to return a KH-15 over Cuba.

The decision went out to the National Reconnaissance Office in North Carolina. For decades, the NRO had been so secret, its existence was only acknowledged after a bureaucratic snafu in 1993. The NRO ordered the Satellite Test Center at Sunnyvale, California, also known as the Big Blue Cube for its architecture, which housed the Satellite Control Facility, the master control for all US military satellites, to adjust the orbit of the nearest KH-15 to make a return pass over Cuba.

Three hours after the initial discovery, a new set of photographs arrived at the White House for the start of the National Security briefing in the Oval Office. President Avery Walker listened grimly, then read the report himself, and ordered a secret meeting of a crisis team of top aides and advisors called the Executive Committee for National Security, or EXCOMM. They convened in PEOC, the President's Emergency Operations Center, a bunker below the East Wing of the White House.

The press could *not* know, not just yet. So the EXCOMM arrived via the underground tunnel between the Treasury Building and White House that John F. Kennedy used in 1962 to conceal the seriousness of Cuban missile crisis from the public. It would be the first of several parallels to those thirteen days in October, 1960, some coincidental, many calculated and deliberate.

"Gentlemen," President Avery Walker continued, "intelligence on the ground has confirmed that Juan Castro has purchased three nuclear warheads." The EXCOMM had suspected a nuclear crisis when they were told of the location of the meeting. The president's Emergency Operations Center was reserved to discuss nuclear crises.

Juan Castro, the son of Fidel's brother and successor, Raul, turned out to be more like his uncle than his father, who forged a historic truce with the US and restored diplomatic ties. Then Raul Castro was diagnosed with the same cancer that killed Fidel. Juan, a die-hard socialist like Fidel, took over and called Russia a more reliable friend. He started turning the clock back. So did the US, secretly funding pro-democracy insurgents to initiate a countdown for nationwide unrest within hours of his father's death. But Raul survived for more than a year, during which time, Juan unleashed death squads, methodically wiping out the opposition, and when Raul died, he reinstated Fidel's authoritarian Communist model. US led sanctions returned. Cuba's economy tanked. But Juan was firmly in power.

Intelligence in coming days would reveal that, in exchange for using Cuba as a conduit for cocaine, Juan Castro got the Medellin drug cartel to use their elaborate global network to purchase and smuggle in the nuclear warheads from the East European black market.

"Can he deliver the nukes?" asked the Secretary of State, halfway down the horseshoe-shaped table.

"He has a dozen SS-19 rockets," replied Baron Hawke, the 55-year old Defense Secretary, whose appearance and demeanor left no room for doubt that he was a militarist through and through. It was no accident he sat where the table curved, to the immediate right of the president. Avery valued Baron's opinion and advice more than anyone in his administration.

"What's their reach?" asked someone else.

"The entire eastern seaboard, and under ideal conditions, Washington." SS-19s were solid fuel intercontinental ballistic missiles that used to be a staple of the former Soviet Union. Old, outdated technology, but just adequate to be dangerous.

"He does not intend to use them," said Avery. "Cuba needs money desperately. Like North Korea, he wants to coerce billions out of us to disarm. I'm not going to stuff the pockets of another dictator. But we cannot let him keep the nukes either. Let's meet again tonight in the Situation Room with pre-emptive options."

Avery received hourly updates, each deepening the crisis another notch. Low cloud cover and hostile atmospheric conditions over Cuba blurred subsequent images for the next four hours. Sure enough, when the weather cleared, the warheads were gone. Avery realized, without being told, it could take weeks or months for intelligence on the ground to develop leads, if at all, to their whereabouts. The EXCOMM returned later that night. A pall of tension hung over the recently renovated, futuristic looking Situation Room located in the basement of the West Wing.

General Jack Powers, Chairman of the Joint Chiefs of Staff, a brilliant thirty-year Army veteran who had risen through the ranks as a Ranger, opened the proceedings. Occupying the chair to the left of the president, Jack outlined a strategy of a massive outward show of force beginning with a naval blockade. This overwhelming buildup would give Juan the world stage he sought for a lucrative diplomatic solution.

"Repeating JFK's maneuvers," explained Jack, "will also draw intense media play."

There were scattered nods. The vice president, a lightweight added to the ticket for geographic reasons, listened in from a secure missile silo outside Lincoln, Nebraska.

Treetop, the Succession Plan laid out by Congress, mandated that he could not be in the same city as Avery for the duration of this crisis.

"Meanwhile," Jack continued, "we unleash an option that can never be traced back to us, one that will not only disarm Cuba, but fulfill an objective US presidents have wanted for five decades." Everyone at the table knew what it was but never believed it would ever happen. Jack's lips twitched to one side in a humorless smile, "Erase the name of Castro forever."

"And finally end communism in our backyard," said Baron, paused, and added what every president loved to hear even more, "without a single American casualty."

"I love the JFK parallels," said Avery. "It will keep the media preoccupied. But Americans don't have the appetite for conflict. No troops. No blockade. Nothing that even remotely suggests that we are getting into a war, with or without boots on the ground." Ever since the ill-advised invasion of Iraq and the interminable quagmire that Afghanistan had become, Avery was yet another president forced to continue the presence of several thousand troops in both regions. Complete withdrawal was unlikely. Ever.

Avery noticed Baron and Jack exchange a quick look. The defense secretary took over. "No problem. This option can succeed with minimal Special Ops support, mostly for mop up work."

Avery tilted his head. "What kind of option is this?"

He trusted Baron. Avery owed his resurrection in the polls during his White House bid to the defense secretary, whose family was as old as the American Presidency. Zachariah Hawke, the patriarch who'd started it all, had fought beside George Washington. Every generation of Hawke since had served one or more presidents at the highest level. Yet, they carried no name recognition with the general population. Avery had asked Baron the reason. "Because," the defense secretary replied modestly, "it was decreed from father to son we should never be overt with our wealth and power." Even though no one in the family had worn a uniform after Zachariah, the president, upon taking office, learned that the highest echelons and innermost sanctums of Washington regarded the Hawkes as the First Family of the Military.

Baron did not answer the question, surveying the horseshoe instead. "Nobody in this room can ever speak of this option because its success is tied to absolute secrecy."

Once he received nods of assurance from every man and woman sitting around the horse-shoe, Baron nodded for Jack to speak. The JCS Chairman went on to outline the option. Nobody in the Situation Room was familiar with it. Pin drop silence ensued for several seconds after Jack finished. Palpable electricity gripped the room. Avery observed a gamut of emotions—pride, disbelief, shock, awe, concern, suspicion, confidence. He himself was astonished.

"I didn't know this even existed," Avery frowned.

"Neither did any president before you, sir," revealed Baron. "It was developed as a DPB."

There were Black Programs, which a handful of need-to-know politicians, including the White House, knew. Then there were DPBs—Deep Black Programs, so strictly confidential, they never left the Pentagon. This option was even more narrowly need-to-know. Later, when they were alone in the Oval Office, Baron briefed Avery further. Three people knew *all* the details, the defense secretary revealed. A remarkable achievement, thought Avery, considering it had taken more than three decades to develop.

It carried a potent code name.

Thunder Strike.

TODAY

Liz ate alone at a sidewalk café in Manhattan. She looked and felt miserable. It had been a tough morning at the office that began badly from the moment she walked in and just got worse. She had never looked forward to getting away for lunch as much as she did today, even though few people wanted to venture out of the air-conditioned comfort of their offices. Hot and humid, New York sweltered in late October like Florida in mid-August. So, there were a lot of vacant tables. The National Weather Service warned there might be no fall. Anything was possible this year, considering that, just a week ago, Hurricane Meg had done the unthinkable. Threaded up the Potomac all the way to Washington DC.

"Liz?"

She looked up and around from her Chinese chicken salad to find her lips being kissed by Billy Madden, one of those lawyers who looked the part. He pulled back with a broad smile.

"Billy." Liz kept a reserved tone, as if holding a grudge. She was.

He drew the other chair out and sat down. Billy had the sharp, angular features of a male model. His full head of black hair met a hairdresser every other week, so he never looked freshly cropped. His eyes were cobalt blue, perfect to hold a jury's attention in a courtroom, soften in sympathy, and harden with accusation. A hunk by any standard, he could've been a hit on a runway had he not chosen a career in the US Justice Department.

"First day back?" he asked cheerfully.

He didn't fool Liz. His lips trembled nervously at the corners. Guilt screamed out through the forced nonchalance. She nodded and didn't say a word. She didn't have to.

"It'll get better," Billy added, reaching for her hand. Liz clenched it into a fist to elude his touch. He awkwardly turned his gesture into a wave for the waiter, then met her hostile stare evenly. "Liz, I'm sorry. I should have been there for you. But I'd just joined Justice and—"

"When shit hits the fan in Washington, ducking isn't reflex, it's the law." Her cool manner turned outright cold and she added bitterly, "No apologies necessary, Billy."

Their young waiter approached. Liz was a keen observer. She could pick up the subtlest clues—a muscle twitch, a nervous fidget, a crack in the voice, any physical symptom—without even trying. It came naturally and unconsciously. A gift she'd discovered early and used deftly to get her way. She knew the young waiter was gay when he'd led her to her table and now his polite cough was hesitant, like he did not want to interrupt. The tension between Billy and her was apparent. She did not miss the waiter's eyes slide briefly to her fingers. He was checking for a ring. Liz could almost hear the queen in him gleefully click off the possibilities. *So, they aren't married. They must've been an item, maybe briefly, definitely intimate, and then maybe the guy bailed on her. But why? It definitely could not have been her looks.*

She was gorgeous. Every man's head had turned when he'd escorted her to the table. Liz was used to it, even enjoyed it, casually flipping her shoulder length hair as she sat down. While the humidity and heat had other women going loose, her sleeveless blouse was deliberately snug to show off her perfect breasts, and those tight jeans were no accident. She had legs to die for and a bubble for an ass.

"The half and half special, please," Billy perused the menu and looked up, completely oblivious and unaware of these micro-dynamics in play. "Caesar salad and turkey sandwich."

"Anything to drink?" asked the waiter.

"Just water." The waiter left.

"You're not here by accident, are you?" said Liz.

"I followed you," admitted Billy.

Liz showed no surprise. The temperature between them dropped another degree. "So you waited before walking over? Why? Did you want to be sure there was nobody here who might recognize you?"

"It's not that at all, Liz. I know apologies mean nothing. I don't blame you for hating me. I wasn't there for you. I was a selfish coward. Believe me, I've been waiting six months for this moment to make it up to you. I tried to visit but they said you were not seeing anyone."

"Why are you here, Billy?" asked Liz curtly.

He leaned forward and lowered his voice. "I got a call this morning. It was almost as if I was being watched. Get this, I walk in. Barely sit down at my desk. The direct line rings. It was a man. He didn't give his name. He knew about us, I mean, he knew I was the one who helped you from the inside. You didn't tell anyone, did you?"

Liz looked offended, "I'm a reporter. I would never reveal my source."

"What about rehab?"

"I didn't tell *anyone.*" Her tone hardened, that short temper flaring.

"Doesn't matter. He knows anyway. He also knew that you were getting back today."

"Maybe *you* bragged to a friend," accused Liz right back.

Billy let it pass. "He'd done his homework. Or he's gotta be with the Feds, or so high up in the White House he must have clearance to classified files, including your rehab."

Liz's eyes went still.

"Yeah." Billy nodded anxiously, "like I said, he knew *everything.*"

"Who doesn't?" Liz shrugged to hide a nervous chill. She'd always known that retribution was a possibility for what she had done but didn't anticipate it would come so soon. "My career's been dissected like a public autopsy."

"He asked me to sound you out."

"For?"

"A bombshell."

Liz reacted sharply. Surprised.

"His words. Not mine," added Billy.

"Shit, tell him yes."

"I already did," grinned Billy, his confidence rising, and slid a piece of paper across the table. "He told me to give you this."

Liz read it. "Admiral Calvin Grant."

Underneath, a phone number and two words: *Thunder Strike.*

"Grant's expecting your call."

As quickly as her enthusiasm leapt, it faded. "Wait, what am I thinking?" Liz pushed the paper back. "I can't do this."

"Why not?" He pushed it back. "Digging is what you do best."

"Yeah, I dug a hole so deep, they buried me in it. *Weekend Leisure.* That's where Tim has me now." *Weekend Leisure* was the afterthought section in the Sunday edition of the *Post.* A rookie's first assignment or a veteran's final stop before oblivion. "And I'm on a deadline to find cruises for under five hundred dollars. It's bullshit."

"You fall off the horse, you get back on. That's how the game is played."

"Failure is not being down, it's staying there. Save the fortune cookie psychology. I got it all in rehab."

Rehab. Harsh memories of her just completed recovery came flooding back, the high walls, locked gates, and barred windows. Jailhouse rules applied 24/7. There were random checks. The nurses could have been guards in a maximum security prison. Her quick temper flared again. A red blush rose to her cheeks as she thought back to the circumstances that led to it all. That was bullshit too.

Liz caught Billy's stare and her manner turned conciliatory. "I'm sorry. It was just hard."

This time, she reached across and closed her hand over his. Her entire manner softened. She used her most striking feature. Her eyes. Foxy light. Altering them from a granite glint to pure silk with literally a single blink. People always forgot that she was unfriendly just a moment ago. The hostility evaporated.

She drowned Billy in her husky voice, "Here you are again, saving me."

"No." He put the piece of paper in her hand and closed her fingers around it. "Starting over."

Liz smiled back. "I've thought about nothing else."

She tilted her head slightly. Billy moved forward a fraction, then hesitated. She let him think for a moment he'd misread her. Then she relented and grabbed his tie and kissed him long and deep. A shadow swept over them. The waiter arrived with their order.

Liz released Billy. Out of the corner of her eyes, she sensed envy in every other guy at lunch. The waiter put down Billy's order. Liz smiled up at him. Just as he turned away, he blinked. She realized he'd placed her. *Shit,* his expression screamed as his eyes softened toward Billy and hardened toward her, all in successive beats.

The doorbell rang. Two longs, two shorts, two longs, two shorts. Billy.

Liz looked at herself in the mirror. She'd settled on a one-piece white dress that clung like a second skin. Liz was temporarily living in her parents' plush brownstone overlooking the harbor. They came up from Detroit often enough to own a place here. Hurricane Meg had wreaked spectacular tragedy upon Washington DC, completely disabling the capital and forcing Congress to evacuate and operate out of New York. That's why Liz rejoined the *Post* at its Manhattan headquarters.

She opened the door. Billy cradled flowers and wine. His smile couldn't be wider. She knew what she wanted from Billy tonight.

"Don't say a word," Liz said, pulled him in, shut the door, and slammed him back against it. Her mouth crushed his, her tongue coiled in, and her hand went directly to his crotch. She whispered she hadn't been with a man in a year to keep him flattered. He hiked her skirt. She wore nothing underneath. He lifted her off the ground. Her legs wrapped around his hips, they plunged into the couch.

Liz was born Elizabeth Katherine Lovell, the only child of Kenneth Lovell, Detroit's top criminal lawyer, and Dr. Elise Lovell, the longest serving pro bono chairman of the Peace Corps Medics, who had led that organization by example to a Nobel Peace Prize. Liz struck DNA gold, inheriting her mother's good looks and father's Machiavellian smarts. She easily won Miss Teen Motor City when she turned sixteen with her perfect '10' body, naturally pouting lips, and curly golden locks. Liz enjoyed playing those who mistook her for another dumb blonde. Few suspected behind that stunning beauty were her father's brains. Then, they all usually cried foul, like in her junior year at Ann Arbor.

Controversy erupted when she won the University of Michigan, School of Journalism's coveted summer internship at the *Daily Post* in New York. Since she was never in the top percentile of her class, fellow students alleged she had more than just submitted a résumé to the faculty member making the decision. She had long ago accepted her looks came with baggage, thanks to her father's public image of questionable scruples. Actually, he was simply a brilliant lawyer. He loved the challenge of taking on known mobsters, murderers, and corporate criminals as clients and winning. Liz never understood why no one would assume she took after her mother, who enjoyed the diametric opposite reputation. Elise's work was the stuff of saints. Anyway, nothing came of the charges and Liz's internship with the *Post* stood.

The Managing Editor of the newspaper with the nation's

largest circulation and online readership was Tim O'Flaherty, a cigar chomping, voluble, arrogant, Irish Catholic divorcé. A throwback newspaperman whose caustic remarks and angry outbursts were legendary. But he also understood that social media was here to stay and Tweets trumped print.

For the final three days of her internship, Liz was assigned to Tim's office. On her last day, Tim asked her out to dinner. Liz had been aware of his glances all day long. After dinner, they returned to his resplendent Connecticut house.

Tim was a kinky old bastard.

At breakfast, the next day, he admitted he played favorites with his reporters, and added that he had a feeling about Liz. He offered to hire her after she graduated. During the previous weeks of her internship, she'd heard about his 'star system.' Tim put his favorite reporters on a fast track. Liz started out in Arts and Entertainment. Within a month, she became bored doing fluff. During a particularly rousing hour of S&M, she asked Tim to assign her to Washington, where, under Tim, *PostOnline* became known for digging up dirt on politicians and airing their dirty laundry.

Liz knew he was no fool. She was beautiful, ambitious, and cutthroat. Perfect for Washington. She was willing to parlay her looks and night life on all the social media platforms. Liz quickly became active in all the right DC circles.The new assignment brought her in touch with the aides and adjuncts of Congressmen and Senators. She was soon posting anonymous exclusives, all written with a salacious pen, and became the most watched online reporter. Her almost instant success ruffled a lot of conventional feathers back in the newsroom.

At a Friday night shindig of young Washington hotshots, she met Billy Madden, a twenty-seven year old, dashing, rookie attorney in the Justice Department. She'd discovered early on that guys, however good looking, were thrilled when Liz went out with them. After a night with her, they usually did anything to keep her. Billy leaked to her that the DOJ was quietly investigating Alabama Senator Jarvis Johnson, who was being groomed by the Republicans to run for president the next time around. She soon knew this story could launch her career. She paid Tim a weekend visit at his Connecticut home. They had dinner and their usual round of unusual sex.

"What do you want?" he bluntly asked, recognizing Liz did nothing without a motive.

Liz told him about the Senator. The story was full of gray areas. A winner. But Liz was here for more, and Tim knew how much more even before she asked him. She wanted to run with it alone. It was unthinkable, even risky, for a rookie not to have a senior reporter share the by-line. It ensured ambition and youth did not color the truth and exaggerate facts. But Tim enjoyed making the newsroom a briar patch of jealousy.

Liz was just twenty-four and Tim already treated her like a first among equals, making the older stars insecure. Nobody suspected Liz was anything more than Tim's new favorite. Everyone knew about his brief affairs with younger women, but they also knew he would never cross the line with a staff reporter. That would be unethical even at a rag like the *Post*, which thrived on scandal. Few realized, in Liz, Tim saw a younger, more ruthless version of himself.

He agreed to let her fly solo.

It took four months, which included threats on Liz's life, to uncover the truth: Jarvis Johnson, a scholar of the Crusades, was arming white supremacists and dispatching them to the Middle East in a reverse campaign of terror against Islamic fundamentalists.

Her exposé divided the country. Half the nation did not view Jarvis, a Southern, deeply Christian gentleman, born and raised in Tuscaloosa, Alabama, as a villain. A twenty-four year veteran of the Senate, he'd been elected with ninety percent of the vote for four consecutive terms. At fifty-nine, the ultra-conservative was respected on both sides of the aisle as a straight shooting, funny maverick. His allegiance to his constituents superseded party loyalty, yet the Republicans wanted him to run for president in a couple of years. National polls showed he could take the White House. The story turned into a national debate. *Are the 'rules of engagement' different in the war on terror? But can 'the end justify the means?' Isn't Jarvis Johnson just 'fighting fire with fire?'* Regardless, it killed his bid for the Presidency before it started.

Liz won a Pulitzer, the first ever for a tabloid. More importantly, it legitimized the shifting trend in journalism. From print to blogs, truth to innuendo, new to entertainment. Tim got as much press as Liz. She silenced her detractors in the *Post*.

The thing about success was remaining successful. Instead, she fulfilled the adage, 'there was nowhere else to go but down,' with a stunning professional and personal freefall that was as meteoric as her rise into a household name. It took her mother's influence and father's negotiating skills to keep her out of jail and save her job.

A part of her life she did not care to revisit.

Liz turned her thoughts to Billy. Her legs tightened around his hips. She grabbed his hair and dug her nails deeply into his back as their breath quickened into each other's ears. Her feelings for Billy were ambiguous. Unresolved. He was cute, sweet, and totally devoted to her. Even now, he was waiting for her. She arched violently for a final time. He pressed into her. She held him tight, enjoying the warmth of their sex carry all the way up her spine. She let out a luxurious moan.

"Liz, I missed you so much," Billy panted into her ear. His lips crushed hers and their tongues wrestled again.

If she could look past his betrayal, he could be the friend and anchor her counselors said she would need during these early months out of rehab. She'd been careful to play by the book. Be a model patient. Even the shrink she was seeing now as part of her mandatory post-rehab program gave her high marks. Little did they know, beneath the outward contrition, she still harbored a ton of unresolved anger and vendetta. Bitterness rose like bile to her throat when she recalled, a year ago to the day, Tim had led the torchbearers, and she'd known he would make her return to work today miserable.

He did.

She had been a wreck this morning. She hadn't slept all week leading up to her first day back. When she walked into the newsroom, it was as hard as she'd imagined it would be. Silence unrolled in front of her like a carpet, then whispers erupted in her wake. The staff tried to look normal, but the veterans did not hide their displeasure. A couple of lightweight reporters were civil and waved, "Hey, you're back." Thankfully, she enjoyed a cubicle and descended into the semi-privacy the low partitions offered. The hardest part was yet to come.

Her nine A.M. meeting with Tim.

It was their first contact since that noon appearance eight months ago before the *Post*'s board during which he'd sat without saying a word. So many times she'd been tempted to wipe his smug aloofness with revelations that could have cost him his job and his reputation. But then her career would be finished along with his.

Liz had waited until the clock began to strike the hour before she took a deep breath, knocked, and entered. Tim's office reflected the man. An ardent student of history with a photographic memory for random facts, it looked like an untidy trivia museum. Original newspapers dating back to the Civil War were piled in front of an early *Believe It or Not* poster signed by Ripley himself. The bookshelf was a mess of autographed first editions. His awards collected dust, stacked three deep on the floor as if he didn't give a shit, like he was above, beyond, and past honors and accolades. Liz stood inside the door for a several seconds. She knew he was pretending to proof some news copy in a power move that was so typical of him.

"You will be randomly tested," he started speaking

suddenly without looking up or even a 'hello.' "If you're not clean, it's grounds for dismissal. I'm reassigning you to *Weekend Leisure*. Every story you write, even if it's a getaway for poodles, will be checked by someone else."

"Is that all?" That quick temper.

Hearing it, Tim's eyes flashed up. "Be careful, Liz, be very careful. This isn't a second chance. It's your last."

Now, almost twelve hours later, she still had to catch herself from reaching boil again. She would need Tim on her side if Billy's 'bombshell' panned out. So much had unfolded while she was in rehab. Cuba had brought a nuclear threat to America's back door. Hurricane Meg crashed into DC. Every day since, a new story was breaking. About Cuba, about Meg's apocalyptic aftermath. There were as many plot lines as journalists in Washington. Yet, she was banned from writing even one, let alone return to DC.

"What's the matter?" asked Billy, drawing Liz out of her thoughts.

"Nothing," she said quickly. There was that anger again. Her short fuse. The one thing she could not keep hidden from her counselors. She'd always been a hothead. By-product of a privileged childhood, her shrink said.

"You just went distant," he said, tilting his head.

"No, I didn't," she said and kissed him in a way that made him dismiss the notion.

They swiveled positions. She straddled him. He squeezed a breast. She leaned forward, rocking again. He plucked at a nipple with his teeth. *Am I ready to forgive him?* He had deserted her too, though he may have redeemed himself with the promise of a story that could get her back on track. Billy would never know that she had started to consider him 'relationship' material when everything had gone to hell in a hand basket. But now…now, she'd never trust him or another guy.

Never. Never again.

"Did you call Admiral Grant?" Billy asked as they sat down to eat dinner.

Liz was a fabulous cook. Another thing about her that was all her own because her parents raised her on take-out. Liz discovered she was a regular Martha Stewart from the first time she'd opened *The Joy of Cooking* for Home Ed in high school. Tonight, since she'd been working all day, she didn't have time to do much. Spinach salad with dressing out of a bottle, chicken potpie that Billy never suspected came out of a box too, thanks to enough of her own concoction of herbs and spices, and dessert, a lemon tart pie off a store shelf disguised under her homemade tangy raspberry sauce.

"Yeah." Liz had dialed the moment they'd separated after lunch.

Grant had answered himself. When she told him her name, he repeated it with a tinge of disbelief after a moment of silence, "Liz Lovell?"

"It's about Thunder Strike," she said. "I was told you'd be expecting my call."

Another beat of silence. He may have been expecting *a* call but not *her* call. Still, he agreed to see her tomorrow night.

"I wanted to start digging but couldn't log on in the office," Liz chattered. "The *Post* monitors my computer. They can, according to the fine print in my reinstatement deal." She smirked and added, "To make sure my ambition did not lead me astray again." She had to wait until she got home. "There wasn't much on him," Liz carried on excitedly. "So I got out my phone and started calling. I still have some friends left in DC." She didn't tell Billy they were all male, all deliberate one-night-stands she knew would come in handy for something like this. "The first four calls went unanswered. That's when the reality of Hurricane Meg's destruction hit home. Like, shit, you know, they could be dead." Billy nodded seriously but she was onto the next thing. "I did get a hold of an aide on the House Defense Subcommittee. He said he helped clean out the West Wing and sat out the storm with the president in the Situation Room. He didn't have much to offer, but confirmed what I already knew. Grant and the president are close friends."

"Aren't you going to ask me how I survived the hurricane?" asked Billy.

"Oh, I'm sorry," apologized Liz and reached out and squeezed his hand.

"I was lucky. I was out of Washington at a conference. I've been hearing crazy numbers, like Meg took out most of Justice, including the AG." Attorney General.

After the last glass of wine, the fleeting touches across the table, brushing knees underneath, soft voices, and coy glances inevitably sizzled into round three. They didn't bother clearing the table and tumbled into the bedroom. When they fell back, they were bathed in sweat from the heat and furious intensity. They could hardly speak.

"I wasn't lying, Liz. I really missed you," Billy said breathlessly, kissing her deeply. Full of tender afterglow.

Liz propped herself up against the pillows and let him kiss his way down past her flat six-pack stomach, thanks to two-a-day workouts in rehab. He got to where he was going and slung a perfectly smooth leg over his shoulder. Liz barely noticed his tongue flicking in and out of her.

"What do you think it's all about?" she asked.

"What is?" asked Billy, without lifting his head.

Liz worked her fingers in his hair but her mind was elsewhere. "Thunder Strike."

The name had yielded no hits. The aide had drawn a blank on the name too.

"Patience," urged Billy. "You'll find out when you see Admiral Grant."

"The guy, did he actually use the word bombshell?" asked Liz, assuming it was Grant who'd called.

"Yes. Now relax and...enjoy." He winked and lowered his head into her.

Liz shifted, pulling herself away and lifting her leg off his shoulder. "I can't relax. I don't work like that."

Billy rolled back into a squat at the foot of the bed. "You don't even know if there is a story. Christ, Liz, I haven't seen you in almost a year. I should have known. All you care about is getting your career on track again."

"You were the one who wanted me to fight back."

"Yeah, and I'll be there for you. But right now? Right this minute?" Annoyed, he began to get out of bed. "Oh, forget it."

Liz lost her edge and changed her tone at once. "Wait, don't go. Please. I'm sorry." She reached out and held his wrist. He looked back at her. She sidled over. "Billy, you know how it is with me. When I smell a story, I work it. Every angle, no stops, all systems go. That doesn't mean I don't care about you. Or us."

Billy shook his head. "Sometimes it's like that's all you care about. Getting the story. Nothing, nobody matters."

"That's not true." Liz leaned over, speaking an inch from his lips between soft kisses. "You do. You matter. More than anyone else." Her light eyes were dead serious. Sincere. Moist with apology. Billy couldn't stay mad. Especially when she held him with that gaze. One that dripped with sex and seduction. She smiled, taking taking the fight and irritation out of Billy, "You're not going anywhere."

Liz used sex without guilt or hesitation. As a ploy. A tool. A means to an end. To her, it was just another weapon in her arsenal. She enjoyed it on a purely physical level with none of emotional strings and baggage. Pushing him into the pillows, she went down on him.

An hour later, Liz sharpened to a faint scrape.

She never fell asleep but Billy was dead to the world, lights out. She glanced over at the bedside clock. Two A.M. Swinging out of bed, she padded naked into the living room. Moonlight sliced through the parted curtains and laid a blue sash all the way to the front door, where a plain brown envelope had been pushed through.

Her heart skipped a beat. Liz picked it up. It was sealed.

Liz hurried into the second bedroom that had been converted into an office. Mahogany desk, deep leather shelves, and bookshelves with classic lines. It reeked of money and class because it served as her father's law office whenever he came to New York. Switching on the antique table lamp, she sliced open the envelope with a letter opener and slid out the documents inside.

Her heart skipped a beat when she saw "TOP SECRET NO FOREIGN" stamped boldly across the type. She realized it was some sort of Joint Chiefs of Staff approval memo for 'Thunder Strike.' A Black Op, clearly. She flipped over the cover page and stared at a message.

PBP/11 TOP TOP SECRET
TO USS WILLIAM J.CLINTON
FOR ADMIRAL GRANT'S EYES ONLY
XH23 65 FDMN001357 TS 18101627
ABORT THUNDER STRIKE.

Liz turned the page over. Another message.

PBP/11 TOP TOP SECRET
TO USS WILLIAM J. CLINTON
FOR ADMIRAL GRANT'S EYES ONLY
XH23 65 FDMN001362 TS 18102108
THUNDER STRIKE PERSONNEL ON BETA LIST.

There were two more pages, both photocopies of newspaper clippings within a day of each other. The first was a bold headline from the *Times*: "CATASTROPHE!" Below it: "Hurricane Meg Levels DC." More sub-heads: "One Million Feared Dead." "Meg a Superhurricane?" "President Never Left the White House."

The second photocopy came from the next day's paper. A small news item lost in the continuing major story of Hurricane Meg.

USAF PLANE EXPLODES IN MIDAIR

Washington, Oct 20: An amphibious twin engine United States Air Force transport plane exploded in midair over the North Atlantic killing all fourteen persons aboard, a Defense Department press release said. The actual cause of the accident is still unknown. No further details were made available.

Liz first placed the two messages side by side. Her eyes studied the top four lines. XH23 65 was some sort of transmission code. FDMN001357 and FDMN001362 she deciphered as message IDs. She couldn't figure out the pair of long numbers that followed.

Nothing, she noted, in the two messages indicated the actual date of transmission. *It must be there somewhere.* And went through them again. *No, nothing at all.*

The date was vital to establish a connection, if any, with the news clippings. She kept staring at the first four lines, the fourth in particular for the next few minutes.

I have it!

18102108 could read as date, month, and time of transmission: 18th October at 2108 hours. She glanced at the other message: 18th October at 1627 hours. She picked up the big storm headline and put it next to the first message, then arranged the second with the news item of the USAF transport plane.

This arrangement immediately triggered alarming questions.

What was the connection between the storm and Thunder Strike? Did the storm come in the way of the operation? Or did the storm abort the operation? Was it compromised? But, first, what was Thunder Strike?

Liz moved over to the second message that simply said,

'Thunder Strike Personnel on Beta List.'

Then fourteen defense personnel died in a plane crash.

Liz sat enveloped in a prickly silence. Excited. Nervous. Butterflies flying circles in her stomach. Her mind racing with possibilities. The exact same thrilling sensation she'd experienced when Billy had told her about Senator Jarvis Johnson.

"Hey."

Liz startled! Caught her breath audibly and snapped her head toward the voice. It was just Billy. She relaxed.

"What are you doing up?" he asked. "It's three A.M. and you're naked."

Liz laughed. He came over and slid into the chair under her, encircling her waist. She settled into his lap and nodded to papers on the table. "The bombshell. Someone shoved it under the door a few minutes ago."

"Admiral Grant?"

Liz shrugged, "I guess."

"Is there a story here?"

She kissed him long and deep and smiled mischievously, "Answer your question?"

"Be careful, please."

Liz looked into his eyes, touched by his concern. "Thank you, Billy."

"My pleasure."

"I can feel it," smiled Liz. "I'm going to be so sore."

Billy hoisted her onto the table with a broad smile, "And my balls are going to kill me."

She barely noticed Billy's thrusts become more urgent. His breath pumped into her ear. Liz's let her reflexes take over the sexual response while her eyes glazed and her mind drifted. Thinking ahead to her next move.

TWO

Liz heard a couple of bolts being drawn. The door opened a crack and a silver haired man peered out. "Admiral Grant? Liz."

"Come in," he said, smiling slightly. He released the chain and opened the door wider, stepping aside to allow her in.

Considering his Navy rank and standing with the president, Liz wasn't surprised he enjoyed a corner suite with a spectacular view in the heart of Manhattan. Unlike the millions who were homeless in the continuing tragic aftermath of Hurricane Meg, the US government paid for Grant's relocation. A dozen similar complexes, hotels, and apartments, had become home to top federal government officials, Congressmen, and Senators. The New York Legislature had been turned into Capitol Hill.

Liz noticed that Grant had done nothing to personalize the suite. It retained that impersonal, aseptic decor of a hotel room even though he could be staying here for several weeks. That was being optimistic. Nobody had seen, not even in theoretical models, the kind of damage that Hurricane Meg had wreaked on Washington DC, so much so 2012's Sandy lost her dubious 'superstorm' label. A timetable for recovery was all speculation.

Grant showed Liz to the square couch. "Please, sit down."

Liz glanced around for the touch of a woman—photographs, flowers. She found nothing. Maybe he'd lost his family in the storm. Almost everyone in DC had lost somebody. Maybe he was single. There was nothing about his personal life online.

"No, thank you," smiled Liz. Either Grant did not know she was just out of rehab or pretended he did not. *He must know*. Considering he was more than just an aide and advisor to the president. "Don't mind me if you want one."

"No, I'll wait," said Grant and returned to take the

straight-backed chair across from her. He was at least six feet tall and a body to go with it. Not handsome in the conventional sense, though he possessed that intangible carriage of old money.

"What can I do for you?"

Liz was ready. Her fingers reached into the unmarked envelope even before he spoke. She handed him the documents. His jaw tightened perceptibly. He flipped quickly through the pages and the corner of his eye twitched when he got to the news item about the plane crash.

During the course of her day, Liz found out that the cover page she had received was the 'implementer' of a Jayspid, or Joint Strategic Planning Document packet. The full packet followed a specific format, she learned, with standardized tabs, so that the Joint Chiefs of Staff making the presentation could find the right page quickly. It contained a coordination sheet, a synopsis of the covert operation, action, background, and talking papers. The implementer was the last document added. It represented the final step: *project approval.* Grant seemed completely unprepared she'd turn up the most sensitive portion of the Jayspid. He should know tha t she did win a Pulitzer.

"These papers raise some very disturbing questions," she said.

Grant stared at her. Liz sensed suspicion. She did not expect a smooth ride with this interview. After all, she'd almost taken down the president, his dear friend. Grant must have followed her fall from grace more keenly than most. He had the clout to access her files.

"I cannot answer any of them," he replied flatly.

Liz didn't miss a beat. Of course. *He wants to know how much more I've unearthed.* "Suppose I tell you what I know. And maybe you can stop me if I get off the track."

Grant nodded after a moment's hesitation. He saw her pen and pad appear almost magically in her hands. "No notes."

"Okay." Liz put them away in her purse. "Thunder Strike

was a chemical or biological attack."

"No."

"A pre-emptive nuclear strike."

"No."

"A pre-emptive strike."

"Yes."

"A WMD."

"Yes."

"Was it ever used?"

"I told you I will not answer any questions."

"It was being tested."

"No."

Liz blinked. "It was used against Cuba."

"That was the plan."

"Thunder Strike was aborted because the crisis defused itself."

"Yes."

"But Thunder Strike was compromised."

"Yes."

"Thunder Strike personnel were aboard the USAF plane that crashed in the Atlantic."

"Yes."

"Beta is code for aborting..." Liz knew the answer even before Grant shook his head.

"No."

She wanted to circle in. "Recalling..."

"No."

"Terminating."

Grant slow blinked. "Yes."

He had allowed himself to be led into it. *Why?* Liz felt a cold hand of fear close around her throat.

———

Hansen was team leader of the three-man stakeout eavesdropping on the entire conversation between Liz and Grant. He looked the part. Big and rough around the edges, his bluntness was matched by a voice coarse from smoking a pack a day since he was thirteen. The men were cramped inside a white, nondescript van that Liz had squeezed past on her way in to see Admiral Grant. Not too old, not too new, it blended with the other cars on the street.

Liz and Grant were on a thirteen-inch TV screen, part of a bank of four surveillance monitors. The other three carried images of Grant's empty bedroom, kitchen, and bathroom. Their voices played over a pair of Bose speakers. The high angle image indicated the cameras inside Grant's suite were mounted close to the ceiling. They were state-of-the-art, wafer thin, and fitted between the slats of the air conditioning vents. Motion and sound sensitive chips triggered a digital recorder on and off in the van. The red 'RECORD' light was on now.

The lens could be pivoted on all axes by a remote joystick in front of the youngest man in the van, Damon. Just as technologically savvy as the kid, Hansen had assigned Damon to be the tekkie of the team. The youngster carried a gun but this was only his third month in the field. Damon had confessed to Hansen he'd used a firearm for the first time in boot camp and had only fired his piece at the practice range.

Flanking Damon on the other side was Hansen's long time partner, Art. Just as bulky and rough-hewn. They wore double holsters with automatics. Like Hansen, Art was no stranger to violence. They had drawn their weapons. And fired. And killed before. In fact, Hansen and Art had carried out a quick execution as recently as this morning on their way to this stakeout.

Murder was a big part of their job description.

They were known internally as the 'cleanup crew.'

"Well, Ms. Lovell—" began Grant.

"Call me Liz. Everybody does."

"Can I ask how you got those?"

Liz sidestepped the question. "Let's just say I didn't have to go out of my way."

"I have to know how you got them."

"I can't reveal my source, Admiral," replied Liz.

"Then your investigation ends here."

"I doubt it. Someone wants Thunder Strike exposed."

"I did not see another name but mine on those papers. You have no more leads."

Liz refused to cave in. Decided to call his bluff. "I'm sorry, sir. I cannot."

Grant didn't blink. He abruptly stood up. "It was nice meeting you." Beat. "Finally."

Liz smiled sadly. "I made my bed."

"Good night and good luck."

Hansen's face tightened. He waited tensely. *How will Liz respond?*

———

Liz gathered her purse and came to her feet. Her mind raced. Grant was right. Without his co-operation, the story ended here, and all hope of a comeback. *Is he testing my journalistic integrity?* Rumors that she betrayed the reporter's 'code of silence' swirled following her downfall. *I have to hold my ground.*

"You probably already figured out that you'll need the rest of that Jayspid package," said Grant. "I know where you can get your hands on one."

Liz zeroed in on his motive. "Why would you do that? You said the success of Thunder Strike depends on its secrecy."

"I never approved of Thunder Strike. And the president was never given the full facts. Considering the history between you two, I don't know if you'd be fair and unprejudiced."

"I'll shield him. I promise. I owe him one."

Grant stared at her.

———

Hansen leaned forward. Rapt. His team and he had been waiting for this.

"I have to think about it," retreated Grant. "I'll call you

in the morning."

"Goddamnit," muttered Hansen gruffly. Seeing Grant move toward the window, Hansen made a decision. He had the authority. "The admiral needs a nudge. Arty, come on."

Hansen and Art piled out of the van. Damon stayed behind to continue the audio-visual surveillance. They stared up at the same time that Grant looked out of the window. The admiral made them. Hansen wanted him to.

Grant turned abruptly. He had to switch strategies. He needed Liz. *I cannot let on that I do.* Liz was reaching for the door knob to let herself out. A sudden urgency leapt into his voice. "You could become a target."

Liz turned, surprised

He asked, "Still interested?"

He could see her asking herself what brought about this sudden change. But she knew better than to ask and replied without hesitation, "Of course."

He held up three fingers. "There are only three copies of the Jayspid package for Thunder Strike. Two have been secured. One has not. It's in DC."

"Washington?" asked Liz, puzzled. "I thought everyone who is anyone is working out of New York since the hurricane."

"I didn't say it was in official hands. A massive manhunt is underway for it."

Grant pulled out a 'burner' phone. He saw one being used on a TV crime drama and went out to Chinatown and purchased it from a store he could never find again. The phone was one of *two* purchases he'd made since returning to the US, when he sensed his life might be in danger after he realized he was being quarantined in New York and refused entry to Washington and contact with the president. He punched a single memory key, but he did not speak. Instead, he texted: "LIZ LOVELL 2CU..."

"When can you leave?" he asked, a snap to every word.

Liz looked flustered. "I can fly out tonight."

He typed: "TMRW." Then faced Liz, clicked off her picture, and sent it off as well.

Crack!

With a wicked crunch, the door knob tore out, smashed into the coffee table five feet away, and cracked the glass. Wood chips flew! Something burned past his cheek. *A bullet!* It lodged in the wall across the room. Liz reacted with a startled gasp. Grant jumped. Since there was no gunshot, he realized it was a silenced weapon. He barked, "Go through the kitchen door! There's a fire escape out the window. Go, go!"

BamBamBam! The door rattled. The gunman was laying his shoulder into it. But the security chain held.

"Who am I meeting?" asked Liz.

The chain atomized with another volley.

"You'll be contacted." He tossed her the cell phone. "Destroy it." She caught it cleanly. "Now, go!"

The timing couldn't have been scripted better. Two men burst in a heartbeat after Liz disappeared into the kitchen. Grant bought her precious seconds. He met the intruders in the living room with his *second* purchase.

A snub nosed .38 tucked in the back of his belt.

He'd started carrying it at all times ever since he bought it. Even slept with it these past few days. His hand did not even get to the gun. *ThunkThunkThunkThunk!* Flame stuttered out of the intruders' silenced weapons. Grant recognized their intent from their steady hands, sure aim, and cold demeanor.

They shot to kill.

Grant first felt force. A tremendous, jarring shove to his chest that lifted him off his feet. Searing, white hot daggers of pain came next. Then he experienced the impact of his spine and skull against the wall. He tried to scream, but heard nothing. His throat shut off air. He stretched his eyes, opened them wide, but his vision faded rapidly. The floor rushed up. His knees were buckling and he lacked the strength or feeling to straighten them.

———

Hansen paused for just a second.

Grant crumpled to the floor. Dead.

The sound of pumps on metal came audible. *Liz.* Hansen kicked Grant's gun across the floor out of habit and followed Art through the doorway Liz had taken. It took them just a few strides to get to the open window. He showed himself without any concern and looked outside. Dark and empty and supported on steel stanchions, the fire escape descended in double flights outside the kitchen door. Feminine heels clicked loudly on the metal. Her silhouette striated between the ironwork.

Hansen did not pursue her. Nor did he direct Art, who stood stoically at the window. Instead, they waited. The rhythm and sound of Liz's footfalls changed when she raced off the fire-escape into the narrow and dark alley which provided access in and out of the parking garage. The urgent and frightened taps of her high heels on asphalt reached up. Hansen couldn't see her but knew exactly where she was. He looked ahead, where the alley emptied into the street.

Her shadow elongated into a light halo on the naked brick wall. A moment later, Liz appeared and stared back. Straight into the killers' eyes.

She was a sitting duck.

But neither man even raised his weapon.

Hansen's earpiece crackled. It was Damon from the van. The young tekkie, who had been monitoring the entire exchange between Grant and Liz, reported just what the Hansen needed to know right now, "She's headed to DC."

"Make it look like a burglary," said Hansen to Art, turned away, and flipped open his cell phone. He dialed unhurriedly.

———

A phone rang in an uptown executive suite not nearly as plush as the one assigned to Admiral Grant. The floor plan was a single cramped space subdivided into a bedroom, office, sitting area, and kitchenette. Inexpensive sconces provided light, none of which were on. Anonymous and nondescript abstracts, typical of mid-range hotel rooms, adorned the walls. A briefcase rested in the chair. Keys to a rental car, a wallet, and a wristwatch lay hurriedly tossed on the narrow office desk along with a ringing cell.

It vibrated precariously along the edge of the table.

It was turned over, the display screen face down, hiding the caller ID.

The kitchenette was done in speckled laminate. A tiny, one-flame cooktop served as a stove, which, clearly, the occupant had never once used. Tucked under the near pristine counter was a below-the-counter refrigerator. Above it, a wall mounted microwave. Next to it, a small glass cabinet with white dishes. Beige venetian blinds were angled for unremarkable views of adjacent buildings but not back into the room.

A prime time movie played on the bulky television set. A tremendous explosion from the frenetically paced film blasted bright orange-white light, revealing a nine-to-five ensemble ready to be worn neatly laid out on the bed: blue shirt, red tie, and a dark pinstriped suit. The sheets and covers were tightly stretched and tucked with the neatness and crispness of a professional housekeeping crew. On the floor, a pair of socks were draped over black dress shoes. The cell continued to ring, vibrating halfway over the edge of the table.

The movie quieted down to reveal the sound of a running shower. The door to the bathroom, located immediately to the right of the entrance to the suite, stood open. Light spilled out. Just inside, a small laundry hamper brimmed with recently stuffed dirty clothes. The tub served as a shower stall as well. The opaque plastic curtains were only half drawn, revealing the bottom half of hot water jetting down in a forty-five degree slant from the showerhead.

Thud. The cell phone fell off the table and simultaneously stopped ringing as the call went to voicemail. "This is Billy

Madden," he said cheerfully. "Give me a reason to call back."

Billy did not answer because he couldn't hear.

He couldn't hear because he was dead.

And he was dead because he'd eaten three bullets.

Two had been fired into his chest and the third had ended his life—blowing away half his face. The other half was a snapshot of terror. His mouth, what remained of it, hung open with the beginnings of a scream. Fear dilated the one eye that remained. The second was a socket, punctured by the bullet. Hot water continued to roar down, enveloping his naked body in updrafts of steam, which had gradually washed the splatter of blood, flesh, brain, and bone off the shiny ceramic tiles into the drain. Some red stubbornly clung to the grout lines. Despite being soaked in moisture since he'd been killed, his body was stiff with evidence of a murder at least twelve hours old.

Billy had returned home after spending the night with Liz to shower and change for work. He did not realize he had been followed back to the suite, nor did he recognize his assailants, two large, rough looking men. He saw them and had time for nothing else.

When it slipped off the table, the cell phone landed display up. The caller hung up without leaving a message, and the display light faded with the ID, "Liz."

———

She knew Billy was dead. *She just knew.*

Her knuckles were white around the cell phone. She stood up abruptly, rushed into the ladies room, entered an empty stall, and dry heaved into the toilet bowl. She shut the stall door, dropped the cover, and slowly sat down. She remained in the stall for several minutes.

Liz was in the departure terminal of the Long Island commuter airport. Waiting for her ride to Washington DC. The president had declared martial law the day after the disaster, opening the capital only to military planes carrying aid for the massive disaster relief effort underway and troops to maintain law and order. Limited commercial flights had resumed to DC earlier this morning. But emergency personnel got priority and they'd taken every seat on every plane.

So, Liz tried the executive jet company that her father used. They wouldn't fly her even after she invoked Kenneth Lovell's name. She pulled out the Yellow Pages and started calling alphabetically down the list of private operators. Most were gone for the day.

A pilot with a 1978 Cessna finally picked up. He wanted a small fortune. Liz agreed. Once face to face, she knew she could haggle him down. And she did, agreeing on less than half what he'd demanded on the phone. Gypsy blood on her mother's side, which also probably accounted for the quick temper.

The pilot introduced himself just as 'Savage,' and looked it. Raspy voice. Gray flecked stubble. Beer gut. Receding hairline. Living rental to rental. He needed her advance to refuel. They went over their flight plan, which had to be an outright lie. They wouldn't be allowed to leave the ground if they wrote down Washington DC as their final destination.

Liz emerged from the ladies room.

Remarkably, she showed no evidence of grief, guilt, or emotional turmoil. She had even redone her makeup. Her counselors in rehab had noticed this about her. The ability to move quickly past remorse. What's the point of dwelling on despair, she told them. Life goes on. It made her sadness seem calculated, an obligation, an act, they said.

"Is it?" asked her shrink last week.

"No!" she'd denied, offended. The way the shrink stared back, she sensed he wasn't sure if she meant it.

Liz knew exactly why.

Eyes were windows to the soul. Hers could be cold, flat, impenetrable. A wall.

———

Tim O'Flaherty declined the National Press Club offer to cancel the dinner in his honor because of the ongoing tragedy in the nation's capital. There would be several empty seats, the organizers warned, since the top reporters, many his own, were in Washington. For Tim, the evening was a damn nuisance anyway that might now actually run shorter than the usual three hours. Lesser attendees meant fewer speeches. Technically, this was a roast, but after twenty years of accolades, he'd heard every joke. So they might as well be speeches. As much as he hated these affairs, he was piqued and insulted if he wasn't honored with regularity. He sought constant reassurance and validation that nobody had usurped his place as one of the most well known names in the media.

The event, a black tie affair, was held in the penthouse of the Trump Towers. The fear of empty tables proved baseless. Politicians became seat fillers. They were working out of New York in the aftermath of Hurricane Meg and turned out in full force. Against a breathtaking three hundred and sixty-degree panorama of NYC, the Congressmen and women grinned, greeted, and swapped around like speed daters.

Tim caught the eye of an exotic, olive-skinned woman with the slenderness of a model at the adjacent conversation huddle. She stood six feet tall. Even without the three inch heels, she'd be five-nine. Tim was so taken by her, he tuned out the drone of the dull Majority Whip from Oregon. Tim casually tugged his ear, a prearranged signal to the reporter he'd brought along from the office.

The reporter hurried over to perform the task that got him this invite, "Tim, news desk wants you to call."

"Deadline emergency," Tim said. "Excuse me, Congressman." When they moved out of the politician's earshot, "Who is she?"

"Sabrina Worth," said the reporter. "She's the president's new speech writer. Started a couple of months ago."

"You know her?" He must, Tim assumed, because the

reporter covered the East Room press briefings in DC.

"Sort of, yeah."

"Introduce us," said Tim.

"She's not your type, Tim. For one, she's almost forty."

"Funny," sneered Tim. His preference for young women—mid-to-late twenties—was well known.

They began a casual walk across.

Sabrina looked over and he saw recognition flash in her eyes. Tim held her gaze. She half smiled. Seeing that he was headed toward her, she extricated herself from the conversation. Tim thought she breathed old world style and sophistication. Her straight black hair that curled ever so slightly at the shoulder suggested a silkiness he could just feel without even touching. Her eyes angled ever so slightly to hint an Asian mix somewhere in her heritage. Her mouth had just the right amount of natural pout that the burgundy lipstick only enhanced. Simple elegant pearls. Then a silvery white evening gown which fit exactly as it must have on the show window mannequin.

"Sabrina Worth," introduced the reporter. "Tim O'Flaherty."

Tim shook her hand and didn't let go. The reporter, who had pimped for Tim before, retreated out of earshot.

"President Avery apologizes for not attending," said Sabrina, her hand still firmly in his grasp. Only, it had gone from a handshake into something friendlier.

Following months of delicate negotiating, the president had agreed to be the keynote speaker this evening. A gesture that indicated Avery had forgiven the *Post*. Tim had done what he never had in forty years as a journalist. Apologized. For what Liz had pulled.

"Why's he still in DC?" New York had become the defacto capital of the United States.

"He feels he'd be abandoning the millions who can't leave Washington."

"It couldn't be that he's ducking the mud bath, could it?"

Sabrina reacted with an inquiring look. "How so?"

"You know, Congressmen and Senators thanking God out of one side of the mouth while playing partisan politics out the other to fill seats emptied by the storm."

Politicians, who hadn't evacuated in time, had perished. They included an inordinate number of Democrats who controlled the other end of Pennsylvania Avenue. Curiously, many of them had been on record decrying Avery's one-vote-margin-of-victory in the electoral college. Now, their seats were in play. One of the *Post*'s reporters was following up a possibility that they may not have deliberately received the storm warning. Hurricane Meg was a mess on so many levels, stories and scandals would unravel for years to come.

Sabrina pulled her hand out of his and defended her president warmly. "You got the president all wrong. He won't even restore water and power in the residence part of the White House until the city has them first."

"When I get any president wrong, you can have my job editing for the *Post*," smiled Tim.

Sabrina eased off. Smiled back. "Thank you, no. Hundred hours a week. Coffee on IV. Ulcers."

"Are you talking about my job or yours?"

Sabrina laughed, gently slapping his arm. Their eyes met. Sparked. Tim knew at that moment they were going home together. His cell phone rang.

"You get that, I'll get the dry martinis," she said in a way that she knew he'd be surprised. He was. "I researched you for the roast." She winked and whispered in his ear as she left, surprising him again, "I know more."

Tim grinned. She slunk away. He looked at the caller ID: *Unknown.* He frowned. Nobody but a select few had his number.

"Hello?" he answered brusquely.

"Tim, this is Liz."

"Why are you calling me?

"This is something big," Liz replied, ignoring his hostility. "Probably the biggest story of the storm."

Tim became instantly curt and distant. "Uh-huh."

"Remember Billy Madden? My source for the Senators' exposé? Last night, he handed me a Joint Chief's memo of a covert op against Cuba called Thunder Strike."

"Just like that?" retorted Tim skeptically.

"There was a name. Admiral Grant. He may have run the operation, he's a close friend of the president. He confirmed there's a story. But it's in DC."

"No," he snapped at once.

"Tim, please, there's something big here."

"We talked about this." He remained firm.

"You once called me a younger, more ambitious version of yourself."

True. That's why he'd had such high hopes for her. "You've been on probation a day, Liz."

"How long before you'd have made your move?"

He snickered.

"We are a team. At least we were, once. I'll pick up all the expenses."

Tim lost his edge. "It's been a year since the scandal. The public may have forgotten, but I don't expect the president has. Admiral Grant is his closest friend. This could be payback."

"Or maybe I'm such a reach, nobody'll suspect until it's too late. I've been out for a year. That's probably why I was an easy choice."

Tim's hackles rose. *Sonofabitch.* No woman manipulated him like Liz. She'd done it again. His edge returned, sharper than before, "An easy choice for whom?"

"Nobody. Jesus, Tim!"

"You're good, Liz. You almost had me feeling sorry for you." Going personal. "You know? I didn't even want you back."

Tim knew she had a temper. It flashed. "I wasn't the one who crossed the line between editor and reporter."

"You could've said no."

"You were the legend. I was twenty-one, awestruck."

"Bullshit. You grew Icarus wings and flew too high."

"You want to test a jury with that defense?"

Tim hit back. "You want to play the blackmail game with me, Liz? I know for a fact you tried to secretly plea bargain your way out of your suspension, offering the White House names of sources you didn't need anymore. If you take me down, you'll fall further." Liz had no answer. He pressed in a hoarse, enraged whisper. "Did you make another deal with them? Nobody just hands a scoop to a blacklisted reporter."

The silence at the other end was deafening. It just confirmed what he suspected.

"You are not telling me something, Liz, what is it?" He didn't expect an answer. None was forthcoming. "Ambition is one thing. Ambition at any cost is another." Tim saw Sabrina returning with the drinks and ended it, "The answer is no. Play by the rules of your probation, or else."

"Or else, what?" snapped Liz.

He knew she would bite. For all her people skills, Liz's temper-on-a-trigger sometimes betrayed her. She gave him the opening he was waiting for. "There isn't a paper on the main line that will hire you. I've checked."

Click. Tim hung up. Liz held the silent phone to her ear for several seconds. She didn't know why she'd even called him. She should have known he'd take the attitude that she'd made her bed and now he'd screw her in it every chance he got.

"Are we leaving or what?" Savage, the pilot, intruded her thoughts.

Liz hesitated. If she defied Tim, it would give him the justification he needed to can her. *Hell with him.* Her face set firmly. "Yes. Let's go."

President Avery Walker guiltily wrung his hands. His face was pale as a ghost. Fear haunted his eyes. He had woken up from a nightmare of a million deaths. He slept alone because he was single. With trembling fingers, he struck a match and lit the bedside candle. He only authorized power for the West Wing from the generators two levels below the ground inside concrete walls designed to withstand a twenty-megaton nuclear strike. General electricity from the city's power grid would not be restored for weeks, which would be when he'd allow himself electricity in the presidential apartment.

Avery climbed out of bed. He did not slip his feet into slippers. The damp carpet barely registered on his naked soles as he padded to the window, mumbling in terror. He carefully opened the drapes a crack and peered outside, afraid he might see the ghosts from his nightmare. Scores of luminous blue cones danced across black sky, each cone a searchlight marking a patrolling helicopter. The light shafts briefly lit up a post-apocalyptic cityscape.

"What's done is done," Avery said aloud in an effort to console himself.

But there were scorpions in his head.

He threw his head back and screamed!

––––––––

Outside Avery's door, Secret Service Agent Connor was not at all alarmed. This eerily Macbethian scene had been playing out all week. A twenty-year, by-the-book African-American ex-marine, Connor was a veteran of presidential details. His wife and he—his kids were away at college—had survived only because he had drawn protection detail the night Meg arrived. As powerful and destructive as Meg was, leveling the city, the centuries old masonry and stone construction of both the Capitol and the White House had withstood the awesome wind and rain.

Connor whispered into his cuff mike, "Episode. Clear the floor."

Avery could be unpredictable. Sometimes, like Nixon had after Watergate, Avery stalked aimlessly around the White House. Not tonight. Connor watched him head into the bathroom, where he soaped and washed his hands obsessively in the candle light. The dancing flame exaggerated Avery's motion into wild shadows on the wall.

The whole mansion reeked of Gothic darkness. Wet carpet and drapes everywhere. Carpenters had begun replacing the windows. All of them had been blown out. The storm had gone through the White House like a barbaric army, destroying antique furniture, flinging entire offices out onto the lawns. The ornate frescoes were cracked, the lavish floors pocked and gouged.

Connor stayed in the shadows till Avery returned to bed, then he shut the door without a sound, and resumed guard. He had been the first to witness the president's strange behavior. It began right after the storm. Avery woke up screaming and had been doing so every night since. Connor had informed his boss. An hour later, he'd found himself standing before Defense Secretary Baron Hawke. Even though Baron had no jurisdiction over the president's protective detail, Connor wasn't surprised. Everyone in the White House knew the defense secretary was the most powerful voice of this administration.

Baron swore the agent to silence and secrecy. These were traumatic times for the nation, he told Connor, and like any other time of national crisis, Americans drew strength from their president. Connor understood. Last night, Baron had brought in a psychiatrist friend, who quietly observed the president's behavior. Connor felt privileged when Baron insisted the agent stay and listen to the shrink's diagnosis. "The nightmares are exacerbations of rage, sadness, distorted grief, and extreme guilty preoccupation caused by the staggering death toll." He called the condition "disaster bereavement."

Avery checked outside. Like an outer wall, a ring of marines guarded the perimeter of the White House. He had walked around the mansion after Meg passed. The symbol of freedom was barely recognizable. It looked as if it had come under intense mortar attack. Not a square inch had been spared the brutal savagery of the hurricane.

Avery retreated to bed and lay down, eyes open, awake for a long time. Crews had been drying out the interior, yet an acrid dampness hung like a mist. He barely noticed it anymore. Gradually, his breathing became even. Sleep came reluctantly in troubled waves. His last thought was the one that had preoccupied him every second of every day since Meg's onslaught.

How could this have happened? How? How? How?

LAST WEEK

THREE

She began as a tropical depression when the illusion of the moving sun, caused by the earth's annual revolution, warmed the ocean and the air. She was weak, shapeless, and remained in this formative stage for a long time. With bulging but not closed isobars, her pressure hovered well above a thousand millibars. She was born where all Atlantic hurricanes were born. Off the west coast of Africa. If she did not want to die, like several other depressions earlier this storm season, she would need a starting mechanism.

It came as an unexplained westerly wave.

This triggered low level air from the surrounding regions to flow into her, accelerating convection. Water vapor, ascending in her moist columns, condensed. Her vertical circulation acquired greater organization. Low level air blew in a circle, giving her horizontal form that familiar cyclonic spiral. Her winds, covering several thousand square miles, curved with greater and greater determination toward a central vortex, where she chimneyed moist surface air upward, releasing the heat that drove her. The pumping action, set up by her large scale vertical circulation, caused a sudden drop in her atmospheric pressure at the surface.

She strengthened freakishly fast into an embryo storm.

Then she began to move westward at fourteen miles an hour.

———

Diane and Sam made out like a couple of teenagers in the USAF jeep on the terrace level of the parking lot at Miami's International Airport. At five A.M. there were few cars. She looked freshly showered because she was on the first plane out so she could head straight to work as soon as she landed in Washington DC. He'd rolled out of bed with her and drove her as he'd promised he would. The intimacy of their hands over each other belied the fact they'd met only yesterday. Their lips let go of each other only to speak.

"Did we talk about long distance romance?" asked Sam with a Southern drawl so deep it had to be genetically embedded.

"Uh-huh," Diane shook her head no, unable to say more because his tongue coiled around hers before she could form another word.

"Let me tell you," said Sam, barely letting go of her lips. "It's the best there is. No man to cook for."

"No one to clean for," agreed Diane.

"Lots of time to spend with your friends," added Sam.

Diane threw in what every man loved to hear, "Sex without strings."

Sam grinned, "It's good for America." He pulled back and looked into her eyes, "Want to give it a shot anyway?"

"Why not?"

They sealed it with another round of intense petting.

Diane had arrived two nights ago in Miami for a job interview yesterday at the National Hurricane Center. Coincidentally, Sam had been there too for a briefing. He'd locked eyes with her the moment she walked into the NHC and wouldn't let go. She ogled back. He beamed, exuding a good vibe. She noticed his eyes boldly do a quick up-down appraisal of her. She wore a conservative pant suit and hoped he'd imagine her in tight jeans and a T-shirt. She was a perky, pretty tomboy with short, dark hair, brown eyes, and healthy curves in all the right places.

Diane smiled, casually inventorying his features as well. Tall, well built, square jaw, broad shoulders, toothy smile, and muscular, chiseled arms. She thought of Errol Flynn the way he wore his leather jacket, collar turned up. Then she noticed the Hurricane Hunters logo on the sleeve. That just pegged the hunk-needle for her. When she came out of her interview, he was still there, making no pretense he'd been waiting for her. He got up and marched over.

"Hi." Typical of Southerners, it came out sounding like 'ha.' Then he more than just introduced himself, "Sam Winger. Dinner at eight?"

Somehow Diane expected the brashness. So, she wasn't surprised. "Can't. I'm flying out tonight."

"Postpone it," he dismissed. "There's a six A.M. flight back tomorrow to Washington that will get you into work an hour late at the most. I'll drive you to the airport in the morning."

"Of course. Then it's settled."

"Excellent. I'll pick you up at, say, seven tonight? No need to dress up. We'll go some place casual and dancing afterwards."

"I was being sarcastic."

"You have to work on that."

"Thanks for bothering to ask my name."

"I was saving that for the getting-to-know-you part of the date."

"Bye." She walked away, praying he would follow her. He did. With a couple of extra long strides, he fell in step beside her.

"Dr. Diane Wood. Lead Forecaster, WFO, Silver Springs, Maryland. Bachelor's degree from UNC, Master's from Penn State, and a Ph.D. from OU."

"You cheated." Diane pulled open the door, nodding toward the fifty-year old black administrative assistant at the desk by the door from which she had just emerged. "You looked at my resume." They stepped outside into a bright, typical South Florida day. It was so hot and humid, Diane felt as if someone just chucked a steaming hot wet towel at her.

"Or, you could call it initiative," Sam persisted, "I found a way to find out more. So I'm not after a one-night stand."

Diane kept walking toward her rental car parked in one of the many 'VISITORS' slots. A social liberal but a fiscal conservative, she'd splurged on a shiny red Porsche in a moment of weakness. "Oh, we've gone from dinner to bed. Aren't we cocky?"

"Freud would say you're thinking what I'm thinking." Sam winked. Diane had to smile. An Oldsmobile pulled into a 'RESERVED' spot. Sam grinned. "I can put in a word. I know the director."

"No, thanks—"

Sam was already waving to a short, stout, balding, sixty-year old bureaucrat, who climbed out in the typical attire for an executive well above middle management. Shirt, tie, and a jacket slung over his shoulder despite the heat. "Hank! Do you have a minute?"

Even if Hank didn't, it was too late. Sam jostled Diane over. She whispered hoarsely, "I'd like to get hired on my own merit."

Sam ignored her. "Diane Wood, this is Dr. Hank Rotas, director of this fine forecasting establishment. Diane just interviewed for the weather girl's job."

Hank shook his head. "Dismiss it as Southern charm."

Diane laughed. "Dr. Rotas. A pleasure."

"When her application comes up for review, call HR and tell them to look no further. Keep it simple so that they don't suspect nepotism. Just say, 'we found her, Mary-Beth! I want her to start Monday!'"

Hank smiled over to Diane, "It was nice meeting you, Diane. If you get the job, it will be despite Sam's recommendation."

Dinner was a blast. It was true a girl made up her mind within the first couple of minutes of a date about sex afterwards. They skipped dessert and ended up in her hotel room.

Sam Winger was a pilot in the 53rd Weather Reconnaissance Squadron from Keesler Air Force Base, Mississippi, the legendary Hurricane Hunters. They flew into severe storms. With the Cuba crisis deepening, the Department of Defense wanted to keep a close eye on tropical disturbances.

Sam and his crew were operating out of Peterson Air Force Base here in South Florida.

Diane had been off men for six months following her bitter divorce to a TV weatherman. She used the word "jerk" as a regular prefix whenever she spoke or even thought of her ex-husband. She didn't mind that he was a vain bastard, in fact, she was attracted to arrogant, self-confident types, Sam being the latest case in point, but her jerk ex cheated on her regularly. She still saw him on the late night news in DC doing the weather on network television.

Diane was the youngest of three kids, the other two being brothers. Her parents were regular worker bees, who'd headed from St. Louis to Los Angeles in search of a better life when Diane's mother was pregnant with her. They moved into the San Fernando Valley and never moved again. So Diane grew up as a Valley girl, that legendary species of California female who'd made a word as unlikely as 'like' famous for starting, filling, and ending sentences, and expressing any gamut of emotions from joy to sadness, surprise to horror, envy to exasperation. Even though she got into Texas A&M, she decided to enroll at Cal State, Northridge, a stone's throw from home, so that she could be close to her parents. They were getting old and her brothers were married and living in Kansas and Nebraska. Few months before school started, her mom and dad were killed in a multi-car accident when a truck hopped the center divider on the Hollywood Freeway.

Desperately needing a change of scenery, she switched schools. University of North Carolina accepted her. Her brothers agreed it would be a good idea for her to get away. They sold the house and divvied up the money at the height of housing boom in California. Financially she was set for life, a luxury few freshmen enjoyed. She packed her car with all her things and drove cross country to start her adult life. Literally. She'd turned eighteen the week prior. Noticing her good grades in science and math, her counselor suggested Meteorology.

She attended Penn State in Happy Valley for her Masters with a full scholarship and then Oklahoma University recruited her to pursue a doctorate in Norman. Once she had her Ph.D., she decided she did not want to teach and got a job at the weather office in St. Louis, Missouri. Her life, it seemed had come full circle. She was back in her parents' home town to embark on her career. It had to be kismet. Diane started out taking hourly observations at the airport, working with spotters, doing surface and upper air observations. During her stint as a junior forecaster, an opportunity opened up in the Warning and Forecast Office in Silver Springs, just outside Washington DC.

"So, how is this going to work?" asked Diane.

Sam and she took the bridge from the parking lot into Miami International Airport. "I don't know."

"We are not seeing other people, are we?"

"No," replied Sam at once, then added on second thought, "Right? I'm Baptist and a serial monogamist. But I've heard some wild rumors about you Presbyterians."

Diane laughed. They were in the terminal. Once she passed through Security, Diane realized, this relationship would be up in the air despite their best efforts and promises. She took a deep breath. "I guess I'll see you when I see you."

"I love you," said Sam out of the blue. Diane stopped mid-stride and stared at him. They were a dozen paces from Security Check. She laughed nervously, at a loss for words. Sam looked dead serious. "You don't have to say it back. I woke up this morning. You were still asleep. I knew looking at you then I'm going to marry you."

"Oh-kay," Diane said slowly. "You have this disturbing habit of skipping intermediate steps."

"Too fast?"

"You think? Have you named our children too?""

"Not at all."

"I was being sarcastic."

"You really have to work on that."

The loudspeaker announced her flight. "I have to go." She turned away and turned right back, "To be honest, I want to say it back. Actually, I wanted to say it back the moment you said, 'ha.'" Her Southern accent was horrible. Her eyes softened and she kissed him long and hard. "I love you."

She pulled away. He let go reluctantly and watched her pass security without beeping. When she got to the other side, he hollered, "Two kids. Twins if you can pull it off. Savannah and Brandon. They can't be identical, or one of them's going to be ugly."

————

Three hours later, juggling her purse, laptop, and briefcase, Diane pushed open the double doors of the Warning and Forecast Office—or, WFO, as weather centers were called—in Silver Springs, just outside Washington DC in Maryland. Her heels clacked loudly across the linoleum.

At the lead forecaster's station, Vick Delhom swiveled the oversized leather chair around, "Where have you been?"

"Sorry," Diane crinkled her nose apologetically. "I stayed over and flew in this morning."

"Why?" he asked curiously. "I thought you were booked on a flight last night." Before she could answer, Vick exclaimed in a low voice, "Oh, my God, you had sex!"

"Shhh!" Diane hissed, looking around to see if anyone heard him.

Thankfully, the Advanced Weather Interactive Processing System, or AWIPS—the nerve center of a WFO—was a large enough island station that his exclamation did not carry to the ten people at the computers around them. Each shift at this Warning and Forecast Office had a Data Acquisition Program Manager, who supervised Hydro Meteorological Technicians, and they watched over the levels of rivers and streams; an aviation forecaster, who made separate predictions for Washington area airports and air routes; a marine forecaster, who monitored the weather all the way to the Atlantic; junior forecasters; and the lead forecaster, Diane or Vick, who drew the local weather picture, reporting facts like the current temperature, pressure, humidity, and wind velocity/direction to the local radio, TV, and other agencies.

"How the hell did you know?" she whispered.

"Honey, I'm your best friend, your shrink, and you know I have that horrible gift. I can just pick up hetero poontang." He logged off and stood up with his hands on his hips. Vick was gay and proud of it. "So?"

"So...what?" Diane tossed her purse in the drawer.

"Details, details."

"He's a Hurricane Hunter." She could never keep anything from Vick.

"Go on."

Diane sat down and logged on to begin her shift. "That's it, V. Now go home."

Vick refused to move. "After a year, poof!" Vick snapped his fingers. "You give it up just like that. There's got to be more."

"No. Now shoo."

Vick changed his tone into a plea, "Oh, come on. Throw me a bone, will ya?" He laughed at his own joke. "Bone, ha-ha, get it?"

Diane made a face. "You know what your problem is, V?"

"I'm thirty-seven, I live with a French interior decorator named Philippe, and my parents still haven't figured out why I'm not married."

"You don't mind your own business."

Vick flamboyantly threw up his hands in a marquee gesture, "If you see any movie this year, see 'She Fell for a Flyboy.' Sequel to 'Bride of A Weatherman.' Another heartbreaker."

"Sam is nothing like my ex-husband."

"But the way you go about getting involved with men is."

"And what way is that?"

"Impulsive."

"Sometimes you just feel a spark."

"How's it going to work? You're in DC, he's in Miami." He looked at her and exclaimed again, "Oh, my God! You didn't agree to a long distance, did you?"

Diane crinkled her face, "Yes?"

"Too polite to say no?"

"No!" Diane replied firmly.

"No? You took a year to work up the anger to walk out on your ex out for sleeping around. You enrolled into meteorology because you were afraid to tell your academic advisor you wanted to do Law. But that was a good call on the advisor's part. You'd have been quickly disbarred for excessive sweetness and decency."

"Hey, I can be hostile," said Diane, huffing it up. "Where's that damn tropical storm research I asked you a week ago?" She was writing an article for publication in the Weather Journal.

Vick looked at her, hurt, "That's kinda mean, seeing as I was doing you a favor."

Diane backed down in apology, "Sorry. I was just kidd— "

"Aha! See? You can't do it!" Then he softened up. "Just be careful, okay? I'm the one who has to sweep up the emotional wreckage."

"You're a queen. You live for it."

"True." Then he became all business, "You were right about all direct access of satellite data from the Atlantic being canceled."

"I told you!" she snapped at Vick.

A Command and Data Acquisition station in Gilmore Creek, Alaska, acquired Pacific data. Another in Wallops Island, Virginia, collected Atlantic data. These two CDAs were the first and only earth contact for data recorded by American geostationary and polar orbiting satellites.

Weather forecasting in the US had come a long way from that day on May 2, 1814, when Dr. James Tilton, Physician and Surgeon General of the United States Army, asked his staff to keep a record of weather. He wanted to study its influence on diseases, and in 1816, the first weather diary came into existence at Cambridge, Massachusetts. By 1838, surgeons were making weather observations in thirteen forts. At the end of the Civil War, this number rose to one hundred and forty-three. With the advent of the telegraph, these observations were used to 'forecast' weather by signaling ahead of advancing storms. In 1849, Joseph Henry, Secretary of the New Smithsonian Institution, persuaded the telegraph companies to transmit weather information free of charge. From this, he constructed a daily weather map for public display at the Smithsonian Castle. Soon, he was predicting weather for Washington, and the model for a national weather service came into existence.

On February 9, 1870, president Ulysses Grant signed into law a resolution to "provide for taking meteorological observations at military stations in the interior of the continent and at other points in the States and Territories...and for giving notice on the northern Great Lakes and on the sea coast by magnetic telegraph and marine signals of the approach and force of storms." Designated as the Weather Bureau within the Signal Service, at seven thirty-five A.M. on November 1, 1870, simultaneous observations from twenty-four stations were transmitted to Washington. Computers began to figure into forecasting when Joseph Smagorinsky established a research office in 1954. His efforts led to the formation of the National Meteorological Center.

Today, the National Weather Service operated with an integrated countrywide network of over a hundred and fifty Warning and Forecast Offices. Each WFO came equipped with a Next Generation Radar, or NEXRAD, fed by satellites with sophisticated payloads, Automated Surface Observing Systems to measure surface weather every minute, Wind Profilers that operated as high as fifty thousand feet, and other state-of-the-art systems and agencies. American satellites, ships, aircraft, balloons, and buoys were responsible for over seventy-five thousand daily observations around the globe.

The *most* by any nation.

The National Oceanic and Atmospheric Administration, or NOAA, the umbrella bureaucracy encompassing all weather agencies in the US, quietly emerged as the single most powerful environmental science center on earth.

Diane had tried to obtain data on current tropical disturbances in the Atlantic on her PC at home. Anyone could read the information directly out of Gilmore and Wallops. But she'd gotten a 'DIRECT ACCESS RESTRICTED BY NOAA MEMO 4Z157' message. She'd even tried it from the AWIPS because all satellite data was available directly to WFOs. She got the same message. When she mentioned it to Vick, he disparaged her computer skills.

With a major in electrical engineering from the Louisiana State University, Vick was the undisputed compu-wiz in the office. A part-time hacker in school, he'd stumbled upon meteorology after reading about sudden, unexplained hundred-mile-an-hour winds and fifty-foot waves that capsized an off-shore oil drilling rig in the Gulf of Mexico. All eighty-four workers aboard perished. The incident caught his eye because he'd taken a summer job on it just months before. He'd needed the money. His parents were black and poor. His father drove a tow truck and his mother worked part time. Vick went online and researched the freak weather. The deeper he delved into how an ordinary disturbance had strengthened to cyclonic proportions, the more hooked he got. Atmospheric pressure had dropped at the rate of one millibar an hour to create a phenomenon called a 'meteorological bomb.' He found recorded cases of other m-bombs burying unlikely regions under snow.

"I should have put money on it," Diane added regretfully.

Vick rarely conceded he made mistakes and she relished when he did.

"You'd have lost." He opened the drawer and drew out a thick stack of printouts. "Atlantic charts from the last seventy-two hours. Including this morning's entry. Direct from Wallops, if you know what I mean? Raw data, baby. Call me a genius. Go on."

"You needn't have bothered, genius." Diane snapped open her briefcase and extracted a similar stack. "I got the same thing. Officially. There's a new access policy, that's all."

"Do you know why? DoD orders."

"Department of Defense? Why?"

"Beats me. Cuba? Maybe they have a secret operation going on down there."

Juan Castro, the new leader down there, was trumpeting his acquisition of three nuclear bombs. The US was naturally perturbed. The headlines constantly recalled John F. Kennedy's similar nuclear confrontation with Juan's uncle, Fidel, back in the 1960s. The media painted doomsday scenarios almost daily, but polls showed Americans did not want to go to war. Not after Iraq and Afghanistan, where US troops were still deployed as peacekeepers. The nation wanted a diplomatic solution. The president seemed to be listening. A die-hard Democrat who believed Avery Walker had stolen the White House, she did concede he was caught between a rock and hard place.

"Come on," chided Diane, "weather satellites don't have the resolution to compromise any secret deployment."

"Resolution! Compromise! Deployment! Someone's been watching way too much TV."

"Oh, shuddap!" Diane whacked his arm.

"So what is the new access procedure?" he asked.

"All satellite data comes out of the SOCC from now on."

Satellite Operations Control Center in Suitland, Maryland, always did function as a central processing center, sorting out data from Gilmore and Wallops according to local needs. For instance, SOCC sent this WFO only those satellite pictures that affected DC unless a moving system necessitated data from other jurisdictions. If needed, Diane could dial up any region of the globe patrolled by NOAA satellites on the AWIPS.

"How did you get those charts?" she asked.

"I broke into the Wallops mainframe," Vick replied in a matter-of-fact voice.

"Shuddap." Diane whacked his arm again.

"As soon as I read the 'Access Denied' message, I had to." He reached into the drawer again and cockily slapped down a tiny flash drive like a winning hand. "I even got you a backup."

"Oh, thank you. That saves me four hours." She'd requested only WEFAX hard copies of Atlantic data, which meant she'd have to manually input all the numerical data. "You are a genius.

"Finally."

She skimmed through his printouts until she came to the satellite pictures. She was in luck. "Cool!"

"217E," said Vick. He knew exactly what she was talking about. The National Hurricane Center ID'd every tropical depression with a number and orientation.

"I don't remember seeing 217E on my printouts."

"Distractions of afterglow?"

Ignoring him, Diane happily thought ahead and aloud, "This is great. Now I can beef up my article with an occurring case study and illustrate why numerical models are a calculated guess at best." Supercomputers were still not fast enough to calculate minute variations in the atmosphere that could radically alter the course of a storm. Diane looked at her watch, "How's the daily forecast looking?"

The WFO issued a report every six hours. In the event of severe weather, the intervals would be shorter. As the shift's lead forecaster, she prepared predictions for the rest of day and the week ahead.

"You can just copy yesterday's numbers," said Vick. The entire East Coast was gripped by historically high temperatures. NOAA could not explain why, except point to two stubborn high pressure ridges over Delaware, Maryland, and Virginia that hadn't moved in days."

"Global warming," Diane repeated it like a mantra.

"Look on the bright side," a new voice interrupted. "Babes in thongs."

Ivory Adams joined them with an oily smile. Ivory was the Warning Coordination Meteorologist. A pale skinned former marine with a slender mustache that stained rather than grew on his upper lip, he spoke in a staccato voice and jumped into conversations uninvited. He filled the mandatory one-asshole-per-office quota. Vick glanced over to Diane, challenging her to fire back.

Diane's face firmed up sternly, "You know, um, that kind of talk, um, that could be grounds for sexual harassment."

Ivory's eyes narrowed toward the pile of printouts. "What are those?"

"Oh—" began Diane, flustered.

Vick stepped in, all acid. "If it's important we'll shoot you a memo. I hear ex-marines who never saw action love firing off paperwork."

Ivory used to be a Marine Corp Engineer. He glared at Vick, tightened his jaw with a humorless smile, and walked away. Ivory was a Tea Party Republican and disapproved that Vick was openly gay.

"Gee, Diane," mocked Vick. "Did you have to be so tough on him?"

"Okay. I can't be mean."

Vick laughed and gave her an affectionate hug. "Don't ever change." He packed his briefcase. "So how did the interview go?"

"Okay, I guess. Sam introduced me to Director Rotas. Hopefully that helps. That's why I want to publish this article." She'd sent in a synopsis to *The Weather Journal* and was invited to submit the entire article. Her topic was Three Dimensional Numerical Models of Tropical Cyclone Track Prediction. More important than the formation of a storm was where it headed. Originally, meteorologists relied solely on statistical predictions—that is, based upon previous cyclone tracks, they forecast the course of a current storm. "I want to show that even with improved mathematical models with all our supercomputers, storm track forecasting is as much instinct as it is science. Did you know that accuracy in landfall predictions has improved less than fifteen miles in the last fifty years?"

"Proving the NHC hasn't evolved much in half a century is going to help you how in getting a job there?"

"Go home." She knew Vick had to be tired. The first couple of days of a swing shift were always hard. Diane had completed hers last week and was on reprieve for another two. They took turns working the graveyard stretches.

"Bye." Vick squeezed her shoulder and left.

"Hey," said Diane. Vick stopped and looked around. "You won't get into trouble for hacking in, are you?"

Vick shrugged carelessly, "What are they going to do? Kill me for stealing weather pictures?"

FOUR

Diane shifted in the deeply cushioned chair and began to study the numbers.

All forecasts started just a few miles away at the National Meteorological Center in Suitland, Maryland, by studying the four fundamental building blocks of weather interacting within themselves and with one another: the sun, the earth's simultaneous rotation and revolution, air pressure, and water. Supercomputers at NMC, working round the clock, assimilated weather data from the world over at the rate of two billion operations per second to produce around fifty thousand different texts and ten thousand maps every day. Called large scale guidance products for their overall view of global weather, NMC then selectively dispatched them to WFOs, who input local conditions to come up with regional forecasts. Since every agency worked from NMC products, weather on TV, radio, and print looked and sounded strikingly similar.

Diane cross-referenced the numerical information with images from NEXRAD to clarify isolated patches of purple haze—areas the radar couldn't read because of interference. NEXRAD utilized Doppler technology. It sent out radial pulses and read the returning radio waves. An approaching cloud increased the frequency of the radio waves, as would an invisible wind. NEXRAD analyzed the frequency changes and displayed visible cloud and invisible wind graphically on a color monitor.

Diane's first priority was to see if she needed to issue a quick update. Every six minutes, the AWIPS synchronously and simultaneously acquired, assimilated, processed, and displayed high resolution data from NOAA's weather satellites, the National Environmental Satellite, Data and Information Service, NMC, local NEXRAD, Wind Profilers, and Automated Surface Observation Systems. Not too long ago, several hundred staff collected this data.

There were no surprises. It promised to be another uncharacteristically hot October day. Daytime temperatures were nineteen degrees hotter than the seasonal averages. Even the Potomac simmered at an unprecedented 28°C. She checked the satellite pictures. The seven-day outlook was identical. Even though tropical disturbances were active this time of the year in the Atlantic Ocean, there was no weather within fifteen hundred miles of the East Coast. If there was a threat from a developing depression like 217E, the NHC would advise them at once.

Diane typed up the numerical data in columns and then the text of her forecast on the word processing software built into the AWIPS. She signed off below the last line using just her first name. With a motion of finality, she hit the keyboard button marked 'NOAAPORT,' the direct conduit to the media, private meteorological services nationwide, government agencies, universities, research organizations, and business interests.

The forecast done, she figured she'd work on her article for a couple of hours. She walked into the adjoining room, housing rows upon rows of seven-foot tall storage towers. Kept under strict temperature control, the towers continuously assimilated local data from nine cuts of the atmosphere. The raw data and every forecast generated in this and every WFO around the country was downloaded into an even bigger storage facility—the National Climatic Data Center in Asheville, North Carolina, the world's largest repository of weather records. Researchers studying global climatology constantly acquired, processed, analyzed, and disseminated information from the NCDC via NOAAPORT.

Diane plugged in Vick's flash drive and returned to her seat. As it always happened, she did not know where she put Vick's printouts. In the active mode, the AWIPS displayed current weather in real time. In the passive mode, it recreated data into a visual display on the monitor. Diane gave up looking for Vick's printouts.

She flipped through the pages of hers. Frowned.

She found no mention of tropical depression 217E.

She checked the page numbers to see if she'd lost a page. *No*. She scrutinized the dates. *No mistake there.* She studied the satellite pictures. *Uh-huh. Nothing at all on my printouts.* She began to look for Vick's and found them just before her frustrations turned vocal.

Diane placed them side by side. Her eyes went still.

Depression 217E and two bulletins from the National Hurricane Center had been erased from the WEFAX she'd acquired via official protocol.

Beepbeep!

Enveloped in her own silence, Diane's shoulders shrank with a start. The beeps indicated the AWIPS was ready with an image of 217E. She brought it up. The legend along the right hand side in a well organized column confirmed it as a tropical depression. Diane plotted a map under 217E. It was halfway across the Atlantic between the American and African continents.

She picked up the NHC's first advisory this past Monday.

ZCZC MIATCPAT1 ALL
TTAA00 KNHC DDHHMM
BULLETIN
TROPICAL DEPRESSION 217 ADVISORY NUMBER 1
NWS TPC/NATIONAL HURRICANE CENTER MIAMI FL
5 PM AST MON OCT 14

AT 5 PM AST...2100Z...THE POORLY DEFINED CENTER OF NEWLY FORMED TROPICAL DEPRESSION 217 WAS LOCATED NEAR LATITUDE 11.7 NORTH...LONGITUDE 38.3 WEST OR ABOUT 1450 MILES...2330 KM...EAST OF THE LESSER ANTILLES. THE DEPRESSION IS MOVING WEST NEAR 14MPH...22KMPH...AND THIS GENERAL MOTION IS EXPECTED TO CONTINUE FOR THE NEXT 24 HOURS. ESTIMATED MINIMUM CENTRAL PRESSURE IS 1008 MB...29.77 INCHES.

REPEATING THE 5 PM AST POSITION...11.7 N...38.3 W. MOVEMENT TOWARD...WEST NEAR 14 MPH. MAXIMUM SUSTAINED WINDS...20 MPH...32KMPH. MINIMUM CENTRAL PRESSURE 1008 MB. SATELLITE PICTURES THIS MORNING INDICATE THE DEPRESSION MAY BE DOWNGRADED TO A TROPICAL WAVE LATER BECAUSE THE SYSTEM IS MOVING INTO AN AREA NOT FAVORABLE FOR DEVELOPMENT.

NEXT ADVISORY WILL BE ISSUED BY THE NATIONAL HURRICANE CENTER AT 11 PM AST.

FORECASTER CLARK

217E didn't weaken. Diane initiated the Rapid Scan Mode and animated the tropical depression from the time it was spotted to the second advisory. A combined Visible and Infrared image of the depression spread across six degrees of latitude with a distinct cirrus outflow. Clark's second advisory twenty-four hours later reported that 217E's winds had accelerated to about thirty miles an hour. Only if they developed distinct rotary circulation and sustained speeds of thirty-three knots or thirty-eight miles an hour would the NHC give it a name. Diane used the AWIPS to project the development of 217E based on the two advisories. Barring any unforeseen changes, 217E looked to develop into a tropical storm.

A hurricane, even.

Staring at the screen, Diane suddenly figured out why direct satellite access had been discontinued, why 217E had been erased from the official bulletins.

Silence suffocated her again.

RingRing!

Suddenly! Her phone rang. She jumped, startled. *Jesus, I'm on pins and needles.* She relaxed, recognizing the extension on the caller ID as her boss, James Vaughn.

She picked up. "Hi, James."

"Diane. In my office, please. Now."

There was something about his tone. Or was there? Maybe she was just being paranoid since his call came on the heels of her realization why data on this tropical disturbance was shrouded in secrecy. Diane hurried upstairs, composed herself, rapped her knuckles on the door with an inserted nameplate: 'JAMES VAUGHN. CHIEF METEOROLOGICAL OFFICER.'

She didn't wait for an answer, entered, greeting him as casually as she could, "'Morning, boss."

James Vaughn had been a meteorologist for twenty-five years. Slight, methodical, sixty-one years old, he sported a pooch belly. He'd been a good and decent sort to Diane for as long as she'd worked here. He clocked in at nine and checked out at five to go back home to his wife of thirty years. They shared an old tract home that was fully paid off. Their two daughters were both married. He kept a picture of his five grand children on the desk. James was a typical bureaucrat —white, suburban, unremarkable. He looked up from a toy catalog over his fatherly bifocals, "Hi, Diane. Sit down."

"Early Christmas shopping for the grandkids?" she asked, forcing it.

If he noticed, he didn't show it. Instead, James nodded with a smile. "How did your interview go?"

Diane shrugged, "Okay, I guess. I hope."

"Good luck." He tossed the catalog down on the table and said in a nonplused voice, "I got a call from the Department of Defense? Someone hacked into Wallops from our AWIPS. Do you know anything about it?"

Diane was no good at lying. She came clean right away. "I asked Vick to do it."

"Why? There was no need to break in. NOAA just instituted a routing change."

"You know Vick," Diane tried to laugh it off. "He couldn't help himself when he saw the 'Access Denied' message."

James didn't laugh. "Why do you need Atlantic data?"

Diane replied in a monotone without a pause, "I'm writing an article on tropical cyclone track predictions and I wanted to do a comparative analysis of Atlantic storms tracked previously by statistical predictors and a developing storm today with state-of-the-art technology and models."

"Hm. Interesting topic. Find anything?"

"No," Diane answered quickly. *Too quickly?*

"Did he make any hard copies?" asked James, then apologized, "I'm sorry, Diane, they want me to ask these questions. Don't ask me why, I mean, we are meteorologists, we should be able to gather and disseminate weather data."

Diane wondered if she should tell him about the two separate sets of data that NOAA was issuing. It had to be illegal. No. A voracious reader of spy thrillers, she knew you don't mess with the DoD. "Vick put it on a flash drive and made printouts."

"I need to have them all back." He grimaced apologetically.

"Sure. I'll bring them right up."

James lowered his voice, "Go ahead and make whatever copies you need, but let's keep it between ourselves."

"Thanks," Diane grinned and left.

She burned another flash drive—she kept one on her keychain—and copied the printouts and stuffed them into the inner recesses of her file. She returned the originals to James's office along with Vick's flash drive. She'd have to buy him a new one. James had left for lunch, so too the rest of the office. She picked up the phone and called Vick. She had to tell him.

Philippe, his partner, answered. French-Angolan by birth, Diane thought Philippe had the coolest accent. After they gossiped like a couple of girl friends for a good ten minutes, he asked, "Do you want me to wake him?"

"If you don't mind."

"I don't." Philippe had a straight-faced, dry sense of humor that always caught Diane off guard. "I can't speak for him."

She laughed. "I'll take the chance."

"He sleeps too much anyway."

Diane heard a couple of thumps. Philippe was probably tapping Vick's head with the phone. Vick awoke with an unpleasant grunt, "Yeah."

"V. Can I swing by your place for a late lunch? I had the spookiest conversation with James. It's about the Atlantic data you pulled this morning."

"Why can't you just tell me over the phone? I hate seeing you twice in the same day."

"Me neither, but this is important."

"Philippe was talking about adopting a kid. I should just tell him we have you. You're here all the time. Bring eighteen ninety-five in exact change.

"Why?"

"You'll want to be fed. That's the cost of all-you-can-eat-and-drink at our house.

She hung up chuckling, turned around and gasped!

Ivory stared down at her grimly.

———

Three days earlier, NOAA 16, an Advanced TIROS-N polar orbiting environmental satellite, had routinely passed over the Atlantic Ocean five hundred and thirty miles above the earth in a sun synchronous orbit. Operated by the National Environmental, Satellite, Data and Information Service, it was the latest of six environmental earth observation systems stationed in space by the US at all times. NESDIS collected a quarter of a million atmospheric and oceanic observations daily from more than four million data points. Five other countries operated the eight other weather satellites for about sixty-two hundred observations.

NOAA 16's sensors picked up a wrinkle in the windflow over coordinates 38.3°W and 11.7°N of the equator. An onboard Direct Sounder Broadcast usually transmitted the data to

NESDIS's Satellite Data Processing and Distribution center in Suitland, Maryland. Twenty-nine readout stations in fourteen countries, including NOAA, received data from a single outlet called GOESTAP, an information gateway created to capitalize on the virtual monopoly the US enjoyed with meteorological products.

Not this Monday morning.

A Department of Defense security trigger activated aboard NOAA 16 and disabled the DSB. Only the Command and Data Acquisition Station in Wallops, Virginia, was able to acquire and time tag the weather anomaly. The CDA at Wallops followed a policy change issued following the eruption of the US-Cuba crisis, transmitting all telemetry, command, data uplink, and data readout to a building on Tinker Air Force Base outside Oklahoma City.

The door only carried an alpha numeral in that familiar military font: 'D7.'

Inside, a state-of-the-art man-computer interactive data access system, capable of processing, displaying, enhancing, overlaying, and animating satellite data, recognized the instability and a beep alerted the military meteorologist on duty. The operator, one of only three with the security clearance to work in this room, tapped a special key marked 'THUNDERSTRIKE," which erased the winkle.

The altered information was transmitted via NOAAPORT to the National Meteorological Center in Suitland, Maryland. The staff at the NMC never realized the data had been reconfigured. They routinely placed the altered data on the Global Transmission System from the Satellite Operations Control Center for national and international distribution. The diversion to D7 resulted in a transmission delay of a few minutes. National and international users never noticed.

Only two agencies were privy to the original data: the Air Force Weather Agency in Offutt, Nebraska, and the National Hurricane Center in Coral Gables, Florida. The NHC forecaster on duty this morning was a twelve-year veteran called Clark. He didn't think 217E would strengthen much.

On its next pass, NOAA 16's Advanced Very High Resolution Radiometer picked up a wisp of cloud. Normally, it would have been recorded on Channel 1 of the AVHRR's five-channel radiometer, downloaded at Wallops, and broadcast in real time via a commercial satellite to the NMC. There, it would have been then processed into polar stereographic and mercator maps of cloud cover for users worldwide.

Not this Monday morning.

The AVHRR images were recorded and time tagged at Wallops, then transmitted to D7 in Oklahoma. Now alerted to isolate all data from these Atlantic coordinates, the Thunder Strike software automatically duplicated the data—one with the instability intact, one erased. The erased signal traveled via NOAAPORT to the NMC for public consumption. Again, nobody noticed the small delay.

The unaltered data went to the AFWA and NHC.

Seeing clouds, Clark, at the NHC, routinely requested data from the Geostationary Satellite in orbit over the Atlantic. Every six minutes, it acquired and transmitted Visible and Infrared imagery to Wallops, where they were electronically calibrated, annotated, and formatted. This was then transponded to the Office of Satellite Data Processing and Distribution. International subscribers then picked it up on a microwave link from the SDPD.

Not this Monday morning.

As soon as the instability had been identified, the satellite images and sounding were routed to D7 to be duplicated. Erased data went to the NMC. The unaltered data traveled to the AFWA and NHC. Clark used Enhanced Infrared imagery to measure the temperature of the ocean surface. It sizzled at a season high 29°C. He confirmed it with Sea Surface Temperature data.

Five hours after NOAA 16 first spotted this instability,

Clark classified it as a tropical depression, the two-hundred and seventeenth of this hurricane season off the east coast and assigned it the corresponding number: 217E. Unable to spot any organized cumulus clouds, he remained convinced this depression, like most, would die. Still, procedure mandated he type up a bulletin.

Clark transmitted it along NOAAPORT, unaware the link for all information regarding these Atlantic coordinates had been closed. Instead of traveling to every Warning and Forecast Office along the East Coast, it went to the AFWA and nowhere else. The NMC, where all public forecasts originated, had no record that a tropical depression even existed.

Until Vick hacked in and downloaded it for Diane.

————

"I didn't mean to startle you," said Ivory Adams.

Diane regained her composure. "I thought I was alone."

"What's that?" He nodded curiously to the AWIPS.

Oh, no! 217E was up onscreen. With a casual tap of the space bar, she erased it off. "Just a research project for an article I'm writing."

Ivory's eyes narrowed. "Looked like a developing cyclone."

"Yeah. Archival." Meaning, a previous storm she'd dug up. Hopefully, he bought it. Ivory was familiar with the AWIPS. Had he read the legend alongside? It clearly tagged the disturbance as 217E with the date and time. She quickly got up and slid her purse up her arm. "I'm starving."

Ivory stood for just a moment more than necessary, then turned, and walked away.

Now that she'd made the pretense of heading out to eat, she had to leave. Diane was a conspiracy freak, thanks to her father's fascination with the death—he called it murder—of Marilyn Monroe. He read books upon books, then, at dinner, recited how the White House had been involved. So, she grew up with a deep mistrust of the government. She did not speak to her jerk ex for a week following an argument over Oliver

Stone's JFK, which they'd caught on cable. Naturally, she believed Stone's coup d'état theory, while he categorized it as bunk. They had a similar argument over the pre-emptive strike on Iraq. She still believed it was an oil grab. Now, confronting this cover-up in the Atlantic, all her apprehensions returned.

She never liked Ivory. His manner seemed sinister. *Is he part of this?* He had to be. Before joining this WFO, he had trained at the AFWA. She looked around as she stepped outside. Ivory had paused too and was staring right back at her. She became convinced.

He knew.

TODAY

Liz could not believe her eyes when she looked out of her circling plane. She had seen pictures of the flooding and storm damage, but she wasn't prepared for this. It looked as if a giant fist had smashed down on the nation's capital and let the pieces drift. More than a week had elapsed since Hurricane Meg had overrun DC, yet Washington looked nowhere near from even starting to recover.

The flight from New York had been unnerving as hell. The Cessna's fuselage had rattled and crackled and moaned all the way over. Whenever they encountered turbulence, Liz felt she was going to die. Oddly, she drew strength from Savage, the unkempt pilot, who chain-smoked calmly the entire way. She'd kicked the habit in rehab. The smell drove her crazy. She almost asked him for a cigarette several times. But she remained strong and did not succumb. *Chalk that up to another small but significant personal victory in my battle against my many addictions.*

They entered DC airspace at daybreak. Meg had leveled the Control Tower at Dulles International Airport. Military controllers handled air traffic from a cluster of mobile units. There was so much confusion on the ground, the ATC—air traffic controller—did not question their claim that they had filed a flight plan. But they were low priority. Looking out the window, Liz saw why. Planes were stacked high, waiting to land. These first commercial flights carried doctors, civilian relief, and few influential residents. The controller said it could easily be an hour, or more.

"What if we tell them we are low on fuel?" Liz asked Savage. She wanted to be on the ground.

"They'd call our bluff," Savage replied gruffly. He did not seem at all enamored by her or her looks, treating her attempts at conversation through out the flight like it was an intrusion. "We would have known we shouldn't be here if we had filed a flight plan."

"Do we have enough fuel?"

"Yeah," said Savage impatiently.

Liz had lived in DC for three years. She knew the city well. As they circled endlessly, Liz recognized familiar skyscrapers dangerously careened at impossible angles. Others had simply collapsed. Cars lay strewn haphazardly in thousands, overturned, smashed, and abandoned. Giant landslides had dislocated entire hillsides. The Potomac and Anacostia rivers still looked swollen, submerging not just bridges, but entire neighborhoods. Rooftops and debris floated aimlessly. She realized the cigar shaped specks were dead bodies. Yachts and sailboats had been carried several miles inland. Smoke from scores of fires, several still raging, created a black haze over much of the capital.

The devastation was Armageddon-esque.

The cockpit radio crackled. They were cleared to land. They'd been circling for ninety minutes. Stepping off her plane, Liz caught her breath loudly. The tarmac was congested with heavily armed soldiers moving tons of food, medicine, clothing, and other relief supplies from mammoth C-14 military transport aircraft. She barely recognized the terminal she'd flown in and out so many times. It was stripped bare of its glass. Entire walls were missing. Pillars had buckled. A 747 Jumbo jet was impaled into the Midfield Concourse. Other commercial liners were scattered carelessly about like cars in a junkyard, without a wing, a tail fin, landing gear. An Airbus had been completely overturned. Another cut in half.

"How much do you want to lay over in DC and fly me back to New York?"

"You can't afford it."

She realized Savage knew if he walked into the terminal and announced he was charging the moon, he would have a stampede of takers. "Try me."

Savage did.

Liz did not haggle. "You have my credit card number. Charge it."

He nodded. "I need an ETD."

"No later than midnight tonight."

"An exact ETD."

"Midnight tonight, then," said Liz, and added at once, "You can't take any other passengers on my flight," He forced a grin. He did not anticipate she'd figure right away that he was not going to just cool his heels waiting for her. He was a hustler. He'd likely begin a shuttle service out of DC.

"Okay. Midnight sharp," he said, trying to regain ground. "Then the deal's off. No refunds."

"Fair enough." Liz walked into the terminal and almost gagged under a pervasive thick, dank stench. Moisture coated the walls, floor, and hung in the air like a physical thing.

Then, she came face to face with the pandemonium.

People teemed chaotically with desperate expressions. Trying to leave on the arriving commercial flights. Bidding on tickets. It looked like a badly orchestrated mop up, where anything went. Airport vehicles and cars had been tossed inside the terminals. Huge, untidy chunks of wall and ceiling were gone. Announcements blared over a bullhorn. Heavily armed soldiers idly stood by and watched. Liz thought she was in a Third World country after a violent military coup. She squeezed out of the gate area only to discover that Meg had taken out the bridge between the terminal and baggage claim. Military jeeps created a corridor all the way to the curb.

The parking structure that she'd used all the time when she traveled on assignment had been pancaked. Cars oozed out the edges like meat out of an overstuffed sandwich. More lay overturned and strewn along the side of the feeder road servicing the terminal. They had been simply shoved over to clear a lane and a half around the airport. A small commuter plane, plucked from the tarmac half a mile away and thrown over baggage claim, protruded out of the wreckage of vehicles.

About thirty yards to Liz's left, a cop let the unruly drivers and pedestrians figure it out for themselves.

She was under no illusions. Someone was watching her. She looked around for an approaching stranger who might be her contact. Admiral Grant hadn't given her any details. No name, no idea if it was a man or a woman. Nothing. Grant had sent out her picture. So, her contact would have to recognize her and make the first move quickly to outmaneuver the surveillance.

A retired cop had trained her in spotting a tail when the threats on her life became real during the Jarvis Johnson story. He had also taught her unarmed combat, how to fire a gun, hot-wire cars, jimmy locks, find food, and live on water. She realized she would need all those survival skills and more, seeing how Meg had blasted Washington back to the Stone Age. She pretended to search for her ride and carefully scanned the faces. Nobody seemed interested in her. Of course not. Her watcher would be a pro.

Liz waited. Nothing else she could do. Half an hour elapsed. At least, it wasn't hot and humid like New York. The temperatures hovered around seventy-five. Pleasant. Her eyelids felt heavy. She hadn't slept a wink last night on the plane, and the night before she'd caught probably a couple of hours of rest between sex, the time she received the unmarked envelope, and getting back up to go to work.

Thunder Strike. *What can it be?*

Billy had been killed for just being a messenger. Before that, fourteen defense personnel in a plane crash. Then Admiral Grant. You couldn't get closer to the president than him, yet he was murdered. She checked around again. She still couldn't spot her tail. Not surprising.

They needed to give her enough of a leash to operate.

Liz's eyes arrested on a man, mid-forties, graying temples, his hair cut short like bristles. He limped to edge of the sidewalk. He had a gimpy left leg. He wore a tight fitting

T-shirt, which he filled out with an athletically cut body and baggy pants with multiple pockets, every one of them filled. He paused ten yards from Liz, met her eyes, and nodded. Liz added up the limp, his tentative friendliness, and genteel appearance.

My contact.

She took a step forward. Traffic, which had come to a standstill, jerked again. That didn't stop pedestrians from stepping off the sidewalk into the spasming cars to get to rides that couldn't pull into the right lane. The same moment that Liz dodged a young couple squeezing in front of her and the gimpy man, a muddy, dented, white Jeep Cherokee swerved aggressively from the left lane.

Straight for her!

————

Philippe drove.

Vick Delhom's partner recognized Liz on the sidewalk instantly. He would have, even if Admiral Grant hadn't sent a picture. Her past had been the stuff of office cooler talk for months. Her name ranked up there with celebrities who so saturated the news, even the uneducated and disinterested American became aware of them. Philippe, like all Europeans, loved scandals, especially those at the confluence of politics, drugs, and sex. He believed Liz had single-handedly put President Avery Walker in office.

He saw Liz squint. She was trying to penetrate the glare slashing his windshield with geometric patterns. She probably got only quick, partial glimpses of him. Even so, she wouldn't recognize him. So, he honked and waved to her.

She looked confused, turning her head from him to the sidewalk. Philippe followed her eyes and reacted as if he'd been punched by a fist full of fear!

He saw the gimpy man. The glare wiped off the Cherokee's windshield and the gimpy man saw him. Philippe slammed on the gas pedal and knifed back into the left lane.

He cut off another car. Ignoring the loud barrage of obscenities from the driver, he accelerated into clear road, but it was just a few open yards. He had to brake hard with nowhere to go.

What Philippe dreaded, happened next.

The gimpy man tore open passenger side door.

A car length opened up in the right lane. Philippe swerved hard and floored the gas. This should rip the gimpy man's grip loose. The Jeep Cherokee leapt. Head-on toward Liz. *Shit!*

Philippe lacked the reflexes to react. She had a second. Less. With a scream, she dived aside. He waited to hear the sickening thump of his fender against flesh. There wasn't one. The Cherokee whipped past her without touching her. He swiveled to the mirror on his side. She was trying to draw the attention of the cop thirty feet back. The cop did not react, did not even see or hear her above the cars in low gear. Philippe lifted his eyes to mirror in the car. Liz just ran into traffic, waving her arms frantically, chasing the Jeep. Horns blared. Brakes shrieked. Traffic gridlocked behind her. It caught the cop's attention. *Good girl.* The cop started forward in a lazy jog.

Slam! The passenger side door shut hard. Philippe snapped around. He thought he'd lost the gimpy man. *No!* He was in the car! He drew a gun unlike any Philippe had ever seen.

The man didn't waste words. He simply said, "Talk."

Philippe could only stare. He had heard about the gimpy man. A merciless assassin. He'd mowed down a room full of people who knew nothing and posed no danger, but they'd heard two words they should not have.

Thunder Strike.

Then he'd gone after Diane and Sam inside Meg.

Philippe gripped the steering helplessly. He could hear himself breathe. The assassin quickly looked over his shoulder. Seizing upon the distraction, Philippe snapped an elbow into the man's chest. Elicited no more than a flinch. A fearsome, hard glint came into the gimpy man's eyes.

With a single swipe of the gun—*crack*—he broke Philippe's nose and repeated, "Talk."

Philippe's face wrenched back and his foot inadvertently jammed the gas pedal. The Cherokee lurched forward. The assassin pressed back in his seat. Philippe hit the power window button and shouted out of the lowering window, "Police! Hel-ahhhhh!"

Thunk! The assassin fired.

The bullet severed Philippe's finger on the button.

He screamed. His right hand slid off the wheel to grab the bleeding stump. The Cherokee began to weave wildly, sideswiping cars. Drivers got out of the way. Triggering more collisions. Grimacing in agony, Philippe caught an encouraging glimpse in the rearview mirror of the cop and Liz break into run toward the Cherokee. Philippe's eyes snapped back to the assassin, who did not say a word. He slanted the muzzle down. A stab of flame!

Crack!

Philippe's knee disintegrated into flesh and bone.

He gasped with another wrenching, agonized cry! His foot slid off the accelerator but not before jamming it down in painful reflex first. The Cherokee staggered without any steering in a dying burst of speed. The assassin put a hand on the wheel, deliberately body-slamming a couple of cars before—*wham!* The Cherokee smashed into a concrete pillar.

"Last chance. Talk."

The pain only steeled Philippe's resolve. He grit his teeth and shook his head. *No.* He was beyond caring now. He knew he was going to die. The assassin shrugged nonchalantly. Pumped two shots into Philippe's heart. One moment, Phillipe was seeing light, life. Then, darkness.

———

The Cherokee horn blared ceaselessly. A hole opened in Liz's stomach and filled up with a dreadful feeling. The cop and she were sprinting between cars. It was dangerous because drivers accelerated, recklessly working forward between the damaged cars. No one wanted to get stuck in this mess.

Liz's picked up a streaking flash. There for a millisecond, perhaps less. *A bullet!*

It wasn't aimed at her or the cop, but the windshield of a Ford Explorer behind them leading the berserk pack. She did not hear the impact. Just saw the glass spiderweb around the bullet hole. Time slowed. Liz's gaze dipped to the wheels. They angled abruptly. Probably wrenched over by the panicked driver. The shallow treads and moist road conspired, U-turned the SUV, and rolled it over. It spun straight toward Liz and the cop. He kept running, unaware.

Liz screamed and yanked him down.

He hit the road face first and was spared the terror Liz experienced. She fell flat on her back and she stared up at the SUV, turned upside down, descending on them. She closed her eyes. Giving up. Waiting to be crushed. Hoping she would feel nothing.

Whabam! The top smashed down. The road shook. Liz felt concussion waves. Realized at once the Explorer had missed them. It hit the asphalt a yard short of her feet! The windows shattered, spraying glass! Then bounced over her and the cop.

She closed her eyes and covered her face. Even so she felt a shadow sweep across. Shrapnel bombarded them as the rooftop glided barely a foot above her face. *Whabam!* Liz opened her eyes. The Ford hit the road beyond their heads and did not bounce back. Instead, it raked the blacktop with an ear-splitting squeal.

Adrenalized by the close call, Liz came to her feet. Ignoring the clash of a second series of collisions, she raced for the Cherokee. She got there before the cop even picked himself up. She grabbed the door open and drew back in horror.

Philippe was a bloody mess.

She lifted his head carefully. His eyes were open. Still.

Lifeless. He was dead.

Her stomach contracted with a sick, empty feeling. Liz wasn't sure how long she remained kneeling there before she felt the policeman's hand on her shoulder. He said, "Don't go anywhere, miss."

Armed soldiers came running. She backed away and stood on the sidewalk. Anger replaced defeat. She should have been more careful. She'd known this could be a trap. Yet, she'd walked right into it.

———

The gimpy man who killed Philippe stood behind the one way glass of the police interrogation room. On the other side, Liz sat alone, her face set in thought. The door opened. A detective walked in. She lifted her head and her expression changed. Becoming perplexed. Nervous.

A thing of beauty, thought the assassin, the way the muscles on her face readjusted, the scheming glint left her eyes and she parted and pouted her lips to lose their pensive thinness. Chameleonic, her silken metamorphosis. *She's damn good.*

He should know, a master of deception himself.

His parents, both steel workers in Pittsburgh, christened him Andrew Tristan. He never used the name anymore. He couldn't. Andrew Tristan Burke, with the social security number and driver's license his parents knew, had been killed in an ambush in Iraq. His body was never recovered. His parents did not know he was even alive.

His transformation from blue-collar kid to assassin started in his freshman year at the University of Pittsburgh. He got in on a GI scholarship. As a part-time soldier, he discovered a gift he never knew he possessed—marksmanship. His CO talked him into quitting college and becoming a full time marine, where his talent earned him a quick transfer into the Special Forces. There, Andrew discovered another facet about himself. He loved killing. Not just enemy soldiers—he proved himself beyond compare at that as part of the advance recon team into Baghdad during the second Iraq war—but civilians. Specifically, women.

Andrew's first victim was a hooker, who he picked up in a dark alley of Austin, Texas, after a particularly dull week at the base. He hadn't been with a girl since high school for a reason he kept closely guarded, a reason he hoped he'd outgrown. The hooker reached between his legs. When he couldn't get aroused, he knew nothing had changed. It was high school all over again. His sweetheart then had been kind to his face, but the next morning everyone knew. His senior year had been hell and humiliating. The hooker had that same sympathetic smile. *Stinkin' whore.*

He roughly shoved her head down. She took him in her mouth and did her best. Staring at the back of her head, the thought of breaking her neck just popped into his mind. And he did it. He snapped her head back with such force, pieces of her spine cut clean through her skin. Blood flew. He went hard at once. He hiked her skirt and spread her legs. Murder to necrophilia, he'd never felt so exhilarated. It became his MO.

Meanwhile, in the much publicized war on terror, Andrew's legend grew as a killing machine. While hunting down Saddam Hussein in Tikrit, a bullet shattered his left knee and left him with a permanent limp. He didn't know he'd been reported KIA—killed-in-action—by the Pentagon.

Until a man named Peter Wilkins called him from the CIA.

Peter wanted Andrew to continue in cleanup, the Agency's sanitized job description for an assassin. Andrew operated in Europe, quietly picking off CIA targets, mostly terrorists flushed out from Afghanistan and Iraq. Off the record, his other depravity flourished. He continued to kill and rape women, in that order.

A week ago, he was flown out of Paris to Andrews AFB, where he received pictures and profiles of eighteen primary targets, all in Washington DC. Peter told him that this cover-up had no margin for error. Everyone had to die. But two got away. Then, yesterday, Peter informed him that the targets were still in DC. The news surprised Andrew. He'd figured the two had left in the chaotic aftermath. There was no way to seal off the city and they were proverbial needles in a haystack. Maybe the bullet wound he'd inflicted on one of them was more serious than he thought.

Andrew stared at Liz from behind the one way glass. The detective who walked in was Buck Stoll. He'd been working with Andrew in Meg's aftermath. Liz shifted in her damp chair. The walls carried deep cracks and large wet stains. Burke noticed the demure manner in which she put the back of her hand to her nose. The assassin knew it wasn't the first thing Buck noticed about Liz. 'Smokin' hot' probably crossed his mind before anything else.

A speaker beside Andrew crackled with their voices.

"Meg busted us up pretty good," Buck said, pulling up a chair and sitting across from her. "Damage everywhere. Roof was flat, so water piled up until it caved in the squad room. You know water weighs five pounds a gallon?"

The police station hadn't escaped Meg's wrath. No structure in DC had. Doors and windows were ripped off the hinges and most of the records lost. A quarter of an inch of water still stood in the holding cells. A 'Boil' order was in effect across Washington because scores of sewer lines had ruptured. The advance team from the Center for Disease Control had taken one look at the scale of the calamity and immediately put out a nationwide call for hundreds of volunteer doctors and nurses. The death toll stood at a million already. Tens of thousands more would die before they even started getting a handle on this massive tragedy.

"I don't understand why I'm here," said Liz.

"Did you know the victim?"

"No." Her hands shook just enough to be perceptible as she picked up the Styrofoam cup of coffee an officer had brought in earlier. "I was just, you know, figuring out transportation. It happened all so suddenly. I've never been an eyewitness to murder. That was scary."

"I understand." Buck tried to be comforting.

Broad, square, and ruddy, he looked like he walked off a hunting show. He couldn't be mistaken as anything but a cop. Andrew shook his head. Buck's sympathy was awkward. "You must be shaken. But I have to ask you a few questions."

Liz flashed a brief smile and nodded. "I understand."

"Did he say anything?"

"No. He was dead when I got there."

The pouch on Andrew's belt buzzed. He unbuttoned the flap and pulled out a slender, state-of-the-art MILSATCOM, a radio phone that battle commanders used in the field. Thunder Strike demanded the same level of secrecy.

He knew it was Peter Wilkins on the other end.

His boss and control officer at ODIA—Office of Denial and Intelligence Activities.

"She's good," said Andrew without even a greeting in that same soft, quiet, and calm voice that he used to strike terror in Philippe. Andrew never shouted—he discovered early on that it served no purpose. In fact, it diminished threat and increased emotion driven actions, which, in hindsight, ended up being mistakes. "Buck's asked her barely three questions and she has him eating out of her hand already."

Andrew didn't much care for politics and was only vaguely familiar with Liz's notoriety. She knew the game and played it perfectly. Kept her story simple. Less chance of tripping up. She told Buck she saw a man pull a gun and called for help. Maybe she got carried away, overtaking the cop to the victim. It was her first day back and the overzealous reporter in her took over.

"Why are you in Washington?" asked Buck.

"This was my beat. I know the city. So the paper sent me."

Andrew smirked. *Liar.* She knew there was no way of

checking. Media outlets didn't have enough reporters covering the disaster. Meg was the biggest story in the world right now, with comparisons to superstorm Sandy and Katrina. History seemed to be repeating on a much bigger scale and with graver consequences since Washington was also the nation's capital and power center of the world. Andrew, who was only half listening to Peter, reacted to what he felt as an admonishment. "I killed him because there was no time to work him."

"You were not supposed to—kill him or work him," snapped Peter uncharacteristically. Andrew had never known Peter to lose it. "Did you get an ID?"

"He wasn't carrying anything. No wallet, nothing."

"The vehicle?"

"A Jeep Cherokee. No license plate."

"What about the VIN?" Vehicle Identification Number. Multiple letters and numbers unique to each car that were inscribed on the dash, the door, and the engine block.

"I didn't have the time." Andrew heard Peter take a breath. "He was black, if that helps. Not African American. He had a French accent. French-Angolan, if I had to guess." A large Angolan population resided in France. Andrew played tourist between assignments, traveling all over the world. He'd sit at sidewalk cafes, walk the streets, visit markets, and watch and listen to people. Studying behavior, habits, culture. He considered it research.

"I thought I made it quite clear to let Liz talk to him first."

"I don't work from behind," said Andrew brusquely.

"You had a week on your own," Peter fired back. "This is two missions in a row you've had trouble with."

Andrew's last target, the reason he was in Paris, escaped unhurt. A Hammas favor for Israel from the Pentagon. He missed the Palestinian extremist. The man jumped out of the sixth floor window, hit the canvas canopy over the entrance below, slid off it onto the sidewalk, and fled. It was pure Hollywood. The French, who had reluctantly allowed the hit on US assurance that it would be clean, quiet, and below the radar, were extremely unhappy. Home to the largest Muslim population in Europe, France feared retaliation and, worse, a public backlash for France turning into another Britain—an American lap dog. Andrew's two assassinations prior to Paris had not been tidy either. There had been two near misses. Three second shots.

Peter started, "Maybe—"

"What do you want me to do?" interrupted Andrew.

"It's inevitable. It happens to everyone.".

Andrew knew exactly what Peter was getting at. *Others became dinosaurs. Not me.*

"I don't know." Peter did not hide his frustration. "Let her go. Use her. That's why she's here."

———

Buck looked toward the one-way glass with a helpless expression. He'd gotten as far as he could with Liz. Buck had no idea what this was all about and preferred to remain in the dark. A DC native for three generations, Buck had never been in a hurricane. Sure, he'd read about them. They usually stayed south, getting as far as North Carolina, not much farther. 2012's superstorm Sandy was a freak, getting all the way to New York and New Jersey. Even though she was a mega-bitch, there was fair warning. Everyone knew she was coming for days.

Meg arrived suddenly, inexplicably without warning. As soon as word came of Meg's impending arrival, every cop, detective to uniform, hit the streets to blare out warnings. But people were asleep. Buck hid out with the rest of the station and their families down in the basement. When Meg hit, they felt her ferocity fifteen feet below the ground. The media was calling her a superhurricane. It fit, even without knowing what that meant.

Immediately following the storm, his uncle, Peter Wilkins, a big shot in the Agency over at Langley, asked Buck to assist a nameless government agent. Buck pulled rank. He had seniority. He took over the station when the lieutenant, who didn't hunker down with them, never showed up. He was probably dead. Nobody questioned Buck moving into the loot's office.

Most of the men and women working here still suffered from "disaster syndrome," one of the cops's wives, a pyscholigst, said. It was a mixed reaction of denial, hysteria, and confusion. Furthermore, the entire DC Police Department was in disarray. Hundreds of cops were still missing. Take-charge officers like Buck were welcome. Aftermath of disasters usually drew people together. Not the case with Meg. The altruism wore off into a wave of fear, bedlam, and desperate scramble for water, food, and shelter.

The phone on the wall adjacent to the one-way glass rang. Buck got up, "Excuse me."

"Let her go," said Andrew when Buck picked it up.

Buck nodded, "Okay." He listened for a moment, hung up, and smiled over to Liz, "You can go, Ms. Lovell.

"I'm sorry I couldn't be of much help." Liz stood up.

"If you think of anything, call me." Buck gave her his card and watched her walk out of the room, marveling her ass. He almost forgot. "Oh, can I offer you a ride? We have a patrol detail leaving in a few minutes."

She turned. He darted his eyes quickly up to hers. He was staring at her ass and couldn't hide his embarrassment. But she didn't seem to notice. Or care. Chicks like her were used to it. She said, "That'd be great, thanks."

Buck put her in a squad car and told the uniform behind the wheel to take her wherever she wanted to go. Liz flashed him a smile. Buck noticed that it never reached her eyes.

The hairs on his back rose. It felt exactly like being in a room with Andrew.

SIX

Peter Wilkins knew this day would come—when he would have to look for a new protégé. It was a tough thing. Andrew and he had worked so closely and so successfully for so long. They'd built their reputations on each other's backs. He sat back stroking his chin pensively. The window of his office, like every other on every floor, was boarded with plywood. He ignored the bulldozers outside, noisily compacting and moving tons of debris Meg had dumped and the river had washed up. It had taken almost four days to separate the corpses. The body bags had been removed only yesterday. But the acrid stench of death penetrated inside.

Peter recalled returning to the CIA Headquarters in Fairfax County outside DC for the first time after the storm. It resembled a building in the heart of a war zone. Swaths of masonry gone. The lawn, once immaculate and green, was shredded like cheap fabric, leaving behind wide tears of bare earth. Huge holes remained where trees once stood. A ring of tanks and heavily armed soldiers guarded the perimeter. Targeted for protection along with the White House, Capitol Hill, the Pentagon, FBI Headquarters, and other vital government buildings, the men and women in green had moved into position almost immediately after Meg subsided.

Peter worked on the third floor office in the wing dedicated to counter-espionage. His door did not have his name or position painted on the half panel of glass. In fact, he did not have a door. Neither did most offices in the whole building. Meg's wind and rain had pillaged every floor of all the furniture and fixtures. Fortunately, there had been enough lead time to remove sensitive documents.

From his sparrow like features to his fastidious neatness and meticulous manner, there was a cold, clinical efficiency in the way Peter looked and worked. He embodied the stereotype of an analyst, though he never set out to be one. Thoroughness just ran in his genes. His father was a tough, by-the-book IRS auditor, his mother an OR nurse. He grew up comfortably in the Jacksonville, scoring consistently near the top of his class at the University of Florida. He got into Harvard easily and graduated with an MBA, hoping to get on an executive fast track at a major corporation. But the CIA came recruiting.

The year was 1980, the Cold War in full swing. America needed the best and the brightest to choose patriotism over money to fight Communists who were staffed with the cream of their IQ crop. Intrigued by the notion of life in the shadows, he signed on.

The Agency surpassed his expectations and more. He loved the game of counter-intelligence. It was cerebral. Fought with just a single weapon: information. Furthermore, the job suited his personality. He lacked social skills. He'd always been a loner. There were a few awkward short-lived relationships with homely women. He never married and lived ten minutes from work so he could spend most of his time at the office. He rose quickly through the ranks. In 1984, CIA Director William Casey entrusted Peter with launching and running a new department that 'didn't exist.'

The Office for Denial and Intelligence Activities. ODIA.

The origin of 'deception and denial' as a military strategy had begun during World War II, when the United States and Great Britain wrapped the location of the D-Day invasion in a series of lies. The Soviets elevated it into a 'policy and procedure.' They created a Directorate for Strategic Deception to deny American satellites clear reconnaissance with dummy roads and matte paintings, fake silos and submarines, sliding roofs and tarpaulins, submarine covers and tunnels, camouflaged hulls and rail sidings, and false impact craters and nighttime tests. To combat growing Soviet sophistication, Casey realized Americans needed to organize their own cover, concealment, denial, and deception.

He introduced Peter to a young DoD Undersecretary

called Baron Hawke.

From their first meeting, Peter felt Baron emanated an aura of old money. Baron's father had no official designation, yet belonged to President Ronald Reagan's inner circle of military advisors. Peter tried to find out more but Baron said little and discouraged curiosity. Together, they created and shaped the ODIA to remain an unnamed and autonomous department, reporting only to the defense secretary, the National Security Council, and the President, in that order.

Thunder Strike had been ODIA's biggest assignment yet. A coup d'état to oust Castro that nobody would have suspected was engineered by the United States. Every aspect of Thunder Strike needed to be cloaked in secrecy for it to work. It began well. Then a tiny low pressure trough, no bigger than a city block, in the Atlantic, changed everything.

The mop-up became sloppy. As point for the operation, Peter shouldered the responsibility. Despite being on the wrong side of sixty, he knew he would not be fired. There was nobody better than him at his job. His record was impeccable. Under him, the ODIA did not have a single failure. Thunder Strike was not going to be the first. He would not allow it.

It was a matter of ego and pride now.

Peter's phone rang. The instrument had multiple lines, each color coded and connected via secure, indestructible direct underground lines to the FBI, NSA, CIA, DIA, NORAD, etc. This call blinked with a blue light.

Defense Secretary Baron Hawke. He was calling from his Virginia home.

Peter answered, "Hello."

"Peter." Baron always began his conversations with no greeting. Just the name of the person he was calling. As long as Peter had known him, Baron had always been soft spoken, deliberate, and measured. His words could never be construed as spoken in haste. He superseded the vice president as the second most powerful man in this administration. "Jack's on from the Pentagon."

"Hello, Peter," growled General Jack Knight. The Joint Chiefs of Staff Chairman was the diametric opposite. His booming voice reflected his oversized personality.

"Secretary, Chairman," said Peter, addressing them as he always did. He never broke protocol even though he'd known both men for almost three decades. He called them Baron and Jack only on the first Sunday of every month, when they golfed together, and at the quarterly conference of NeoCon—a neo-conservative group founded by former Vice President Dick Cheney in the 1980s and radicalized even further by Baron when he took over a few years ago.

"Liz is in DC," said Peter.

"I don't trust her," snapped Jack.

"We were getting nowhere," Peter responded. "She comes in. We have movement."

"How much did Liz find out about Thunder Strike from Admiral Grant?" asked Baron, ignoring the brittle exchange between Peter and Jack

"Nothing at all," said Peter, unruffled. "We moved in before Grant gave her any details."

Baron did not answer. Peter heard familiar creaking. Whenever he relapsed into thought, the defense secretary rocked his antique leather chair. Peter knew that because Baron had mentioned it during golf. For as long as they'd known each other, none of the men had ever visited each other in their homes.

"And when she finds out? Then what?" asked Jack.

"We won't let her get that far," Peter replied.

"It was never supposed to get this far or take this long, Peter," Jack crackled. "I haven't seen my wife since we evacuated our families to New York. I've been living out of a suitcase, hand washing my underwear, and bathing out of a basin."

Peter realized Jack had spent his life following orders

and living strictly between the rigid covers of the military code book. Now, they were operating outside the lines, treading dangerous, unprecedented ground. A decorated veteran of actual ground combat, Jack wore his emotions on his sleeve. But lately, he had begun to second guess their every move. It was becoming worrisome. Peter sensed that Baron had noticed as well.The creaking stopped. Peter sharpened.

"The president, "Baron said, "he had another episode last night."

With Congress in New York, they had kept Avery's nightmares under wraps. But politicians were expected to start trickling back into DC from New York soon. As early as tomorrow. Tragedy always provided great political mileage and a goldmine of images for campaign ads. The defense secretary needed to solidify his grip on power before the Cabinet found out something they never suspected.

Baron was running the country, not President Avery Walker.

"Father," said Warren, "it's time for me to leave."

Baron looked over, covered the mouthpiece, and said, "Let me walk you out." Then he told Peter and Jack, "I'll see you shortly."

The defense secretary disconnected and put an arm around his 19-year old son as they headed down the sweeping, grand staircase that encircled a magnificent, twenty-foot wide chandelier hanging from cathedral-shaped dome four stories above floor level. The crystals glittered with morning sunlight, which first dappled through the canopy of centuries-old trees outside, then entered as golden shafts through the tall, stained glass windows, each handcrafted more than a hundred years ago by artisans brought in from Florence.

Baron Samuel Hawke was born to the kind privilege regular people could never comprehend. Construction of this mansion, which overlooked the James River, began in 1792. It took a decade to complete and became the second great

American estate in Virginia.

Family founder and pioneer, General Zachariah Hawke, brought in masons, sculptors, and painters from as far away as India. Built on a footprint of half an acre, every Hawke since had added, upgraded, and modernized it into what it was today: an imposing, three-story, multi-terrace, eighty-seven thousand square foot edifice to money and power. It stood at the end of a three mile-long uphill driveway. The Hawkes could see below and around, but the trees permitted the ordinary citizenry only small, mysterious slices of the mansion, befitting the family's stature as anonymous kingmakers and the power behind power.

Zachariah had chosen this site partly for its perfect proximity to DC, which was neither too close nor too far, and partly for its history. The first official Thanksgiving had been held in 1619 on the Berkeley Plantation nearby. But he chose the site mainly to challenge the owner of Virginia's first great estate: John Ulysses II, whose father had received a land grant and settled here fifty years before Zachariah showed up. Zachariah's audacity—no surprise to anyone who knew this giant of a man with an even bigger persona—served notice that the Ulysses were no longer the single most influential family of the time.

Overtly, the Ulysses were the biggest land owners in the county. Covertly, they were America's earliest lobbyists and the first family of diplomacy that nobody knew. Every Hawke, since Zachariah, was educated about the history of the Ulysses, and vice versa. John Ulysses II's father gave young George Washington his first job surveying and mapping their vast acreage. Both highly intellectual men, John and Washington forged a lifelong friendship. John recognized Washington as a special leader, charismatic, experienced, and educated from civics to military. The Ulysses recommended Washington to the Second Continental Congress in 1775, which was key to his appointment as the Commander-in-Chief of the American Army.

Here, Washington met Zachariah Hawke, a brash, outgoing, battle tested patriot. Zachariah's brilliant battlefield acumen made him Washington's most trusted military advisor. Fighting shoulder to shoulder, they too became fast friends. Zachariah even saved Washington from capture with an ingenious escape following their defeat at New York City. But when it came to hold an infant country together with a fragile alliance of states, militias, and the French, Washington needed the diplomatic skills of John Ulysses II.

In 1789, after Washington became the first president of the United States, he called upon Zachariah and John to be his military and political counsel respectively. Neither wanted an official post and agreed to advise Washington privately. Already sworn enemies and bitter rivals, aggravated further by Zachariah's nerve to begin construction down river from the Ulysses home, they battled for Washington's ear to forge diametrically opposite visions for a new nation seeking an identity.

Zachariah was a fan of Roman history. He declared that if the world saw America as the difference in the ongoing war between Britain and France, the US could emerge as a fearsome military superpower—he was allegedly the first to coin the term. John vehemently opposed the idea and prevailed. Washington issued the Proclamation of Neutrality, which laid the blueprint to keep the US from joining foreign conflicts. Zachariah found himself on the outside looking in.

Then, rebels in Pennsylvania defied federal authority. Diplomacy failed. Zachariah rode at the head of the army with Washington to decisively quash the Whiskey Rebellion. John's influence faded. War with Britain loomed. Just when it seemed the Hawkes could not be deposed, Washington saw the wisdom in a peaceful resolution. He signed the Jay Treaty, which ushered a decade of peace with Britain. The Ulysses roared back.

So began this militarist vs. diplomat see-saw, one which

grew and intensified with each successive presidency. Soon, the Hawkes and the Ulysses were deciding who would square off for the Oval Office. They chose to work unobtrusively from the sidelines, realizing notoriety would spark public outrage. The two families even gave their secret, alternating grip on the most powerful office on earth a name.

Storming Freedom.

On account of the fact Ulysses was overheard making a snide observation about Zachariah's gait, always 'storming' in and out like a petulant street thug. Zachariah mocked Ulysses as an overzealous 'freedom' lover who believed the US should be helping every country achieve democracy. Dictators, Zachariah believed, better served American interests.

Storming Freedom turned out to be an apt phrase. Whether the world was at war or at peace depended on which family controlled the dark shadows. Both strived to oust the other entirely because owning the dark shadows meant absolute power absolutely. It remained to this day the ultimate but elusive prize every time the Oval Office went up for grabs. Neither family could ever completely conquer and possess the dark shadows.

Until the 16th president of United States.

Abraham Lincoln had refused to compromise on slavery, dooming diplomacy. The Confederate States seceded. The president held it against John Ulysses III for staying in Virginia while the Hawkes left their family home to stand with him. Excommunicated from the corridors of power, the Ulysses came to the brink of irrelevance. For the first time, absolute power came within reach of the Hawkes.

Ironically, it was the diplomat who drew first blood, when John Ulysses III rewrote the rules of the rivalry. He was the Genghis Khan of the Ulysses line. Cunning and ruthless, he hatched a plot as bold and brilliant as it was simple. To this day, John Wilkes Booth was believed to have acted alone. With Lincoln's assassination, John Ulysses III raised the stakes.

The president was a mere pawn and fair game.

This became an MO of the Ulysses if a president threatened to end their relevance. They used loners to ensure the motive would be credited to madness. Booth was a fanatic. Charles Julies Guiteau, who shot James Garfield, was a zealot. Leon Frank Czolgosz, who gunned down William Mckinley, was an anarchist. On the other hand, as brilliant as the Hawkes were with military strategy, their first and only murder was almost their last.

JFK.

With John F. Kennedy, the Ulysses came as close as the Hawkes had with Lincoln to control the dark shadows entirely. Following the Bay of Pigs fiasco, John Ulysses IV single-handedly resurrected the charismatic young president's public image by calling the Soviet bluff with a naval blockade around Cuba. Soviet Premier Khrushchev was disgraced and toppled soon afterwards. The Hawkes outsmarted themselves, adding layers to the plot to muddy the investigation. Nothing went right. Oswald killed JFK, but it was caught on film. Ruby killed Oswald on live TV. The fiasco spawned conspiracy theories that never went away.

At the time, it triggered whispers of a cabal controlling the Presidency. In a rare show of unity, the Hawkes and the Ulysses shut down and withdrew from the dark shadows entirely. The legacy of secrecy called Storming Freedom survived. Their insatiable appetite for power returned stronger than ever, with the Ulysses masterminding the pullout from Vietnam under Nixon, who had aspirations of going down in history as a superstatesman. The Hawkes engineered his downfall with Watergate, only to lose to the Ulysses again with Jimmy Carter's victory. The Hawkes controlled the dark shadows for most of Ronald Reagan's tenure, but the Ulysses returned when it came time to cement his legacy. John Ulysses V became a secret advisor to Mikhail Gorbachev, whose collaboration was vital to the fall of the Berlin Wall, the

Soviet Union, and communism.

Over the two hundred-plus years of this rivalry, many 'rules of engagement' evolved. They never targeted each other, preferring the sport to the kill. Neither stooped their influence beyond or beneath the White House. Even though Republicans and Democrats drifted apart, the families were bipartisan. Power and control trumped ideology. Like folklore, nothing was written. The history, legacy, and importance of their clandestine war were passed down by word of mouth from father to son. Remarkably, the first born of every generation had been male.

Baron was the eldest of three siblings, the other two being sisters with little interest in politics. They married businessmen and lived on the Left coast. Baron graduated from Princeton at the top his class. His wife bore him a single child, a son, Warren, who was headed to Submarine School. He would be the first Hawke to enlist since Zachariah.

Father and son stood framed in the giant front doorway. The resemblance was unmistakable, down to the formality in their manner. Baron put both his hands on Warren's shoulder. "You have no peers. Others' loftiest aspirations can be nothing more than your stepping stones."

Warren nodded. Like his father, he rarely smiled. "Of course, father."

When Baron turned sixteen, his father had gradually exposed him to this secret battlefield. Warren had been receiving the same private tutoring. So, he knew what was expected. Baron added, "Never for a day—for a moment—forget that you shoulder the burden of writing history. Not yours, not ours, but this nation's."

Baron hugged his son. Warren stepped back. "Yes, sir."

"Make me proud."

Warren climbed into the waiting black Bentley. The chauffeur shut the door without slamming it. Baron heard a light footfall. It was his wife. She breathed wealth and

Southern elegance. He circled her waist. Warren looked out and they exchanged waves. The Bentley pulled away. Baron's proud smile faded into an anxious frown.

His wife noticed. "Give him time," she said. "He's only nineteen."

By saying nothing, Baron conveyed his disappointment. He wanted to be afraid of Warren, as his father had been of him. From his first lesson, Baron relished the intrigue and subterfuge. He never gave his father pause about his ability to operate in the daunting world of the dark shadows. Warren did. The boy was petty, cruel, and material. He was consumed by their wealth, which surpassed kings and sultans, but seemed unable to grasp the staggering universe of influence he was being groomed to inherit—power which had no walls, a floor, or ceiling. There was always more to be had.

"I won't be back for dinner," Baron said and pecked her lightly on the lips.

He climbed the stairs and entered his bedroom, which was the size of a tennis court. Picture windows offered a spectacular view of the James River. As always, his wife had selected and laid out his clothes. He dressed quickly and picked up his briefcase. A manservant waited outside the bedroom in an electric car. He climbed in and rode a quarter of a mile of hallways and rooms to the south wing. An elevator deposited him on the roof. His personal, fully armed, and luxurious Sikorsky waited on the helipad. The estate also contained a private airstrip for his two Lear jets, one of which roared into the sky as he strode across the terrace. It was flying Warren to Submarine School in Groton, Connecticut.

Baron sighed. Maybe he was being too harsh.

The Hawkes had to wait two centuries for Baron, their Genghis Khan.

———

John Ulysses VI was the opposite.

A brilliant scholar, sophisticated, cultured, and full

of knowledge of the world and its politics, he abhorred violence. John regarded it as savage and hardly the answer. He disapproved of the blood his forefathers had shed. He loved the US Constitution and believed peaceful solutions endured while settlements reached at gun point were not only dangerous but short-lived. He thought he'd raised his son, John Ulysses VII, with those same values.

This morning, he wasn't just disappointed, he was stunned. John was rarely blindsided, but his son had succeeded in doing just that.

"It's my life, dad," the young man known as YJ—short for Young John—faced off, defiant.

"Why did you hide it from me?" asked John, who'd found out just moments ago what his son wanted to do for a career. YJ had successfully concealed it. He had walked into John's study a few minutes ago on his way to his new school, and dropped the bombshell.

"To avoid this exact exchange. I'm not cut out to be a diplomat, dad. Parker's your guy." His kid brother. "He's seventeen, already working toward getting into Law School. He can have the V-I-I moniker. John Parker Ulysses VII."

"You are stepping out of our domain," bristled John. It was not his personality to raise his voice. But his frustration and anger ran so deep right now, YJ was testing that restraint and dignity.

"You mean no Ulysses has ever joined the force? From the time I was little I was like no Ulysses. I was never an ambassador for peace. I kick ass. That's what I do, that's who I am." He saluted and started for the majestic front door. "I'll call you when I get there."

"Have you told your mother?" She was in DC helping with the humanitarian effort.

"Called her on my way to see you. She was okay with it."

Of course she is. Unlike Ulysses wives before her, who stayed home to manage the estate, John's wife—a former

Olympic Gold medalist—was an outspoken social worker. It came from the fact that she had breast cancer. So she had a different view of life, that it was uncertain and should be lived in the now. YJ embraced and embodied that spirit.

"Wait," said John, following his son outside. The Ulysses home was magnificent and grand—modeled after British castles, with soaring stone walls and turrets—which every generation had also renovated, if nothing else, to match and surpass the Hawkes' improvements. "But Submarine School? In the same class as Warren?"

"Last time I checked this is a free country, dad. It's not my fault we were born two months apart." The Hawkes and the Ulysses sent their first born to the same private school. Another unwritten 'rule of engagement.' Familiarity helped intensify the rivalry. YJ had consistently outperformed Warren academically and socially.

He straddled his Ecosse Titanium. John had purchased it last year as a gift for YJ's eighteenth birthday—the most expensive motorcycle on the market. John noticed that it was packed for the long ride to Groton. "'Sides, if Hawkes have military in their blood, Warren shouldn't feel threatened." YJ flashed his perfect teeth in a wide, roguish grin. "If he does, even better. Bye, Dad."

He slipped on his helmet. *Rrr*! The 2150cc polished billet aluminum V-twin engine snarled. YJ revved it once and accelerated away with the speed and style only 200 horses and 210 ft-lbs. of torque could deliver.

John knew he ought not to be surprised. He'd watched YJ grow from cute to debonair, mischievous to daring. He was a gifted student, and his intelligence came with street smarts. With maturity, these traits would have married into a winning combination, especially since John knew for a fact that Baron feared Warren was utterly inferior competition to YJ and ill-equipped mentally to fight the next generation of this war. It had never happened before. The families had always been evenly matched intellectually.

In their own first head-to-head in the dark shadows, John had outmaneuvered Baron when the older president Bush preferred to form an international coalition against Iraq. The ignominy of exile continued under Bill Clinton. Baron tried and failed to oust the 42nd president with a sex scandal. When it seemed that John was destined for an unprecedented fourth term in the dark shadows under Al Gore, Baron used his influence in the Supreme Court to intervene and overturn the popular vote. The younger George Bush was an intellectual lightweight who deferred to his vice president, Dick Cheney, Baron's ideological soul mate. Fate beamed upon this dream ticket for the Hawkes with the terror attacks of 9/11.

Baron seized the dark shadows.

Moving swiftly, with the knowledge and blessing of the vice president, Baron packed every level of Defense with Hawke clones: militarists. President Bush heard what Baron wanted him to hear. The Proclamation of Neutrality, which had withstood the test of time since 1793, went by the wayside. The United States launched the first ever pre-emptive strike, invaded Iraq, a sovereign nation half a world away, and occupied it.

John feared America was treading a fine and perilous line between greatness and infamy. The latter came to pass. The war backfired. Anti-American sentiment swept the globe. With the historic election of Barack Obama, the Ulysses returned to take back dark shadows. The 44th president imposed upon John to call in favors and contacts in the deepest corridors of power that only two hundred years of working at the highest echelons of influence could access. But the Bush-Cheney atrocities were so severe, when President Obama left office, radical Islam was spreading across every continent. Much peace-making work still remained. John needed another term to complete laying the framework for lasting peace between America and the Middle East.

The Republicans were grooming Alabama Senator Jarvis Johnson to challenge the Democrat's choice, the competent and respected female Homeland Security Secretary. There was a cache about Jarvis that the Ulysses feared could edge him into the White House. John knew Jarvis was a two-faced son of a bitch, with a public persona of an inclusive maverick, but behind closed doors he was a bigot. While agonizing how to take Jarvis down in a way that would satisfy his intellectual approach to this rivalry, John ran into Tim O'Flaherty at a fundraiser in Washington. They were acquaintances. Like always, Tim came with a young, ravishing blonde, who he introduced as his new Washington correspondent, Liz Lovell, and joked, "In terms of ambition, she's well ahead of me when I was her age."

John was taken by Liz. It was rare to meet a woman as beautiful as she was smart. He decided she would be the one to bury Jarvis. A scandal-hungry rag like the *Post* was a fitting cemetery. The Ulysses and the Hawkes constantly made and broke careers of men and women they used and abused in their high stakes war. Liz surprised John and won a Pulitzer for destroying Jarvis. Democrats seemed assured of victory. Their candidate jumped to a double digit lead over the Republicans' hasty replacement for Jarvis—the governor of Indiana, an unknown political novice named Avery Walker. John badly underestimated Baron, who masterminded Liz's downfall and Avery's comeback for a stunning upset win.

Then, Baron shocked John, breaking away from tradition, leaving the sidelines, and taking a cabinet post. But he discreetly shunned the limelight, diverting the attention to his friend and colleague, the Chairman of the Joint Chiefs, Jack Knight, who became the face of Defense. The crisis in Cuba gave Baron an unchallenged opportunity to steer America in the direction Zachariah had envisioned.

A couple of days ago, John received a call from Admiral Grant, who came from old money and was consequently an old friend. The admiral had been John's conduit to Avery's ear. With Baron as defense secretary, Ulysses's efforts to organize a political solution to the US-Cuba crisis did not get far with the president. Grant confided in John that Baron had launched an audacious and dangerous secret operation codenamed Thunder Strike to depose Juan Castro. Grant did not divulge the details. John's decency, a trait previous Ulysses would have condemned as an unacceptable weakness, precluded him from prying them out of the admiral. John knew and respected Grant as a man of honor and principle, who would never violate the sacred trust of secrecy that covert ops demanded. Grant did make it clear he strongly disapproved.

Then, without warning, Meg happened.

The hurricane did not reach the Ulysses and Hawke estates. The area felt rain and strong winds but none of her fury. James River ran higher than normal but did not flood. John flew over DC and was speechless. The response was woefully inadequate and incompetent, affirming his opinion of Avery—a governor who was in over his head as President.

In a phone call two days ago, Grant sounded particularly despondent. He had just returned to New York following the sudden and stunning end to the US-Cuba standoff. Grant confessed he could look past the frustration of being isolated in New York and kept away from the president. But he felt responsible for the lives of the survivors of Thunder Strike and could never live with himself if the manhunt claimed them.

"What is Thunder Strike?" John finally asked.

When Grant told him, John was shocked and outraged. He realized why the EXCOMM had all perished in the storm. The rumors that some Congressmen were deliberately not evacuated were likely true too.

"They have the last Jayspid," Grant told him.

"Expect a call," assured John. "Don't be surprised who it is."

John knew who he wanted. Liz. After she'd taken down Jarvis, her own life and career had unraveled. Baron had brilliantly manipulated her downward spiral into a public disgrace to ensure her fall would elevate Avery into the White House. But John remembered she was tenacious and could use a second chance. It took him one phone call to discover she'd just gotten out of rehab.

He reached her like he did before.

Anonymously, through Billy Madden.

John sat down behind the desk of his study, which surpassed Baron's for the views the 270-degrees of tempered glass afforded. The phone rang almost immediately. It was his direct line. Only a select few had the number. He recognized the caller as an informant. Like the Hawkes, the Ulysses had sources in every branch and level of the public and private sector.

"She's here," reported the male voice. John was expecting her arrival. But he was not expecting the man to continue speaking. The informant detailed the fatal shooting at the airport.

"Thank you," said John, disconnected, and sat back. Troubled.

He dialed Admiral Grant's cell phone. The call went directly to voice mail. He hung up without leaving a message. His anxiety took on a sense of foreboding. Another phone call to another highly placed source in the New York Police Department confirmed what he suspected—Grant and Billy were dead.

Murdered.

John quickly recreated the timeline and easily surmised Baron was onto Liz.

———

"It's a shock, isn't?" said the uniformed cop, who introduced himself to Liz as Deputy Stan Kruk.

Liz rode shotgun in the squad car. Just one lane was open in each direction of the Dulles Airport Toll Road. Damaged and overturned vehicles piled high on the left shoulder. Overpasses were down everywhere. Bumper-to-bumper traffic snaked forward at an agonizing crawl.

Following the terror attacks on 9/11, then Hurricane Katrina, and superstorm Sandy, the federal government mandated that local governments across the country create an Emergency Operations Master Plan and Procedures. Exercises were conducted every year, but even the worst scenarios did not prepare them for the suddenness of Meg's arrival and the crippling aftermath. Liz had read that the storm threw the capital's Office of Emergency Services in disarray. The mayor, police chief, and heads of the city's utilities and essential services perished in the Emergency Operations Center in the early hours of her onslaught. This should have automatically activated the secondary and mobile EOC units. Meg had taken them out too. Bureaucrats and city council members further down the chain of command never took over because they never showed up. Feared dead.

The responsibility came to rest with the President Avery Walker at the White House. But Meg destroyed power and all lines of communication necessary to marshal the emergency management system, suspend state statutes, release funds, and mobilize relief and rescue. She wiped out entire police, fire, and other emergency response units. This vacuum erupted in lawlessness.

Street gangs took over. Looters moved in. Quickly, food, water, and shelter became the most valuable commodities. Local TV and radio stations had gone off the air with the first blast of wind and rain. A lot of journalists died. The bloody violence worsened. Media arrived from neighboring states. The first pictures of storm damage, the unbelievable death toll, and prevailing bedlam went on the air. The horror that the nation and the world saw was Hurricane Katrina plus superstorm Sandy times a hundred.

"Anarchy, plain and simple," said Deputy Kruk. He turned on his siren and lights to move over to a rare stretch of open shoulder. Liz nodded absently. Looking around. Just trying to get a handle on the scope and scale of the devastation. She tuned in and out of his incessant chatter. "The president declared the Washington Metropolitan Area a disaster zone. An understatement, if there was one."

The president federalized the rescue effort and called in the marines. Literally. Twenty thousand troops of 101st Infantry moved in. The nation's most decorated ground combat force made little difference initially due to the lack of a unified command. Who should give orders? Who could follow them? It seemed as if no lessons had been learned from the travesties of incompetence that followed Hurricane Katrina in New Orleans. Finally, the president declared martial law, clamping down a twenty-four hour curfew, with broad shoot-to-kill orders. The soldiers treated DC like a battlefield. Military, Reserves, National Guard, and police were only now, more than a week later, beginning to return law and order.

Liz's eyes swung to the mansions of Mount Vernon, or what remained of the wealthy colonial style homes. Meg had smashed most of them out of existence. Reston's newer tracts fared even worse. A powerful bomb could have gone off and left more recognizable wreckage. A tent city full of refugees occupied the rolling green country of Difficult Run Stream and Meadowlark Gardens, two of DC's more picturesque parks.

"Of course, the rich get served first," observed Kruk wryly.

"Hey. It's still America," Liz said, looking at him with a light laugh.

Liz suspected it made Deputy Kruk's day. He laughed back. At ease. Flattered. Liz had been aware he was stealing glances whenever he could. Men were always trying to impress her. He should know she was way out of his league.

They turned south onto the George Washington Memorial Parkway. Throughout the drive, Liz found herself momentarily disoriented. Familiar landmarks were missing. The Kennedy Center was a shell. All twenty-six square miles of Arlington lay leveled. Just two protruding stubs on either were left of the Arlington Bridge. Across the river, the Lincoln Memorial crumbled. West and East Potomac Parks were submerged. So was the Arlington National Cemetery. Not even tell-tale wreckage of the George Mason and Arland Williams Jr. Memorial bridges remained. When she thought that she could not be shocked anymore, Liz caught her breath loudly. The shoulder ahead was blocked.

By half a mile of body bags two rows deep.

"City of DC had only fifty thousand bags," explained Kruk. "Death toll is several times that."

The stench of death penetrated the squad car even though the windows were rolled up. Swarms of flies buzzed overhead. Liz gagged a few times. She saw the driver of the car beside her throw up right into his own lap. It seemed like an eternity before they passed the corpses.

Liz asked Kruk to get off when they reached Alexandria. The historic center of commerce and politics, where the founding fathers met to debate freedom and discuss the revolution, looked like London after the Nazi blitz. Traffic, predominantly army and paramilitary combat units, wound along a single tortuous lane between layers upon layers of debris. Soldiers stood guard upon these mounds. At the corner gas station, cars stretched as far as the eye could see. A couple of marines, perched on a tank, supervised gas being rationed with a hand pump. In the fight for street control during the first days of lawlessness after the storm, thugs set scores of stations on fire. Many still burned. There were no resources to fight them. Distinctive corkscrewed skyward all over the city.

They turned toward Old Town. The quaint shops did not stand a chance. Meg ripped out the cobblestone alleys. Home to several Department of Defense buildings, none made it. Liz looked for Crystal City, a huge complex. Couldn't find it. A big-top replaced the Salvation Army headquarters. Refugees lined up in thousands. Their restive mood was palpable. Kruk continued his barrage of stats.

Meg had killed a million at last count. Left around two million homeless in the Washington Metropolitan Area, which included the entire District of Columbia and parts of Maryland and Virginia. Meg did not reach Baltimore, unraveling before she could. Just drenching that city with a foot of rain. There was minor damage from the sixty-mile an hour winds. In DC, the Marine Corps of Engineers had drained fields, cleared debris, and erected about fifty refugee camps. Each accommodated about five hundred refugees. Thousands tried to occupy them. Triggering riots. This morning, the first C-17 transport planes arrived with donations of food, money, blankets, and clothing from all over the nation. "Soldiers had to suspend distribution and fire shots at a lot of locations. There were casualties. Like we need more."

"Turn left here," Liz interrupted.

They cruised between shelled out structures that used to be densely packed luxury apartments and condominiums. Now they were just mountains of rubble. The familiar smell of death ebbed and flowed with the breeze, sometimes faint, sometimes so harsh. Liz held her breath. She saw flies, dogs, and birds preying upon the corpses. People too. For money and belongings to buy food, water, gas.

"You'll get used to it," remarked Kruk, seeing Liz shake her head.

"Left," nodded Liz, seeing a street full of single family homes.

Liz sensed what Kruk was thinking. She probably lived here amidst the forty percent of Alexandria's hundred and fifty thousand residents with a gross income of half a million dollars or more. The residents had all fled, leaving the streets littered with their affluence. Designer furniture, bricks, stone, all kinds of high-end toys and house wares. Liz studied the expensive cars flung every which way, hoping to find one that was roadworthy.

A few homes in, Liz said, "Stop."

Kruk pulled up and followed Liz's eyes to the single-family house. "Yours?"

"Uh-huh," lied Liz. She lived in the neighborhood, but in a townhome several blocks from here. Alexandria was the chic address to have. It was six miles from downtown, home to thousands of Washington professionals, with a vibrant political club scene where hotshots networked. She'd given up the townhome when she'd admitted herself into rehab.

"Shit, sorry," he sympathized. Splinters of roof survived above the few walls that were still standing. "I thank God everyday. My apartment survived, sort of. It's still standing and habitable, which is a lot more than could be said about thousands of others. Meg only took out the windows and trashed the inside of every unit." Liz got out. "Are you sure you're going to be okay?"

She nodded. "I'll be fine."

"It's dangerous out there. There's a shoot on sight order for looters. We're not broadcasting it, but the storm tore up all the prisons. Nobody knows how much of them scum survived. There being no place to lock 'em up, there's no point in arresting them, if you know what I mean?"

Liz looked at him sharply. Reading between the lines. Cops were meting out street justice. Taking out criminals. She brushed her hand over his and flashed him a radiant smile. "You've already gone out of your way giving me a ride. Thanks."

"No problem." Kruk almost danced into the car.

Liz was surprised scavengers had not looted all this high end storm debris. Then she saw a private security car with two armed officers cruise by and instantly knew why. Deputized to fill the vacuum, they were probably exercising those broad 'shoot to kill' orders. Meaning, anyone who looked out of place here was fair game. They stared down Liz. Her sophistication met and exceeded their bar of who belonged and who did not. They also saw Kruk. Nods exchanged. They turned at the next corner and disappeared from view.

America always went apartheid in a crisis. "It's our security blanket," Kenneth Lovell, Liz's father, told her after 9/11, when innocent Arab Americans were rounded up in scores on tips from white neighbors. Neither of her parents was remotely racist and they raised Liz to be color blind, but Kim maintained, "Being white'll get you a free pass." He was right. Especially during a tragedy so vast and sweeping. Liz was not morally or ethically averse to exploiting the prejudice. *Hey, it is what it is.*

Liz turned away. Her eyes fastened on a silver Mercedes Kompressor parked nose in. Partially buried in what was once a garage. Meg had ripped off the roof and two walls.

She heard Kruk start the squad car and turned and smiled again, making him feel like he'd made a connection. He waved. She waved back, knowing he'd most certainly allow himself another peek in the rear view mirror. So she confidently walked up the drive as if it belonged to her. She also figured he was on the radio, calling out her location. He'd probably park out of sight and keep an eye on her. The instant he turned out of sight, she moved with purpose and precision, quickly, methodically, examining the car.

The windshield was not broken. The passenger side window had shattered. No big deal. No body or chassis damage. The car looked in good shape. Just like she thought. She knew cars. After all, she was born and raised in Detroit. She crouched under the steering column, ripped out the ignition wires, and began to expertly hot-wire the Kompressor.

———

Around the corner, Kruk did not stop. He passed a military green Humvee, with Andrew behind the wheel. The assassin had followed them. Andrew ignored the uniform's friendly wave, got out, and briskly stepped across a littered yard. He reached the corner and peered over a crumbling wall. He couldn't see Liz, but saw smoke eject from the tailpipe of a silver Mercedes. It did not start. He retreated to his Humvee. In no hurry.

He knew what she planned to do.

The engine died and fired again, this time grinding continuously. It sputtered and coughed up white smoke that rose high enough for Andrew to see. Then it growled alive. Revved. A few seconds later...*scrawl!* A metallic sound rent the air.

That would be her pulling out from under the collapsed awning, Andrew figured. He fired up his Humvee. There were multiple sounds of collapse mixed in with pistons pumping with effort. *Crash!* She was out. Andrew eased the Humvee forward, clearing what remained of the corner home. There was an impenetrable cloud of dust rising from the fallen walls. He expected to see the Mercedes backing out.

But there was no sign of it. Yet he heard engines. Loud. Accelerating.

Shit. He realized Liz didn't back out of the drive. She'd plowed forward into the backyard. He heard the loud splinter of wood as she mauled through rear fence into the driveway of the house behind. She was heading onto the street in the back. Andrew U-turned swiftly. She would veer right and head away from him. Her only chance of losing him would be to she get to the end of street and turn out of sight before he appeared at the far end behind her. The Mercedes roared, accelerating hard. Andrew was familiar with the specs on her car. Zero-to-sixty in four seconds.

Andrew pedaled down. The Humvee leapt with even more horses. He blasted past the corner house. A fallen tree blocked his view. *Goddamnit!* He swerved. His Humvee came around. His eyes confirmed what he suspected the moment prior—the few seconds he'd needed to clear the tree was all Liz needed.

She was gone.

Andrew throttled down, raced to the end of the street,

hoping to get to the end of the block before Liz made another turn. Too late. When he got there, she'd disappeared. Amateurs normally turned right. So he did. Soon, he realized he'd guessed wrong. He searched the neighborhood for the next half hour. He ground his teeth angrily. *Crafty bitch.* Finally, he forced himself to accept that he'd lost her and reluctantly reached for the MILSATCOM.

It rang before he could dial.

"Peter," Andrew greeted brusquely, answering on the first ring.

————

Peter Wilkins did not return the greeting.

He had gone back to the surveillance dossiers on the personnel of the WFO in Silver Springs. As soon as he knew Meg might strike DC, Peter had taken it upon himself to move all his department's documents into the vaults two floors below the CIA HQ. Peter perused down the background research. He found Philippe's name buried in the dense type. A French-Angolan. Even though things had been hectic last week, Peter scolded himself for missing the fact that lead forecaster, Vick Delhom, was gay and lived with a partner.

"I have an address that I did not think was relevant any more," said Peter.

LAST WEEK

She continued to move northeast, hungrily enriching her moisture in her middle and lower troposphere. This dramatically increased her area of disturbance. Winds in her bowels grew stronger, becoming a particularly large flow where her pressure caused masses aloft to be removed from her environment. This prevented air from recirculating and weakening her.

She formed spiral bands of deep cumulus clouds, which rotated cyclonically and enhanced her convection, transporting heat and moisture toward her center. Her centrifugal force spun the air parcels tangentially some distance from the center, creating an eye wall. This was as far as her inward spiraling air would penetrate.

Here, with the viciousness of a horsewhip, her strongest winds lashed at over thirty-three knots. Waves, thirty feet high, crashed across. With the development of the eye, her transformation into a tropical storm became irreversible.

She earned a name.

Meg.

———

"Hello, hello!" Diane hollered, pressing her nose to the pane of glass on Vick's front door.

"Boo!" Vick snuck up behind her.

Diane jumped and swiped him with the papers in her hand. "Don't do that!"

From the looks of it, he'd been gardening around the side of the house. "Hey!" interrupted Philippe, opening the door. "Don't hit my little honey-bunny. He bruises easily."

"Hi, Philippe."

Philippe wore a South Beach muscle shirt and short shorts that showed off his chiseled body. Both Vick and he worked out religiously and it showed. Diane was always struck by how good they looked as a couple. Physically and emotionally, they ying-yanged each other. Vick's light chocolate complexion and hard masculine energy complimented Philippe's darker shade of black and soft and delicate demeanor.

Vick nudged Diane inside and shut the door. Philippe and he had a really neat place. Unique. At the bottom of the grade in a neighborhood nestled on the leeward side of two slopes. Philippe, an interior decorator, had done a great job. Their home had been featured in a bunch of magazines and TV shows.

"Lunch will be ready in about fifteen," said Philippe.

"What are we having?" asked Diane eagerly.

"Your meal is not guaranteed until I evaluate what it is you have to tell me that you couldn't have told me over the phone," said Vick.

"Ignore him," said Philippe. "Want anything to drink?"

"Diet anything."

"Don't make her feel at home," Vick growled. "She's already freeloading."

"What's with you?" asked Diane. "Why are you so grumpy?"

Philippe walked around the kitchen island to the refrigerator. "He's having a spell over the renovation."

"Toucan orange and blue?" Vick accused Philippe and looked to Diane for help.

"Looks great," said Diane. "I love it."

Vick turned on her, "That's not the point. I didn't get a vote. And I found the house."

"Get over it." Philippe slid Diane her soda across the granite counter and shared his iced tea with Vick. They settled around the coffee table in the living room. The furniture was all vintage rattan, hand-upholstered with bright colored fabric from India.

"You won't believe this," began Diane, spreading her papers.

"If I won't, why bother telling me?"

"I know why they erased the data off the official weather bulletins." Diane set down the two reports, one with the tropical depression 217E and one without. She had plotted the projected track as a dotted line. It showed 217E—a tropical storm by now—traveling east, carried by the equatorial current, one of several gigantic streams of water that moved about the oceans. The Mississippi river would be a minuscule brook by comparison. Diane ran her fingers to the end of the dotted line and pronounced, "Cuba. That's why."

"The surface temperature of the Atlantic as it approaches the island is a blistering 85°F. AWIPS extrapolates 217E will be a C5 when it makes landfall." Category 5 represented the most powerful storm designation. "Without warning."

Cuba relied on an obsolete Soviet Data Collection Platform for all its meteorology. The DCP's primary mission had been espionage during the Cold War. It got all its data from a French weather satellite, which also carried just a communications payload and read off a US geostationary satellite.

"Juan Castro won't know what hit him until the punch has already landed," said Diane. "The hurricane destroys the nukes. Maybe a small invasion to mop up in the aftermath. End of crisis."

"I think that's damn clever," said Vick.

"Wow," exhaled Philippe, impressed.

"Using the storm is brilliant," agreed Diane. "Looks right on paper, perfect in theory."

"But?"

"They are gambling the storm track will hold."

"Why won't it?"

"What if a low pressure trough forms in the lower left quadrant?"

"She'll stall, curve northeast, and dissipate in the mid-Atlantic. No harm, no foul."

"Not exactly. The Southerlies are strong this year. It's hot, it's fast, and it's already across the Equator. If the storm even as much as pauses, the Southerlies'll grab it."

"I'm sure that possibility has already been dismissed."

"Humor me," persisted Diane, finding a track projection she'd run. "Here's a what-if scenario?"

Vick looked at it and shook his head, "That's an unprecedented course."

"Because meeting up with the Southerlies is unprecedented."

Set in motion by wind systems, the nature, strength, and direction of ocean currents varied from year to year. In the past decade, rapid industrialization, exploding population, and indiscriminate deforestation had resulted in gradual but significant global warming. This in turn affected air patterns, destroying a few that had been around for centuries, creating new ones like the Southerlies, which had emerged over the last couple of years. The Southerlies came up from below the equator and their effect on terrestrial climate was yet to be assessed.

"Hurricanes just don't run amok," persisted Vick. "It's the basis of your own thesis."

"I know." In her article, she stressed the predictability of most cyclone tracks. "Still, the Southerlies can conceivably carry the storm all the way toward us."

"Wow," Philippe said.

"Check this out." Diane shuffled her papers.

"Instinct? Or science?" asked Vick.

"An educated hunch." Diane placed a pressure cell over the US map showing a massive high pressure ridge over Virginia and Maryland. "It hasn't moved in a week and it's the reason for the unseasonably hot climate."

"It will also keep the storm from making landfall."

"Yeah, from making landfall along the usual hurricane targets." She ran her finger from Florida up to North Carolina, historically the most vulnerable. "But that second HPR over Greenland is sliding over." Diane superimposed the other stubborn high pressure ridge settling over the Delaware. That created two half circles facing off each other. Diane raised her eyebrows. She didn't have to explain. "See what I mean?"

"It's never happened," dismissed Vick.

"But it could."

Trapped between the two high pressure ridges was the Potomac River. Even Philippe understood what she was getting at. "Wow."

"Oh, for God's sake," dismissed Vick. "No storm has ever come up the Potomac. Never will."

Diane wagged her finger with a smile. "Never say never." She flipped through her research. "Last year, there were two hurricanes, Orlene and Paine."

"I remember." They arrived within days of each other. The NHC issued warnings up and down the eastern seaboard. Neither made landfall because Orlene traveled straight north. Unprecedented climatologically, then made a U-turn in mid-Atlantic and dissipated. Paine birthed two weeks later, followed Orlene's track almost exactly, and dissipated at almost the same coordinates. Meteorologists were still scratching their heads. Vick quickly glanced over the pictures and data. "The Greenland current," which flowed south, "will meet the storm mid-Atlantic and take it back south away from us."

"There's a fifty-fifty chance they could miss each other."

"Okay. Say all your what-ifs come true, the water is too cold."

"Wrong," said Diane. "The heat wave we're having has SST at eighty-four degrees." She clarified for Philippe, "Tropical storms thrive on water seventy-nine degrees and hotter."

"Wow," said Philippe repeated.

"World climate is in a state of flux," said Diane. "There's been a startling jump in the number of depressions strengthening into tropical storms and cyclones. Take our 217E, for instance. It started out as a depression that even the National Hurricane Center advised in its first bulletin as disorganized and likely to weaken. Instead, you have the opposite."

"Wow!"

"I think you've mastered the single syllable exclamation," said Vick. "Try two."

"Bite me?"

"Good one," howled Diane and gave Philippe a high five.

"Won't the TV networks see it and warn us even if the government doesn't?" asked Phillipe.

"Not until she comes within four hundred miles of the coast," explained Diane. "That's the maximum range on the radars TV stations have."

"What are the chances those two HPRs will line up to thread the eye into the Potomac?" asked Vick skeptically.

"Ten percent, according to our local model."

"Are we in danger?" asked Philippe anxiously.

"No," Vick said adamantly. "One, and you can thank me for it. Our house, this entire neighborhood actually, is behind two slopes. So we are safe. And two," Vick leaned into Diane and raised his voice, "DC is too far north and inland!"

Diane poked his chest with every word, raising her voice just as loudly. "Unless she becomes a superhurricane!"

"What's that?" asked Philippe.

"The exact moment Diane lost her mind," replied Vick.

Diane ignored him and explained to Philippe, "For a long time we thought hurricanes can survive only over water. Now there is a hypothesis that if eyewall gusts exceed five hundred miles an hour, a hurricane becomes such a powerful thermal engine, it becomes self sustaining and can tear across land without losing strength."

Philippe caught on quickly. "Like a tornado?"

Diane pointed a finger at him. Exactly. "With torrential rain."

"You've gone from a hunch to wild speculation and now to ridiculous conjecture. Let's eat before you predict the end of the world by the weekend."

It was a fun meal. It always was at the Vick's. Philippe

and he bickered constantly.

"Why did you really come here?" asked Vick as they began to clear the table.

Diane batted her eyelids and crinkled her face in a plea. "I need more storm data."

"I don't know. They probably changed the locks at Wallops." The satellite downlink station in Virginia.

"What about the NHC?" National Hurricane Center.

"Mmm," went Vick. "That's a possibility."

———

At the National Hurricane Center, Director Hank Rotas looked up. The door opened and he took an instant dislike to Peter Wilkins walking in. Hank didn't know what Peter did exactly, but knew it was something unsavory. Peter fit Hank's preconceived mental picture—the type who loved the power trip of keeping secrets because it compensated for his physical shortcomings.

Peter's arrival culminated a series of troubling conversations that began on Monday, just hours after tropical depression 217E had birthed off the West Coast of Africa. Hank was coming off a wonderful weekend, fishing alone. Almost as soon as he'd walked into the office, he'd received a call from Defense Secretary Baron Hawke himself.

"Mr. Rotas," Baron spoke first without a greeting. "Can I call you Henry?"

"Hank."

"Hank, this morning, your National Hurricane Center reported a tropical depression. 217E?"

"Yes." Hank had seen Clark's advisory, but paid no more than cursory heed to it. Global warming had left the oceans almost half a degree hotter, which explained the higher number of storms. Last year, twenty-three received names and thirteen reached hurricane intensity. This year, of the thirty named storms, twelve had strengthened into hurricanes, and miraculously, none made landfall.

"It's unlikely this will develop into anything significant," said Hank, feeling the first cold fingers of suspicion encircling his throat.

"If it does," said Baron, "we'd like to classify it."

And there it was.

He should have known, realized Hank, who still carried painful memories of lies he'd once shared with the DoD. Lies surrounding seven years of weather warfare over Laos, Vietnam, and Cambodia thirty years ago. Every year, monsoon rains battered Southeast Asia, making roads and trails impassable. The US devised a covert op to increase rainfall sufficiently in selected target areas, soften road surfaces, cause landslides, and wash out river crossings. Hank, a young and ambitious meteorologist in the Research Flight Facility, Miami, jumped at the opportunity to be the liaison between the National Weather Service and the DoD. As the mission progressed, he became more and more disillusioned.

Weather knew no boundaries. Neither did it discriminate between military and civilian targets. The death toll rose as the US expanded the operation from the Laos panhandle area into Cambodia and North and South Vietnam. Even after president Lyndon Johnson announced a halt to bombings above the 19th parallel in March 1968, the weather warfare continued. At final count, Americans flew more than two thousand six hundred sorties, dropped almost forty-seven thousand five hundred seeding units, and utterly devastated the ecology.

New York Times legend, Jack Anderson, broke the story in 1971. What Anderson uncovered stunned Hank. The entire operation, codenamed Popeye, was so wrapped in secrecy, even then-Deputy Assistant Secretary of Defense, Dennis J. Doolin, knew nothing of the seven-year rainmaking program. Crews, in the guise of performing aerial weather reconnaissance, carried out extensive seeding operations. They made normal factual weather reports through regular unclassified worldwide weather channels. Secretly, special reports were transmitted through classified communication channels to the president and the National Security Council.

"Why?" asked Hank, and knew the answer the moment the question left his mouth.

"It's need-to-know at this stage," replied Baron quietly and left it at that.

Weather products had been withheld as recently as 1992. On the eve of the first US-led coalition attack on Iraq, visibility data was falsified. Meteorologists forecast dense fog and low cloud for the night January 16, 1991. Instead, Baghdad enjoyed clear, starlit skies, and the US flew over a hundred sorties, catching Saddam Hussein and the media off guard. That, Hank thought, was a forecast for dense fog and low clouds. Not a potentially devastating tropical storm.

"This conversation remains confidential," said Baron. "We'll talk again tomorrow. Same time."

"You may have a problem," Hank began his report when they'd spoken again the next day. 217E had continued to strengthen against all odds. "We have a Southerly windflow." Even though he suspected the defense secretary had probably been briefed by military forecasters, Hank explained that a wind system was sweeping up from below the equator. "Four of our track guidance models show an encounter. If that happens, the storm could get caught up in these winds and be carried toward the northeast."

"How many models are there?" asked Baron.

Like he didn't know. "Nine track guidance models and four intensity models," replied Hank.

"The other five show the storm just slipping ahead of the Southerlies?" asked Baron.

"Yes," replied Hank. It hadn't been hard to figure out why the DoD wanted to the storm a secret. To devastate Cuba and win this nuclear standoff.

"When will you know for certain?" asked Baron.

"Tomorrow."

"Okay." Baron concluded their call in his usual polite, measured voice, "Let's talk then."

In the ensuing twenty-four hours, despite all models predicting otherwise, 217E's winds passed thirty-three knots. Categorizing it officially as a tropical storm. The thirteenth for the season. Hank hoped it wasn't an omen. The thirteenth name on the alphabetical list this year was a short one.

Meg.

The history of hurricane names went back to the West Indies, where they were named after the particular saint's day on which a storm struck. Thus, there was Hurricane Santa Ana, which hit Puerto Rico on July 26, 1825. The first use of a woman's name for a storm evolved from a novel by George R. Stewart and became a regular practice in World War II. Until then, the US had used the phonetic alphabet— Able, Baker, Charlie. In 1978, men's names were included. Every year, two six-year lists of names in alphabetical order were prepared separately for the Pacific and the Atlantic. This year's list would be used again in six years. Names carried an international flavor. They were selected from library sources and agreed upon at the World Meteorological Organization. The use of names quickened communication and reduced confusion when more than one tropical storm occurred at the same time.

But Meg had no competition.

Not in the Atlantic or the Pacific. There wasn't another storm worthy of a name. Small mercy, thought Hank, more concerned by Defense Secretary Baron Hawke's late evening call yesterday, informing Hank to expect Peter Wilkins. Baron did not elaborate about who Peter was or what he'd be doing here. Hank knew better than to ask. He'd be fed the need-to-know mantra. Baron told Hank that Peter would need a private office and complete access to all discussions about Meg.

Hank knew Peter would not be late. Peter wasn't.

Disengaging from Peter's handshake and sitting back

down, Hank realized he might as well hand over his chair too because he'd just ceded authority of the NHC to the Department of Defense. Hank didn't delude himself. He could not have stopped it even if he'd tried. Still, he was angry at himself. His staff would hate what was happening too. But people like Peter thrived on the dislike. It just made the power trip that much sweeter.

"Don't mind me," said Peter. "I'm here only to ensure there is no security breach."

Sure. Hank didn't buy the friendliness for a moment. "I have a storm discussion scheduled in about half an hour."

"I don't have to be there," replied Peter.

"Don't you want to meet the Department heads?" asked Hank, a little surprised.

"I'll introduce myself once I get situated," Peter shrugged casually. "Just point me to my office."

Hank called his assistant in and Peter left with her. When the door closed behind them, Hank took a deep breath. When the defense secretary indicated he wanted to classify Meg, the frightening reality was that it was possible. The NHC was the central and only clearing house for severe weather in the world.

It had always been that way, ever since the NHC's beginnings in Barbados in 1847. Lt. Colonel William Reid of the Royal Engineers of England established the first hurricane warning display system based upon barometric readings. It wasn't until 1870 that Father Benito Vines, the director of Havana's Belena College, used movement of upper and lower clouds to devise the first scientific system of hurricane forecasts and warnings. During the Spanish American War, President Mckinley declared that he feared hurricanes more than he did the Spanish Navy. He set up observing stations throughout the eastern and central Caribbean. In 1955, the Miami office became the National Hurricane Center. In 1982, meteorological satellites evolved as the primary observing tool for tropical storm analyses. The World Meteorological Organization mandated that the NHC disburse advisories and warning without prejudice.

Even to an enemy. Even during war.

That was about to change.

Hank had the unenviable task of breaking it to the three men who walked in. Ray Powell was the academic looking head of the Specialist/Forecast Unit, Clyde Welch, the portly head of the Tropical Satellite Analysis and Forecast Center, and Assistant Director Gerardo Sanchez of the Hurricane Research Department, as fiery as he was brilliant. Gerardo would be the most upset.

"Gentlemen," said Hank, coming straight out, "The DoD wants to keep Meg secret." These were smart men. He didn't have to spell out why.

"What about commercial shipping and air traffic?" asked Gerardo, then added acidly, "They are re-drawing trade routes?"

"Yes," replied Hank, and he wasn't kidding. "Flights and ships are being re-routed at least four hundred miles away from the outermost spiral. So nobody can even report a visual. This storm doesn't exist." He let that sink in. "You and your staff, this entire office is now under the National Secrets Act. Any breach is treason."

"So that's why that weasel pencil pusher is here," realized Gerardo. "To police us."

———

Anger flared in Peter's eyes even though he expected trouble and resistance from this brilliant, Cuban meteorologist nicknamed 'hombre.' Peter had read the bios of every employee here. He'd locked the door of his new office to watch the discussion on one of several unmarked flatscreens. CIA techs had rigged and rewired the room to be a teleconference center. What Hank and his staff did not know was that the techs had also installed surveillance devices through out the National

Hurricane Center. Peter's office was the monitoring station. He had the principals up on the teleconference screen.

"We don't have a choice but go along, hombre," said Hank helplessly. "Any questions?"

"No," said Gerardo. "But I have an opinion."

"We can guess," smiled Rotas, then added seriously, "NMC, TPC, and EMC have been excluded."

All three men straightened in surprise.

"So where are we going to get our models from?" asked Gerardo. His Hurricane Research Department studied the structure of hurricanes using two-dimensional models created and updated by the Tropical Prediction Center and three-dimensional models that came out of the National Centers for Environmental Prediction's Environmental Modeling Center. Gerardo's HRD then produced nine independent track guidance and four intensity models for each forecast cycle.

"AFWA," said Hank. Air Force Weather Agency, Offutt AFB in Nebraska.

"They're qualified," shrugged Ray. "After all, they are the official backup."

"We are the only ones generating forecasts, I hope," said Ray. His Forecast Unit used HRD's track and intensity models to issue bulletins.

Normally, the National Meteorological Center in Maryland and meteorologists at the WFOs in target areas also came up with their own forecasts based on local conditions from those same TCP and EMC models. They would all confer on the NWS Hurricane Hotline. Forecasters from the Heavy Precipitation Branch, National Severe Storms Forecast Center, local WFOs, AFWA, FEMA, and other relevant local, state, and federal agencies listened in. The entire conversation was logged, and differences, if any, resolved. The NHC had final say in all track and intensity forecasts ultimately issued to the public. But these weren't normal circumstances. With Meg, the NHC was the only civilian agency preparing track and intensity forecasts.

"What about NESDIS?" asked Clyde, referring to the National Environmental, Satellite, Data and Information Service, whose Satellite Analysis Branch worked closely with his Tropical Satellite Analysis and Forecasts. During the early stages, when erratic cloud cover obscured the eye, they verified each other's 'eye-fixes' of the storm to create 'best track' models.

"Out of the loop," said Hank. "Too big and bureaucratic."

"Shit," said Ray. "So we have no one concurrently verifying our forecast except for AFWA."

Gerardo snorted unhappily. Hank called his assistant. "Tell Roland we are ready for him."

Roland Tucker carried the title, Chief, Air Reconnaissance Coordination, All Hurricanes. A US Air Force employee, he occupied a liaison office at the NHC to coordinate aerial weather missions called synoptic flights.

Aircraft reconnaissance, still indispensable to forecasts, provided the only detailed measurements of the winds, atmospheric pressure, and temperature from inside the storm. These, along with broader information from satellites, ocean data buoys and ship observations, constituted the total "package" needed to run numerical models. Also, eyewall measurements, accessible only to aircraft, were vital in determining strength and estimating subsequent speed, intensity, and direction. In October 1989, when the NHC had no aerial weather reconnaissance, Hurricane Jerry posed several forecast and warning problems because of incorrect remote observations and consequently poor numerical guidance. This resulted in contradicting reports and severe property loss.

Roland walked in. Crisp. Clean cut. Not a crease out of place. Hank couldn't remember ever seeing him out of the USAF uniform in the office. Military through and through, right down to the clipped speech pattern. Over his breast pocket, he wore the insignia of the "Hurricane Hunters," and sown to his sleeve was the emblem of the 53rd Weather Reconnaissance Squadron, Keebles AFB, Mississippi.

"Hank. Gentlemen."

"What's the status on AWR?" asked Hank about the Aerial Weather Reconnaissance.

"Why the delay?" Gerardo jumped in with an irritated tone. "We should have had one flight already."

Roland looked at him sharply. They disliked each other even after a decade together in this office. "I just got DoD clearance. Ask them."

"And they want track predictions yesterday," grumbled Gerardo.

Hank intervened, "We have approval. That's what matters."

"Damn bureaucrats have all of Washington to shit on," grumbled Gerardo. "Why ruin the only agency that actually works for the people?"

Hank knew Gerardo's resentment ran deeper than just Meg's classification. Like Hank, Gerardo did not like the way Meg had birthed. Where did the wave that triggered her into strengthening come from? She reminded him of Orlene and Paine last year. They'd formed identically within about a week of each other—depressions the NHC had also ignored because they had nothing going for them. Both just did not strengthen, they strengthened so rapidly, NMC's supercomputers, the fastest in existence simulating numerical models, couldn't keep up. That had never happened. High pressure troughs appeared on either side in contradiction to all the numbers, taking both storms on an unprecedented, arrow straight, south to north course. Then, without a recognizable steering current, they each executed a cycloid loop, or complete circle, and dissipated as mysteriously as they had birthed, strengthened, and moved. Gerardo and his HRD team still hadn't solved the mystery. Fortunately, Orlene and Paine died over cooler waters in the upper latitudes without making landfall.

The DoD expected the opposite from Meg.

"Wind velocities passed thirty-three knots around noon, our time," said Gerardo. Wind vectors were derived by automated programs studying visible reflectance, infrared radiation, and water vapor radiation of successive satellite images. Then he needled Roland, "These are only guesstimates. So too her eye-fix."

"I guess you can go over the rest with Roland," said Hank. The men left.

Hank had been studying storms for twenty years. No two were alike. Nature never repeated herself. One unforeseen factor, and Meg could become a whole new ball game. He pensively settled back in his chair, nagged by certainty that there was more to this operation than what he'd been told. *Do I want to know?*

Arriving at Miami's Patrick Air Force Base, a ball of fear, excitement, and sheer thrill bounced around in the pit of Sam's stomach. Even though he'd been doing it for five years, flying into a hurricane was a novel experience every time. Despite the enormous advances in aviation and thousands of flight hours into storms over more than half a century, it remained as dangerous and unpredictable as the first one by Colonel Joseph Duckworth on July 27, 1943. When he took off in a single engine, propeller driven, AT-6 Texan trainer into the eye of a hurricane threatening Galveston, Texas, little did Joseph know that he would begin 'one of the US Air Force's largest, continuing, humanitarian efforts—the tropical cyclone reconnaissance mission of air force weather reconnaissance units.'

During World War II, after suffering massive losses in typhoons and storms, the US formally established the Army Air Force Weather Service on February 14, 1944. They flew B-24s into the eye of storms and earned the name Hurricane Hunters. In 1946, they switched to the four-engine, propeller driven WB-29s. In the early 1960s, the WC-130 Hercules became the primary aircraft for all premeditated missions into tropical cyclones. Today, aerial weather reconnaissance came under the jurisdiction of the NOAA's newly formed Office of Aircraft Operations. In the forty years that the US had been involved in aerial weather reconnaissance, only three aircraft and their crew had been lost, none since 1974.

Sam parked his jeep and jogged indoors. He winked toward Ethel Gipper behind the front desk, "What-up, EG?"

"From the bags under the eyes, obviously you," shot back the forty-five year old, heavyset smart mouth. Sam had asked her about night clubs yesterday. As a woman, she wanted to know why. He tried to lie. As a mother of teenage sons, she didn't buy it. He told her about Diane. She pointed him to The Jade in South Beach.

Sam winked, "I owe you one."

"Really? How drunk was she?"

"Not at all. Because a Southern accent, if properly employed, can be just as intoxicating."

Ethel howled. Sam disappeared into the locker room. His crew was already on the tarmac. Preflight preparations for missions into a hurricane were very precise. He zipped on his overalls, picked up his flight gear, and emerged outside in time to see a B-52 Stealth bomber being towed into a hangar. Probably back from a surveillance mission over Cuba, figured Sam.

He headed toward the Lockheed WC-130 Hercules, a mammoth four-engine turboprop, bearing the NOAA and the 53rd Weather Reconnaissance Squadron insignia. Sam, his crew, and the plane came out of Keesler AFB near Biloxi, Mississippi. The guys were behind the refueling truck.

"Ranger!" Sam greeted his African American copilot with a high-five, then slapped his bespectacled navigator on the back. "Quince." Shook hands with his more formal and reserved flight engineer. "Knoll.

"The ARWO and DO are out of AFWA," whispered

Quince, referring to the Aerial Reconnaissance Weather Officer and Dropsonde Operator, the remaining two members of the crew. Quince had clearly been waiting to blurt it out.

"Really?" reacted Sam, just as intrigued. "Air Force Weather Agency. Mmm."

Ranger nodded eagerly. Knoll, taciturn as always, raised his eyebrows. They headed up the rear ramp together as if they needed to draw strength from numbers when they met the two men from Nebraska, who looked like Laurel and Hardy, sans the humor.

"Pfifer, ARWO." He was beanpole thin.

"Schultz. DO." Plump, complete with a toothbrush moustache.

Sam shook their hands. "Sam Winger. And I have two forms of ID to prove it." Neither man even smiled. They brusquely returned to their pre-flight prep. Sam and the guys headed forward to the cockpit. Sam whispered, "What's with all-military?"

"Exactly," Quince whispered back.

Ranger and Knoll shrugged. They all strapped in.

"Where's the MFP?" asked Sam, looking for the familiar clipboard. The Machine Flight Plan plotted a fuel efficient route from Patrick AFB to Meg taking into consideration weather, load, and other variables.

"Sealed," replied Pfifer, unnerving everyone. He'd snuck up without a sound. As Aerial Reconnaissance Weather Officer, Pfifer occupied a workstation on the flight deck behind Sam, coordinating the acquisition of data at flight level. "I have orders to give it you upon takeoff."

Sam wasn't surprised. "Roland hinted we might be in for a few changes on this recon. There is some DoD interest in this storm." Pfifer said nothing. Sam kicked off the pre-flight checklist. "Windshield heat."

"Warm up," replied Ranger.

"Cabin signs."

"On."

"Parking brake."

"Setting pressure to normal."

There were eighteen items. Finally, Sam said, "Start engine."

Ranger turned on number three first, then the outboard turbine of number four, then number two on the other wing, and finally number one.

"NOAA two-one, you have clearance," crackled the tower.

"Ready to copy," said Ranger, and read back the clearance.

The Hercules rolled forward onto the active runway and paused, revving.

"Ready for takeoff," reported Sam.

"Cleared for takeoff," the tower replied.

"NOAA two-one rolling." Sam took his feet off the brakes.

The Hercules picked up speed. The four engines sucked in the clear, hot South Florida air. At a hundred and thirty-eight knots, the Hercules passed decision speed. At a hundred and fifty-three knots, it cleared the ground and the nose assumed an angle where the wings attained optimum lift.

"NOAA two-one, report reaching three thousand feet."

"Roger," copied Ranger.

Sam rolled the flying laboratory into a steep bank and they cleared the Florida coastline.

Pfifer leaned forward with two sealed envelopes. He handed Quince the first one. "Your flight plan to the storm." Pfifer raised the second envelope. "This will be opened after we spot the storm. It lays out our course to the eye."

He pocketed it.

"Oh-kay," drawled Sam, shaking his head, nonplused by the secrecy.

————

Just as the Hurricane Hunters climbed over the endless blue Atlantic, President Avery Walker took his seat at the head of the horseshoe in the Situation Room. An EXCOMM intelligence briefing led by Defense Secretary Baron Hawke got under way. The display was at 'DEFCON 2,' the second highest level, and the terror threat at 'orange,' or heightened. Participants outside the Situation Room, like the vice president, came up on the video screens via IAS, DoD's Integrated Automatic Digital Network System with SVS—Secure Voice System, which encrypted all phone-in participants.

The mood was somber.

Returns from an Aurora spy plane were in. Its vast array of sophisticated camera gear produced photographs of such fine resolution, threat analysts could identify Politburo members entering or leaving the Communist Party Headquarters in Havana.

"Shouldn't we take a wait-and-see approach, at least initially?" said Admiral Grant from the flatscreen labeled, 'USS WJC' or *William J. Clinton*, America's newest aircraft carrier that he commanded. "They could be resolving this internally."

Since last week, the Politburo's three-a-week meetings had been replaced by erratic conferences. This came accompanied by unconfirmed rumors that dissent brewed in Juan Castro's inner circle. The leader of the opposition was seventy-year old Elian Santos, Minister of the Interior. Reports indicated his support might be as much as a third of the Politburo. Such dissent would have been unthinkable under Fidel Castro or his brother, Raul.

It signaled a ray of hope that Juan did not have as firm a grip. But Juan's brother, Carlos, was Defense Minister. Profiled as a thirty-five year old, young, ruthless womanizer in a Politburo where the average age was sixty-two, Carlos shared the same closeness to Juan as Fidel and Raul had. Carlos's Ministry of National Defense, along with the Party's Military Commission, under General Roberto Melchor, controlled all branches of the armed forces. The relationship between Carlos and General Melchor was unclear, but there was no evidence of acrimony.

"The Aurora's returns indicate the Politburo hasn't met even once today," reacted Baron quickly. He suspected Grant was voicing a private plea from John Ulysses VI. The instant this crisis broke, Baron knew the Ulysses would have diplomatic 'irons in the fire' inside the Politburo. To regain a toehold in the dark shadows, John needed to pull out a political solution. From the outset, Admiral Grant had not been shy about expressing the fact that he found Thunder Strike's collateral damage—loss of innocent lives—unacceptable. Baron added, "It could be that Juan Castro is quashing Elian's revolt."

"True," Avery nodded, "We don't know if Elian's even alive." He looked at Grant. "What's the status of Thunder Strike?"

"Underway," replied Admiral Grant. The *Clinton* was serving as the operational headquarters for the black op.

Baron pointed to another screen. "That's the latest satellite picture. It shows the storm, now called Meg, acquiring the familiar spiral. An indication she's gaining strength."

Avery looked at Peter beaming in from the NHC. "Peter. How is it going with Dr. Rotas? Does he have any reservations?"

"If he did, he didn't say," replied Peter.

"He is a bit of a maverick," said Baron to the president.

"In what way?" asked Avery.

"Congress gave the NHC autonomy and he's been at the helm fifteen years. So, he knows where the lines are. He doesn't cross them and is not afraid to point it out if we do."

"He doesn't like to be told what to do's what you're saying?" smiled Avery.

Baron nodded. "He's pretty much his own boss."

"AFWA can handle all storm discussions, sir," suggested Jack.

"I like the fact that we have strong civilian oversight at

every stage of Thunder Strike," said Grant.

Spoken like a Ulysses. But Baron bit his tongue. Avery nodded. Non-committal. Baron relaxed. He may be pulling the strings as a Hawke but he wanted to go into the history books as Baron, the architect of Thunder Strike, the most important weapon of war since the invention of the firearm. That's why he did not brief the president or the EXCOMM that there had been an unauthorized access of raw satellite weather data this morning by Vick Delhom and Diane Wood—a pair of low level meteorologists at the WFO in Silver Springs.

Peter had faxed him their résumés. Vick profiled out as trouble. Diane was highly educated, almost an academic. Harmless. Baron asked Peter to lean on James Vaughn, the Meteorologist-In-Charge, by all accounts a pencil pusher who was easily intimidated. *Make him handle it.* James was a year away from retirement and looking forward to it. *Threaten his pension.* James agreed to retrieve the data discreetly. He reported back that Vick had obtained the data for an article Diane was writing. Peter verified it. James assured him that she had turned over everything Vick had downloaded.

Baron trusted Peter, who had, over their decades of friendship, shown an acute sixth sense which set him apart. Made him the best. So, Baron did not even hesitate when Peter asked him permission to wiretap not just the phones at the WFO but personal cell phones of everyone there. Peter suspected they hadn't heard the last from Diane and Vick.

EIGHT

"Hark! My hurricane hunters!" sang Quince, the navigator and a bohemian at heart. "You should be seeing something soon."

"Negative," said Sam, scanning for tell tale wisps of clouds ahead. The sky was clear. The Atlantic Ocean below enjoyed a rare placidity.

"You will," said Quince.

Pfifer, dozing in his station, stirred awake. He spoke quietly into his headset. "Schultz."

As Dropsonde Officer, Schultz was relegated to the cargo compartment near the right paratroop door. He acquired vertical atmospheric soundings from the flight level to the surface of the ocean.

Instrumentation aboard these aircraft had come a long way from basic drift meters. Today, they flew into hurricanes with a NEXRAD on board and sophisticated dropsondes, which were sensors that Schultz would drop into critical sections of the storm for continuous measurements of pressure, temperature, humidity, wind speed, and direction. Radio used to be the only line of communication between the aircraft and the National Hurricane Center. Now, Aircraft Satellite Data Link connected the computers on the aircraft to those at the NHC. ASDL permitted superimposition of wind observations, temperature, pressure, humidity, and cloud patterns over digitized radar data in real time. Rapid Scan Imagery allowed the NHC's forecasters to animate the images into a moving picture of the internal structure, mesoscale features, and dynamics of the storm as the aircraft flew through it.

"I have visual at eleven o'clock," said Ranger, sharpening everyone's attention.

Detached, delicate, fibrous, and silky looking, white strands heralding Meg's outer spirals snaked toward them.

———

A collective sigh of relief went up at the National Hurricane Center.

"At least she is where she is supposed to be," said Clark, the lead forecaster, who had drafted the first report when Meg was still a tropical depression that he did not think would develop into anything significant.

"Now let's hope she concurs with our satellite pictures," yawned Gerardo Sanchez, the volatile Research chief. He had been here since eight this morning and it was past eight P.M.

Hank wandered over. "Always skeptical."

"Just cautious." Gerardo had been doing this too long and he knew there would be surprises they'd been spared by remote satellite images and soundings. He pulled up a chair, stirring the first of what he knew would be many cups of black coffee.

The Hercules showed up as a blinking dot entering Meg's outermost spiral from the lower left quadrant. Gerardo looked over to Clarke's screen and stiffened sharply. *Is it my imagination?* He blinked and leaned closer. Nothing but purple haze, or unreadable data. He thought he saw something in the lower left quadrant, but didn't see it again.

"Your flight plan to the eye of the storm," said Pfifer, holding out the second envelope toward Quince as the first wisps of cloud formed a soft carpet over the Hercules.

"Everybody ready?" asked Sam over the intercom.

"No," replied Quince at once. "Hold on." He adjusted his crotch, drawing grins from Sam, Ranger, and Knoll. "Now, I'm ready."

Pfifer wasn't amused. "How long have you guys been together?"

"Too long," sighed Sam.

"Let's rock," said Quince, settling in. As navigator, he would guide them all the way to the storm center to accurately mark the position of the eye when they reached it. He worked off a color coded satellite image of the storm superimposed over an Atlantic grid. Red designated heavy precipitation and strong winds. Meg's numbers were approximate because they'd been measured from a satellite. Quince studied the constantly updating satellite image of the storm to determine the easiest way in.

Out of the corner of his eye, Sam saw Quincy crack open Pfifer's envelope and look up at once, surprised, "We are entering at thirty thousand feet?"

"Really?" reacted Sam. The usual protocol was to enter the storm from a stagnation point at much lower altitude. Pfifer offered no explanation. Quince shrugged. So did Sam.

Headsets on board crackled with the first order from the NHC, "Release a dropsonde."

"So soon?" asked Sam.

"Hombre saw something," replied Clarke. "Let me correct that—or he thinks he did, and doesn't want to take any chances." Sam was good friends with Gerardo and respected him as a guy who had a gut instinct about hurricanes.

"Dropsonde away!" replied Schultz.

One of a series of red lights on the instrument panel in front of Sam snapped on indicating Schultz had opened the AXBT launching tube. A split second later, the adjacent red light snapped on too, when a small door at the bottom of the fuselage opened. Sam peered out the side window. The dropsonde—a slender, lightweight cylinder—fell away. The tube auto sealed shut. The red light turned off. The dropsonde contained a Radio Direction Finder, which tracked the speed and direction of the wind at various levels, and other devices to measure temperature, relative humidity, and air pressure Beeps commenced as the first readouts began to arrive.

The thin whitish veil of underlying cirrostratus clouds soon thickened into heads of nimbostratus. Dark, ominous, and ugly, these rain bearers were gray, wet, shapeless, and feebly lit by powerful strokes of lightning deep within. Sam ordered everyone to check the harnesses and ties securing the payload one last time.

"Here we go," announced Sam and the banked the Hercules.

The mammoth plane shuddered like a toy, signaling they had entered the outer spiral. Edging in a counterclockwise flight pattern and losing altitude at the same time, they would, if all went well, burst into the eye at fifteen hundred feet. A crosswind fiercely attacked the aircraft. The Hercules shook violently.

"If that's thirty knots," said Ranger, "my mother's a man."

"She's not?" Sam couldn't help himself.

The Hercules bumped and rattled.

Pfifer called out, "It's going to be like this all the way."

"So autopilot's out?" Sam shot back. He didn't know why he was trying to lighten the mood. Pfifer and Schultz had not smiled, let alone laughed, since coming on board.

The Hercules banked into the first rain bands. These were the active storm clouds that spawned off deadly tornadoes on landfall. Dramatically stronger winds lashed out. The claps of thunder pierced the insulated walls. Blades of lightning slashed close enough to sometimes make the crew recoil. Soon, all Sam could see was an oily mass splattering the windshield. His eyes squinted with concentration. Conversation thinned. Quince became their eyes and ears. Knoll closely monitored the Hercules's mechanical systems. For the next hour, they corkscrewed deeper into Meg's cloudy terrain. It got rougher and rougher.

"Coming up on fifteen thousand feet," reported Quince.

Schultz released two more dropsondes for spatial and temporal coverage of the storm. Computers on board recorded readings from three levels of the atmosphere. The last and most critical reading came just before the dropsondes hit the water. It provided surface and near surface wind speeds, temperature, and pressure. Meteorological, nuclei, radiation, cloud physics, and miscellaneous sensors combined into a multi-channel data acquisition system, issuing over a hundred samples per second per channel in real time via the ASDL to the NHC.

"The home stretch to the eye of the storm," announced Sam and turned the wheel gingerly.

They were entering the annulus of clouds around the eye where the strongest gusts prevailed. Moist air spiraled in ascending columns to fill the low pressure void that was Meg's eye. The closer the air spun to the eye, the faster it gusted. Simply put, the eyewall was a lethal tower of wicked turbulence, continuous thunder, and incessant lightning. It was the most terrifying part of AWR. And the most exciting.

"I love this part," grinned Sam.

Slap! Meg greeted them with a vicious updraft! Tossing the Hercules up a hundred feet. Sam barely leveled the Hercules, when Meg swung at them again, landing a giant size punch. The Hercules careened out of control! Momentarily. Sam steadied the plane again.

"Jesus!" yelled Ranger. "She's no tropical storm."

"That was a fifty knot nudge back there," confirmed Schultz over the intercom.

"NHC underestimated her strength," said Pfifer.

"You think?" said Sam.

The Hercules, a solid fortress of a plane on the ground, appeared ludicrously puny in Meg's endless murky darkness of unabated turbulence. Every blade of lightning hungered after the plane. Every gust aimed to knock it out of the air. Every dark cloud sought to smother it in a deadly embrace.

Suddenly!

Without warning!

The Hercules dropped like stone!

"Shiiiit!" Sam reacted.

This time he could not regain control.

The Hercules continued fall.

"Pull up! Pull up!" yelled Ranger.

"Losing altitude hundred feet a second!" screamed Quince.

Sam remained calm. Pulling the wheel. Working the flaps. Doing everything he could. The Hercules did not just continue to drop, they could feel the nose angle steepen. Threatening to turn the plane belly up. This beast of a plane was not built like a fighter to right itself on a dime.

The altimeter needle ripped below a thousand feet.

Quince screamed again, "Eight hundred feet!"

"Nose angle at sixty," reported Ranger.

"Knoll!" yelled Sam.

"No failure!"

Then!

Just as suddenly!

The tail of Hercules dropped! The plane flatbottomed hard! Bouncing with jarring intensity as if it had struck a solid floor. They'd been saved by a goliath updraft.

Sam grabbed back control.

"There goes the secret flight plan!" Quince shot at Pfifer, whose fingers couldn't grip his seat handles any tighter. He barely reacted.

"Which part of this do you love, again?" Ranger found his voice. He felt he had to say something to release the pent up terror.

"The still being alive part," replied Sam.

"Contact!" Quince yelled, shock raising the pitch of his voice.

"What?" Sam whipped his head around.

"Contact!" repeated Quince. "It's heading directly for us!"

Before Sam could react, a US Navy FA-18F Super Hornet screamed out of the opaque black clouds. He yelled, "Jesus!"

And was half way over with the wheel when Ranger shouted, "Hard over!"

The Hercules was too big and too heavy to respond immediately. It lumbered into a slow bank. *Too slow.* The Hornet approached fast. *Too fast!* The sleek fighter's wings angled. Going vertical. *Too little, too late.* In that terrifying split second, the image of a fiery death from a head-on collision at a combined velocity well over a thousand miles an hour flashed in front of Sam's eyes.

The two cockpits came face to face.

Got so close, he saw white faces in the FA-18's cockpit.

Splat! The Hornet's afterburners smeared the Hercules's windshield with high octane emissions. Startling as that was, it also signaled the fighter had miraculously eluded the bigger plane's nose. The Hercules and Hornet passed, angled steeply in diverging turns, bellies barely a yard apart!

The FA-18 disappeared behind the thick clouds. Sam leveled off. The terror of the close call was so intense, they felt no relief of escaping alive, not yet. The incredible roar of the storm permeating inside registered as utter, pin drop silence. Nobody spoke.

Sam found his voice first. "Everybody OK?"

"Fine," replied Ranger.

"My shorts are brown, but otherwise I'm fine," Quince joked with a nervous cackle.

Pfifer just nodded. Schultz, who had not been privy to the terrifying visual of the near miss, sounded the calmest over the com. "I'm okay."

"What's a Navy jet doing in here?" Sam wondered aloud.

Nobody had an answer. Pfifer's expression betrayed nothing.

The next moment, the noisy rattling ended abruptly. So did the stormy violence outside. They were in Meg's ill-defined eye, forty miles in diameter.

Huge amounts of spray stood suspended in the air. An eerie sight of spinning eyewall clouds surrounded them. Conditions starkly contrasted from just a second ago. It was like flipping a switch from turbulence to serenity. They obtained the first eye fix by visually picking the calmest spot in the center of the boiling ocean.

Sam guided the Hercules out of the eye but not out of the

storm. As unnerved as they were, they had to circle back into Meg's agitated bowels and penetrate the eye again. And again. And again. At least three more times.

To determine if Meg continued to move forward.

———

At the National Hurricane Center, Gerardo anxiously paced behind Clark, his lead forecaster, who was still trying to clarify the purple haze in Meg's critical lower left quadrant, where the Hercules released that first dropsonde. The computers had to process several channels of information, remap the display, and overlay a wide variety of atmospheric variables. A slow process.

Gerardo checked around the room. The rest of the staff sat glued to their terminals. They used the data pouring in from the first pass through the eye to develop Satellite Interpretation Messages, or SIMs—graphic analyses of significant features and trends—that assisted regional WFOs in the preparation of local forecasts and warnings.

"Hombre!" called out a forecaster. "Need you here." Gerardo shuffled over, sipping his umpteenth cup of coffee. "I'm showing conflicting windflows."

Masses of color onscreen moved clockwise and counterclockwise. Gerardo frowned. With audible concern, he said, "Isolate the storm."

The forecaster nodded. His fingers flew over the keyboard. The data was color coded. Meg separated out as a white spiral and the Southerlies appeared as a serpentine red smear. Tiny crimson fangs appeared and disappeared, extending into and retracting from the jittery cotton ball that represented Meg. The Southerlies were much closer than Gerardo anticipated. He was hoping for no interaction, but clearly that was no longer the case.

"Gusts from the Southerlies are interacting with Meg," he surmised.

Clark hollered, "Hombre!"

Gerardo snapped his neck around. Something in Clark's voice roused goose bumps of apprehension. Gerardo hurried over. He saw that Clark had just finished replacing the purple haze in Meg's lower left quadrant with accurate sea surface temperature and pressure. Gerardo had been right about the alarm in Clark's voice.

"It's a low pressure trough," said Clark grimly. Realizing Gerardo's fears.

"Hombre!" called out another forecaster monitoring eye-fixes. Gerardo could see his screen. The forecaster knew he did not have to elaborate what was on his computer.

Clark's report wasn't the worst news. This was.

All eyes swiveled. The noise level in the room dropped dramatically. Gerardo punched up the intercom. "Hank."

Hank asked at once, "What's wrong?"

Sensing a shadowy movement, Gerardo looked over. Peter took an anxious step forward, but remained well out of everyone's way. Their eyes locked, Gerardo said, "Meg's stopped moving."

———

Diane was fast asleep on the couch when the phone rang and startled her awake. Her glasses, perched precariously on the tip of her nose, crashed to the hardwood floor. She realized Sam in handcuffs, naked across the window bars, was a dream. The ringing was not and answered before her voice mail kicked in.

"Hello." Her voice crackled with sleep.

"Didn't you say you're going to be up and working on your article?" scolded Vick.

"What time is it?"

"Barely ten-thirty."

"Really?" Diane checked her watch. "I didn't sleep last night. I was in Miami, remember?"

"With a man who's put half an ocean between you two after a one night stand."

"Very funny."

"Get online. I just sent you a NHC movie called Meg."

"What?" Diane's fingers flew over laptop.

"Tropical depression 217E is now hurricane Meg."

"Tropical storm Meg, you mean."

"That ship sailed a few hours ago. The last AWR pass recorded eyewall gusts of well over seventy-five miles an hour." The threshold wind speed to classify a system as a hurricane.

"That must be some kind of a record."

Diane opened the Satellite Interpretation Messages. Her stomach knotted and asked in a fearful drawl, "V. How did you get these SIMs?"

"Like you told me to. I entered the NHC mainframe and hooked into the live AWR images. Sam?"

"Yup. He told me he was flying out when I left him."

"Compare his fourth pass through the eye to the first.

"The coordinates have not changed."

"Meg's stalled. The first of your 'what-ifs' has come to pass and your Potomac scenario just upped to twenty percent."

"Never doubt a woman's intuition." Diane studied the legend on the right side. "Look at her stats. Eyewall pressure near nine hundred and falling. Sustained gusts of eighty miles an hour, sporadic gusts at one-twenty."

"And rising," added Vick.

"I can't believe we still haven't received anything from the NHC."

Normally, the National Hurricane Center, upon recognizing a storm heading toward the North American coast, promptly relayed SIMs and bulletins to the National Meteorological Center in Maryland and the targeted WFOs. Local forecasters would then begin running their own models, integrating local conditions into the large scale guidance from the NHC and NMC.

"In fact," said Vick, "official satellite imagery out of

NESDIS and data out of NMC to users worldwide still does not acknowledge the existence of the storm. Guess what? NMC, NESDIS, TPC, and NCEP are all out of the loop. Do you know who's running models? AFWA."

"So, when Meg starts moving, how are they going to explain why she suddenly showed up in our weather maps?"

"Good point–what the hell?"

"What?"

"Ivory just walked in."

"What is he doing there?" asked Diane suspiciously. "He's not on the night shift. You know, he snuck up behind me this morning. Maybe he saw something and now he's curious."

"I recorded everything. I'll hide the drive in my drawer. Bye." Vick hung up.

Filled with nervous apprehension, Diane paced in circles, her thoughts jumping all over the place. Ivory was a Warning Coordination Meteorologist. He must know about Meg. Did James Vaughn know? As the Meteorologist-In-Charge, he must. What would the DoD do if they discovered how much Vick and she had figured out? She was excited her hunch had come to pass, but she also worried about the twenty percent chance of landfall. The northeast should take precautions. *Who can I talk to? How can I substantiate a threat when the official weather maps don't even show one?*

———

Dr. Hank Rotas entered Peter Wilkins's office for the first time and saw the array of flatscreens he'd heard so much about from the staff. "Each is a video teleconference monitor," Peter explained. They were not labeled. Deliberately, realized Hank, so as not to reveal the agencies reporting to Peter. Hank could guess who they were, but there was one more screen than his mental count.

Rather than apprehension, Hank had felt a sense of relief and even a little elation that Meg had stalled. He walked in hoping to end the secrecy. Take back the NHC. Video callers came onscreen one by one. Hank did not know how many would participate. Defense Secretary Baron Hawke appeared from his home in Virginia, unflappable as usual. JCS Chairman Jack Knight beamed in from the Tank, as the Joint Chief's Conference Room at the Pentagon was called. Behind him, his top aides looked tired and worried.

"What happened?" asked Baron

"An unexpected low pressure trough in the lower left quadrant stalled Meg," answered Rotas.

"What does that mean?" asked Jack anxiously.

"I don't know," said Rotas frankly.

"Don't know?" exploded Jack. "I have more than a dozen Special Forces teams at sea."

"My office is still studying the consequences."

"Just answer me this," said Jack bluntly. "Will Meg make landfall in Cuba like you predicted?"

"I never predicted that," retorted Hank curtly. "In fact, my office has yet to issue an official storm track and landfall prediction." His deduced quickly that the only other agency privy to Meg must have jumped the gun—Air Force Global Weather Agency. "Was it AFWA?"

Baron did not answer. He asked, "Is the Cuba scenario dead?"

"More likely than not," nodded Hank. He knew the AFWA had probably come to the same conclusion, since the NHC was using their models.

"But you are not sure," Peter interjected, looking at Hank in the chair next to him.

The military forecasters must be concurring with the NHC's pessimism, or Baron and Peter would have been quick to point out that Hank's team was wrong. "We won't be able to say until she begins to move again. Initial projections suggest the northeast as a possible target." He waited a beat and said what he came to say, "I want to declassify Meg."

Baron did not flinch. "That is not a priority, Hank."

"I will make it mine if she poses a significant threat."

"Does she?" asked Peter with an edge.

Hank knew the AFWA probably already told them that the models projected Meg would be a tropical wave at best. "Not at the present time. But that could change, and I will issue appropriate warnings."

Jack said shortly, "That is not your decision."

Hank put his foot down. "As director of the National Hurricane Center, I have final say on all severe storm discussions. So, it is my decision."

Baron, the consummate politician, capitulated, "Of course. When would you make it?"

"By the time we issue our six A.M. bulletin." Hank nodded toward Peter, "I'll keep Peter posted."

"Okay," said Baron. "Thank you, Hank. Goodnight."

"Thank you, gentlemen." Hank nodded and left the office, sensing everyone was waiting for Peter's signal that he had left the room.

―――――

"Do nothing until you hear from me," Baron dismissed the Chairman, Joint Chiefs by switching off Jack's screen.

"There is another developing situation," said Peter. "The Silver Springs terminal that accessed information yesterday from Wallops did it again less than an hour ago. This time from the NHC."

"The same two meteorologists?"

"Yes. Vick Delhom and Diane Wood."

"Do you know what they accessed?"

"Meg," said Peter. "Straight off the aerial recon."

"Any mention of Thunder Strike?" asked Baron.

"No." Nobody at the NHC knew the name of the operation.

"Any risk they might find out?"

"No. But I have been impressed with Vick's ability to hack in at will," said Peter.

Baron knew from Peter's response where this was going. "What about the woman?"

"Diane's not the problem."

Baron paused. Peter did not have to spell it out. He looked straight at the analyst, and with the briefest of nods, said, "Okay."

———

An hour later, Vick took his usual break for a bite to eat at the all-night convenient store across the street from the WFO. There were no clouds, but smog buildup due to the relentless heat during the previous day blanketed the stars from view. The neon store sign flickered with age. Vick stepped on the curb. The neon jittered off. The sidewalk went dark. In that moment of blackness, Vick saw a flash. Recognized it as metal.

A blade!

Then a white hot streak of pain tore across his neck. His hand instinctively shot up to dull it. Instead, his palm filled with blood spraying out. Vick's brain relayed one last message—*I'm being mugged.*

He let out a scream. A muted croak, nothing more, emerged. His head flopped forward. His knees buckled. *Crack!* His skull struck the pavement, ripping another shockwave of agony through his body. He lay on the sidewalk, eyes open, acutely aware that he was losing consciousness gradually.

TODAY

NINE

"There is only one reason we are all here tonight, handing this man yet another award," the familiar network anchor from *Evening News* had opened last night's awards dinner to introduce Tim O'Flaherty, Managing Editor of the *Daily Post,* onto the stage. "Abject terror." Laughter had roared through the hall even though the tongue-in-cheek remark was no joke. A few weeks ago, when Tim heard his name was the answer to a question on the most popular TV quiz show, he knew he'd become an icon—an impressive achievement for an aging journalist in the youth-driven social medial.

It had been a long, hard road getting here.

Tim considered himself an utterly uncomplicated guy with just a hard work ethic that he'd inherited from strict working class parents. His father was a middle-management drone in a faceless global corporation in Columbus, Ohio, and his mother a real estate broker. Tim was the youngest of three male siblings. They were an ordinary family until it became apparent Tim was growing into a remarkable physical specimen. He won a scholarship as a defensive lineman at the Ohio State University, a football powerhouse. The boys were all diehard Buckeye fans, having been born and brought up in the university town. Tim became a local hero for staying home and going to school at OSU.

His four years playing this violent sport shaped the man he became. Disciplined, tough, aggressive, and unafraid of new challenges. As good a football player as he was on the college level, even making the game-saving tackle that won them a National Championship, Tim was smart enough to know he was undersized to play at the professional level. So he took up writing as a freshman and honed his flair for languages. He spoke French, German, Italian, Russian, and Spanish. Naturally, upon joining the *Times*, he quickly rose to become the European Bureau Chief. He married his college sweetheart. It didn't work out. He was brash, impatient, curious, and adventurous. He liked to move and explore. He had a roving eye. Always blunt, forthright, and honest to a fault, he told his wife he was not a one-woman kind of guy. He never married again. In fact, he refused to even be in a committed relationship.

A decade later, he returned to Washington as the Deputy Managing Editor with a reputation for flair, flourish, and flamboyance, which immediately clashed with the 'respectable' tradition that the newspaper was unwilling to give up even though readership was declining. TV and online-anywhere-anytime-news saw the inevitable marriage of journalism and entertainment.

Tim believed that print news faced extinction if it remained dry, hardboiled, and serious. He quit the *Times* and shocked his peers by taking over as Managing Editor of the Daily *Post* in New York, a notorious tabloid that symbolized yellow journalism. Undaunted, he set about reforming its image without losing his core base: middle and low income readers at check out stands of grocery and convenient stores across the country. He introduced catchy, bold, giant headlines that soon became the *Post*'s signature front page. Combining the staff's expertise reporting sordid entertainment gossip with his extensive beltway expertise, he masterfully shifted the paper's focus to unearthing salacious political skeletons.

Sales spiked. He'd not only connected with the public's morbid curiosity, suspicion, and dislike for elected officials, but grabbed young viewers too. Seizing on this untapped niche, he molded the reporting and writing style to compete with the immediacy and audiovisual appeal of TV and websites. Articles read like gripping short stories. He introduced gritty and incisive Editorials. Weaving facts, rumor, innuendo, sex, and violence, the *Post* transformed into the nation's premier eavesdropper in 'the city of conversation,' Henry James's name for Washington DC. Liz's Pulitzer validated this new docu-dramatic style of news he liked to call 'infotainment.' Tim was hailed as its pioneer.

He garnered 'prestige,' which Dean Acheson called 'the shadow of power.' Tim knew it and would never allow it to be wrested from him. So, he made sure he wasn't hurt by the scandal surrounding Liz. He'd suspected the allegations against Liz might have some merit long before they even broke. He wrote a guarded editorial to stake out lines of integrity that even he, while pushing the envelope and stretching the rules, would not cross. But he was also no fool. The scandal involved politics, drugs, little towns, rising stars, and murky truths. People loved to watch public figures fall. Especially beautiful celebrities. Liz was that and more. At the height of her popularity, she was linked with movie stars and musicians. Adding fuel to the curiosity was the fact it was entwined with a compelling presidential race.

The whole affair evolved into a kind of journalistic 'perfect storm.' Tim and the *Post* enjoyed the catbird's seat. The feeding frenzy became a national pastime. When everything went to hell in a hand basket for Liz, he used his editorials to come off as a victim of the trust he'd placed in a star he helped launch. It moved him another step higher in the ladder of legends.

Tim sat down behind the perennially messy desk inside his office. The different stories to appear now on the website and tomorrow in prin needed his immediate attention. He had spent the night with Sabrina, the White House speech writer he'd met at the awards dinner yesterday evening. They planned to meet again for dinner at his Connecticut home tonight.

As he settled in, his assistant walked in. "Tim," she said, "Liz did not come in today."

"Did you call her?"

"I wanted to check with you first."

"Don't bother. I warned her. She's fired." He resumed reading. The assistant simply stood there. She did not know if he was being serious. He looked up irritably, "What part of that didn't you understand?"

"I-I got it," stammered the assistant and withdrew.

Tim heard a buzz erupt from the newsroom. There would be few tears, if any at all.

———

To stay alive and relevant, Liz realized she had to keep a step ahead. Those were the deadly rules of the game she had signed up to play. She didn't know the name or significance of the black guy in the Cherokee. He was dead when she got there. Fortunately, she'd never discarded the prepaid cell phone that Admiral Grant gave her last night. When she looked at it, the display showed a 'missed call.' It had come in last night when she'd been in the air onboard the Cessna. Under 'outgoing calls,' she found the number Grant had texted last night. The numbers matched. She called it.

There was an answer.

Liz did not know who was at other end of the line.

But she received an address.

Traffic crawled along the Capital Beltway, which had survived Meg's beat-down to become the only connection across the river. Nobody was getting anywhere quickly. The Mercedes Kompressor that Liz had hotwired dipped down and climbed out of a pothole so deep, the massive steel rebars showed.

The foundation of emergency management was preparedness. People paid little attention to threats from natural disasters in their daily routine. They believed the government would warn them of impending catastrophes. Hurricane Meg had arrived with little or no warning. The destruction in every direction was a snapshot of total surprise. Earlier, in Alexandria, Liz saw the tail end a freight train precariously hanging off the edge of the west bank. The railway tracks, locomotive, and the other cars were gone. Presumably, they had plunged into the river. For that to happen, the train must have been halfway across, unaware a hundred-mile wide hurricane was bearing down.

That just did not make sense.

Just when Liz thought the traffic couldn't move any slower, it stopped entirely. The big rig in front of her stalled. *Oh, great.* Hazard lights on the eighteen-wheeler started to flash. Luckily, she was right at Indian Head Highway, which she needed to take heading north. Before anyone behind her realized the traffic nightmare that was about to unfold, Liz swung the Mercedes onto a short stretch of shoulder.

Liz settled back. Checked her rear view for any tail. None. She floored the gas. Zipped down the exit ramp. With the luxury of distance from the whirlwind of quick decisions she'd been forced to make in the last forty-eight hours, she realized how this assignment turned out rested squarely on her shoulders.

————

Six miles back and five minutes later, the ripple effect of the stalled rig reached Andrew Burke. He pulled up his Humvee. Thought nothing of it. Leaned back in his seat. Ten minutes later, traffic remained frozen. Andrew saw people getting out of their cars and stretching. *Damnit.* He picked up the MILSATCOM. Peter answered at once.

"I need a chopper," said Andrew.

"Where are you?" asked Peter.

Andrew passed on his coordinates off the GPS readout on the MILSATCOM. He told Peter to order a tow truck for his Humvee, which he was abandoning where he'd stopped. He walked away empty handed. His gun, attachments, and ammo were dismantled into pieces and tucked into the multiple pockets of his specially tailored pants.

He worked his way down the embankment. Meg had twisted and knotted up the side rails like flimsy string and flung them all over the undeveloped land that ran alongside. Whatever weeds and vegetation had been there before the storm were now gone, leaving behind a barren, slushy field, littered with mud-caked death that had hardened with rigor mortis. Andrew breathed through his mouth to neutralize the stink.

He always won this game of death without contest because he never had to work under the pressure of outrunning someone he could not simply eliminate first. Careful prep and precise execution had elevated him into a league of his own. Liz made him hurry. Move quickly and improvise. But she'd given them the break they needed when she led them to Philippe. The ball was rolling again. So why was she still in the hunt? What was Peter's endgame? There was no way he'd let her leave DC alive. Unless—

An improbable thought entered Andrew's mind.

Unless Peter was recruiting her. *Or, has he already?*

———

Liz caught her breath. Coming down the exit ramp off the northbound Indian Head Highway, she saw the remnants of an Oxon Hill mall that she remembered as brand spanking new when she'd left DC to check into rehab. Half a dozen black kids sifted hopefully through the crushed stores. Suddenly, two men in uniforms–cops or private security, she couldn't tell–darted out of nowhere! Opened fire! The kids scattered!

The uniforms gave chase. Like predators in a jungle, they zeroed in on the weakest and slowest kid, an overweight teen. He took two bullets in his back, one from each uniform, and crashed face down. The uniforms, who laughed and joked through out this brief shootout, saw Liz. They stared at her. She sped off, taking the first turn that put her out of their line of sight. They did not follow her. So, reports about DC being under siege from itself were true.

Washington had the most comprehensive emergency management in the nation. It was slanted heavily to guard against a terror attack, which, by virtue of being launched by an enemy, united people. Natural disasters were a different animal altogether. It evoked survival and self preservation. Hurricane Katrina revealed that race and class shaped those basic instincts. In the Washington Metropolitan Area, behavioral science studies had not been updated to account for the fact its five million residents stood on the verge of crossing the majority minority threshold. Institutions, built and run by whites, had transitioned from the bottom up into Hispanic and Asian hands. A Guatemalan immigrant had wrested the Mayor's office. African Americans suddenly found themselves outnumbered and sidelined.

Liz knew all this because she had researched the capital for a story about DC housing the only citizens in America without a right to vote. The city was unique. It was managed and run by Congress. An archaic law denied the people representation in government. To delve deeper, she'd spent a couple of nights with a hunky urban planner, who dug up several hush-hush studies the city had authorized following Katrina. One of them discovered 'negative feedback loops,' which measured stability of neighborhoods. Not surprisingly, affluent neighborhoods came out stable. They were also predominantly white. Apparently, they monitored their ethnic populations carefully. These interviews, conducted as part of the study, were buried because the revelations were explosive. Residents associated blacks and immigrants with negative value. Real estate agents in the area knew it and conspired to ensure the 'color' of the community did not change. So the poor settled 'around' the wealthy white enclaves, creating racial, social, and economic envelopes of disenchantment.

Watching, waiting, seething.

A tinderbox of angry sentiment.

Meg provided the spark. These gated communities had been plundered. Residents, who dared to return, shuffled amidst the ruins, shoulders drooping, heads dejected. Walking corpses recovering memories and piecing their lives together again. Without cathartic discussions with other survivors, reunions, and any semblance of hope or relief, symptoms like psychic numbing, survivor syndromes, and depressive sorrow predominated.

Liz braked to allow a pair of tanks by. A gun rat-a-tatted somewhere. The soldiers perched on the turrets did not even look in the general direction. Neither did Liz. She'd been in DC barely four hours and already the gunfire had become part of normal city ambience. The tanks passed. Liz fed gas to the Kompressor. The pistons growled coarsely and powered the car uphill.

She reached the crest and was pleasantly surprised by a starkly different image. The unusual geography of being on the leeward slope of two hills had saved most of these homes. Meg had still gotten to them but not with devastating fury. The damage here wasn't beyond repair. Liz saw families patching holes, fixing windows, clearing debris. She heard laughter and saw smiles for the first time.

The address she wanted was at the bottom of the slope. The damage to the designer home seemed minimal compared to what Liz had witnessed elsewhere. Meg had stripped the paint. A couple of walls looked off plumb. The glass in the windows was shattered and the roof punctured in places. Liz climbed the steps under the porch that leaned precariously. She saw blades of glass impaled in the siding. Liz knocked loudly.

She heard no footsteps. The door opened almost at once. Whoever was inside had been watching and waiting.

"Hi. I'm Liz."

"Diane Wood." She nodded Liz into the house.

———

Approaching rotors drew Andrew's attention skyward. Behind him, traffic hadn't budged an inch. The wind shifted suddenly. Black coils of smoke from a gas station fire on the other side of the Beltway drifted toward Andrew. Sunlight dimmed as the chopper drew closer. The dark smoke spiraled clear and a Bell 206B3 Jet Ranger III banked into view. Puddles of water and uncertainty about the saturation of the ground made it too dicey to land. The helicopter hovered with a steady *whupwhup* of propellers, and a youngster—presumably the copilot—winched down a rope with a foot-buoy at bottom.

Andrew put his head down and fought across the concentric rings of slush rippled out by the downdraft. Andrew reached the rope. Wet soil drenched the soles of his Timberlands that sank an inch deep. He kicked off as much of the dirt as he could, fastened the rescue harness, and climbed onto the foot-buoy. Upon his thumbs-up, copilot reversed the motors. The Goodrich winch reeled up the rope.

Andrew's weapons-laden pants threatened to drag him off the buoy. He pressed down with both feet. Ribs on the buoy and his Timberlands provided traction. His bad knee throbbed whenever he shifted his weight onto it. The doctors told him the bone bruise would never fully heal. He held his breath and his grip until he grabbed the outstretched hand of the copilot who hauled him in with the greeting, "Howdy. I'm Brent."

Andrew nodded curtly. Made no return introduction. He squeezed up front into the seat beside the pilot, hearing and ignoring Brent's sarcasm, "Please. Go ahead. Take my seat."

The pilot looked over, "Cale. Welcome aboard."

"Do you know where we are going?" asked Andrew, strapping himself in.

Cale nodded. "44-45 Lincoln Court. We have a ground unit leading the way."

Andrew's jaw tightened. *This is a first.* Peter had ordered backup. Andrew looked out. A squad car, lights flashing and siren wailing, raced into view.

"I know them," said Cale. "We sat out Meg together."

Without prompting Cale went on. Officer Douglas had the wheel and Officer Hess rode shotgun. They were ten-year veterans, who, along with Cale, had survived Meg's landfall because they had been fortunate to be on duty at the time. They'd hunkered down in the holding cells in the basement of the precinct along with the rest of the shift. "To open up space for families, we released all prisoners," said Cale. "Don't reckon many of them made it. Not that anyone is going to miss them, right?"

The onboard speaker crackled. "This is Delta eight-oh."

Cale recognized the voice. "Hey, Hessie. Come in."

Andrew unclipped the mike in front of him. He noticed Cale's face tighten and did not care that the pilot disapproved his cockpit being usurped. Andrew wasn't surprised that Cale said nothing. He probably recognized the distinct clash of metal from Andrew's pockets as weaponry. Actually, he probably had never seen pants like these. The dispatcher had also probably revealed the call for this pickup came from the CIA. But most likely, Andrew suspected, he intimidated the hell out of Cale.

"How far is the address?" Andrew asked the cop directly.

"Ten minutes?" replied Hess in the form of a question.

———

Seven days as a fugitive had taken a toll on Diane. She had not noticed how much until this morning when she'd looked at herself in a shard of mirror. Her face was pinched. She was pale, disheveled, and tense. Her eyes were dull, the sockets sunken. For the first time she'd asked herself, where was that vibrant, light-hearted, happily-in-love meteorologist of just a week ago?

As part of her job, Diane attended seminars on post-traumatic symptoms and disorders. Survivors of a disaster felt a brief sense of relief having beaten death. In her case, the stress and fear never eased up. She'd witnessed cold blooded murders in addition to the storm toll. She had been running for her life during the entire duration of the hurricane. The threat persisted in the aftermath. She was slipping into a state of chronic anxiety, emotional fatigue, and loss of initiative. She felt helpless and unable to stop the descent into the mental state of recurring morbidity called 'death imprint.'

"Would you like some tea?" Diane asked. "I have a kettle on coals."

Without electricity or gas, wood, paper, and charcoal emerged as the fuel of necessity. Everything in the house was still drenched from the wind and rain which had whipped through. Furniture had been tossed about, some with such violence they'd carved out huge holes in the drywall.

Liz turned around. "No thanks. I don't think we have time, Diane. We have to hurry."

Diane sharpened anxiously.

Liz explained, "They'll find this address sooner than later, if they haven't already."

"You're right," Diane nodded. She had been on pins and needles ever since Philippe left this morning for the airport. She wanted to go. But he wouldn't let her. He said he was expendable and she was not. When he didn't return after four hours, she began to fear the worst. Then Liz called and confirmed what Diane suspected. The gimpy-legged assassin, who had pursued Diane during the hurricane, had been laying in wait.

Diane felt guilty she didn't have any more tears. Philippe had been a lifeline in the aftermath. He stood in line for hours and brought home Red Cross and FEMA relief packages because it was too risky for her to go out. Shelters and relief centers were obvious first choices for surveillance. Diane found a set of clothes in the closet from the time she'd house-sat for the guys a month ago.

"Admiral Grant said you had a military document detailing Thunder Strike. Where is it?"

Diane hesitated, startled by how quickly Liz cut to the chase. "Look, I just lost a friend."

Liz seemed surprised, as if Admiral Grant's text message were credentials enough.

"So did I," said Liz. Diane found herself drawn into the reporter's eyes. "My boyfriend. Last night."

Diane swallowed fearfully and shared her grief. "Oh, my God. I'm so sorry."

The edge left Liz entirely. "He did not know anything about Thunder Strike. He just heard the name and paid for it with his life."

"And you still came out?" asked Diane, her comfort growing.

Liz's lips thinned. "I want payback. Don't you?"

Diane nodded angrily, "Yes."

"Admiral Grant said the truth is out here in DC." Liz paused and added on second thought, "With you."

Diane's guard went up instantly. Liz was lying. Admiral Grant had laid down ground rules during their very first conversation over unlisted, prepaid cell phones. "Be careful what you say and how you say it. It's all in the semantics. Say the Jayspid is in DC or the Jayspid is not here. Never use names or even reference people. That way, you'll never reveal who or how many of you are out there with access to the Jayspid. Or even if there's more than one copy of it."

"You have to understand," Diane said tentatively, wondering suddenly if Liz was who she seemed, "I, I need time, uh, to verify, uh...get to know you?"

"I was with Admiral Grant when he called you," Liz said in an insistent voice. "It was around eight."

"Yes—" Diane felt Liz painting her into a corner. "Trust nobody," Grant had warned. "They will lie, deceive, and use any means possible to retrieve the Jayspid. Do not give it up unless and until I tell you." So they'd agreed on a code. Three numbers somewhere in his message.

He did not include them in his text last night.

Also, when Diane got Grant's message, her first reaction had been alarm. *Liz Lovell? That can't be right.* Like much of America, Diane had followed the whole scandal. To confirm, she'd called Grant back last night. He did not pick up. It went directly to voice mail. This morning, Liz returned the call on his cell phone. Diane's first instinct had been to leave as soon she hung up after giving Liz this address. But Liz's voice had evoked trust and security. Now, meeting her face to face, Diane wondered if she should have gone with her first instinct. There was something sly and calculating about Liz. *Is that why Admiral Grant did not insert the code in his text?* Did he not trust her either?

Two leads had become two victims in Liz's wake.

"He gave me his phone," pressed Liz. "He pointed me here to DC."

"And now he's dead too." The words came out laced in suspicion and accusation. The conspiracy freak she was, Diane couldn't help suspecting if Liz, under the guise of exposing Thunder Strike, was playing bait to draw them out one by one for the assassin to kill?

Liz owed the White House.

What a return favor burying Thunder Strike would be!

At the same time, with Grant dead, there was no more help coming. One option after another had been systematically eliminated. Liz could be it. The last hope to survive this ordeal. So, Diane could not afford to make an error in judgment. She'd stayed glued to the window to make sure Liz came alone, leaving the back door open for a quick getaway if she saw or sensed danger.

"You don't trust me?" Liz sounded hurt.

Her tone touched Diane. She felt bad. Guilty. *Am I judging Liz based on the past?* Liz had flown all night and risked her life to get here. Liz was a reporter—being persistent came with the job. Maybe her motives were genuine. Exposing Thunder Strike could turn Liz's career around. It was that big, that explosive.

"Like I told you this morning, he was being watched," said Liz. "Look. We only have a small window."

Liz's demeanor in this brief encounter had encompassed a gamut: comfort, edge, sympathy, pressure, hurt, aggression. What was an act, what was not? Diane couldn't tell. At that moment, the sound of rotors seeped into audible range.

————

The Jet Ranger carrying Andrew stayed low, keeping pace with the mud speckled squad car that ignored the winding roads, cutting across the devastated terrain instead, bouncing and crashing over and through debris. Andrew figured Douglas and Hess, the two officers inside, were accustomed to driving this way. Meg had destroyed all distinction between what was paved and what was not. The squad car slewed onto a stretch of cracked blacktop. Andrew stared ahead. The ground rose steadily in front. The ridge ran too high to see over it. The siren joined helicopter engine for a loud, threatening symphony.

————

Liz and Diane turned together. Liz grabbed the possibility. "We've got to get out of here!"

"Do you think they are coming for us?"

Even if the helicopter and siren posed no danger, Liz used them ratchet up the urgency. "Do you want to take a chance they are not?"

Diane reflexively looked over toward the approaching sound.

"Make up your mind," Liz pressed. As a journalist, she constantly searched for weaknesses to exploit and buttons to push. She had sized up Diane as timid and non-confrontational. Typical of people with careers that required little or no social interaction. They lacked manipulative skills but were vulnerable to them. Sensing that Diane felt trapped, Liz brought the pressure. "Are you in or out?"

Diane swiveled her eyes back and forth again.

Liz stepped closer. "Do you have the Jayspid?"

"Not here," blurted Diane.

Liz hid her disappointment. "Where, then?"

"Across town." Liz couldn't tell if Diane was lying to buy time.

Liz nodded. "Okay. Fine. Let's go."

Diane grabbed a backpack from behind the couch. Liz noticed it was stuffed with something bulky and square. Like a binder. *The Jayspid?* The two women emerged outside. The siren and rotors blasted so loudly, they seemed right on top. Liz reacted apprehensively. Saw nothing. She noticed Diane shared her anxiety.

"They must be just over the hill," said Liz and broke into a run. Diane sprinted after her.

They climbed into the Mercedes. Snapped on their seat belts. Liz observed Diane cradle the backpack tightly into her lap. Liz slammed the gear into Drive and gunned the Kompressor forward. As she did, her eyes drew to the rear view mirror. "Shit!"

Diane whipped her head around. Rotors of the Jet Ranger rose above the ridgeline. But the cockpit was yet to clear it. The flashing light band of a squad car appeared, moments away from coming over the top.

"Does this road let out?" asked Liz, stepping on the gas.

"Yes. Make a right at the tree."

An uprooted oak blocked half the road. Liz reached it and braked hard, skidding the rear wheels on the muddy blacktop. Her tail lights glowed brightly.

———

The cockpit cleared ridge. So did Andrew's eyes for an unobstructed view of the descending road.

It was empty.

Below him, the squad car roared along the empty street. Neighbors stopped and stared. While the helicopter put down in the middle of the road, its thirty-three foot-wide propellers whipping up loose debris, Andrew ordered Douglas and Hess to go ahead and storm the house. Douglas appeared out of the car first, unholstering his piece. Andrew recognized it as an automatic. A Beretta. Hess straightened, breeching a shotgun. They raced up the drive.

Andrew straightened out of the helicopter as the two

uniforms knocked the door down and burst in, shouting together, "Police! Show yourself!"

Andrew walked into the house as the two cops re-entered the front room.

"Nobody here," said Douglas.

Andrew showed no reaction.

Eeeeee! Shrill! Prolonged!

The men reflexively lifted their guns. Andrew caught Douglas and Hess stare at his. Likely, they'd never seen anything like it. The wouldn't have. It was a prototype 'Offensive Pistol' issued by the US Joint Special Operations Command.

Andrew led the way into the kitchen. A kettle shrieked over coals in the kitchen. Douglas kicked it off the makeshift stove to kill the ear-piercing whistle. Scalding water sloshed free, struck the glowing red hot charcoal, and erupted into steam with a loud hiss. Andrew's eyes went still with realization.

"It's still hot. They must have just left," he said quietly. "Get outside and tell the chopper to sweep for a silver Mercedes." When Deputy Kruk had dropped Liz outside the house that she claimed was hers, he'd written down the license plate number of the silver Mercedes.

"Yes, sir." Douglas exited running.

The Jet Ranger lifted off as Andrew and Hess emerged outside. Douglas was already behind the wheel. Once again, Andrew rode shotgun, relegating Hess to the back seat.

"Which way?" asked Douglas.

"Back toward DC," said Andrew.

Sparse density and utter devastation left few places to hide in the suburbs south of here. Also, Diane and Liz belonged to that breed of young urbanites who loved living in the District. Like criminals, amateurs sought the security of a familiar environment.

————

Pilots Cale and Brent were relieved Andrew was not

flying with them. He emitted an unsettling vibe. They began a quick circle of the neighborhood. The Jet Ranger III came equipped with a state-of-the-art moving map display; as the terrain changed so did the map. Multiple underbelly 360-degree swivel cameras fed images that switched from normal to infrared with a flick of a switch. They didn't expect to find the Liz and Diane. So they weren't disappointed.

"Report back," Cale told Brent.

Andrew answered the radio. "They won't take the Anacostia Freeway. It's one lane, it's jammed, and they'd be sitting ducks. Concentrate your search on surface streets."

"Ten four."

Cale leaned into the wheel. The Jet Ranger banked over decapitated buildings of Martin Luther King Jr. Avenue. Meg had scattered everything inside them across a mile-wide radius. Brent joysticked the multiple cameras around, zooming in and out of the suspicious cars.

Nothing.

———

Brought up by her parents to be honest and good and fair, Diane had a hard time lying. She did not want to inadvertently reveal something that Liz could use to elicit more. So Diane politely thwarted Liz from striking up a conversation. Liz seemed to understand and left her alone. Once again, Diane second guessed herself. *Am I being bitch about Liz?*

They crossed back into DC. Without the Mercedes hood ornament jutting up and out in front, the sports car looked like just another mud splattered compact, indistinguishable from the rest of the cars on Capitol Street. They passed one leveled and flooded neighborhood after another.

A chopper advanced. Both women held their breath.

It chattered by without slowing down.

"We have to get across the river" said Liz.

"Eleventh Street bridge is the only way."

When they got there, traffic bunched up into a-mile-an-hour crawl.

———

Brent straightened sharply. "Hold it!"

The downslope of the 10th Street exit ramp tilted the trunk of a silver compact skyward. The sun caught the car maker's rear insignia. It flashed brightly. *Mercedes!* The license plate was caked and hard to read. Brent switched on the camera's heat-seeker. This was standard equipment in most urban police choppers. It outlined two thermal signatures. Internal algorithms, another standard feature born out of a quick way to verify and evaluate hostage situations, did a quick match of anatomical stats. The readout called with 100% certainty that the driver and passenger were female.

"Found 'em," grinned Brent and activated the TL—thermal lock—option. Each human heat signature was unique. Now, the two women could not shake their pursuit.

Cale banked left. Aimed the chopper for the Mercedes. He saw smoke spurt out of the exhaust. The Kompressor leapt. "They made us."

Cale crushed the throttle. The Jet Ranger surged. Gained on the car in a flash. Drew overhead within seconds.

"What are our orders?" asked Brent. "Do they want the bitches dead or alive."

"Didn't ask," smirked Cale, "don't care."

Brent shared his bloodthirsty rush. "Pancake them."

Cale dropped toward roof of the speeding car. The two pilots waited for the sweet scrawling sound of chopper's skis ripping through Mercedes. None came. Instead, empty road rushed up and the trunk of Kompressor receded away to their right.

"Goddamnit!" screamed Cale, snapping his head around.

The women had waited until the last second, then swerved hard onto Pennsylvania Avenue. The chopper flew straight on, descending fast. They were going eat asphalt.

"Pull up!" yelled Brent, the color draining from his face.

Cale threw his shoulders back. Yanked the stick and

turned the wheel. Both men yelled, horror and fear dilating their faces. One moment they were leaning forward, staring at a fiery death, the next they slammed back into the seat, looking at destroyed buildings and slices of haphazard sky juxtaposing wildly in crazy angles. The Jet Ranger had responded. Its nose lifted sharply and unevenly. The chopper slewed around hard and fast. By the time Cale steadied the Jet Ranger and turned it around, the women were racing past 8th Street.

"They are headed west on Pennsylvania," Brent panted into the radio.

———

Lights and the siren came on. Andrew grabbed the dash. Douglas bounced onto the shoulder of the 11th Street bridge and floored it. The squad car dangerously hugged the edge. Andrew stayed calm. Meg had ripped out the safety railing for extended stretches. It was a sheer drop to the river. The shoulder narrowed ahead. Without decelerating even a bit, Douglas did the only thing he could to create space.

He broadsided the traffic!

Loud slams of metal on metal rent the air. Drivers honked and screamed. He left a mess of cars turned completely around in his wake. Traffic gridlocked. The squad car came flying off the 10th street exit and veered onto Pennsylvania Ave so fast, they were on two driverside wheels for the entire turn. *Bam!* The other two tires returned violently back to earth. Rocking Andrew with a spine-jarring thud.

———

Ahead, Liz thundered into 7th Street. Fueled her pistons. She saw an open manhole. Too late to swerve. She hoped her speed would crash the wheels in and out of the gaping hole that oozed sewage. It did. The Mercedes dipped down and rose so hard, the women smacked their heads against the roof.

"Watch out!" screamed Diane.

Liz took one look ahead, punched the horn, and didn't let go. A few thousand mobbed the historic Eastern Market, now a FEMA distribution center. People along the edges reacted, pointing toward the Kompressor with shouts of alarm. Liz glanced into the rearview mirror. The Jet Ranger appeared, taking the corner so sharply, its propellers were almost vertical.

This set off a roar of panic and triggered a melee.

The crowd parted.

The Kompressor passed through. Liz did not ease up. Diane clutched the dash and closed her eyes. Even Liz thought there was no way somebody wasn't going to be fatally hit and run over. The car passed so close to people, Liz felt their breath. The Mercedes miraculously emerged on the other side without contact. The helicopter leveled off ten yards above the stampede. The sound was fearsome.

"Liz!" Diane yelled.

An armored car stood parked across the intersection. Liz didn't hesitate. Cranked the steering left. Floored the brake simultaneously. The rear wheels locked. The tires stopped spinning. A shrill peal! An acrid smell! Rubber tattooed the road! The Mercedes skidded onto 'A' Street. Even before the grill aligned forward, Liz throttled down.

She'd surprised the chopper again. It flew straight.

Liz caught her breath loudly. 'A' Street teed off at the Library of Congress, which looked like historic ruins. Chipped and pockmarked like it had been through a war. Two collapsed pillars blocked the cross street. Yellow tape cordoned them off along with other fallen architectural details to preserve pieces of landmarks until construction crews could restore them.

With no place to go, Liz U-turned, and spat, "Shit!"

Flashing lights appeared at the far end. The squad car. It used the divide in the crowd that Liz had created outside Eastern Market to make an easy left.

"Out, out," said Liz, throwing open the door.

The women abandoned the Mercedes. Diane pointed, "This way!"

Liz lost the squad car approaching at breakneck speed

when she sprinted around the corner a step behind Diane. Liz tripped in shock when she glanced over at the Supreme Court building. More fallen columns. The entablature missed chunks of the familiar relief work. More yellow tape around the fallen remnants.

The women reacted to the sound of brakes. Looked back. Two uniforms unloaded from the squad car. One carried a handgun, the other a shotgun. Then they saw the gimpy assassin. The sight of him catalyzed both Diane and Liz. They cut across the ripped turf and walkway between the Library and the Court. As they cleared the buildings, Liz stumbled in astonishment again.

Meg had beheaded the most enduring symbol of democracy, the US Capitol. Only an uneven circle of jagged blocks remained of its signature dome. Barely a course high in some places. Pillars angled awkwardly. Deep, long cracks riddled the exterior all around. Not a single pane of glass had survived. Restoration and reconstruction of the Capitol enjoyed the same high priority as the White House. Scaffolding was up all around. Crews had already commenced repair work.

Diane grabbed Liz. Steadied her.

"It was a helluva hurricane," gasped Liz.

"You had to be here," replied Diane.

Then it struck Liz—the strength of this country, functioning without missing a beat even though Meg had ripped out the very heart of government. She followed Diane around the corner. Staying one turn ahead of their pursuit, they burst into the National Mall, that great American backyard known for its spectacular carpet of immaculately manicured green lawn flanked by groves.

"Shit," breathed Liz, running out of expletives.

It was now an overcrowded tent city.

Diane led Liz past the reflecting pool. Once sparkling, the water had turned brown and filthy from refuse, bathing, and laundry. The women ran down the steps into the crowd.

Meg had taken a giant bat to every surface of the Air and Space Museum, Art Gallery, Natural History Museum, and Smithsonian. Liz and Diane weaved between the dense mass of people.

The helicopter thundered in over the Capitol.

They looked up and saw the copilot lean out. Point down at them.

———

Douglas had his Beretta out. The shotgun hung from Hess's pumping hand. Andrew was nowhere in sight. The chopper pilots chattered into their earpieces. Locked into the women's heat signatures, Brent relayed their position down. The two cops ran roughshod over the refugees.

"Stop those two women!" yelled Douglas.

They kept running. Refugees looked at the cops. None reacted. The women disappeared under flapping tarp. The pursuit zigzagged between tents, trailers, open kitchens, endless lines of laundry, and temporary toilets that reeked from lack of refuse management. The women hit an open stretch. The Marine Corp had run out of temporary housing past 12th Street. Here, people camped out in sleeping bags, cardboard boxes, newspapers, or nothing at all. The stench of sweat, piss, shit, and people assaulted the senses with almost physical force.

The cops saw the blonde gag and trip. The other grabbed her arm, helping her regain her balance without sprawling. It allowed the two cops to catch up.

"Stop running!" shouted Douglas.

Liz and Diane plowed on, leaping over people, avoiding kids. The refugees looked on passively, still dazed.

"Oh, screw this," said Hess, aimed his shotgun up, and fired a volley into the air. That elicited an instant reaction. Anyone standing quickly hit the ground. Simultaneously, the women skipped over rubble and passed behind the Washington Monument.

The cops cursed. Resumed the furious foot chase.

———

Diane knew she could not keep up this pace. Her breath came in short, sharp, wheezing gasps. A week of half-meals to stretch the rationed food affected her stamina. Several times already during the foot chase her knees had buckled. She felt faint, but every time she came to the verge of blacking out, she thought about Sam, Vick, and Philippe. Vendetta pumped adrenaline, renewing her will to keep going.

Diane noticed Liz's eyes snap in surprise yet again. They'd ducked around the renowned obelisk, now on the ground, toppled over and broken. The women skirted past the remains of the World War II Memorial and plunged through a visible column of mosquitoes—the standing water and filth of the reflecting pools had brought the blood suckers out in indestructible swarms. They disappeared behind a cluster of Red Cross medical tents and out onto the streets again.

Electric poles, fallen trees, wrecked cars, and building debris littered these streets, which, on a routine working day, buzzed with politicians, lobbyists, bureaucrats, and awestruck tourists. Here and there, live power lines sparked dangerously.

The helicopter appeared over the decimated buildings of the Federal Reserve and State Department. Diane led Liz into a jungle of collapsed and charred masonry and beams that used to be The Gourd, one of DC's trendiest eateries. The gas line had ignited, burned, and gutted the structure. The women disturbed a flock of birds. Squawking irritably, they flapped noisily onto the ravaged ledges higher up, waiting to fly back down and continue to peck on a badly decomposed body– human or animal, it was hard to tell. Two dogs, also feeding on it, backed away with bared teeth and territorial snarls. Their jaws dripped with coagulating flesh.

"Oh, God." Liz covered her nose, disgusted.

They heard footsteps. Pounding in and stopping short. Silence fell and stretched. The women crouched. Liz pointed.

Diane saw the cops. *Where's the assassin?* The two uniforms exchanged a hand signal. They were going tactical. Diane lost them when they separated and flanked out to the either edge. She looked over to Liz, who shook her head. She lost them too. They couldn't hear even a footfall. The uniforms were consciously avoiding loose debris that could crunch and give them away.

Whupwhupwhupwhup! The walls and the ground throbbed. Reverberation loosened dirt down the walls. Birds fled. The quiet hide and seek shattered!

Cale brought the helicopter in low over the ruins. The chopper hovered and moved. Hovered and moved. Hovered and moved. The swirling dust and the Jet Ranger's heat emissions in the confined space corrupted the thermal images. Brent discerned two outlines. Close to each other. He knew Douglas and Hess had singled off. The silhouettes had to be the two women.

Brent tapped the slight conical bulge on the signatures and smirked, "Tits."

Cale was too eager. Lowered the chopper too far. The rotors churned up dust. The thermal screen went berserk. Blinding the pilots.

"Sorry," muttered Cale and picked up altitude quickly.

Brent lost the women, but snapped, "Wait. Look."

Brent drew Cale's eyes ahead. They pilot grinned and radioed to Douglas and Hess, "It's a dead end."

The women used the precious seconds of zero visibility to splash across a puddle. They were in the back of the restaurant. Past what remained of the rear kitchen wall was a back alley. The structure next door had collapsed, blocking off street access.

"Shit," muttered Liz, recognizing there was no way out. The dust thinned. They couldn't move, not without being seen.

They stood under a dangerously poised roof.

Trapped.

"Hold up," Liz said, hearing uneven static.

A live power line on the ground sparked weakly. She had an idea. Picked up an ornately turned piece of wood that was once a table leg in the restaurant. Meg had shredded the expensive furniture. Liz used it to maneuver the live wire into the puddle. Electrifying it.

Diane smiled and Liz knew she'd cut into the meteorologist's distrust. It was going to take more baby steps like this one. Staying under the damaged roof, they backed off behind a pile of twisted stainless steel that used to be The Gourd's kitchen.

The two uniforms appeared.

———

"Jersey eight-oh," Douglas radioed, "where are they?"

"Straight ahead," Brent replied. "Behind some kind of mangled steel." Data presets in the TSD—thermal signature dictionary—identified over a thousand material signatures.

"You got the only way out covered," added Cale exultantly.

Douglas and Hess advanced closer to the electrified puddle. And stopped.

Six inches from the water.

———

Diane clenched her fist. Exchanged a frustrated glance with Liz. *Crunch.* A stealthy footfall. The women froze.

"'Morning, ladies." Soft. Quiet. Full of threat.

Diane's heart pounded. Terror paralyzed her. The sound of a shoe settling on loose debris came from right behind them. Liz and she turned slowly.

Andrew melted out of a shadowed niche.

———

In the chopper, Cale and Brent saw the two women appear through a hole in the roof. They couldn't see Andrew, who stood under a concrete awning, which also prevented

Brent from getting a thermal read of him.

"We take 'em out," Brent said over the radio.

Diane found herself unable to move when Andrew turned his eyes and attention entirely toward her. He said in a dreadfully calm voice, "End of road."

He took half step forward. His eyes flickered ever so slightly off her. He nodded to Douglas and Hess. "Hold your fire."

Douglas repeated the order, "Hold your fire."

Diane assumed it was to the lurking chopper. Andrew nodded to the backpack. He recognized it from his pursuit through the storm. "Is the Jayspid in there?"

"No," said Diane. "Just food and water."

"Open it."

Diane slipped off the backpack, zipped it open, and peeled back the flap which had a bullet hole in it. She noticed Andrew's lips twitch in recognition. He'd put it there. The straight edges were imparted by a couple of MRE—Meals Ready-to-Eat—packets and two square bottles of water.

Diane caught Liz's eyes meet Andrew's ever so briefly.

Did they just share a look of disappointment?

Almost as soon as the thought crossed Diane's mind, Andrew surprised her. He swung the gun smoothly and deliberately toward Liz! "Start talking or your friend dies."

The barrel came to rest between Liz's light eyes, which widened in surprise.

Is that a genuine reaction? Diane replied, "She's not my friend."

Liz reacted sharply.

"So you don't care if she lives or dies?" asked Andrew

Diane answered, "Not really."

"Okay." Andrew tightened his finger around the trigger.

Diane looked at Douglas and Hess. The cops relaxed and took step forward. Diane second guessed herself when she saw

Liz's throat roll. *Oh God, what am I doing?* Just as she was about to stop Andrew, the two cops stepped into the puddle together.

A rage of current engulfed them! Twin screams tore out of their throats! They convulsed wildly. Douglas involuntarily pulled the trigger of his Beretta.

Bullets sprayed every which way!

————

In the helicopter, Brent saw bloody holes pop all over Hess for what seemed like an eternity. Hess lost his shotgun and crumpled to the ground. *Crack!* One bullet strayed through the glass of the helicopter. The bubble glass spider-webbed. Brent heard a grunt. *Shit, that came from inside the cockpit.* He snapped his eyes toward Cale, who did not even know he was hit. It angled into his neck, severing his neck at the spine. Killing him instantly.

Slumping, Cale's hands slipped off the controls.

The helicopter plummeted.

Brent recovered. Tried to wrest control with a guttural cry. He desperately yanked the column all the way and hung on, urging the helicopter to respond, "Come on, come on!"

The Jet Ranger wobbled wildly. Everything slowed to a crawl as Brent helplessly observed the sixteen-foot long overhead propellers meet the ground. The velocity of their rotation crumpled the cockpit. The force ripped out his seat. Ejected him through a chaos of shooting glass and engine parts!

————

Dust kicked up sharply. Turned into a twister. Blinded, Andrew retreated. The chopper's rear rotors swung straight for him, forcing him to dive behind the stump of a counter.

Boooom! Jet fuel ignited.

A spectacular fireball consumed Hess, who was already dead. Douglas still twitched with the last throes of life in the puddle. Andrew heard him scream. Waves of flame rolled past with diminishing intensity until the violence finally dissipated.

The stillness crackled with settling wreckage and fire.

Andrew stood up. Dusted off. He skirted the smoldering crash and counted the bodies. He found only three. All male.

The women had not only escaped, they'd vanished.

Andrew's eyes iced up into narrow, angry slats. He'd been furious with himself when he didn't eliminate all the targets during Meg's assault. The frustration mounted when he hadn't been able to finish off the assignment in the aftermath. Liz's arrival only festered the venom building inside him. Their escape brought his hate to critical mass. He needed to vent. Kill somebody. Anybody.

"Hey," a voice pleaded weakly.

Andrew turned and saw Brent. Astonishingly, the young copilot was alive and largely injury free. He just needed help with a section of copter that pinned his feet. The patches of third-degree burns looked non-fatal. Andrew could save him. Instead, he raised his gun. With an unforgiving rage, he emptied his gun into Brent's chest, pumping him with bullets long after he was dead and even the brain had stopped sending post-mortem jerks.

Andrew still felt unsatisfied.

————

Defense Secretary Baron Hawke had come straight to the Situation Room in Sublevel B underneath the White House when he got there this morning after seeing son, Warren, off to Submarine School. While Meg had wrecked the rest of the White House, including the elevator shaft, stairs, and corridors leading down, she had been unable to lay a scratch on the Situation Room. The reinforced concrete kept out even the smell of moisture that pervaded the rest of the mansion. The president, his secret service detail, closest aides, and their families had sat out the storm in here.

Baron occupied the president's chair at the head of the horse-shoe. Jack fidgeted in the VP's seat, a far cry from the decorated, confident general, who had laid out the bold option to take out Juan Castro in this very room. He pursed his lips pensively. Peter Wilkins, on the large flat screen labeled 'CIA,' had just completed a briefing.

"This changes everything, doesn't it?" said General Jack Knight, the Joint Chiefs Chairman. "I told you involving Liz'd backfire."

"We don't know that," said Peter.

"You lost them."

"Diane is not going to trust Liz right away."

Jack poured angry sarcasm into his tone. "And you base this observation on..."

"The psychology of amateurs, General."

Jack's sarcasm only increased. "As opposed to you professionals who did not even bother to check what seemed like an obvious address after the storm?"

Baron peripherally listened to their exchange. Peter said, "My mistake."

"Another critical one." Jack was being Jack and wasn't going to let Peter off that easy. "First, you bring in an operative, who by your own admission, has been in the field a few missions too many." He lifted up and dropped a dossier. "I've been reading his profile. He's psycho."

"He's an assassin, General," said Peter acidly. "Well adjusted candidates don't usually apply."

Jack snapped, "Don't get smart with me, Peter. Is the Agency is so depleted of qualified candidates, we couldn't do better than a cripple?"

"Don't be fooled by the bad leg. He compensates with a perfect eye."

Jack snorted in disbelief. "Jesus. You're in as much denial about him as he is about himself. Can we replace him?"

"Not without losing ground," replied Peter bluntly.

"Are we monitoring Liz?" asked Baron, speaking finally as he came to the end of his own train of thought. He rarely, if ever, took the war of words between Jack and Peter seriously. For as long as he'd known them, and they'd known each other for over thirty years, they'd never got along. Early on, as neo-conservatives who began to develop a powerful shadow network in the Pentagon, CIA, and the Department of Defense, Baron had tried to find some sort of common ground where Jack and Peter could operate without sniping. He soon realized some personalities just clashed.

"She's got only one out," said Peter.

"Tim O'Flaherty at the *Post*?"

Peter nodded. Jack still worried, "These two women are using those prepaid cell phones that you cannot trace."

"Not O'Flaherty."

"I have wiretaps in his office and home. I also assigned his surveillance to the cleanup crew who neutralized the threat posed by Billy Madden and Admiral Grant. They can move in on Tim within thirty seconds."

Jack shook his head angrily, still unsatisfied. "This mess is about to become quicksand. Do you know the history of Thunder Strike? Thirty years it took to get it operational. And now a weather girl and a second rate reporter—-"

"I wouldn't call Liz a second rate reporter," said Peter. "Take away her one mistake, she's damn good."

"How is that supposed to be reassuring?"

The cell phone on the table in front of Baron purred. It looked like another consumer flip-out, but was actually specialized piece of military equipment configured for secure conversations and issued to everyone in the EXCOMM since the start of the Cuban crisis. Baron checked the caller ID on the display and answered.

"Agent Connor," said Baron.

The man in charge of president's protective whispered, "The president's headed to the Oval Office, sir."

———

Avery entered the main corridor of the West Wing. He

passed the gaping hole that used to be the northwest entry into the Oval Office. Meg had taken out the door and deposited it clear across the room. He waved distantly to the Chief of Staff and about a dozen men and women still engaged in the tedious process of resettling.

Avery sat down and swiveled his chair around to face the three south-facing, double-paned, bullet proof windows. Construction crews had prioritized sealing the outer walls of the West Wing. They had dragged in a makeshift desk into the Oval Office along with a leather chair, sofa settee, and four straight backs. The floor and the walls remained untouched, badly bruised and scarred from Meg's beating. Outlines of discoloration remained where paintings that had been fixtures for decades had been removed before Meg's arrival.

Avery's eyes were bloodshot. He'd cut himself shaving this morning and missed a couple of spots under his jaw. He looked unkempt. Hardly presidential. Last night had been the worst so far. He'd barely slept. Avery stared out and remembered his inauguration two years ago. What a bittersweet day that had been. He'd come all the way from the bottom of a crowded Republican field to capture the nomination. An unlikely presidential candidate, considering he never completed his first term as Governor of Indiana.

The son of staunch conservatives, both professors of theology at Notre Dame, he'd fallen in love with politics after an internship for the re-election of his Congressman, a family friend, to the House of Representatives. Stumping from door to door and meeting voters, he discovered a new generation of young Republicans who shared his concern that the party was drifting toward religious fundamentalism. A record number of young voters carried him from the Indianapolis School Board to the governor's mansion. Two years later, he announced that he was running for president.

Raised in the era of a carnivorous media, but having had the advantage of deciding as a teen that he wanted a career in public service, Avery had consciously kept a clean image. Thought he before spoke. Shunned controversy. Kept his personal life clean and discreet. Girls he dated were classy, the kind who would never kiss and tell. Monitored his social media. He did not even smoke or drink. Still, a tabloid journalist called Liz Lovell, who had made her reputation burying Senator Jarvis Johnson, a fellow Republican with even more impressive credentials, found dirt on Avery that triggered a media feeding frenzy.

It threw Republican Party into chaos. Liz had already destroyed their #1 choice, Jarvis Johnson, who had quit without even announcing his candidacy. Now she was going to ruin Avery, a distant second choice. He had squeaked out a nomination on the backs of moderates and centrists. Conservatives threatened to stay away from the polls, mocking him as "not even the best of the worst." When he got no bump after the Convention, the media called this election for the Democrats a full two months before the polls closed. The attractive and charismatic Homeland Security Secretary led by double digits. Preparations for the 'coronation' were on.

Avery's denials were met with public skepticism. It looked utterly hopeless. Most Republicans distanced themselves, some called for him to quit and convene an unprecedented extraordinary GOP session to nominate a new candidate. Avery retreated to the governor's mansion in Indianapolis.

It was his darkest hour.

Baron Hawke came to visit him.

Unannounced. Uninvited.

Avery knew Baron from Republican retreats as a one-time Undersecretary in the Department of Defense who'd served on the Iraq Committee, the secret think tank that ran the ill-fated war.

"I believe you," Baron said simply, then came through in a big way, helping Avery close a double-digit deficit over the course of a the next six weeks, which went down as one of the most eventful and memorable in the history of US presidential elections.

Baron buried Liz, and with her, the Democratic candidate. Opponents called it a sympathy vote. Regardless, the election left the nation deeply divided just like it had after George W. Bush took the White House without winning the popular vote. Avery barely squeaked by in the states he carried. In those he did not, the margin wasn't even close.

His motorcade that twentieth day in January two years ago had been appropriately shrouded in a thick fog. He was evenly cheered and booed. Two years later, he remained unpopular. Then the Cuba crisis happened. As always, Americans rallied behind their president. Last week, his approval climbed to sixty points—unthinkable a year ago. Americans recognized he was in a difficult position. Trying to disarm a dictator without going to war.

Hours after those numbers came out, Meg made landfall.

Avery stared out dejectedly, watching the night shift hand off to the day crew. Armed military men and women exchanged places around the White House, in tanks, and armored cars. Overhead, a fresh fleet of heavily armed Blackhawks took over. New sharpshooters on the roof appeared. Avery saw them only as shadows on the Rose Garden—now a mess of uprooted turf, bald flower beds, fallen trees, and debris carried in off the street. Marine One personnel changed. The First helicopter stood at the ready on the South Lawn, parked there from the moment it could land after the storm had passed in case Avery needed to be evacuated hastily. Meg had left a behind security nightmare, made worse by Avery's insistence on staying in the White House.

A million dead. *A million!*

Avery simply could not shake free of the storm toll.

"God, please forgive me," he said, an incantation he repeated at least a dozen times every day. Instead of alleviating, his guilt only deepened. Depression replaced the sadness and unrelenting despair. He could not eat, sleep, or work.

Avery was touched that Baron was concerned enough to consult a psychologist, who said this kind of mental turmoil afflicted people of high morals and good conscience. Avery was entrenched in chronic grief—a morbid disaster bereavement syndrome. So, Baron consoled, it was not entirely unnatural that the president indulged in apologies, calls for forgiveness, and conversations with the dead. Avery awoke this morning with a realization he could not shake—*be that as it may, it's no excuse.*

This was the most powerful office on earth. He was neither upholding his oath of office nor carrying out the duties of the president of the United States of America.

He had a decision to make.

LAST WEEK

TEN

During the hours that the unforeseen low pressure trough in her lower left quadrant detained her, she fed greedily upon the limitless moisture and unseasonable warmth of the Atlantic. Her sustained gusts passed a hundred knots. Around the eyewall, where she concealed her fiercest gusts, the wind sporadically raged to two hundred miles an hour. Pressure on her fringes dropped rapidly toward her eye in one of the steepest gradients ever recorded in so young a hurricane. Torrential rain fell from her decks of cumulus and cumulonimbus clouds. Her high altitude winds swept the condensing water vapor in her upper atmosphere as wisps of icy cirrus clouds. Turbulence whipped her cloudy terrain with almost continuous flashes of lightning. The ocean under and around her heaved in turmoil. Violently breaking waves climbed up to almost forty feet. The surface water foamed, almost eighty percent white.

She measured an awesome 17 on the Beaufort scale. Her disaster potential, if she made landfall at this point, was Category 3 on the Saffir/Simpson Scale. She could blow away mobile homes, destroy vegetation, break moorings, carry small craft inland, and trigger flooding hours before she even arrived.

But she was like a car spinning its wheels in a quagmire, seeking traction to climb out of this low pressure trough and move. The giant push came from the Southerlies blowing in from the hemisphere beneath equator. In her upper troposphere, where she was evacuating tremendous masses to retain the integrity of her heat engine, these masses concentrated into powerful outflow jets. She propelled herself into motion once again. She drove out of the low pressure trough. The Southerlies became her steering currents, carrying her within their flow.

She headed northeast toward the United States.

"Can I tell him?" asked Gerardo with childish glee.

The temperamental head of the Hurricane Research Department at the NHC was in Hank's office along with Clyde and Ray. Hank looked at Ray. As the chief of the Forecast Unit, it was Ray's job to issue official track and intensity predictions.

"Be my guest," smiled Ray.

Hank called Peter Wilkins on the intercom. Peter arrived a few moments later. Nobody had gone home. Barely did Peter step inside, when Gerardo, unable to contain himself, blurted, "Cuba is no longer a target."

Peter showed no emotion. He nodded, "Okay. Does that mean you are going to declassify Meg?"

Hank answered. "If the forecast models hold, yes. We will advise Weather Forecast Offices along target areas in the northeast in our six A.M. bulletin."

Peter looked at his watch. It was one A.M. "Thanks for the heads-up."

"That was anti-climactic," said Gerardo, disappointed, after Peter left.

"I think I'm going to crash on the couch here," said Hank, yawning.

"Go home," said Gerardo. "We can handle it."

Ray nodded. "Yeah. Sure."

"Nah," said Hank. It would not be fair to put his department heads on the frontline facing off the defense secretary. Hank also worried about Gerardo's temper in case things got heated. Clyde nodded, sharing his sentiment. "I should be here when we officially take the wraps off Meg."

———

Damn fools have no clue I'm monitoring their every word and move. Peter smirked as he walked back to his office. He closed the door and called Baron. As unearthly as the hour was, he knew he would not be disturbing the defense secretary. During crises, Baron had revealed after a couple of drinks during a rare unguarded moment several years ago, he slept on the couch in the library of his Virginia mansion. He said did not want to disturb his wife, though she'd told him often that she didn't mind the phone ringing in their bedroom. But there were matters of state she could not hear. They'd been married twenty-eight years and she'd learned never to press or pry.

Peter heard a momentary thickness in Baron's voice, but the defense secretary came awake quickly. When Peter finished speaking, Baron simply said, "Get Robert."

———

Dr. Robert Mclaurin looked like a throwback to the Third Reich. Fair skinned and clean shaven, his close-cropped, thinning blond hair was slicked tightly over his skull. He wore rimless bifocals. Behind them, his eyes gleamed. Penetrating and hypnotic. Oozing intellect and intensity. Whatever the hour, Baron had never known this high strung scientist to look tired or unkempt.

The same could not be said of the EXCOMM gathered around the horseshoe for this two A.M. emergency session that Baron had summoned. The three high ranking women in President Avery Walker's cabinet came sans makeup. The men were unshaven and heavy-lidded, including Avery. The president, however, did not exempt them from showing up in a formal suit. He believed that the White House demanded a dress code appropriate to its lofty stature as the symbol of freedom. He removed his tie only in the privacy of his upper floor residence.

Baron sat in the VP's seat next to Avery. The vice president participated from Air Force Two. He was on his way to Europe for a trade summit. Jack beamed in from the Tank. He was alone, his entourage of aides and officers excluded, as always, from all EXCOMM discussions. For a man who probably had the least sleep, the Joint Chiefs Chairman looked almost well rested. Baron was aware Jack had been fine tuning the Special Ops missions in the aftermath, which included taking out Juan Castro and the Politburo should Meg fail to claim them. The change in storm track jeopardized what, just an hour ago, promised to be the crowning jewel of his illustrious military career.

"Go ahead, Doctor," Baron gestured.

Dr. Mclaurin clearly needed no introduction. He exuded a compelling aura, commanding the room even as a remote feed on the flatscreen labeled, 'USS WJC.' Admiral Grant sat in the chair behind Dr. Mclaurin.

"The low pressure trough," Dr. Mclaurin said unapologetically, "well, was an act of God." His clipped tone caused him to sound impatient, as if he was irritated that he had to pull himself away from important work and educate a roomful of idiots. Over these past few days, the EXCOMM had come to accept his abrupt manner as normal demeanor.

"We just heard Meg is no longer moving toward Cuba but north toward us," said Avery.

"Yes," replied Dr. Mclaurin. "She got entangled in a northbound system called the Southerlies."

"The NHC is saying our northeast is threatened."

"Poppycock!" dismissed Dr. Mclaurin, his face scrunching in utter disdain. "Watch."

Heads lowered in unison to individual flatscreens built into the tabletop in front of each chair of the horse-shoe. An atlas of the Atlantic and the North America appeared. Meg showed up as a white spiral symbol and the Southerlies as a red arrow.

"The Southerlies should take Meg to about eight hundred miles east of the Delmarva Peninsula," explained Dr. Mclaurin, using a telestrator to move Meg upward, "where she will encounter a high pressure ridge." He drew a yellow, convex crescent blocking Meg's track. "The high pressure ridge will act like a roadblock. It will stall her again." He extended a blue arrow down from Greenland. "The timing will be such that she will be picked up by this south-moving annual flow from Greenland, which will take her right back down to Cuba as an even more devastating storm than originally projected."

"How is it Dr. Rotas is not seeing this scenario?"

"He doesn't know about the high pressure ridge."

"Why not?" asked Avery.

"It hasn't formed yet. So his little models haven't adjusted," said Dr. Mclaurin twisting in a little scorn. Baron smiled to ensure nobody missed it. "Once they do, they will project the track I outlined."

"When do you anticipate this turnaround?"

"Tomorrow afternoon."

"That won't work," said Peter.

"Actually it works out even better than the original scenario," snapped Dr. Mclaurin. "Meg will come down on Cuba just past midnight. Catch the bastards sleeping. Literally." Dr. Mclaurin allowed himself a crooked smile that made him look more intimidating than amused. "It'll be a miracle if the commies even find their senses after Meg's done with them."

Laughter rippled around the horseshoe. Jack loved it. "From a military standpoint, a night time landfall is ideal."

"No," clarified Peter, "it won't work because Dr. Rotas plans to declassify Meg in his six A.M. bulletin." Everyone looked at their watches reflexively. The deadline was less than four hours away.

The Secretary of State, seated in the middle of the horseshoe, asked, "Can we let Meg go and wait for the next hurricane?"

Baron glared at the Secretary of State for even suggesting it, then looked at Dr. Mclaurin. Admiral Grant, sitting in the chair behind the scientist, blinked. Baron realized that Grant noticed the subtle eye signal. Baron didn't care. It didn't matter. The power in dark shadows belonged to the Hawkes. How appropriate that this episode the "storming freedom" would be defined by a storm ushering freedom. All Grant could, and would, do is report the minutes of this session to the Ulysses.

Baron suspected John Ulysses VI was behind the gradual surge in support for Elian Santos, the seventy-year old Minister of the Interior in the Politburo, who opposed further escalating the nuclear confrontation with the United States. A peaceful solution would wrest Baron's control of this Presidency. So it was imperative that Thunder Strike proceed to its devastating conclusion as quickly as possible.

"We are at the tail end of the hurricane season," said Dr. Mclaurin. "Westward moving currents are weakening dramatically. They may not be strong enough and warm enough to sustain and carry a storm across the Atlantic. Frankly, I don't see another opportunity until the hurricane season next year. But why are we giving up on Meg? She is still viable."

Baron next flashed his eyes at Jack, then arrogantly back at Grant. The Joint Chiefs Chairman jumped in, "Multiple teams are already at sea, ready to deploy. All the pieces are in place, Mr. President."

"We may never have a shot like this again," added Baron and looked down the horseshoe. Heads up and down the horseshoe nodded.

Grant remained stoic. Baron twitched his lips triumphantly. They were ganging up on Avery and the admiral could do nothing about it.

Avery looked at the NHC screen. "Peter, can Dr. Rotas be convinced to change his mind?"

"He'll want to know why, sir," said Peter.

"Mmm." The president knew Hank would never reach the level of security clearance necessary to be included in Thunder Strike discussions.

"There is an alternative," said Dr. Mclaurin. Grant sharpened. To oppose it.

"Jack and Baron have briefed me," said Avery first, without revealing how he felt.

Dr. Mclaurin added, "The track I have projected is climatologically unprecedented. Some of the NHC models, which rely on historical data, will be unable to cope."

"So?"

"Rotas cannot think outside the box. Last year, he became so alarmed by two storms, Orlene and Paine, that did not traverse traditional tracks, he overwarned the eastern seaboard."

Avery remembered. Evacuation routes became jammed. The storms did not make landfall. "So, he might not be so quick this time to raise a warning."

"Knowing him and his obsession to play it safe, it could firm his intent to declassify Meg," said Dr. Mclaurin.

"Can't say I blame Dr. Rotas," said Grant, speaking for the first time. "He doesn't want to be left holding the bag."

"What bag?" snapped Dr. Mclaurin, turning around. "Even if Meg makes landfall, his own models show she'll be a Category 1 or less." He returned his eyes to the EXCOMM. "That's about as intense as a severe thunderstorm. It doesn't even warrant evacuation, for Chrissakes." He wanted to go off on Hank, but held his tongue and added after a noticeable beat, "Mr. President."

The respect on second thought brought an uncomfortable silence to the horseshoe. Baron tensed. Avery let it go. Baron relaxed. Among brilliant men in the world, Dr. Mclaurin probably ranked in the top five. The president obviously recognized that kind of intelligence stood above and beyond common reproach and reprimand.

The CIA director's cell phone rang. Avery used the distraction. "Thank you, doctor. I don't want to detain you any more."

"Good morning, then," nodded Dr. Mclaurin curtly, stood up, and turned on his heel. On his way out, he delivered a withering glare toward Grant. It wasn't lost on the EXCOMM, who had long ago concluded there was no love lost between the two. They'd been witness to Dr. Mclaurin lambasting Grant as an adversary just waiting to shut down Thunder Strike.

After the door closed behind him, Avery asked Grant, "Do you believe Dr. Mclaurin?"

Baron concealed the shadow of concern on his face by averting his head down and shuffling his papers. As close a working relationship as he had with the president, he knew Avery and Grant shared something deeper. Their friendship went back to their college days at Notre Dame, where they'd met as freshmen. In their second semester, they became roommates. Both had a deep passion for history and religion. Grant came from a lineage of seamen, all eventual commanders of their own boats. Their parents met and clicked as friends too.

In this administration, Grant was Avery's conscience. He shared John Ulysses's mindset and Baron regarded Grant as a credible threat to the Hawkes' grip on the dark shadows. So, he had asked Peter to place an Intelligence Officer aboard the *William J. Clinton* to watch the admiral.

"I don't doubt him," Grant answered carefully.

Baron did not intrude with a comment. While receiving high marks for his firm yet restrained handling, Avery had also raised expectations. What Grant did not know was that it was no accident that the only successful and satisfactory resolution was the complete nuclear disarmament of Cuba. Baron had carefully planned and skillfully executed this escalation and expectation. Thunder Strike would crush the enemy without overt military action. Open the way for massive humanitarian relief. Win hearts and minds. Grab world sympathy along the way. All Ulysses strengths...that now the Hawkes could usurp. Avery was no fool. Thunder Strike could define his legacy in his first term if he killed communism in Cuba.

The CIA director got off his cell phone, his face ashen. "Mr. President. General Roberto Melchor has been given complete command of the nuclear warheads."

"Dear God," whispered Avery. General Melchor controlled Cuba's military and answered only to Defense Minister Carlos Castro, Juan's tyrannical brother.

"It gets worse, sir," the director continued. "He has

permission to launch them without Politburo approval."

"I can't see Juan giving up his finger on the button," reacted Grant.

"Me neither," agreed Avery.

"My agents on the ground cannot discredit this intelligence," said the CIA director.

"Any possibility it's a countermove?" suggested Grant.

The US had intensified an underground propaganda campaign that a D-Day style surprise attack from the air, sea, and land was in the works using pro-democracy pamphlets that could not be authenticated, and phone calls from Cubans in the US to their friends and relatives known to be double agents.

"True," nodded Avery. "Juan doesn't know if we're bluffing. This could be his gut check."

"South Florida is already on edge," said Jack. "Last thing we want is Castro starting a panic there."

"Regardless," said Baron, "the stakes just went up enormously. They have no established checks and balances for a launch. If true, we have to worry about a trigger-happy field commander."

A deathly hush descended around the horseshoe. Avery interlaced his fingers and tapped his chin pensively. He issued orders one after the other. "Let's go to Defcon One."

Baron nodded to Jack, who picked up the phone in the Tank to relay the message.

Avery then said, "Ask the governor in Florida to go Red." Taking the domestic Threat Level to its highest. Severe. The FBI director ran with it. Avery added, "Tell him to keep it classified until we have further intelligence." Avery then turned to the CIA director, "Any word on Elian Santos?"

Baron caught the CIA director's eyes before he answered. He had briefed the director that the president should not be allowed to see any glimmer of hope in Elian. The director said, "Nobody has seen him."

Baron added, "There's a strong possibility he's been arrested or killed, correct?"

"Yes," nodded the director quickly.

As Baron moved his eyes away, he caught Grant's disbelieving stare. The sign on the Situation Room wall changed to 'DEFCON ONE.'

"Thunder Strike is our only option," said Baron.

"Or," said Grant, bringing up an alternative nobody in the EXCOMM would dare suggest. "You could call the UN secretary general."

The UN secretary general got on Avery's shit list, when, the morning after the election, he warned the world to be prepared for four years of instability. This US president was weak and unpopular, he'd said in an interview, and the country divided too deeply. This speech also doomed any shot the Ulysses had of even challenging Baron for a toehold in the dark shadows.

"That would be a disastrous retreat," said Baron at once. "Even Juan dismissed the secretary general's request for an audience."

"Only because we sidelined the UN," said Grant.

"I agree," said Avery, turning to Grant. *Taking his side?*

Baron felt the covert gazes in his direction. They would see nothing. He never let his emotions get the better of him. Never reacted out of reflex.

Avery added after a moment, "Opening talks with Juan is the same as us blinking first. No way."

Grant did not hide his disappointment. Baron nodded once with a thin smile.

"Take the NHC and Dr. Rotas out of the loop," said Avery decisively. "Let's show Juan Castro a real WMD."

———

Timing to tactics, weather had influenced warfare from the dawn of combat. World War II saw the introduction of specialized weather services into the US military. In 1950, the

Korean War brought forecasters onto the battlefield. The Air Force launched the first Defense Meteorological Satellite in 1965 to support combat operations in Vietnam. A new agency called the Air Force Global Weather Central set up shop at Nebraska's Offutt Air Force Base, hooking up the military in southeast Asia with weather data being downloaded stateside via a new Solar Observing and Forecasting Network and a high speed Automated Weather network. Over the years, as the need arose, the military created new products, programs, services, and offices. On October 15, 1997, the various fragmented weather services, including the AFGWC, were streamlined under one centralized command, the Air Force Weather Agency.

The architect of this reorganization, Lt. General Gary Gueretin, slept in his riverside home located minutes away from Offutt AFB, the headquarters for the AFWA. Ever since Thunder Strike went operational, he'd kept his cell phone within arm's reach at all times. It rang now on the nightstand. He heard it but did not wake up until he felt his wife prod him in his ribs.

"Your phone," she mumbled. A military wife, who'd spent much of her marriage raising their two children on her own, she'd learned to accept his dedication to his work.

Gary opened his eyes and checked the time. Half past three in the morning. He came fully awake in an instant as only a trained soldier could and answered, "Hello."

"Gary. It's Peter."

"'Morning," said Gary. He swung out of the bed and continued out of the room.

Peter did not waste time with a return greeting. "Remove the NHC from all Thunder Strike discussions. That's direct from the president."

The order wasn't entirely unexpected. Peter had called last night, asking Gary to be ready. Gary knew Hank, and was aware that the NHC director never fully got on board. Gary did not fault Hank, who took his job just as seriously as Gary did his. War or peace, foe or friend, the NHC was established to be blind and nonpartisan. Hank was simply adhering to the mandate and guarding his autonomy.

Though Peter never officially briefed him, Gary quickly deduced Thunder Strike entailed keeping Meg a secret to mount a massive military op in the aftermath. He thought it was brilliant. The storm toll of innocent citizens was acceptable collateral damage if it meant the end of communism in Cuba.

Gary admired Peter. They knew each other from NeoCon retreats. Both chose the careers they did to stop the Red Threat in Vietnam. Gary signed up for multiple tours of duty. In 1992, he masterminded the logistics of the coalition effort during the first Iraq war. His skill for organization, combined with his degrees in electrical engineering and business management, brought him to Offutt, Nebraska, in 1995. With absolutely no budgetary constraints, the National Military Command asked Gary to streamline the military's meteorological services under a single Weather Directorate. He'd been the AFWA's first and only Chief.

"When do you want to start?" asked Gary.

"Half an hour ago," said Peter, "when the president gave the order." Gary did not laugh. Looked at his watch. Peter said, "The NHC's next forecast is at six A.M. It gives us a little more than two hours. Is that enough time?"

"An eternity."

The AFWA worked closely with all agencies of the National Weather Service and served as their primary backup, including the NHC. So, the AFWA not only received data from every NOAA source, it also collected information from classified terrestrial and space based military observation platforms. The uniformed staff of more than seven hundred, just as highly qualified as their NOAA counterparts, operated the same state-of-the-art hardware and software, plus secret prototypes that were technologically years ahead. Centralized under one roof against the stunning backdrop of the Missouri River, the AFWA's organization chart reflected military-tight control, with Directorates for Operations, Communications and Information, Plans and Programs, Air and Space observations, Combat Climatology, and Combat Weather.

Gary had created the AFWA as a weather superstation.

Designed for exactly what the president wanted to do: take over any or all of NOAA's operations without NOAA even being aware.

Gary speed dialed. The phone rang at Tinker AFB outside Oklahoma City, where the only AFWA department outside Offutt resided. Gary deliberately set it up there so that it could serve as a "need-to-know-only" terminal of the AFWA.

It carried that cryptic alpha numeral: 'D7.'

Gary simply said, "Go."

———

Sam Winger came in on his final approach. He knew this airstrip well even though the Avian Atoll barely registered on satellite images and did not merit more than a speck on an atlas. It was that tiny.

The atoll had been discovered by accident in June 1943 at the height of World War II, when a US frigate, separated from its fleet in dense fog, almost ran aground on its miniscule beach. The Captain, Justin Hanges, recalled its existence ten years later. He was part of a Cold War counter-espionage subcommittee within the CIA looking to maintain an eye in the sky over the North Atlantic to monitor Soviet subs and ships.

Over the next five years, a million-barrel, all weather, subterranean fuel tank went in. An airstrip, thirty-five hundred feet long, kissing either edge of the island, was laid atop the tank. Six bunker-style buildings that could withstand the ferocious Atlantic weather were constructed, complete with hangars, offices, control tower, a sophisticated ops and communication center, living quarters, recreation, and canteen. More than fifty years of regular upgrades later, Avian remained a vital refueling base for US spy planes, long range bombers, and jets from carrier fighter wings. At the peak of its operational glory, thirty-two men and women lived and worked here. When the Cold War ended, Avian was declassified. Today, the military maintained a rotating staff of seventeen. A regular visitor was NOAA's Aerial Weather Reconnaissance.

Hurricane Hunters routinely used Avian as their layover between recon missions into Atlantic hurricanes. A thick Atlantic fog blanketed the Atoll. The runway lights showed up as dim smudges. Sam let the Control Tower guide him in. The Hercules put down. He engaged the brakes instantly. Reverse thrusters roared. The landing strip was only seven hundred feet longer than the minimum length required to land the huge C-130. Sam slowed to a halt within five hundred feet of the end and turned toward the tight cluster of concrete buildings. Lights were on. The Hurricane Hunters were expected.

Sam looked beat staggering down the rear ramp. He empathized with Ranger and Knoll, who couldn't crash just yet. They had to stay behind and brief the maintenance crew on refueling and coordinating a quick check of the plane. Meg had abused the giant bird quite a bit. Sam and Quince headed inside. Pfifer and Schultz, the two men from AFWA, lagged a few paces behind. Quince went straight for the food. Sam hit the head.

When he emerged, somebody hollered, "Lt. Sam Winger?"

Sam turned and saw a pilot wearing a US Navy uniform. He asked carefully, "Who wants to know?"

"Lt. Gene Fellow. US Navy." He was about six feet tall, close cropped and square jawed.

"I don't owe you money, do I?"

Gene blinked. "No, uh—"

"Then I'm the guy you're looking for."

Gene saluted smartly. Sam, who was bringing his arm up to offer a handshake, changed direction and saluted back casually. "I got orders to fly you out."

"Me?" Sam jerked his head like a rooster. "Where? What for?"

"The *USS William J. Clinton* to see Admiral Grant."

"I know the ship, but never heard of the admiral."

"I'm not surprised."

"Are you sure you got the right guy?"

"Are you Sam Winger, the lead Hurricane Hunter?" asked Gene.

"Yes."

"Then, yes."

"I have to be back on AWR, I'm guessing in six hours."

"I'm sure the admiral is aware," said Gene.

Sam sensed discomfort. The guy seemed like the taciturn type. Sam knew how to use his easy going nature to make people talk more than they usually did. He asked casually, "What's all this about?"

"I can't say."

"Let me tell my guys. They tend to miss me. We are very close."

Gene did not smile. "I'm parked in the hangar."

When Sam showed up, Gene was standing beside a FA-18F Super Hornet. Sam grinned, "Ooh. That's what I call extreme limo service. Can I drive?"

"Have you flown one of these?"

"No. But I'm a fast learner. I mastered Spanish in a single drive from Pensacola to Biloxi. Okay. I could say hello, goodbye, your breasts are in good hands."

Gene let the joke pass again. "Did you start out in the Air Force?"

"Nope," said Sam. "UPS." Sam saw Gene hesitate, wondering if it was a joke. "Seriously. Overnight delivery. That was me." They climbed up the fold-in ladder. "Sweet," Sam whistled, taking in the all-digital cockpit, with touch-sensitive, liquid crystal, upfront control displays. He slipped on the helmet that came standard with night vision goggles.

They were towed out. Ranger, Quince, and Knoll stood

outside and waved. The look of puzzlement had not left their faces. First, Pfifer and Schultz showed up from the AFWA with classified flight plans; then a close encounter with a Hornet like this one in the eye of the storm; and now a mysterious summons by the commander of the America's newest aircraft carrier. *What the hell's going on?*

The jet exhaled a plume of fire. A giant fist punched Sam back into his seat. The FA-18F roared down the runway and took off. Within seconds the fog swallowed the sight and sound of the fighter. Sam was so tired, he nodded off, until radio chatter in his helmet awakened him. He checked the luminous dial of his wristwatch. They'd been flying an hour.

Gene banked sharply and headed in for a carrier landing. Accustomed to generous runways built to accommodate the Hercules, the *William J. Clinton* looked the size of a postage stamp and didn't get much bigger. Sam's stomach tightened as Gene took the Hornet into a steep turn toward the stern of the ship. A slender, truncated ribbon of lights represented the landing strip atop the flight deck. It was five hundred feet long. Nowhere near enough for high speed, heavy jets to put down safely. That's why a plane landing on an aircraft carrier needed to engage its tailhook into one of four intricately woven, high-tensile steel 'arresting wires' stretched across the deck. Sam, who manifested his nervousness with a smart mouth, clamped it shut. He did not want to distract Gene. The Carrier Air Traffic Controller cleared them to land. A fire engine moved into place. Rescue personnel got ready, just in case.

The Landing Signals Officer took over guiding the Hornet in. Sam could hear him in his helmet. Always in command, Sam found himself gripping his wheel helplessly. Gene listened to the LSO's instructions and watched the 'lens,' a system of lights and Fresnel lenses mounted on a gyroscope that shot lights out from the *William J. Clinton*. Different colors indicated different angles of approach. The lights turned amber, or "meatball," as Sam heard the LSO holler happily.

Confirming Gene was right on target.

"That was the easy part," Gene said.

"Cool," Sam shot back acidly, "I live for the hard part."

"Don't worry, I ranked in the top percentile for consistently snagging the third arresting wire with my tailhook."

A pilot's promotion depended on it, Sam knew. Now came the actual landing. The ocean started going by faster and faster as they descended lower and lower. The FA-18F passed the edge of the deck at a hundred and fifty miles an hour. The carrier was a blur.

Sam was certain they'd overshot the runway.

Bumpbumpbump! The tires hit the flight deck. Sam bounced in his seat. Stopped breathing. The landing lived up to the terror. Sparks streaked. Rose above the cockpit glass. Gene wouldn't know if his tailhook grabbed the wire until it actually did. Sam felt the Gs lay into his chest again as Gene pedaled down, feeding all the power the Hornet had back into the engines. The fighter jerked with power.

Oh, shit. Did we miss the runway? Do we have to do this again? Then he remembered. It was SOP. Gene accelerated in case the tailhook did not engage and he needed to take off again. The landing strip was tilted fourteen degrees to help "bolters" slide off the side and regain altitude, preventing a collision with planes on the other end of the deck.

Without warning! Sam jerked forward with a force that made him gasp violently! The snug harness kept him from flying through the glass canopy. The tailhook caught the third arresting wire perfectly. *Snap!* Stretching it! Attached to the two ends of the wire were hydraulic cylinders below deck, which absorbed the momentum of the sixty-thousand pound Hornet traveling at over two hundred miles an hour. Stopping it dead! Sam crashed back. He started breathing again.

"You okay back there?" asked Gene.

"Define okay," said Sam.

"You're okay."

Flight deck personnel in float coats and cranials ran over. They unlatched the canopy and swung it back. Gene waited for Sam at the bottom of the ladder. "Follow me."

"Oh. I was going to wander off."

"Sam," Gene advised gravely, "the admiral is very serious."

The long walk to the flag bridge, Admiral Grant's inner sanctum, prepared Sam. The formality intensified the nearer they got. A sailor with a side-arm in a spotless uniform and knife-edge creases saluted crisply. Gene returned the sailor's salute. Sam did the same. The sailor did not come to ease till Sam went through the door and closed it.

The quarters on the other side of the door looked straight out of a luxury yacht. Grant had his hands clasped behind his back, waiting for the two men. Sam assumed the admiral had watched them come in, and after a few years on this crate, he pretty much could guess how long it took to get up here from the flight deck. Gene clicked his heels and saluted crisply. Sam did the best he could. He took Gene's cue and stayed at attention. It had been a long time since he was around this level of military code of conduct.

"At ease," said Grant. "You must be hungry."

Sam smiled gratefully. "Ravenous, sir,"

Grant pressed the intercom. "Steward. Three cups of strong coffee and one large dinner." He looked up. "Sit down." They settled into comfortable leather couches. A couple of folders and packet of cigarettes lay on the coffee table between them. "Cigarette?"

"No, sir. I don't smoke."

"Do you mind if I do?"

"No, sir."

Grant loosened a cigarette out of the packet and tapped the filtered end on his thumbnail. "You must be wondering why you're here."

"I was—am still perplexed, sir."

Grant lit up, giving no indication he was amused. "There was a breach of security when your plane encountered Lt. Fellow's Hornet inside the storm."

Sam looked over to Gene. "That was you?"

"You were not supposed to be in those coordinates," said Grant. "Why did you change your flight plan?"

"We did not, sir. We hit turbulence and got knocked off course. The storm stats we went in with were nowhere near what we encountered."

"That's your Personnel file." Grant pointed the burning end of his cigarette to the folders on the table.

Sam shrugged, puzzled. There should be nothing damning in it. Born and raised in Memphis, Tennessee, he had a normal and typical childhood. His father, Sam Sr., was a tremendous salesman, who had started out in used cars when he turned eighteen. His mother worked as an accountant at one of the lots. They met, fell in love, and married. Soon, they owned their own Toyota dealership. Sam grew up in a happy home, inheriting the gift of the gab from his father. After high school, Sam decided to attend the U—as alumni liked to call the University of Miami—to pursue a degree in, surprise, surprise, Communications. He got a part time job behind the counter of a Flight School.

The owner loved Sam because the kid could enroll a dish cloth. He rewarded Sam by taking him up for a free lesson. Sam was hooked. Within a year, he was good enough to be an instructor. His parents visited him frequently. Smitten with the colorful lifestyle of South Beach, they sold the dealership and moved into a houseboat there once Sam graduated and found a job as a pilot for UPS, the largest private mail carrier.

Sam did not know where Grant was headed. "Sir, I haven't slept in thirty-six hours and I have a second date with a hellacious bitch called Meg. So, what's this all about?"

———

Grant took a deep breath. He was taking a huge gamble

that Sam would go along. Counting on a kid he'd practically abducted. Whose reaction he was guessing from a resume. In the planning stage of Thunder Strike, Grant had pulled the backgrounds of the two teams of Hurricane Hunters stationed in Biloxi, Mississippi, and selected Sam and his crew to run recon missions because of one entry.

"You lost your parents in Hurricane Camille."

Sam nodded. "They disobeyed the mandatory evacuation order and snuck back onto their houseboat, figuring they'd ride out the storm. Their bodies were never recovered."

"Lt. Fellow here," Grant said somberly, "lost his parents to Sandy." Grant made it a point to familiarize himself with every frontline man and woman under his command. If something happened to them, his sympathy would be genuine and not sound like a form letter.

Gene had been in his first year at the Academy. His parents lived on Staten Island and boarded up their home like the other neighbors. The house withstood the hundred-mile-an-hour winds and rain quite well, until a rafter in their bedroom gave way. The roof caved in. They could have been saved, but it happened in the middle of the night and they were asleep. So were the neighbors, who did not hear the collapse above the roar of the storm. When they rushed over in the morning, it was too late.

"Myself?" continued Grant. "I'm a career seaman. My father was one, my grandfather too and his father before him. I respect and fear Nature." Grant tapped the ash off the end of his cigarette. He could offer no proof. What he feared was remote, at best. A bad feeling born out of the sea in his veins.

Grant had been steadfast in his opposition to Thunder Strike from the day Baron revealed this option. The admiral and the defense secretary had never met until that first EXCOMM session. Each had been aware of the other as part of an invisible triumvirate that came to be on Day One of this Presidency, with Avery playing the apex of balance to the two diametric angles that Grant and Baron provided. Neither could deny a quiet resentment when the president leaned one way or the other. Baron guessed early on that Grant was the invisible voice and hand of John Ulysses VI reaching in and clawing for relevance. Much of Grant's rhetoric came from his long philosophical discussions with John. With Thunder Strike, tension turned into animosity. Grant's skepticism ran just as deeply as Baron's passion for it. They waged a battle for the president's ear.

It was Hawke vs. Ulysses all over again.

Baron won it decisively this morning.

Grant and John spoke afterwards. The admiral sounded discouraged. John suggested a countermove. Grant feared it could jeopardize everything. The president's trust in him. Their friendship. National security. His career. "Forget Cuba," said John, "these are American lives now." He convinced Grant was duty bound and morally obliged to act.

Knock! Soft. Polite. The door opened and an impeccably uniformed steward wheeled in the coffee and Sam's dinner.

"Eat first," he said. "Then we'll talk."

———

Diane couldn't believe it. Vick was dead. She'd had lunch with him just yesterday afternoon. Now he was gone. Slit across the throat and killed. She stared into the mirror. Her eyes were red and puffy from crying. She felt an overwhelming sense of loss coupled with an insane rage. Everyone in the WFO shared her stunned, angry grief. Footprints around the scene of the crime indicated a single assailant. The cops were calling it a fatal mugging with robbery as the motive. There was nothing to indicate otherwise.

Diane emerged from the ladies room. Her boss, James Vaughn, was talking to a cop in a suit, who he'd introduced to her earlier as a detective. Philippe pulled up and got out of his Cherokee, wild eyed. Diane could not even begin to understand how he must be feeling. Philippe rushed to the stretcher. The policeman pulled the sheet back and he broke down. Vick was a gory, blood-sodden mess. Diane went to Philippe's side and took him in her arms.

James came over. "Philippe, I'm sorry."

Philippe nodded wordlessly. They watched the police load Vick into the ME's van. It pulled away.

"The body'll be released after the autopsy," said James. "The police will contact you. Should be a week."

Soon after the police departed, the staff headed back in. Philippe looked numb. Diane promised to stop by later. Turning away after his Cherokee pulled out, she saw James waiting.

"Can you complete Vick's shift?" he asked. "I'll ask Ivory to take yours."

She nodded. James left. Everyone returned to work. A grave hush hung over the entire office. Diane sat lifelessly at the AWIPS. It brought back memories of her parents' accident. Good people dying horribly. *What kind of divine justice is that?* After a few minutes, she snapped out of her sorrow and opened the drawer for a pen.

The contents were in total disarray.

Untidiness was so unlike Vick. He was always on her case for the messy way she worked. The trash can was overturned, the bag missing. *Shit!* Vick had promised to leave the memory stick with the AWR data in the desk drawer. It was gone. Recovered whoever searched the drawer and removed the trash bag.

Ivory Adams.

His name popped into Diane's head at once. *Who else?* Especially after the way he'd snuck up on her yesterday. It could not be coincidence he'd shown up during Vick's shift earlier. Ivory had walked in when Vick was talking to her on the phone.

With a growing fear, she ran her tongue over her lips. They were parched. So was the rest of her mouth. She looked around. Everyone was back at his and her desk. She asked nobody in particular, "Anyone seen Ivory?"

"He was here," said the Hydro Meteorological Technician on duty.

Diane returned to her station.

Obviously Ivory had recognized the storm over her shoulder yesterday. Then he'd caught Vick and probably reported it to the DoD. *But is that reason enough to—wo, slow down.* Even if her theory about a military campaign in Meg's aftermath was true, it was still only a storm that was being concealed, nothing that deserved—she stopped herself again, though this time, she could not help following through with the inevitable deduction.

Was Vick mugged? Or murdered?

Her blood ran cold.

ELEVEN

Sam Winger followed Gene Fellow outside. They wore heavy oilskins. A harsh drizzle blanketed the *USS William J. Clinton.* The aircraft carrier, which was as long as the Empire State Building was tall, barely twitched in the choppy ocean. Carrying eighty-two aircraft, about fifty-five hundred sailors, and more firepower than the entire allied navy during World War II, the *William J. Clinton*'s primary objective on this mission was to provide operational support for Thunder Strike and enforce a zero air-and-sea-traffic zone around Meg, whose outer spirals were responsible for this inclement weather.

The two men reached the FA-18F Super Hornet. Sam paused. Gene walked around the jet. Sam looked up and saw Admiral Grant on the bridge. Intermittent stabs of lightning briefly reduced him to a silhouette. Sam stripped off the oilskins and handed it to a waiting sailor. He climbed inside, still digesting the contents of Grant's talk and tour.

Wow.

It was all he could muster as reaction to Thunder Strike.

He came out of his thoughts when Gene slapped the fuselage, signaling the Hornet looked okay on the outside. The plane captain, called a Brown Shirt, had refueled and checked the FA-18 earlier, but it was customary for the pilot to do it as well. Gene climbed in. The canopy dropped shut. It was opaque with mist and condensation. He turned on the cockpit heaters. While the glass cleared up, he ran the routine preflight checklist written on a long piece of cardboard taped over his right thigh.

Gene started the engines, moved the twin gray-white throttles to idle, and waited for the deck crew to break down the plane. Once the chains were unhooked and the chocks removed, Yellow Shirts directed Gene across the four and a half acre roof. Blue Shirts, supervising the flaps and control surfaces, waved their blue wands. Red Shirts, nicknamed ordies, moved in front of the thermal-sensitive noses of the Hornet's modified missiles. Hearing a distinct hum, Gene gave the ordies a thumbs-up. A Green Shirt raised a lighted board inscribed with the Super Hornet's takeoff weight.

The catapult officer swished the green wand in his right hand horizontally. Gene pushed the throttles to full power. The engines exploded with noisy power. The FA-18F strained to break out of the holdback bolt. He tested the rudder pedals, moving the black control stick between his legs. The catapult officer slashed his green wand vertically. Gene throttled all the way. The engines breathed fire, lighting up the jet blast deflector. The fuselage trembled. The holdback bolts continued to restrain the fighter. The hookup man duckwalked quickly under the plane for one final check. Gave his thumbs-up.

Gene turned on the red and green navigation lights, signaling he was ready for takeoff. The catapult officer went down on one knee, faced the bow, and touched the deck with his green wand. The Green Shirt pushed the red 'FIRE' button.

Sixty-five thousand pounds of steam exploded! The holdback bolt broke. Sam and Gene slammed into their seats. The Hornet shot forward.

The catapult hook's 8-wheel trolley raced along the flight deck tracks with an ear-splitting rattle. The fighter left the edge of the flight deck. Dipped. Then climbed. The afterburners disappeared behind the opaque curtain of rain.

"My father was a pastor," said Gene, as they began a steep climb. Sam noticed that, following Admiral Grant's briefing of the mission ahead, Gene had become friendlier and more talkative. Probably because he realized they were a team now—two against the world. "A Southern Baptist, renowned for his fiery sermons."

"So I'm guessing you took after you mother." Sam tried to force levity.

Gene nodded. "She was a quiet and dignified lady. Never wore her religion on her sleeve My dad's diametric opposite.

He was all about following your conscience."

"I know this goes beyond your call of duty," Admiral Grant told Sam and Gene while they stood on the catwalk looking down at the Thunder Strike ops center, "but I could not think of asking anyone else." Sam and Gene knew he was referring to their personal losses in hurricanes. "Should my fears be unrealized," Grant continued, "just say you were following orders. I'll take the fall." The admiral was not just risking thirty of service, seniority, and commendations, he was laying four generations of his family's valiant service to the Navy on the line.

Sam had to say yes. He looked at Grant and couldn't resist adding, "But not for all those noble reasons. I get to see my girl."

Grant and Gene laughed. At that moment, instead of alleviating the pressure of the daunting mission ahead, Sam felt its enormity even more. His chest tightened. These were two of the more serious people he'd ever encountered. *Shit. And they look scared.*

The Hornet reached cruising altitude. Gene picked up again, "My father never told me the right thing to do may not always be the right thing to do."

"So what are you saying?" quipped Sam. "Are we doing the right thing or are we doing the right thing?"

"Does it matter?"

————

The seconds and minutes seemed to stretch longer with each hour. Diane had set up NOAAPORT to alert her when the NHC's six A.M. bulletin came in on the AWIPS. Official satellite images of the North Atlantic issued by the National Meteorological Center continued to be uneventful. Without Vick, she had no way of knowing Meg's status.

Diane's frustration mounted.

The NHC knew adequate lead time was critical in an evacuation, particularly along the northeast, which was so heavily populated. The warning and preparedness process involved the coordinated effort of several local agencies. It began with the vulnerability of the coast using the "sea, land, and over lake surge from hurricanes," or SLOSH, model.

Developed by a man named Jelesnianski in 1985, it outlined the potential dangers for various scenarios. After every storm, the Techniques Development Laboratory of the National Weather Service compared the actual water rises and falls to hypothetical models, determined highest surge that could be expected called maximum envelope of water, or MEOW, and refined the model by including geographical features that had been excluded in the initial simulation. From historical information of intensities, tracks, and flooding for a family of storms most likely to make landfall, the National Hurricane Center then simulated up to five hundred different scenarios. Various evacuation plans were drawn up based on transportation analyses, shelter analyses, and population behavior studies. No plan existed for a hurricane coming ashore into the Washington-Baltimore Metropolitan Area.

"Diane," a forecaster interrupted her thoughts, "do you have the morning update?" Local TV networks and radio stations received one for their morning newscasts and broadcasts.

"I just sent it," said Diane. "No change." Temperatures hovered in the upper 80s for the second week in a row.

Beep! Diane straightened sharply. The six A.M. NHC bulletin was in. She punched it up eagerly on the AWIPS. Her enthusiasm died as sharply as it spiked. The Atlantic remained clean and blue. There was no sign of Meg.

Where are you?

———

The same question baffled the forecasters at the NHC. Half an hour after Peter walked into Hank's office to hear Gerardo say that Meg threatened the Northeast and the NHC would be declassifying her in its six A.M. bulletin, she began to unravel. Quickly. Hank studied the data for the umpteenth time. "It looks she won't even make it half way up the Atlantic."

Gerardo frowned. Tapped the Sea Surface Temperature data onscreen. "But SST is still at eighty-four." Ideal to sustain a storm.

Clyde waved his Tropical Satellite Analysis Branch printouts. "I think the Southerlies disrupted her somehow."

Ray nodded, "I agree."

"Something smells," growled Gerardo.

"We are dealing with a first," said Ray, whose Forecast Unit analyzed Sanchez's models for twenty-four to seventy-two hour forecasts.

Hank was unsatisfied like Gerardo, but he knew Ray's comment was valid. Being a new, largely manmade windflow, the Southerlies had never interacted with a tropical storm. So, there was little data and no precedent for the models.

"The increase in forward speed may be killing her too," said Ray.

"Your forecast, then?" asked Hank.

"There are signs of a new HPR," high pressure ridge, "about eight hundred miles east of the Delmarva Peninsula which should stall Meg. Then the Greenland current, heading south, will pick up what should, at best, be her carcass and finish her off around the mid-latitudes. But if the HPR doesn't develop, or hold, and Meg breaks through before the Greenland current gets there, a couple of models show her reaching the Potomac." Ray pointed to the two High Pressure Ridges facing off each other on either side of the Bay. "Then these come into play. Meg could conceivably thread up to DC."

Gerardo twisted his lips in an evil smile. "And drown politicians? That would be karmic."

Hank smiled and shook his head. "What are the chances of that?"

"Remote. More likely Meg'll make some noise along the northeast."

"Ten percent," Hank read off the forecast screen. "What's the AFWA saying?"

"None of their models show landfall," said Ray.

"Surprise, surprise," added Gerardo sarcastically,

"So it's my call," said Hank.

Gerardo's eyes widened. "You're not changing your mind, are you?"

Ray agreed. "Hank, we are in the business of forecasting severe weather. If she does make landfall, Meg's still going to pack forty-five mile-an-hour winds, heavy rain, possible flooding. You should go with at least a watch in the six A.M. bulletin."

A hurricane watch announced the possibility of cyclonic conditions within the next thirty-six hours. A hurricane warning was associated with sustained winds exceeding seventy-four miles an hour within twenty-four hours. The NHC sometimes issued a warning if dangerously high water threatened the coast even if the wind gusted below hurricane force.

Hank hadn't forgotten the embarrassment of what happened with Orlene and Paine last year. He'd gone with Gerardo and Ray both times. Issued advisories within a week of each other up and down the Carolinas. Neither storm materialized. Although the NHC did not get a bad rap publicly, Hank had been reprimanded behind the scenes by the heads of both NOAA and the National Weather Service for the panic, inconvenience, and a price tag of forty million tax dollars that local, state and federal emergency services spent to mobilize each time.

Clyde read Hank's mind. "I don't see Meg being anything significant."

Gerardo snapped at him. "Oh, you're a forecaster now?"

"No, but—forget I said anything." Clyde threw up his hands in the air and backed off. He obtained satellite storm fixes, soundings, and extrapolate data for initial model inputs before they were confirmed by aircraft reconnaissance.

"She'll most likely be a tropical wave," said Ray.

"Are you a hundred percent sure?" asked Gerardo.

"No—"

"We all thought Meg wouldn't get out of being a depression. We were wrong. Then we thought, okay, she'd be a tropical storm at best. We were wrong. We thought she would never reach hurricane force. We were wrong."

"Okay, we get it, hombre," said Ray. "We were wrong."

"And we could be wrong again." Gerardo looked at Hank. "Who do you think will be sent up shit creek without a paddle?"

Gerardo was right. The NHC was damned if it did, damned if it did not. Hank nodded toward Peter's office and whispered, "Is he in?"

"With his ear pressed to the frikkin' wall, I bet," smirked Gerardo.

Indeed he was. Peter eavesdropped with growing trepidation on the unmarked flatscreen. Seeing Hank leave the huddle, he turned off the surveillance monitor and turned his face into a genial mask when Hank knocked and entered. "'Morning, Hank."

"Peter."

"Sit. What's the verdict?"

Hank took a deep breath as settled into the chair. "There is no immediate threat of landfall. So I will go along and keep Meg classified."

Peter hid his surprise. "I'll advise the defense secretary."

"However," cautioned Hank, "There is still a ten percent chance of landfall along the northeast. Should that increase, I am reserving the option of issuing a watch."

"Fair enough," said Peter.

"We can issue a watch without mentioning Meg by name. She'd be disorganized, allowing us introduce her into the weather maps as a rapidly escalating severe storm incident."

Peter understood Hank's logic. It eliminated the need to lie and cover up how she came to be. The Director would have have loved to give Washington and the DoD the proverbial finger, but Peter figured Hank for a survivor, who knew when to put his foot down and where to compromise. After the Orlene and Paine fiasco last year, another over-warning could cost him his job. Peter and Baron would see to that. Since there was no obligation to promote someone from within the NHC, he was afraid they'd appoint a lackey. Bring in a company-man from the AFWA.

Peter slapped the table. "Well. That's it, then, I guess. I have nothing to keep me here."

Hank frowned. "You're leaving?"

Peter gave a 'yes' nod. "Meg is no longer an option. Her declassification was the only thing keeping me here."

"Should it become necessary to issue a watch, we will do it in our next bulletin at three in the afternoon."

"Can you give us a heads up either way?"

"Sure."

"That would be great," said Peter cordially, stood up, and extended his hand. "Accept my apologies for the rough spots." When he left here, the NHC would be irrelevant.

Thanks to two men and one woman a time zone away.

———

They were working on two hours of sleep at Tinker AFB outside Oklahoma City in that cookie-cutter military building stenciled with the cryptic alpha-numeral 'D7.'

Short for Detachment 7, the planet's most comprehensive environmental database.

Owned and operated by the Air Force Weather Agency in Offutt, every weather observation, including data from other countries, was archived here, as were all recorded preliminary and final storm reports. The simple, single, unimposing door opened into the largest two-storied warehouse in the state of Oklahoma. The enormous space was needed because D7 stored a copy of every item found in the National Climatic Data Center, NOAA's vast and staggering weather library located in Asheville, North Carolina.

As soon as 217E became a cyclone called Meg, the two men and one woman had begun scouring D7's archives for storms with similar stats. They found nineteen cyclones going as far back as 1945. Environmental conditions of eight closely matched the SST and other storm data. Three of those had changed track around the coordinates where Meg had stalled. One headed into the Gulf Coast, weakened, and made landfall as a Category 2 Hurricane. One swiped Florida's South Beach with more wind than rain. The third curved north. Like Meg did a few hours ago.

They combined this storm's stats with a fourth hurricane that they had discovered earlier, which had dissipated in the mid-Atlantic where Meg was expected to stall again. They sent the information out to the AFWA, where modelers and forecasters from the Combat Climatology Center mocked up hundreds of track guidance and storm intensity scenarios. They fudged the numbers to ensure they would pose a ten percent landfall threat. They sent these bogus numbers back to D7. So, when General Gary Gueretin called D7 some two hours ago with the "go" order, the two men and one woman were ready.

D7 was also the location of the 'THUNDERSTRIKE' key, the automatic command that erased Meg from all weather satellite imagery being distributed to the National Weather Service and consumers worldwide every six minutes. Only the NHC and AFWA had been receiving unaltered data. Beginning with the transmission immediately following Gary's call, the data going to the NHC was modified gradually. An hour later, the NHC received completely reconfigured data that baffled its forecasters and led them to predict Meg's surprising demise.

Hank would not discover the switch.

When and if he did, it would be too late.

———

Dawn smeared the eastern sky. The FA-18F Super Hornet arced in from over the Atlantic Ocean. Below, the Washington Metropolitan area sprawled endlessly. The jet roared across low. Sam straightened, yawning. He craned his neck and saw the fuel gauge. "Are were running on empty?"

The needle was lodged below 'E.' Gene replied, "We've been flying on a wing and prayer for the last five minutes."

"Pastor humor?"

Gene didn't laugh. "Do you have a runway?"

"Still looking," said Sam.

Their radio came alive with the bored and tired voice of an ATC—air traffic controller—near the end of his shift. "Identify yourself, please."

"I'm turning off the radio," said Gene.

"So," Sam surmised, "he's going to try contacting us a couple of times. "

"Then the shit's going to hit the fan." The Hornet was within the Dulles International Airport's Terminal Control Area. Since 9/11, all aircraft needed prior approval to enter DC air space. "Jets will scramble into the air. I'd say we have five minutes. By then we'd be out of fuel and luck."

"You ran away with the Optimist of the Year crown, didn't you? But I'm afraid none of your gloom 'n doom scenarios will come to pass. Not today. Runway, two o'clock."

Gene eased back on the twin gray throttles, skidding the plane around at three hundred and twenty miles an hour. He activated the wings forward for more lift and maneuverability at this speed. A thin black ribbon came into view. "You have to be kidding me!"

Sam's choice for a landing strip was the westbound Capitol Beltway. Deserted at this hour. The engine sucked up the last few drops of fuel and unwound.

"Flameout," gasped Gene

"You were saying?"

"Never mind." Gene opened the landing gear doors. The

heavy wheels of the fast descending fighter fell free. High rise apartments loomed in front. He slammed the control stick forward and left. The jet banked sharply and rose minutely. Enough to sneak them over the soaring rooftops! The altimeter needle fell rapidly.

"Power lines!" hollered Sam.

"I see them," said Gene. The Hornet barely cleared the high tension wires, straightened over the freeway and touched down. Streaked along the westbound freeway. Empty. Until—

An eighteen-wheeler appeared suddenly! Roaring up the ramp in front.

"You could/ve landed on the other side. Same freeway. Right direction."

"Too late," Gene snapped angrily.

Boom! One of the jet's tires blew! Rubber melted into the concrete. The Hornet slewed like it was on ice. Ran amok. Chasing the eighteen-wheeler.

"Eject, eject, eject!" yelled Gene. He reached between his knees for the yellow-and-black ejection loop. Pulled it powerfully.

Three consecutive explosions shattered the morning calm!

The first rocketed the canopy clean off the jet. The second blasted Sam's seat up the rails. The third did the same to Gene. They shot fifty feet into the air, their parachutes opening as they began to descend. Below them, the Hornet's nose gear collapsed. Its left wingtip grazed the center divider of the freeway and turned the jet around! The right wing slammed to the ground. Sent the Hornet cart-wheeling in a rage of sparks. Then it flat-bottomed onto the concrete with a volcanic thud! Simply atomizing the rest of the landing gear.

Missiles broke loose!

Rolled free of the violence!

Detonated!

Instead of fire, an impenetrable white mist exploded into the air. It grew and spread, enveloping Sam and Gene. They crashed into the undergrowth beside the Beltway. The sharply sloped embankment protected them from a hailstorm of debris. They heard the Hornet continue to skid with an ear-rending screech for another two hundred yards before exploding into a spectacular fireball.

A giant tremor shook the ground.

"Shit!" shouted Sam. Chased off the freeway by the erupting remnants of the jet, the eighteen-wheeler took out the side rails and plummeted straight toward Gene, who was hung up in the branches.

Sam unclipped his chute with a single motion. Raced forward. There was no way he'd get to Gene, who squirmed violently. *No way.* The eighteen-wheeler loomed, two stories high, a heartbeat away from crushing the pilot. Sam leapt across the face of the grinning grillwork! Body-slammed Gene, hoping momentum would carry them clear of the truck. Sam felt the scalding heat of the engines. *Oh, crap.*

Gene's entangled parachute acted like a tether and swung them into the air like a trapeze act. The cords stretched. They soared up. Over the hood. They passed so close to the windshield, Sam saw the driver's face distended in horror. The danger was hardly past. They flew toward upright chrome exhaust, belching hot smoke. It was going to cut the men in half. Sam twisted hard. They dodged it by an inch—less!

The eighteen-wheeler passed underneath them. Gene's fingers, at that moment, found the purchase to unclip the straps. The two men dropped. Hit the ground. A second later—

WhoomWhoom!

Two fighter jets thundered low overhead!

———

The pilots saw a protruding tail through the mushrooming white mist and flames. They did not see any markings. Memories of 9/11 slammed their brain cells with fear and alarm! Both hit their radios simultaneously. Galvanizing law enforcement. Mobilizing emergency services. Sending shockwaves through

Homeland Security.

Waking up Peter, Baron, President Avery Walker.

———

"Holy moly," Diane heard a forecaster exclaim and swiveled around. She joined everyone else in the WFO to stare up at the TV set. The plane crash on the Beltway saturated the news. All the reports went with the terrorist attack angle.

Someone said, "This has been one depressing shift. First Vick, now this. I just want to go home and stay out of everybody's way today."

Everyone echoed his sentiment. Diane's cell phone rang. Her brow furrowed. *Who's be calling at this hour?* She looked at the display. The caller ID came up as 'Sam.' *Sam?* They'd exchanged cell phone numbers in Miami. It couldn't be. If it was, he could give her Meg's location. She brightened and answered. "This is Diane."

"Nice entrance, huh, hon?"

"Sam!" Diane shot out of her chair. Her eyes jerked to the TV where the story of the crash continued. In a hoarse whisper, "Holy fuck! That was you?"

"I won't have you using that kind of language in front of the twins."

Diane heard another voice scold, "Stop with the jokes."

"Who's that with you?" asked Diane.

"My grouchy driver. Lt. Gene Fellow. I think he was carrying Liability Only insurance with a high deductible."

"He's right. Stop with the jokes. What's going on? Why are you here?" Before Sam could answer, she exclaimed in a low voice, "Meg! She's headed here!"

"You'd think that would be the scary part, wouldn't you?"

The reason, she discovered when she went to pick them up from an alley ten blocks from the crash where they hid out because their flight suits hardly afforded them anonymity, was so far beyond the realm of reality, it was diabolical.

TODAY

TWELVE

Evidence of rage was everywhere.

It seemed as if every possible worst-case-scenario had come to pass. In retrospect, it wasn't surprising they had. While being one, Meg was also another kind of perfect storm. Washington DC's crumbling, crime-ridden housing projects were characterized as the second worst in the United States. The capital was almost forty percent poor. During the incredible real estate boom at the turn of the millennium, the government poured hundreds of millions of dollars to gentrify plush, predominantly white pockets, ignoring depressed neighborhoods with blacks and immigrants, like Ivy City and Trinidad, located less than five miles from the White House. The inequity created decay and decline, loading up a gun of discontent. Meg discharged the chambers.

Diane and Liz had stopped running when they'd reached Mount Vernon Square, which now looked like a dumpsite. Like so many other famous intersections in DC, where the old and the new once stood cheek to cheek, little remained to distinguish recent architecture from historic landmarks. Meg had turned building parts into devastating missiles. The satellite dishes and transmission tower of National Public Radio lay in the ruins of the Techworld office development, huge chunks of which rested in the rubble of white marble that used to be the City Museum. The Washington Convention Center, the largest building in the city, teemed with refugees despite huge holes in the roof and walls. The sights and smells of overcrowding were overwhelming. Remnants of Mount Vernon Square could be found two blocks south in Chinatown, where Meg ripped through the recent two-hundred-million dollar renovation that had transformed the area into a trendy hub of dining, shopping, and entertainment.

"Where are we going?" asked Liz between huge intakes of breath.

They kept moving. Diane panted hard. When the two cops had stepped into the electrified puddle, everything that followed was a blur. Bullets flew! One cop went down. The chopper crashed. Liz grabbed Diane by the hand. They fled through a blinding storm of fire and dust. As they put distance and time between themselves and danger, Diane's panic and fear lifted.

She replayed the mayhem in her head.

As lightning fast as it had been, the assassin had time to get off at least one shot. After all, he had them trapped at point blank range. *Was he bluffing when he threatened to kill Liz?*

"I'm asking because I need to know if we need a car?" added Liz when Diane did not answer.

"Bethesda," said Diane reluctantly.

"That's almost ten miles. Let's find a car."

"A car? Where?" asked Diane.

Liz gestured around them. "There's gotta be one we can drive."

They were walking up 7th Street. It was littered with vehicles, some overturned, some lying on their side, all haphazardly tossed by Meg. She'd dumped a few from as far away as a mile. Refugees, who'd been turned away from relief camps, had converted the vehicles into homes.

"You're going to steal a car?" asked Diane incredulously.

"See an open rental anywhere?" Liz quipped.

Diane smiled. Relaxing. Immediately second guessing her misgivings about Liz yet again.

They skirted around the JFK Recreation Center and entered urban in-fill. From top to bottom, Meg had eviscerated the high priced condominiums and apartments above designer stores and restaurants. Birds swarmed in and out, feasting on death.

Liz darted her eyes around for a car. She said, off-handed, "I'm not your enemy, Diane."

Diane reacted sharply. Her lungs had stopped heaving.

She responded after a moment, "Admiral Grant—we never talked about going to the press."

"How else did you plan to expose Thunder Strike?"

"We did not plan to expose it at all. The admiral didn't believe the president authorized a cover-up and was trying to reach the White House to get the president to call off this manhunt."

"Well, obviously he realized once you gave up the Jayspid, you were not safe."

"I could have backup copies."

"Do you?"

"I can't say," Diane replied smoothly. She was on guard, now that she knew that Liz was good. "I'm sorry."

Liz didn't press. "We have to be at Dulles by midnight. I chartered a plane. It's waiting to fly us out."

"That must have cost a fortune," said Diane.

Liz just smiled. "I want to break this story, Diane. But I can't. Not until and unless you start trusting me."

There was no easy way to tell Liz that she wasn't ready to do that yet. So Diane simply nodded.

"Look," said Liz, "I'm not the reason Admiral Grant and your friend are dead. It was only a matter of time, whether the admiral talked to me or not. Every agency, the CIA, FBI, cops, Defense Intelligence, are looking for that Jayspid."

"I know I'm safe as long as I have it." *Oh, crap. I just let slip that there weren't any copies.* She'd referred to the Jayspid as 'it.' *Did Liz catch on?* Diane couldn't be sure.

"At some point you have to give it up," Liz said.

"As soon as I know we are safe."

"That looks like it could work." Liz looked away toward a Ford pickup, turned on her heel abruptly, and headed toward the truck.

Diane blinked. *Did I see a flash of anger in Liz's eyes?* Diane stood for a moment with an unsettled stomach. It was a see-saw with Liz. One moment, Diane felt safe. Protected. Liz showed a complete lack of fear. In the next, Liz turned cold. Calculating. I just cannot get a read.

She followed Liz across the lawn, which looked as if someone had turned over a giant trash can of building debris, house wares, and dismembered body parts, some animal, some human. Liz circled the pickup, looking for a way to climb into the cab, which was exposed, but the flatbed was buried under a pile of framing and drywall.

A DCPD squad car cruised into view.

"Cops," whispered Diane hoarsely. "There's a—"

"Shoot-to-kill order on looters," said Liz. "Yeah." Nicked up. Dusty clothes. Sweaty faces. They looked scruffy. "Play along."

Diane nodded and lowered her head in trepidation. She picked up a two-by-four and tossed it aside. Liz kicked away trash. Diane couldn't even bring herself to look up. Her heart thumped loudly against her chest. Her hands trembled and she fumbled a broken lamp.

Liz was the opposite. "Give me your backpack."

Diane obeyed. Liz knelt down and unzipped it, casually removing a bottle of water. She twisted the cap off and chugged down a big gulp. Diane wondered what she was doing, then got it. Liz pretended to see the slowing squad car for the first time.

The young cop, riding shotgun, revealed his piece, resting it deliberately on the ledge of the window. He was about twenty-five, if that. Sandy hair cut short. Blue eyes. His lips met in a stern line. He looked like he was born to join the force.

"Hi," waved Liz.

Diane continued to lightly clear away the debris around the truck, her face averted. The squad car's brakes emitted a prolonged squeak. It was pulling up. *Shit.* Diane held her breath. Liz casually tossed the curtain rod in her hand and started forward.

"Anything the matter, officers?" asked Liz, taking another sip. The bottled water somehow justified the sweat and dirt.

"Is this your house?"

"Yes." Liz looked over her shoulder. "That's my friend, Diane."

Diane swallowed hard and turned and smiled. But the nervousness got the better of her and the mangled piece of metal fell out of her sweaty hand. She hoped she didn't give herself away. *What if they ask us for a Driver's License?* The address would not match. If it crossed Liz's mind, she did not show it.

"We were lucky," Liz said. "We were in Baltimore when the storm hit. We waited a week and figured things had settled down enough to come and check out the house." Liz came up to the car and casually brushed a lock of hair from her eyes.

Diane tensed. *Does fluffing still work?*

The cop relaxed. *It does!* "Just keeping an eye out, miss."

"Appreciate it," she smiled warmly. Sipped some water and deliberately flicked her tongue across her lower lip.

Diane had to suppress a smile. Liz was working the kid. The cop put the gun away. Diane could see his brain working. He knew her from somewhere and was struggling to place her. Diane's stomach coiled up like a tight spring. If he recognized Liz, the charade was over. Liz remained calm. Subtly seductive. She must have ice running through her veins.

"Be careful," said the driver. He was older. He behaved like he outranked the cop riding shotgun.

Liz leaned down and patted her purse with a radiant grin. Not a trace of tension anywhere on her face or in her movements. "I have my pepper spray. Diane's got a tazer. We are good."

Liz straightened, flipping her hair. The cops smiled. They drove off. The car turned out of sight. Diane exhaled. "That was close."

"It was."

"I could never do that," smiled Diane.

"Do what?"

"You know? The hair flip," laughed Diane. "I grew up with two older brothers. Too much tomboy."

"Nonsense," said Liz. "You're beautiful." Diane was flattered, her unease from a few minutes ago forgotten. Liz looked past Diane. "Aw, crap." The passenger side rear wheel leaned out unnaturally because the axle had buckled under the weight of the roof, which had collapsed on to the flatbed. "We have to find another one." They resumed walking. "You gotta remember with guys, they have just enough blood to rush from one head to the other, but never enough to both at the same time."

Diane laughed, her guard dropping further. A young distraught couple appeared around a mound of masonry, taking turns to call out, "Mary! Mary!"

They saw the two women.

"Have you seen a little girl?" asked the father. He sported a week-old stubble. He was dirty, tired, and overcome with anxiety.

"She's ten, blond, about this high," said the mother, raising her hand about six inches above Liz's hip.

"No," said Liz, full of sympathy. "I'm sorry."

"We live out of our van," said the father, feeling the need to unburden. "She was with us. Then she was gone."

"We've been looking for the last two hours," wept the mother. "Oh, god, I hope some animal didn't take her."

"You'll find her," said Diane. "I'm sure she's safe."

"Good luck," said Liz, squeezing the mother's hand.

The couple kept running and calling, "Mary! Mary!"

Liz watched them go out of sight and shook her head. "It's hard enough to lose someone you love. But your child? That must feel even worse. I can't believe someone, anyone could not have stopped this."

Diane was drawn into Liz's eyes, which were gentle and moist with sadness.

"We tried," said Diane. "Believe me, we did."

———

Seven blocks west of the women and half an hour later, Andrew limped into Logan Circle. With one powerful slap of wind and rain, Meg had reversed the decade long revitalization that had sent property values here skyrocketing. She'd wiped out the trendy Whole Foods Market, which had started it all. Until then, this area had been stigmatized as a haven for drugs and prostitution. The thriving galleries were shells, pillaged by Meg of all the artwork. The U Street Corridor, responsible for much of the economic development, resembled a wasteland. The center of gay Washington now served as a supply depot for military units patrolling the northwest District. Andrew walked along the endless stretch of concrete barrier until he came to a makeshift guard gate topped off by coils of barbed wire.

"I'm with the Joint Chiefs," he told the soldier on duty without revealing his name. "Picking up a Humvee." Andrew had abandoned his on the Beltway.

The soldier made one call. Within minutes, a Humvee appeared. Andrew climbed in. There was a full tank of gas. His conversation with Peter, after he'd lost the women in The Gourd, had been tense. They were sharp and curt with each other. A first.

"You work behind Liz," said Peter. "I thought I made that clear."

"I let them go, didn't I?" Andrew shot back. Peter did not know that the women could have died.

"Now Diane probably suspects Liz even more."

"Look for another friend or relative, and we'll be back on track."

"Thank you," said Peter acidly. "I have been doing this for just as long as you have." Andrew said nothing. "I'm taking a lot of heat covering for you. So, let's be perfectly clear. No more confrontations until you have that Jayspid."

"Understood," said Andrew. "I need a car."

"Let me have Jack arrange one you can pick at a supply depot close to you." Peter paused. "I'll call you when I have something."

So, now, Andrew had some time to kill.

He drove west and turned on the radio. Reception was limited to Baltimore stations. Another expert was analyzing the meltdown in DC. "Emergency management procedures for a major metropolis," he said, "begins with a study of microsystems and macrosystems. Microsystems contain a detailed emergency plan, an adequate staff to coordinate it, reliable sources of information during a crisis, and the means to manipulate the information. Macrosystems include damage and risk forecasting, behavior science, cost of eventual recovery, and public policy." The two were then integrated into local maps, topography, demography, transport, communications, building safety, and other information to simulate a 'geophysical model,' which identified vulnerable areas, and a 'socioeconomic model,' which revealed how people would behave and property affected. From these models emerged the Damage Probability Matrix, which estimated a community's vulnerability to a wide variety of hazards. The radio guy revealed, "No DPM existed for a wet weather incident in DC on the scale of a hurricane. After Katrina and Sandy, how could they not have one?"

Andrew smirked. The chaos, civil unrest, and suffering afforded him the anonymity he needed for his kind of R&R. He arrived at Dupont Circle, home to the nation's most prestigious think tanks like Brookings, Carnegie, and others. They were deserted wrecks now. He drove past the remains of the Phillips Collection. Andrew had heard talk around police cooler that the Collection's centerpiece, Renoir's Luncheon of the Boating Party, was gone. Stolen? Or did Meg carry it away and destroy it? Nobody knew. Zealous disciples stood guard around the very first Church of Scientology. Two blocks removed from the Circle, on the curbside of Johns Hopkins University, which had been turned into a shelter, Andrew found what he came for.

A couple of hookers.

Caked in excessive makeup, they looked out of place. Nobody knew how and why JHU became whore central in the aftermath. They wanted fifty bucks each. He did not haggle.

"I'm Candy," said the one sliding into the front seat beside him.

The other climbed in the back. "Then I'll be Sugar."

They reeked of cheap cologne.

He said curtly, "Take your clothes off."

"We have time," said Candy. "Where we goin'?"

Slap! Without warning, Andrew struck her cheek with a full, flat palm. She fell back with a wrenching cry. He snapped, "Now!"

"Take it easy, guy," said Sugar.

"Bastard," cursed Candy, starting forward.

Andrew delivered a threat, full of deadly intent, via just a glance. She shrank back.

He figured the hookers were no strangers to abuse. They'd probably discovered that many soldiers liked to play rough. These two were thinking maybe this geezer did not even question their rate. They'd have taken as little as twenty each, he knew. Cash, being so hard to come by, was gold. With banks and ATMs destroyed or robbed, most people could only trade jewelry, clothes, and other valuables. Hard currency went a lot further.

The girls took off their clothes. When they were naked, Andrew pinched Candy's nipples. She grinned. Sugar breathed heavily into his ear and reached down for his fly.

"Don't," said Andrew shortly.

She withdrew her hand. Flicked her tongue over, around,

and inside his ear. Kissed his neck with exaggerated sighs. Caressed a hand down his chest. Candy worked her hand slyly up his thigh.

"I said don't," warned Andrew again.

His slap was still imprinted on her face as subsiding red welts. She pulled her hand away and guided his fingers between her widening legs. Sliding his thumb into her, she rode it in and out with fake moans. The two pretended to work themselves into a frenzy as Andrew pulled into a dead-end alley. The women thought he'd want sex now and began get all over him.

"Get out!" said Andrew, shoving them back.

"What?" asked Candy, surprised.

"Get out." Andrew drew his Offensive Pistol.

"Shit, dude," said Sugar.

"Easy with that thing, cowboy," said Candy.

They weren't alarmed. Andrew did not expect them to be. They'd likely seen every kind of fetish and figured he wanted do it at gunpoint. Andrew stood on the other side of the hood. He pointed in the direction of the dead end. "Run."

"Hell no," said Candy

Sugar nodded. "We ain't takin' a step without our money—"

Bang! Andrew fired. Burned a round past her cheek. Both girls jumped.

"Shit, asshole!" she reacted, feeling her cheek for a bruise.

Andrew raised his voice just a decibel without losing that menacing quiet. "Turn around and run, or I will splatter your brains."

Fear jumped into their eyes. They didn't say word.

Andrew repeated, "Turn around and run."

They turned around and ran.

His eyes turned to granite. His lips twisted. Muscles twitched over his cheekbones as he clenched his teeth. His face became a picture of hatred. He dispassionately watched the girls recede, their flabby white asses jiggling with cellulite.

Their bare feet echoed on the asphalt that was littered with crap. The alley was in complete shadow. The sun descended quickly, already halfway over on the western sky. Night arrived earlier every day to DC in winter.

Andrew rested his elbow on the hood of the Humvee. Sighted along the barrel of his gun, lengthened by the addition of a silencer that he'd screwed on before he picked up the women. He sniffed once. An unconscious habit that signaled he was ready to pull the trigger. He waited for them to look back over their shoulders. They did. Simultaneously.

Fantasy and reality became one.

Andrew saw Liz and Diane.

Running scared.

Thunk! His gun coughed once. Moved a fraction. *Thunk!* Coughed again. The women took a bullet each so quickly in succession, the impact seemed simultaneous. The soft nosed rounds shoved them forward powerfully. Their mouths opened. A shriek wrenched out their throats. *ThunkThunk!* Andrew unleashed two more shots that took out the back of their heads and abbreviated their death cries.

They crashed to the ground at full clip.

Dead before their skulls hit the pavement with a violent crack of bone.

Andrew walked up and turned over Candy. The bullet had emerged through her nose and split her skull wide open. Sugar was better preserved. An erection strained against his trousers. Necrophilia put him in a hypermanic state of mind. That's when he functioned best. He unzipped his fly and straddled Sugar's corpse, driven by Peter's answer to his last question before they disconnected.

"Is Liz working for you?"

———

President Avery Walker did not leave the Oval Office. His head lowered, his brow furrowed with concentration, he wrote furiously on a yellow legal pad. Words flowed out of his pen. There were balls of crumpled pages in the trash can under the table. Several false and unsatisfactory starts. So immersed was he in what he was writing, he did not hear the knock on the door, looking up only when he heard Baron's voice.

"You wanted to see me, Mr. President?"

Avery nodded him to the chair. "Yes." He waited until Baron settled in. "Baron, you've been a rock."

Avery saw Baron blink, puzzled. It was an odd start to a conversation. Baron replied, unsure, "Thank you, sir."

"You know," said Avery," you were my first choice for running mate."

Baron tilted his head. Shrugged, "I know."

Avery recalled the phone call—one of the most difficult he had to make. He knew Baron was expecting this call—to be offered a spot on the ticket. Instead, Avery said, "I think I need a moderate to put blue states into play."

"Water under the bridge, sir," said Baron with a thin smile.

"I'm sorry," said Avery. "I guess I'm looking for forgiveness from someone. Anyone."

"Why, sir?" asked Baron, concerned.

"I have asked the vice president to return to Washington tomorrow." The VP was working out of New York. "I'm going to tell him I want you in the number two spot when I'm gone."

"Gone? Sir?"

Avery had never known Baron to look surprised. The defense secretary appeared genuinely taken aback. "You might as well be the first to know. I am going to address the nation tomorrow. Come clean about Thunder Strike." Anxiety rippled across Baron's face. Avery saw it and said, "Don't worry. It may've been your baby, but I'll shoulder the blame entirely. I also intend to announce that I am resigning."

"Don't you think that's a bit extreme?"

"Extreme? A million people are dead, Baron. Kids are orphans because of me. Wives are now widows. So unnecessary." Broken thoughts spilt out. "I see ghosts of the dead. Faces of ordinary people haunt me." Words cut through his lips like a razor, "They blame me and they should. I hear their cries at night. Mr. President, Mr. President." Avery clutched his head. "Imagine scorpions in your head. That's what it's like when I close my eyes. I'm afraid to sleep at night. I can't work. I can't look outside without being wracked with guilt." He stared down Baron. "My mind is made up."

Baron retreated, "It'll be a shame to see you go, sir."

Avery nodded gratefully.

"Then I have to get your signature on a couple of funding bills that were couriered in from New York. I thought they could wait till tomorrow."

"Just come on upstairs," said Avery, pushed his chair back, and stood up. He shook his head with a sad smile. "You know, ever since I was a teen I dreamed of being president." With a wan smile, "Be careful what you wish for, huh?" He patted Baron on the back.

"It was not your fault, sir," consoled Baron.

Avery shook his head. "How could it not be?" The buck stopped here with him when he authorized Thunder Strike. "A weapon that turned against its maker."

LAST WEEK

THIRTEEN

She swept northward, majestically orchestrating more than a million cubic miles of atmosphere. She had shed all her ambiguous and erratic cloud cover. Satellites, monitoring her unchallenged march, captured the fearsome yet breathtaking spectacle of her powerful, tightly coiled, well-defined form.

She stood upon the ocean fifty thousand feet tall, a whirlwind of devastating violence. Her presence could be felt as deep as the ocean floor sediments, where her approach was heralded by gigantic internal waves that would persist in her wake for several weeks after her passing. She had grown rapidly as a tropical cyclone, earning the dubious 'Category 5' stature on the Saffir/Simpson hurricane scale when her sustained gusts surpassed one hundred and fifty-five miles an hour. She could level most structures and submerge the beach front as far inland as ten miles with flood waters fifteen feet high.

Replicating the most intense hurricanes before her, she had developed a distinct cloud-free eye. Air entrained laterally and updrafted below the cloud base in her eyewall, resulting in subsidence. This warmed her atmosphere and dissipated the clouds in her eye, stabilizing her thermodynamically. Here, in her innermost recesses, whipped by a turbulent radius of maximum winds, mere hours after reaching Category 5, her gusts sporadically reached three hundred and fifty miles an hour. Her spiraling rain bands were afire with nonstop lightning. She plucked sixty-foot waves out of the ocean. The associated foam and spray served as an additional source of water vapor, intensifying her cumulus activity. To retain the integrity of her heat engine, she remained anti-cyclonic aloft and cyclonic near the surface.

Carried by the Southerlies, her forward speed picked up to forty miles an hour. This acceleration should have inhibited her intensification, weakened, and killed her.

Such was the law of Nature.
But she was not a natural storm.

———

The *USS William J. Clinton* gently swayed in the rough weather while the other ships of the fleet rocked madly. Waves clawed up the hulls, wrapping around the deck like giant serpents, seeking to embrace and overturn them. The wind came in sharp, violent gusts. A hard, driving rain poured down. Thunder growled incessantly. The extended bolts of lightning provided the only respite from the intense gloom cast by the thick, dark, swirling cloud cover.

Dr. Robert Mclaurin strode into the Thunder Strike ops center, a technological marvel.

A weather superlab.

He clapped his hands, drawing the attention of his fourteen-member team. Giant flatscreens displayed awesome satellite pictures of Meg from different angles——some overhead, some from the side; three-D and two-D wire frames that were updated every six minutes by Combat Climatology at the AFWA; images from cockpit cameras of fighters inside the storm; and banks upon banks of screens scrolling with data.

"Gentlemen," began Dr. Mclaurin. He had no women on his team, except for his personal assistant. "I called this review because I sense skepticism. I've been hearing talk of Nature being this Goddess of Mystery, full of surprises and secrets. Nonsense! Wasn't the rising sun once a miracle that was worshipped? Tides were ascribed to an angry God. Nature is no more enigmatic than a brick. Every one of her so called secrets is a scientific equation away from being explained. Yes, Meg did not make landfall as planned. Rather than a setback, it affords us the opportunity to show our detractors that we are truly weathermen of the new millennium, who no longer report the weather, we control it!"

Dr. Mclaurin was aware, even as child, that he was

mesmerizing. He could command a room, be it unseen over a speaker phone, or an image on a remote feed, like when he addressed the EXCOMM. In person, however, he was another animal. Nobody budged. There wasn't even a cough or rustle of fabric. Not an eye left him. The storm outside did not penetrate into these bowels of the *William J. Clinton.*

"Four days ago, Meg was a sluggish depression. Look at her now! Her sustained winds reached three hundred miles an hour a few minutes ago. We clocked her eyewall gusts at almost three fifty. Already, there has been nothing like her. Imagine when she makes landfall. She will not only be the first manmade hurricane, but one that has only been theorized, and skeptically so.

"A superhurricane!

"Now! More important than the making of the storm is our ability to direct this incredible weapon that packs the power of three million atom bombs where and how we wish. Overcoming Nature's habit for boring consistency. Targeting places untouched by cyclones. Steering her along unprecedented tracks. And that! That is the challenge ahead."

He let the silence stretch a moment longer than necessary. Then, he caught them unaware with a loud clap. Shoulders tightened as the sound shattered the absolute quiet like a bomb. "Let's get to work!"

With a chorus of "Yeah!" the men dispersed to their stations. Dr. Mclaurin walked over to the meteorologists working on the High Pressure Ridge east of the Delmarva Peninsula. Isobars—lines of pressure—bunched together in convex curves.

"It's taking shape," said one of them.

Dr. Mclaurin ran the numbers in his head and snapped, "It will not hold." The Southerlies would want to drag Meg all the way north and west across the Peninsula into Maryland and Virginia. So, the HPR needed to be strong enough to stop and hold Meg until they could steer her into the Greenland current that would carry her back South toward Cuba. "Increase the HAARP transmissions."

Over the years, there had been no shortage of reports and rumors that the High-frequency Active Aural Research Program in Gakona, Alaska, was really a geophysical weapon. They were effectively dismissed. HAARP maintained an open-for-the-world-to-see website. Overtly, it did study the ionosphere. Covertly, it was a quantum next step above and beyond the Soviet 'Woodpecker' and the US 'GWEN' systems, both primitive weather modification projects that fired ELF, or extreme low frequency, waves into the upper atmosphere. The project had been originally inspired by the work of Nikola Tesla, a Russian immigrant to the US, who had worked at Westinghouse and Edison during the infancy of electricity. He'd discovered that the atmosphere changed when it was bombarded with low frequency radio waves.

Experiments involving firing ELF into the ionosphere began secretly as part of the Star Wars program and continued when the HAARP facility went online in Gakona in 1993. It contained a hundred and eighty antenna units, organized in fifteen columns by twelve rows. By the turn of the millennium, they perfected shooting ELF waves to converge at specific coordinates, disrupting scalar fields, or lines of temperature and pressure, thus acquiring the ability to alter the course of jet streams and set up weather blocks like low pressure troughs and high pressure ridges.

Dr. Mclaurin had been in charge of HAARP's covert experiments. It was another moving part of his bigger, more elaborate Thunder Strike project. No one outside this ops center knew that the HPRs facing off on either side of the Potomac River had been created in a day as a dry run. When Dr. Mclaurin stopped the HAARP transmissions, they should have dissipated instantly, but an unexpected confluence of upper atmosphere events caused them to linger, not only bringing unseasonable heat to the east coast, but dangerously warming the waters of the ocean and the rivers to equatorial temperatures.

"We have never attempted an ELF transmission of this intensity," said the meteorologist. Nobody knew the consequences, but this third and most important weather block, to stop and hold Meg, needed to go up in hours.

"That's why those who go first are called pioneers," said Dr. Mclaurin.

The meteorologist smirked proudly.

As Dr. Mclaurin walked away, Eva, his personal assistant of several years, the only nontechnical person who enjoyed the same security clearance as the rest of the team, hurried over. Fifteen years his junior, a Swedish immigrant, she'd become his assistant at twenty-one. Mousy, content to be in the background, and happy to stoke his enormous ego, she went to his home every weekend and cooked and cleaned for him, handled his bills, appointments, and mothered him during illness. Dr. Mclaurin considered personal relationships a distraction and never married. Eva also filled the void of intimacy in his life. Sex was infrequent to rare. He suspected she didn't much care for it either. He even acknowledged to her he was a lousy lover. But he promised her he would never look, let alone stray. In return, she was jealously faithful. He knew she would take a bullet for him.

"Doctor," Eva said with a broad smile, "AFWA has taken over Thunder Strike." She called him Robert behind closed doors of the bedroom. Never elsewhere or otherwise.

"Finally," said Dr. Mclaurin brightly. "Is the NHC out?"

"Yes. As of six A.M. eastern time."

He grabbed Eva's shoulders and squeezed them. "Outstanding!"

There was no love lost between him and Hank Rotas. Their hostility went back thirty years. The news added a spring to Dr. Mclaurin's step. He sat down with his cloud physicists. At middle latitudes, colder air penetrated the cyclonic vortex, cooling the warm core. This acted like a thermal brake on further intensification, dooming tropical disturbances to a swift demise.

"But she is holding up well," observed Dr. Mclaurin. "Though, when we stall her, the diametric opposite flows of the Southerlies and the Greenland current will disorganize her spiral."

"Seeding sorties have to be almost continuous," said someone.

"Not almost, but continuous," said Mclaurin. "We have to control Meg's secondary updrafts while they are in a state of flux."

"Come and get me when we stop her," he said, looked at the satellite pictures of Meg with a fondness a father would only reserve for his child, and left.

Robert Mclaurin had been a child prodigy. He came from a family of brilliant academicians. His father taught quantum physics at MIT and his mother theoretical math. He graduated from high school at ten and obtained a bachelor's degree at thirteen in Computer Science. Around graduation, his father was invited to submit a paper on cloud physics for the National Hurricane Research Project, which had been commissioned to prepare a comprehensive report that encompassed a variety of topics: hurricane formation, hurricane structure and dynamics, hurricane forecasting, and means of hurricane modification. Young Robert, desperately seeking a direction for his genius, became instantly captivated by the speakers who presented papers on human control over hurricanes. Within a couple of years, he earned a master's degree and doctorate in meteorology.

He started work at the NHRP in 1962.

He was seventeen.

Over the next fifty-some years, Dr. Mclaurin and weather modification embarked on a rollercoaster of fame and ignominy. He was recognized as the author of dramatic discoveries and condemned as the villain of dashed hopes. Eventually, he outlasted his critics with the crowning achievement of his persistence, Thunder Strike.

Weather modification began as research into techniques to turn damaging hail storms into crop saving rain. Once scientists had identified clouds as the building blocks of weather, they embarked upon replicating Nature's miracle of making clouds rain. The first, and until today, most important discovery of weather modification came on a hot and humid summer day in 1946 at the General Electric Research Lab in New York. A scientist called Vincent Schaefer tirelessly strove to discover the chemical that would induce clouds to rain. He modified his deep freezer into a cold chamber to simulate cloud conditions. Apprehensive the summer heat might adversely affect his experiment, he slid a block of dry ice into the chamber. To his amazement, he saw ice crystals form instantly. Vincent had chanced upon the discovery that would become synonymous with weather modification: cloud seeding. His colleague, Bernard Vonnegut, discovered that smoke containing silver iodide had an identical effect. But neither could explain how or why dry ice and silver iodide induced the ice crystals to form.

For four-and-a-half decades, scientists could only point to the rain after a cloud seeding run and claim credit. It was not until the early 1980s that 'Nature's miracle' was deciphered and the mystery of the internal processes of cloud seeding solved. Warm, moist air rose, cooled, and condensed into microscopic droplets of water light enough to be suspended in the air. Called the cold rain process, a mass of these droplets gathered together to create a cloud, which essentially contained ninety-nine percent pure air. Despite the freezing temperature at the altitude where they formed and resided, they remained unfrozen, leading them to being called supercooled clouds.

If these supercooled clouds came into contact with a solid particle, like dust, the water droplets immediately formed a crystal of ice around it. The crystal gained weight, collided with other similarly developing crystals, and finally became heavy enough to fall earthward. Whether they came down as rain, hail, or snow depended on geography, temperature of the atmosphere, and other local conditions. Cloud seeding merely used chemicals resembling ice to induce crystal formation. Thus, human intervention was merely a catalyst. Once triggered, Nature still had to do the rest.

The US government's involvement with weather modification began with Project Cirrus. On October 13, 1947, the first cloud seeding of a hurricane was undertaken from an experimental aircraft. Observers aboard reported changes in the appearance of the clouds. But the most significant change occurred in the track of the storm. Heading northeast before the seeding, she suddenly reversed westward and slammed into the coasts of Georgia and South Carolina. Unable to explain this drastic behavior and fearing a scandal, the government quickly halted further modification efforts.

In the mid-fifties, three hurricanes devastated the eastern seaboard, claiming four hundred lives and causing over six billion dollars in property damage. With the tragedy of 1947 a distant memory, the US Weather Bureau established the National Hurricane Research Project to collect aerial weather reconnaissance data on hurricanes. Six years later, the NHRP organized a seminar of the best minds in America, including young Robert's father. In 1961, evolving from this study, and almost coinciding with seventeen year-old Dr. Mclaurin's arrival at the NHRP, Project Stormfury was launched.

Dr. Mclaurin became deeply involved in the preparation of the Stormfury Hypothesis. It postulated that the eyewall of a hurricane was unstable with abundant supercooled clouds. Therefore, seeding the eyewall could dissipate the clouds into rain and cause the diameter of the eye to increase, resulting in the radius of maximum winds to inevitably suffer a sharp reduction. On September 16, 1961, a naval aircraft flew into Hurricane Esther. Her pressure had been dropping a millibar an hour. After eight canisters of silver iodide were dispensed into the eyewall clouds, the pressure stopped deepening. Radial profiles of her wind fell significantly too. Scientists declared the experiment an unqualified success.

Dr. Mclaurin's standing in the NHRP rose dramatically, when he pioneered the introduction of computers to replace the cumbersome and time consuming task of assimilating observations manually. He engineered the creation of the earliest numerical models of convective bubbles, which allowed researchers to simulate the effects of seeding on isolated cumulus clouds.

With recognition came difference of opinion. The numerical models of hurricanes were now augmented by the first meteorological satellite pictures. Dr. Mclaurin believed that hurricanes did not contain enough supercooled clouds for seeding to be effective. Project Stormfury, he wrote in the Bulletin of the American Meteorological Society, should abandon seeding and concentrate on a more deeper understanding of microphysical and dynamic processes of hurricanes. Critics blasted his findings. Mclaurin fell from boy wonder to outcast, excluded from all Stormfury discussions.

He began work on non-hurricane cumulus clouds and discovered that their high vertical velocities made them the largest reservoirs of condensed water. However, rainfall from these clouds was small. After a year of experimentation, Dr. Mclaurin demonstrated that, with careful seeding, he could suspend the particles in the vertical currents until they grew into large size hail. When discharged, the cloud yielded torrential and devastating precipitation.

The Department of Defense contacted the twenty-three year-old scientist. Dr. Mclaurin received the call with a great deal of apprehension. He assumed it had to do with the draft that he had been dodging. Instead, the DoD invited him to demonstrate his claim at the National Weapons Center in China Lake, California.

Mclaurin did. Successfully.

The DoD wanted him as Project Director of Operation Popeye, an extensive, top secret, rainmaking operation over specific trails in Laos, North Vietnam, South Vietnam, and Cambodia. This appointment, they said, would fulfill his draft requirement. He accepted the assignment without hesitation.

Vietnam provided the first glimpse of the effectiveness of weather as weapon of war.

The seven-year rainmaking effort produced critical data and innovations Dr. Mclaurin could never have obtained from simulations and field experiments at a civilian agency with budget constraints like the NHRP. That the innovations came at the price of civilian fatalities and irreversible environmental damage in Southeast Asia did not bother him. He'd always been a strong advocate of animals for research as well as willing human guinea pigs. Science could never advance without sacrifice.

In Popeye, the silver iodide was placed in a metal container three inches long, with a candle assembly for delayed ignition. The container and candle were enclosed in an aluminum photoflash-type cartridge case. The units were carried aloft by RF-4C reconnaissance aircraft and released at half mile intervals. They burned for about thirty-six seconds as they dropped three thousand feet down shafts of active updrafts. Typically, each seeding run influenced an average of four to five cloud groups and drenched a diameter of twenty miles with heavy precipitation for about six hours. Along the main Ho Chi Minh Trail, Dr. Mclaurin used emulsifiers, a chemical used by oil drillers to impart slipperiness in soggy mud. Enemy movements dropped from nine thousand to less than nine hundred. Rainfall rose to an unprecedented twenty-eight inches, culminating in the floods of 1971, which devastated North Vietnam.

Popeye was a career-making success. Dr. Mclaurin returned home to accolades. At twenty-eight, he became the youngest director of the Oceanic and Atmospheric Research, the premier civilian weather research facility in the US. In his absence, Project Stormfury had languished. His suspicions of a decade ago, that hurricanes may not have enough supercooled clouds, were supported by discoveries of ice in storm clouds. The government killed Stormfury. Soon afterwards, even Mclaurin's brief honeymoon at the OAR ended.

In 1974, New York Times correspondent Jack Anderson exposed Operation Popeye. The Foreign Affairs Committee summoned Dr. Mclaurin, after Hank Rotas, testifying for three days, named him as the architect of the program. Dr. Mclaurin was reprimanded and forced to tender letters of apology to the governments of Vietnam, Laos, and Cambodia. The humiliation did not end there. The president unceremoniously fired him as director of the OAR.

Dr. Mclaurin never forgave Hank Rotas.

Dr. Mclaurin found work at the North Dakota Atmospheric Research Board, one of the longest running programs in the United States exploring weather modification. Working with cloud physicists, Dr. Mclaurin developed a tracer gas, which could be tracked on a complex computer program, to follow the path of silver iodide used in cloud seeding. The results were eye-opening. Contrary to popular belief, silver iodide did not mix with the supercooled clouds upon release. Powerful updrafts within the storm clouds shot the silver iodide to the top. Crystallization occurred as it drifted down.

Dr. Mclaurin's genius surfaced again.

If the strongest updrafts in a developing system were targeted for seeding, the silver iodide would rise. On the way down, as crystallization occurred, the latent heat released would add to the buoyancy of the updraft and strengthen it dramatically.

A weak disturbance could be triggered into a powerful storm.

But he knew that more important than the formation of a storm was where it headed. At cyclonic proportions, the main updraft worked on the same scale as several million atomic bombs and was beyond human modification. Smaller updrafts around it were not. They could be worked like a steering wheel, effecting turns in the storm by selectively seeding them to achieve an asymmetric distribution of energy. "In conclusion," Mclaurin wrote in a report seeking federal funds for more research, "the United States will not have to ever deploy a single man to fight wars, if the forces of a hurricane can be marshaled and directed at the enemy."

His report found its way to the desk of a young Undersecretary of Defense.

Baron Hawke.

Thunder Strike was born.

Dr. Mclaurin spearheaded top secret experiments in the Atlantic. It took time and money. Baron was patient. Ten years passed. Then, another decade. Dr. Mclaurin used Star Wars to test the prototype of what would become HAARP. In 1993, he took over the covert Directorate of the facility. His team invented Composite Seeding Agents that packed almost ten thousand times the chemical potency of silver iodide. At the turn of the millennium, more than twenty years later, Dr. Mclaurin began for-real experiments. Instead of their usual payload of firepower, missiles carried CSA. Three fighter jets, working in tandem, flew sorties into developing storms. The first plane released tracer gas to identify the updrafts for the second plane, which was equipped with complex sensors to pinpoint the updrafts. The third released CSA into the updrafts.

A year ago, Dr. Mclaurin informed Baron he was ready to create the first hurricane. He selected a tropical depression in a dormant region with minimal external steering currents. Weak updrafts, which would have otherwise died and killed the disturbance, were nurtured to strength. The depression grew into a tropical storm and then to Hurricane Orlene.

The lack of external steering currents allowed him to seed smaller updrafts and direct the storm where he pleased.

He was able to direct Orlene in an unprecedented, arrow straight, south to north track. For the sheer flamboyant hell of it, he made her execute a cycloid loop, then like an emperor tired of a mistress, he drove her into cooler mid-latitudes to kill her. Now he had to demonstrate success on a statistical level. He had to prove he could repeat this, so that the results were distinguishable from natural behavior.

He did. With Hurricane Paine.

Stringent, impenetrable security surrounded these experiments, since the DoD was operating in violation of the World Meteorological Organization's mandate banning weather modification experiments for nonpeaceful purposes. The National Weather Service's agencies responsible for Atlantic discussions treated the two storms as they would any other. The National Hurricane Center performed routine aerial weather reconnaissance and made normal factual reports through regular unclassified worldwide weather channels.

The Pentagon classified Thunder Strike as a viable weapon ready to be integrated into all Joint Chiefs of Staff strategy discussions. Since its success was contingent on its secrecy, when the time came to replace the existing Geostationary Orbiting Environmental Satellites, Dr. Mclaurin worked with DoD tekkies to install a switch capable of ceasing direct broadcast of all meteorological products on the next generation of GOES. The same feature was installed on the newly deployed Polar Orbiting Environmental Satellites. NOAAPORT, a communications link that could selectively shut data flow to any agency, became a part of National Weather Service's modernization and restructuring.

The waiting game began for an appropriate crisis to unveil Thunder Strike. Cuba's acquisition of nuclear missiles seemed tailor-made. Baron knew Avery would go for it. His Presidency teetered on the verge of irrelevance after his controversial win. Following the morning EXCOMM session, when the Avery announced the startling developments in Cuba, Baron ordered

Thunder Strike on the front burner, with a request for 'a full JCS package with talkers, background papers, point papers, all the right tabs, Jayscap, and UCP.' The request came with a 'suspense' notation and permitted 'shotgun coordination.'

A 'JCS package' or 'Jayspid' referred to a complete report, specifically formatted for the Chairman, Joint Chiefs of Staff, who then presented it to the EXCOMM. 'Talkers' fielded questions. Since Thunder Strike was a Deep Black Program, the talkers were just Baron, Jack, and Dr. Mclaurin. 'Background papers' and 'point papers' detailed the project's risk, impact, etc. 'Jayscap' was Joint Strategic Capabilities Plan and 'UCP' the Unified Command Plan. 'Tabs' along the right hand side of the package identified the location of documents. A staff officer, called an action officer, put the package together. Since he faced a 'suspense' date, or deadline, he made several copies and simultaneously distributed them to the various Pentagon offices contributing to the package—a process, in Pentagon jargon, called 'shotgun coordination.' Again, being a DPP and the defense secretary's 'gold watch,' or pet project, Thunder Strike was given to a 'spook.' He handled sensitive front burners. All Thunder Strike requests remained behind 'green doors,' where highly sensitive activities took place and only 'elephants,' or the highest Pentagon officials, had access.

As Baron anticipated and assured Dr. Mclaurin, Avery gave his preliminary green light at the second EXCOMM session. Realizing Thunder Strike would 'rattle some chains,' Baron asked Dr. Mclaurin, an impassioned speaker with incredible charisma, to make the presentation.

Dr. Mclaurin hit it out of the park. Almost.

Alone in his opposition, Admiral Grant cast enough doubts that the president wanted to sleep on it. But next morning, Avery 'sprinkled holy water.' Thunder Strike was a go and classified as 'Brick Bat,' a JCS urgency designator that made it top priority with defense contractors. Baron introduced Dr. Mclaurin to Peter Wilkins, who came on to organize the 'denial and deception.' Peter suggested that everyone outside the EXCOMM be led to believe that Thunder Strike was merely a covert Special Forces mop up in the aftermath of a natural storm.

Dr. Mclaurin handpicked a team to join him aboard the *USS William J. Clinton,* which went through an extensive modification to incorporate the very specialized ops center. A direct satellite link allowed Mclaurin to access information from any satellite and weather office, including the AFWA and NHC without their knowledge. He was privy to numerical models as they were being run. The Aircraft Satellite Direct Link permitted him to directly receive aerial weather reconnaissance data. The *William J. Clinton*'s Super Hornets were modified to identify and seed updrafts. The pilots ran through an intensive training course of working in tandem trios. Speed and precision were imperative once a disturbance was identified. The instability in an infant weather system altered with such rapidity, mere minutes separated capturing it for further development and losing it forever to natural dissipation.

Mclaurin's hypothesis of steering a storm relied on minimal external currents. But the Southerlies began their annual journey north over the equator. He did not bring up this wrinkle, afraid the powers-that-be might call off Thunder Strike. Lack of experimental opportunities could kill the project. He was not getting younger and with a nation weary of war, this crisis was likely his last opportunity to test the effectiveness of weather's most potent force, a hurricane, as a weapon of war.

Mclaurin and his staff began to run numerical models incorporating the Southerlies. They drew upon statistical data from the Atlantic, Pacific, and Indian Oceans, with similar wind flows and their effects upon tropical storms. The results were not encouraging. He hoped and prayed he could outrun the storm past the Southerlies.

When Mclaurin received the green light, a sluggish tropical depression, 217E, was the only available disturbance. Air needed to be triggered into an easterly wave. Disguised as a secret underwater test, he detonated a nuclear device. The incandescent heat created an instant low pressure. Air from all around rushed in. Since the explosion was never reported, the National Hurricane Center was caught off guard by the sudden development of updrafts over 217E. Air missions commenced to identify, nurture, and strengthen the disturbance. Soon, wisps of cloud appeared. Within seventy-two hours, Mclaurin turned 217E into an embryo storm, then hurricane Meg.

Like the NHC, Mclaurin had been handicapped by Meg's early erratic cloud cover. The nonstop missions to strengthen her from a depression delayed aerial weather recon. He needed AWR. So they let a Hurricane Hunters team fly in with a flight plan that would keep them away from the cloud seeding FA-18s. Even as flight paths unexpectedly crossed, threatening security, the recon revealed a low pressure trough in the lower left quadrant. While others like the NHC needed computers, Dr. Mclaurin could do the complex spatial math in his head. He knew at once that Meg would stall and her internal flow would merge with the Southerlies. Mclaurin lost control of her. But in the process he had created a superhurricane, another theory he pioneered, one that was dismissed as utterly fantastical. He'd proved those doubting bastards wrong again.

Dr. Mclaurin entered his office. A bank of smaller monitors and computer alerts allowed him to keep tabs on Meg from here. It was going to tricky. Stalling Meg was not the problem. Steering her into the Greenland current could be. The south flowing Greenland current was a much weaker system than the northbound Southerlies. Once he accomplished the switch, he did not doubt his ability to carry her south to Cuba. Her strength would so catastrophic, he doubted a Special Ops mop up would even be necessary. There would be nothing left. The entire island would look like Hiroshima did at the epicenter of the atom bomb. He'd be surprised if the entire Cuban population numbered more than few thousand.

"Hmm," he chuckled proudly.

Vietnam was a cute little rainmaking program by comparison. Thunder Strike was human control over hurricanes, a goal that had so captivated him as a boy and lured him into a stormy love affair with meteorology. Finally, now, he was the unquestioned master in a field of study he had pioneered. It had been a difficult road. He'd endured unjust scorn, but he'd never complained, taking the limelight and obscurity in stride.

He'd always looked upon himself as martyr.

They'd have to kill him before he'd abort Thunder Strike.

———

Peter was on a CIA Learjet flying back to Langley from Miami. They reached cruising altitude. Hoping to catch some sleep on the flight back, he stretched out the leg rest, flattened his seat out into a bed, and closed his eyes, recalling how he'd reacted to hearing about Thunder Strike for the first time.

"We have to make a hurricane disappear," Baron had said to Peter without any preface an hour after the defense secretary had presented Thunder Strike to the EXCOMM. Then, Baron had gone on to describe the military option to Peter, who was shocked that he never knew it existed.

"Okay," Peter replied, desperately trying to hide a thrill snaking around his mind and body. He always worked on the assumption that nothing was impossible, but this was more than just a challenge. History would declare the effort as the greatest covert op ever. He began with an analysis of the organization chart of the National Oceanic and Atmospheric Administration. He wanted to see if he could cherry pick who could know and how much, and who could be excluded entirely.

NOAA comprised of six agencies. The National Ocean Service did what its name indicated. Peter excluded it from all Thunder Strike discussions, as he did the National Marine Fisheries Service, which operated within two hundred miles of the American coast. The Oceanic and Atmospheric Research had labs in Boulder, Norman, Princeton, and Miami. When Dr. Mclaurin headed it, decades ago, the OAR worked with the Office of Defense Research on clandestine combat weather programs. They'd been part of Operation Popeye. In 1973, under Dr. Mclaurin, they investigated equipping US ships with 'cold cloud modification subsystem' devices to provide operational capability for manipulation of the atmospheric environment in which naval operations were conducted. The OAR also actively helped quell an insurgency in Thailand with a covert weather modification operation. After Hank blew the whistle on Popeye, the DoD launched the Defense Meteorological Program to remove civilian involvement in all weather related R&D for the military. The OAR now just worked on improving models and developing new techniques to forecast severe weather. Peter excluded the OAR.

That left the two agencies he thought he could not do without. Intricately entwined, they were also NOAA's biggest bureaucracies. One was the National Environmental Satellite, Data and Information Service, which received, broke down, and distributed satellite imagery to the other, the National Weather Service. NESDIS had one positive. Its operations were centralized in Suitland, Maryland. But the NWS was a behemoth, with nationwide Warning and Forecast Offices, River Forecast Offices, the National Data Buoy Center, National Meteorological Center, National Severe Storms Forecast Center, Tropical Prediction Center, National Center for Environmental Prediction, and National Hurricane Center, all interdependent.

Baron had been absolutely firm that no one could know Thunder Strike was a manmade storm. As Peter studied how the two agencies operated, he realized it was going to be extremely difficult to sort, select, separate, and feed the various departments on a need-to-know. He narrowed in on the NHC. It operated autonomously. So it could be contained. But the NHC relied on the TPC and NCEP for storm models, which in turn depended on NESDIS for satellite imagery that came from a Command and Data Acquisition station in Wallops, Virginia. Peter stopped counting after he reached fifty, and he'd just covered the civilian staff at the NHC, TPC, and NCEP.

Peter found himself at wits end. He looked at his watch. He'd been working for eighteen hours without a break to eat or drink or even pee. He drove home, depressed. Denial and deception was his forte, yet he was going to have to call Baron and concede that, despite DoD triggers on the satellites and in NOAAPORT to selectively shut off direct broadcast, the NWS's structure made it impossible to keep a lid on a light drizzle let alone a hurricane.

Peter lived alone in Clearview Manor, south of the CIA Headquarters. He parked his car and entered the house through the garage. The address fit his desire to maintain a low profile. The single-story, single-family home was in a tract of identical floor plans. Walking in, he placed, rather than tossed, his keys and wallet on the credenza in the hallway. Everything about the décor reflected the man. The furnishings were sparse, cold, and impersonal, purchased to be functional not decorative. He had nothing he did not need like a vase, flowers, and ornamental knick-knacks. Befitting his job as a tactician who worked in the shadows, there were no personal pictures. The walls were barren, devoid of paintings too. He was careful not have anything that could identify who he was and what he did. All utilities were maintained in the name of a dummy LLC. But every room had a clock. In the bedroom and living room, there were several, each representing a time zone, identified by a label under clear adhesive tape.

Peter opened the pantry closet. It was stacked with a variety of precooked meals, bottled water, and cans of vegetable juice. He'd never used the stove or the oven that came with the house. Selecting beef stroganoff, he punctured holes in the plastic like the instructions said and placed the carton in the microwave.

Of the two bedrooms, one served as his office. He changed, tossing his work clothes in the hamper. He always washed them after one use. Though he could afford a maid, he did the laundry and cleaning himself. He brought his work home and could not risk a stranger in the house. So he reserved Sunday mornings for domestic chores.

A meticulous creature of habit, he had the timing down. He was walking back into kitchen in his pajamas when the microwave beeped. Peter emptied the dinner onto a white porcelain plate and neatly set the table for one. Tonight, he allowed himself a glass of red wine, an indulgence he saved for the weekends. He ate alone, completely preoccupied.

He absently rinsed the plates, put them in the dishwasher, and went to bed. It was one A.M. An hour later, he snapped awake! Groggy for a moment, he realized what had brought him out of his sleep. His eyes brightened alertly. He swung out of bed, hurried into his office, and found a number off his rolodex. He did not bother checking the time. Picking up the phone, he dialed ten digits of a number clear across the country. He knew the man at the other end of the line would not mind being roused.

A gruff voice, hoarse with sleep, answered, "Hello?"

"Gary. Peter." He remembered Lt. General Gary Gueretin headed the AFWA and had provided combat climatology for the second Iraq invasion. They were also neo-con acquaintances. Without revealing the specifics of Thunder Strike, Peter outlined the challenge he faced.

"You should visit Offutt," said Gary.

Within the hour, Peter was flying to Nebraska. After a tour of the Air Force Weather Agency, Peter realized he'd been wasting his time dissecting NOAA. Gary had created a duplicate entity. Quickly, all aspects of denial and deception fell into place. It was Gary who told Peter that he'd overlooked the International Space Station, which had a bird's-eye view of the planet. The president informed the ISS's member nations what everyone outside the EXCOMM believed: Thunder Strike was an operation to keep a storm classified so that the US could mount a military campaign in the aftermath against Cuba. Nobody objected. They all wanted the communist island disarmed.

Peter ended up needing the experience and expertise of the NHC. The AFWA had never handled severe weather alone. Even Gary agreed that Thunder Strike was too important to be the first. Peter pulled the Hank's dossier and discovered the director had blown the whistle on Operation Popeye. So, Peter scripted Baron's briefing when the defense secretary first approached Hank.

"Sir," a woman's voice intruded, "your phone is ringing."

Peter blinked his eyes open, feeling a gentle, persistent shake. He'd fallen dead asleep. The stewardess was kneeling by his seat. Peter became aware of the soft purring from the seat-side handset. A CIA agent herself, she knew better than to answer it.

"Oh, thanks," said Peter. She walked away quickly. He picked it up.

It was Baron. He brought Peter up to speed about the plane crash in DC.

Five minutes after the Dulles Air Traffic Controller alerted the Counter Terrorism Unit about an unidentified, fast moving plane in DC air space, two F-16 Fighting Falcons scrambled into the air from nearby Andrews AFB. Six minutes later, they did their first flyby and called it in. The phone at the Homeland Security Secretary's bedside rang four minutes later. Twenty-seven minutes after the crash, Baron and the president found out almost simultaneously that a plane had crashed on the Beltway. Since Avery had raised the Threat Level to Red last night, law enforcement and anti-terrorism agencies were already on high alert. Forty minutes later, the first responders identified the plane as "one of our own." They sent out its serial number and reported that there were no bodies. It would be another thirty minutes before the driver of the eighteen-wheeler and other eyewitnesses confirmed they saw the two pilots eject. That report arrived the same time as the Hornet's serial number returned an ID.

It belonged to the air fleet aboard *William J. Clinton.*

Baron said the next call had been to Peter, waking him on the Learjet.

Peter immediately contacted the intelligence officer on the *William J. Clinton*, then spoke with Gary, who conferenced in Pfifer and Schultz, their spies on Hurricane Hunter team. Eleven minutes after Baron's call, Peter called the defense secretary back with an accurate recreation of events leading up to the Hornet's crash landing.

"Are you sure?" asked Baron.

"Yes, sir," replied Peter. "Grant personally authorized auxiliary fuel tanks on the Hornet."

———

Baron was still at the Hawke estate in Virginia. His wife had walked in on him transfixed to the TV coverage of the crash. He did not have to tell her a crisis was upon them. She knew the drill. She would instruct the staff that they were not to disturb him. She would carry the breakfast tray herself into the library, which became his private sanctuary until he left for Washington. There were Confederate touches all over the décor. Management to menial, if the estate's all white staff wasn't hint enough about where Baron's social conscience lay, one piece of art left no doubt how he really felt. It was a tabletop brass plaque, inscribed, "If I knew then what I know now, I'd have picked my own damn cotton."

Baron sat down pensively. They had been so preoccupied that Hank Rotas at the NHC was the loose cannon, they did not consider Admiral Grant would blindside them and jeopardize

Thunder Strike. Baron believed Grant would not do anything to hurt his friend, the president. Baron realized he must brief the president carefully. Avery should feel betrayed in a way that ended Grant's influence. With the admiral out of the picture, it would dash the Ulysses's hopes of infiltrating the dark shadows for the rest of this Presidency, and if Avery ran again, four more years.

"I wouldn't tell the president anything," said Peter, almost as if he was reading the defense secretary's thoughts. It was not the first time Baron had noticed Peter's uncanny ability to be a step ahead. "Not yet, at least."

"Why not?" Baron could usurp the personal friendship that he enviously watched Grant enjoy with the president.

"We may need the admiral." Baron heard the phone ring on Peter's end. "Do you have to take that?"

"Yes, sir. This could be more information."

"Go ahead." Peter put Baron on hold. While he waited, Baron deduced why Peter did not want to implicate Grant. Securing Thunder Strike was paramount. As long as Grant was unaware that they were onto him, he could provide vital leads to the weather girl and the two pilots.

Admiral Grant had to be the last to die.

Peter came back on the line. He said, "Sam contacted Diane."

———

Meg's strength astonished Diane. Sam and Gene showed her the weather report Admiral Grant had given them. Meg was moving northwest. She'd gone beyond Category 5, already stronger than any Atlantic hurricane in history. Diane had also read Dr. Mclaurin's plans for Meg.

"It's dicey what he's trying to do," said Diane. Even with the latest high resolution soundings from satellites and more advanced man-computer interactive data analysis systems, accuracy in numerical forecasting was restricted to tropical and subtropical regions. At mid-latitudes, models relied on quantitative data, making predictions suspect.

"But you are applying natural laws on a manmade storm," said Gene Fellow, wolfing down his breakfast like a hungry dog.

They'd stopped off at a tiny coffee shop. Sam ordered a three-egg Denver omelet with all the fixings. Diane did not want to stuff herself, going with a short stack of butternut pancakes. Gene got toast, two scrambled eggs, and corned beef hash. They all ordered coffee and gulped down the first cup like it was water.

Diane had briefly perused the hefty Jayspid, awestruck. It laid out the historical, conceptual, experimental, and operational phases of Thunder Strike. The Jayspid was a smoking gun. Any document that detailed the most audacious weather modification program would be. No wonder Vick had been murdered. He'd died just this morning, yet it seemed so long ago.

"A hurricane has never done what he's planning in the recorded history of this planet," said Diane.

"Dr. Mclaurin lives and breathes weather," said Gene. "Man's a frikkin' genius. I was part of the seeding when he made Orlene and Paine do what no hurricane had done in recorded history."

"Those were Category 4s," said Diane, soaking her last pancake with maple syrup. "This is going to be a superhurricane, if she isn't already. It's the difference between stopping a bike and turning around a runaway train."

"Say he pulls it off," said Sam, his mouth full. "Meg will head south. Then DC is out of the woods, right?"

"Sure," said Diane. "But the turnaround is going to happen eight hundred miles offshore about ten tonight. That's past prime time on TV. Working folks'd have gone to bed. So timing is critical. That's the dilemma here. If he fails, Meg will make landfall around four A.M. tomorrow."

"It's a Catch-22," said Sam. "It'll be over-warning before

she starts moving and too late if you wait and see."

"Out here, I'd go with over-warning."

DC was unfamiliar with hurricanes. Usually landfall targets had a week to prepare. People stayed tuned to their radio and TV for updates as the National Hurricane Center escalated awareness and narrowed where a storm would come ashore. In 1989, during Hurricane Hugo, some people evacuated target areas before the first formal advisory. Throughout the storm's life span, the local Warning and Forecast Office effected a gradual stepwise increase in perceived threat. More recently, advance warning enabled south Florida to escape Hurricane Andrew with minimum fatalities. With Katrina, New Orleans had adequate warning. Most people left. But nobody anticipated the levees would break. With Sandy, casualties would have been in the thousands had mandatory evacuation not been implemented.

"If it were up to me," continued Diane, "I'd order evacuations regardless of whether Meg makes landfall or not."

"That's what Admiral Grant figured," said Sam. "Down in Florida, we have it down to a science. What about here?"

Diane's train of thought suddenly shifted. Everyone at the table had lost their parents to tragic events that could have been prevented. "We don't. Not even on paper. Exit routes here are not equipped to handle an exodus from the Metropolitan area in eight hours."

Tropical storm warnings followed a three step process. Step one, the NHC determined if a threat existed, then contacted the local WFO, and authorized warnings. Step two, the Meteorologist-in-Chief at the local WFO contacted the local Emergency Operations Office, which in turn advised local and state officials. Step three, the media got involved, broadcasting warnings to the public. Since the NHC continued to deny Meg's existence, Diane had to jump to step two.

"We have to start with my boss, James Vaughn."

"Will he believe you?" asked Gene.

"Don't you think he's in the loop?" asked Diane.

"No," said Sam. "Admiral Grant said nobody is, except the AFWA and NHC."

"Any warning has to begin with him." Under normal circumstances, the NHC activated NAWAS—the National Warning System hotline. All Emergency Management Offices were directly tapped into it. Diane would then issue a variety of evacuation orders, from mandatory to voluntary. She set her cell to speaker phone so that the guys could hear and dialed.

After a couple of rings, James answered. "James, this is Diane."

"Hi, Diane," said James. "What's up?" His tone suggested he was alone and halfway into another routine morning.

Diane told him about Meg.

"Are you serious?" he reacted. Diane believed the sincerity of his surprise. Being from Oklahoma, where a forecast for thunderstorms brought out a tornado instead, James grew up measuring advance warning in terms of lives and damage. She told him about Sam, Gene, the plane crash on the Beltway, and Thunder Strike. It led to a long silence.

James asked, "Is that why Vick died?"

"Yes."

"Don't speak to anyone. Come straight here. I'll call the NHC."

"No," said Sam. "Don't call anyone. Not until we are there with you."

"I understand."

"Thanks," said Diane. "We should be there in thirty."

———

Peter smiled. He'd guessed right when he patched into the National Security Agency's surveillance mainframe and waited patiently for Diane to use her cell phone. He heard every word of her conversation with her boss.

The aft section of the CIA Learjet was an electronics marvel—a fully equipped audio-visual command center. Peter had been trained to operate the complex gear. Several such planes had been first retooled for covert ops during the war on terror in Afghanistan and Iraq. These flying command centers proved so successful, the Agency made this standard equipment in every new aircraft they added. Peter's Learjet was the newest. So, all the electronic goodies were the latest incarnations. Peter had informed the stewardess not to enter unannounced and strapped himself into the bolted down seat which swiveled three hundred and sixty degrees.

His elation quickly passed when he had a moment to reflect. The two pilots, then Diane, and now the Chief Meteorological Officer at the Silver Springs WFO—the number of people who knew real truth about Thunder Strike was increasing. He needed to contain the circle from widening further.

He called the Agency. "Send a cleanup team to the WFO in Silver Springs."

————

James sat in thought, wringing his hands. Diane's bombshell did not come as a complete surprise He'd had a nagging suspicion that there was more when Vick's computer break-in of a routine Atlantic download prompted that first call from the DoD. One ghost from the past did startle him—Dr. Mclaurin.

When Diane mentioned the name, he instantly flashed back to the one time he'd heard the scientist speak at a conference over fifteen years ago. Like everyone there, he came away absolutely awed by the man. Despite his checkered past and reputation as the Josef Mangele of meteorology, Dr. Mclaurin's work was pioneering—the stuff of meteorological lore. Over the years, James had also heard whispers and rumors at seminars and retreats of DoD funded weather making projects. When Diane connected the two, James instantly remembered Operation Popeye. Every meteorologist from the 1970s knew about it. It was almost like 'required knowledge.'

What Dr. Mclaurin had done was groundbreaking. It was only logical Pentagon would have continued the research. So, James did not disbelieve Diane.

If Dr. Mclaurin was involved, Thunder Strike was real.

James's stomach tightened. Vick had been murdered to keep the storm a secret. Meaning, Diane, the pilots, and he could be on the hit list too. *If I sit tight and do nothing, nobody'll realize I know anything.* Ten minutes later, a knock sounded on the door. He looked up, expecting Ivory, who was scheduled to take Diane's shift.

Instead, two men in suits, carrying silenced guns, entered.

They did not introduce themselves. They wore barely visible earpieces, which James recognized, thanks to his kids, as the newest Bluetooth device. The older suit uttered only the three words to James, "Keep your routine."

Then the two men took up positions on either side of his window. James pretended to work. Twenty-five minutes later, the two men straightened. So did James. Subtly. The older suit nodded, "I see them."

He clicked off, pulled out his cell, and speed dialed.

James craned his neck. He recognized Diane's car drive into the parking lot of the WFO. She parked in her usual space. Diane climbed out first, slinging her purse over her shoulder and elbowing the door shut. Two men in military brown jumpsuits covered with patches and insignias—the Hurricane Hunters—straightened out of the passenger side.

"They are out of the car, sir" the older suit reported to the number he'd just dialed. He lowered his head, listening to his next order. He nodded, disconnected, raised his eyes, and stunned James by barking, "Take them out."

———

Diane waited for Sam and Gene to flank her before starting across the parking lot.

"Diane!" A staccato shout.

Diane glanced over sharply.

Ivory appeared above his car a few spots away. He waved, "Wait!"

Then, in the matter of a second, all hell broke loose.

Two men emerged from the WFO on the run. Two more leapt out of a van parked at the far end of the lot. These four men, dressed in suits and ties, awakened the conspiracy freak in Diane. Alarm bells went off. She saw their hands appear. They carried guns. *Shit.*

"Back into the car," Sam said in a low voice.

"Stop!" shouted the older suit, seeing them retreat.

Diane never locked her car when she parked here. This innocuous habit earned them precious seconds. Sam, Gene, and she each grabbed open a door and dove in simultaneously.

Schik!Schik! Two harsh eruptions of gravel!

"Bullets!" yelled Sam.

Diane slammed the door, heard Sam and Gene do the same. She jammed the key into the ignition. Turned it. The engine fired. She looked up into the rear view and glimpsed the suits sprinting. She reversed directly toward them, forcing them to leap out of the way.

Bam!Bam! A couple of sharp metallic hammer blows. Close! She snapped her neck, thinking the suits were pounding on her truck.

"They're shooting, go, go, go!" barked Sam.

Diane thrust the car into Drive before it stopped completely. Stomped on the gas pedal and wildly slewed out of there. She looked into the mirror on her side and saw James race outside. He gestured angrily. She couldn't see Ivory.

"They were waiting for us," said Sam.

"Your boss sold you out," said Gene.

"No, it's the other guy, Ivory Adams," said Diane breathlessly, her mind working in overdrive. Ivory had climbed out of his car. So, he must have been waiting to identify her for the suits. Diane told Sam and Gene about Ivory, an ex-marine who used to work for the AFWA, how he'd showed up at the

WFO unannounced last night, and hours later Vick had been killed.

"You spoke to your boss, not Ivory," observed Sam.

"Did you tell anyone about Sam and I?" Gene asked in an accusing voice.

"No," said Diane defensively. She got on the westbound Suitland Parkway and weaved between lanes, constantly checking her rearview mirror. Nobody followed them. "I left right after you called me on my cell—shit!" She whipped her head toward Sam. "You think they have my phone bugged?"

Gene answered, "They probably wiretapped your whole frikkin' office when you and Vick hacked in."

———

In the CIA Learjet, still an hour out of DC, Peter did not lose his cool when his cleanup crew reported that Diane, Sam, and Gene got away. Following 9/11, one of the many hidden amendments in the Patriot Act allowed the CIA to issue an All-Points-Bulletin directly over DC police frequencies. Peter sent out a description of Diane's white Toyota Camry.

He heard a DCPD helicopter, on routine patrol in the area, pick up the APB and report he was over the Suitland Parkway. Peter called up the police dispatcher, presented a security code that allowed him to talk directly to the pilot—another post-9/11 amendment to dissolve enforcement jurisdictions. Peter linked into the images of the chopper's underbelly cameras and realized at once that the white sedan would be hard—impossible—to distinguish from the sky on the busy freeway.

———

The DCPD helicopter passed right over the trio. Sam reacted, "They know this car. We have to dump it."

"I'm still making payments," Diane protested. The Toyota Camry was barely a year old.

"Not if you're dead," growled Gene.

"Okay," said Sam, "let's park it somewhere then."

They passed the Washington National and Lincoln

Memorial Cemeteries. Diane changed lanes.

"Good thinking," Peter complimented the young copilot of the DCPD helicopter, who suggested using the prevailing speed on the Suitland Parkway, the suspects' approximate time of departure from the WFO, and calculate the EDT—Estimated Distance of Travel.

The helicopter's onboard computer was linked to DCTC—District of Columbia Traffic Central—an underground, futuristic looking, electronic hub downtown. Here, sensors embedded in the concrete and asphalt of the freeways and main arteries reported back with green, yellow, and red lights on a giant street map of the capital. Green represented smooth traffic flow and maximum speed, red the slowest. They received the EDT computation almost instantly.

"We have to turn back," said the copilot, reporting they were well beyond the envelope.

"Do it," said Peter, then listened peripherally to the police chatter while he ordered in two more cleanup units from the Agency onto the surface streets within the EDT envelope.

———

"That chopper is turning around," Gene said urgently, looking over his shoulder.

"Let's get off," said Sam.

Diane pulled into the right lane.

"Shit," Sam suddenly realized, "Hurry. Separating from the freeway traffic will make us stick out. We need to get down that ramp fast!"

Diane floored the gas pedal, glancing up into the rear view mirror. The DCPD copter was halfway into the turn.

———

The pilots' eyes swung forward a heartbeat after the car disappeared down the steep slope of the exit ramp. The DCPD copter accelerated. Peter's voice came over the speakers, "Spot 'em?"

The pilot replied with casual confidence, "Matter of time, Chief."

———

Diane heard the chopper approach. They were the only vehicle on the ramp. She exclaimed, "They are going to see us!"

Sam snapped, "Under the tree!"

At the bottom, where the ramp let out into the street, stood an oak. The rotors got real loud real quick. The helicopter was upon them! Diane pulled up under the branches. *Did we make it in time?* Even if they did, was the foliage wide enough and dense enough to shield them?

Diane, Sam, and Gene held their breath. The DCPD chopper flew right past them. Diane joined the guys in letting out a huge sigh of relief. She quickly merged into the street traffic.

———

9/11 had also triggered the installation of cameras into traffic lights at all strategic nodes through out the capital. DCTC hooked up Peter to live images from the surveillance platforms within the EDT envelope. He spotted the Toyota as it crossed from Maryland into DC, where Branch met Southern Avenue. But there wasn't a squad car in the area.

Peter smiled coldly. It allowed his two mobile cleanup units free reign.

———

Diane turned onto Erie Street. An unmarked Ford raced up alongside and slowed abruptly. Sam shoved her head, yelling, "Down!"

Her forehead cracked into the bottom half of the steering wheel. A microsecond later—*boom!* A shotgun blasted her eardrums. The window on her side shattered. A million shards of glass showered down. *Boom!* A second deafening blast. This one took out the rear windshield. More glass rain.

"There's a second car behind us!" yelled Gene.

"Floor it!" said Sam.

Her head still in her lap, Diane hit the gas pedal. The car surged! Diane, Sam, and Gene surfaced. They pulled ahead of their pursuers, who had slowed down, figuring them for dead, or at least wounded. Diane checked her mirror. The other car was a Ford too. They gained on her Toyota, running side by side, hogging both lanes behind her.

"Damnit!" she muttered. She was up against traffic.

"Onto the sidewalk," ordered Sam.

Diane cranked the wheel. The car climbed the curb with a nasty jolt that rattled their teeth. Their pursuers copied her move, falling one behind the other. A Delivery Guy exited the office building ahead, pushing a dolly loaded with packages. Diane was traveling too fast to react. She jammed the horn. Delivery Guy abandoned the dolly and threw himself out of the way.

The edge of Diane's fender smashed the dolly!

The packages flew into the air and came down on the windshield of the Ford immediately behind her. They contained something solid and weighty because the impact carried a huge cracking sound and spider-webbed the glass into an opaque sheet. Blinding the assailants. Slowing the pursuit.

Diane seized on it. Veered into two vacant car lengths in the right lane.

Boom! Another shotgun blast!

Diane and the guys ducked instinctively, but it wasn't meant for them. Diane surfaced. The driver in the lead Ford blew out his windshield to see. The volley had an immediate effect on the traffic. Cars screamed to a halt. The Fords got off the sidewalk and got behind Diane. But she didn't give the gunmen a clean shot, wriggling recklessly between lanes.

"You got mad driving skills, girl," grinned Sam.

Diane had no idea where she was getting them. Traffic lights loomed ahead. She sailed cleanly past the intersection just ahead of the cross-traffic. Their pursuers weren't so tidy. The second Ford smashed a frantically braking car out of the way. It set off a series of collisions that carried all the way to Diane, Sam, and Gene.

"Chopper!" warned Gene.

The DCPD helicopter swung over them, low.

"I watch police pursuits on TV all the time," said Diane. "Never in a million years did I imagine myself to be in one."

"And the bad guys never get away," said Gene gloomily

"Doesn't apply," quipped Sam. "We're not the bad guys."

"Yeah," Gene retorted with angry sarcasm, "make jokes."

Diane zigzagged at breakneck speed. The Fords stayed on their tail. She looked at the speedometer. She was doing eighty. Erie had a posted speed limit of thirty-five. The Toyota approached 30th Street, which emptied of cross traffic because the light was about to turn red and go green on Erie. Diane bulleted across before the change.

"Watch out!" shouted Sam, recoiling reflexively.

A VW Jetta on 30th, trying nip across on yellow, accelerated into the intersection. The driver slammed on the brakes and wrenched the wheel! To escape being T-boned, Diane whipped left. The Toyota skidded around ninety degrees onto 30th St, her tires tattooing the road with four black streaks. The Jetta did a ninety too, missing the Toyota by an inch, no more! The driver's eyes bloated in terror! Diane realized why. He'd turned head-on toward the lead pursuer.

Whabam! An earsplitting collision.

"Oh, fuck," exclaimed the DCPD copter pilot.

The copilot and he took their eyes off the Toyota to watch the Jetta spin around one-eighty. The lead Ford shot into the air, rolled over, and in a freak piece of timing, descended upside down squarely on the second Ford that swerved and seemingly escaped the accident. The roofs of the two cars kissed explosively. The window stems on both cars snapped! Crushed the occupants. Glass sprayed, laced with human and auto fragments.

The ground pursuit was over.

When the pilot looked ahead, the Toyota had vanished. "Crap."

———

Diane turned left onto Naylor, then made an immediate right into a narrow, nameless alley. Rotors advanced.

"Under there," pointed Sam to an awning behind a warehouse.

Diane was going too fast. She jumped on the brakes, overshot the awning! The chopper came hard and fast. She punched the car into Reverse. The chopper's rotors reverberated, almost on top of them! She pulled in beneath it. Once again, they held their breath, not knowing if they'd escaped unseen or not. The helicopter swooped across and away.

Diane breathed again.

They abandoned the car there and fled south on foot. The chopper crisscrossed over them. Every time it got close, they ducked into a doorway or sprinted under an overhang.

———

"Afraid we lost 'em, Chief," the pilot reported.

His cavalier tone made Peter clench his teeth. If these two idiots only knew the enormity of the stakes. Peter pulled up a hybrid map of DC—a satellite picture of the capital overlaid with the names and notations of a street map.

He knew at once where Diane was headed.

———

"There it is." She pointed to the Naylor Road Metro Station across the road.

The Green Line to DC had just pulled in. Passengers unloaded. Others hurried across the parking lot to catch it.

"Let's go," said Diane. They quickly joined the criss-crossing human traffic of arriving and leaving commuters. Some glanced over curiously at the airmen in uniform.

———

Peter told the police dispatch again he was going direct

to the   ground units. He punched up a call sign that appeared in all the squad car computers as a blinking all-caps notation, 'HRHP!' High Risk High Priority, a classification of emergency reserved for Homeland Security, the FBI, and CIA. He called for a 'rushed action' to the Naylor Road Station. Peter got an immediate response from one unit, which reported being less than a minute away from the location.

Peter then ordered the DCPD copter to focus on the station.

———

Diane pointed. Sam and Gene snapped their head around. The copter was turning sharply back around. But they were already safely under the platform roof. Out of the pilots' line of sight. A bell chimed once as a prelude to the soothing, recorded voice that announced, "Departure in one minute."

"Let's go," said Diane and started forward. Gene hugged close.

"No, wait," said Sam, grabbing them back. "We could be trapped on the train. Staying out in the open on the platform offers more avenues of escape." Barely did the last word leave his lips when sirens screamed. "See?"

Diane peered around the corner. A police car peeled in. Two cops spilled out and hurried through the thick crowd on the platform. Combing faces. Diane looked away. Sam and Gene dropped to the ground and out of sight, pretending to tie their laces. Her dry mouth contrasted sharply with the rest of her body, where her sweat glands had opened the floodgates. The cops passed them, hopped into the last car, and hastened down center aisle, back to front, looking left and right.

Chime. Announcement. "Departure in fifteen seconds."

Diane watched the cops reach the first car. Sam had a hand each on her and Gene, holding them back. They waited for his signal. He whispered, "Now!"

The cops stepped off the train. Two cars behind them, the trio snuck onboard. Timing the crossover perfectly.

Diane peered carefully between the crush of standing passengers. The cops stood on the platform. One of them unhooked his radio. Clicked it on and shook his head from side to side as he filed a negative report.

Chime. Announcement. "The Green Line is ready for departure."

The doors slid shut. Brakes released with a squeal. Wheels grated on the rails. The Green Line moved forward. Gathered speed. Diane found the courage to peer out. The cops on the platform receded.

———

Peter was convinced Diane, Sam, and Gene were on the train. He ordered police units to the stations ahead. It was only a three-minute ride to the next stop at Southern Avenue, too short for a unit to respond, he was told. Peter dialed into the Station cameras—they did not disembark. Congress Heights was a six-minute train commute from Naylor Road. He brought up the platform surveillance.

"Goddamnit!" the exclamation escaped aloud in a rare display of frustration. He saw only TV snow. There was no time to reach the station manager and he could not risk the possibility that Diane, Sam, and Gene would stay on the train indefinitely.

Two units reported they could be at Congress Heights in ninety seconds.

Same as the train.

———

Diane, Sam, and Gene disembarked. No cops. She checked her watch. It was eleven thirty A.M. Less than fifteen hours to landfall if Meg broke through Dr. Mclaurin's High Pressure Ridge.

Time was ticking away.

They hurried out of the parking lot. Crossed the street. Just as they stepped onto the curb on the other side, sirens screamed around the corner. The trio darted into a store a microsecond before two squad cars hurtled into the station.

––––––––

Peter only half listened as the cops swarmed onto the train at Anacostia, the next station. He knew they'd turn up empty. Past the anger of losing them yet again, he clasped his hands behind his head and rocked back and forth in the chair.

What will Diane do next?

FOURTEEN

"A secret hurricane?" Elliot Brand, the articulate, fifty-three-year old, African-American public servant laughed. "That's a good one, Diane. This is DC. You can't even have a private thought."

Elliot had looked surprised when he saw her enter. Diane had shown up without an appointment with Sam and Gene. They had walked from Congress Heights Station to 2720 Martin Luther King Jr. Avenue, where they entered a contemporary building with a predominantly glass façade and a half-arch for a roof—headquarters of the Homeland Security and Emergency Management Agency. Elliot was its director.

"Diane!" he'd greeted her genially.

They knew each other fairly well, but on a purely professional level. Whenever severe weather, usually heat waves and excessive snowfall, threatened the city, they spoke on the phone several times a day. They also ran into each other at NOAA seminars and Emergency Management Committee meetings.

"Hi, Elliot," Diane had greeted back and introduced Sam and Gene.

Elliot's brow had furrowed with instant curiousity, reading the airmen's patches that identified Sam as a Hurricane Hunter and Gene as a Fighting Redcock. After the obligatory round robin of handshakes, Elliot had asked lightly, "What brings you here?"

"A hurricane," said Diane. He looked at her incredulously

"There isn't even rain in the forecast." He pointed to the bulletin neatly pinned on the board behind him. Diane noticed Ivory Adams had issued it. The HSEMA received reports over NOAAPORT every six hours. Elliot thought she was joking. Diane bugged him all the time about the shortcomings of DC's severe wet weather response.

"I know." She told him about Hurricane Meg and that

the DoD had classified her, which had elicited the repartee that DC was no place for secrets.

Neither Diane, Sam nor Gene smiled. She nodded and Sam outlined Thunder Strike. He pulled the Jayspid out of Diane's backpack and showed it to him. "This is called a Joint Strategic Planning Document and details it." Elliot flipped through it. "Only three copies exist. One with the president. One in the Pentagon. And this one is from the *William J. Clinton,* the operational headquarters for Thunder Strike."

When Diane added they were the pilots of the Hornet that had crashed on the Beltway this morning, all jocularity left Elliot's face. He looked at Diane. "Does James know?"

"Yes." Diane told him what happened to Vick in the wee hours this morning and to them when they showed up at the WFO.

"What about Ivory?" asked Elliot.

"I think he is on it. He's originally from the AFWA, who, by the way, are the only agency outside of the NHC handling Meg. NMC, NESDIS, they are all out of the loop."

Elliot looked at them helplessly, "Look. James or Ivory must advise this office, before I can call an EMC meeting." He translated for Sam and Gene. "Emergency Management Committee."

"That's not going to happen," said Diane bluntly.

Elliot rubbed his forehead, at a loss. "Maybe there is no threat. Like you said, we won't know if there is or not till tonight when she moves again."

"If Meg breaks through," said Diane, "there's not enough time for people on the Delmarva Peninsula, who'd be in her outer spirals by midnight."

"That fast?"

Diane nodded. "In mid and upper latitudes, the winds blow harder, speeding up storms moving north." On September, 21, 1938, one such fast moving hurricane was reported a hundred miles east of Cape Hatteras, North Carolina. Six hours and three hundred and fifty miles later, she crossed Long Island, New York. By eight that night, she passed Burlington, Vermont. The storm, at times, reached forward speeds close to seventy miles an hour. "Once Meg starts moving, she's going to come hard and she's going to come fast."

"The two HPRs facing off each other could meet up in front and stop her," Elliot argued.

Diane shook her head. "They haven't moved in weeks."

"Still. All the way up to DC? How do you know she won't deteriorate?"

"She'll be a superhurricane—"

"I don't even know what that is. How do you propose I convince the Mayor and all the other department heads from Virginia and Maryland?" They included Police, Fire and Emergency Medical Services, Health, and other District and federal agencies, as well as utility companies and the Red Cross and the Salvation Army.

"There are theories—-"

"Theories?" Elliot shook his head. "Theories won't fly, Diane. Not if you're talking about evacuating the capital of the United States. I need something more substantial. Solid. Someone who can prove Meg exists. First hand."

"What's wrong with us? I flew a recon mission into her yesterday," said Sam. "And Gene was part of the seeding missions."

"Not just Meg," added Gene. "I've been part of the prototypes. Orlene and Paine."

"Still," said Elliot firmly, "I have to convince a whole lot of bureaucrats there is a five-hundred mile hurricane we cannot see and she's threatening to do what no hurricane has ever done."

A despondent silence descended over the table.

Sam spoke up suddenly. "Okay. You got it." Diane and Gene looked at him puzzled. Sam asked, "Can you listen in on ham radio frequency?"

"We have a radio at the Emergency Operations Center," said Elliot. The EOC was located in the basement level of Ronald Reagan Building at Pennsylvania and 13th Street, just east of the White House. It became a nerve center during manmade and natural disasters and emergencies in DC.

"Can you get whoever needs to be there at, uh," Sam looked at his watch again, "say, at five o'clock sharp?"

Elliot nodded. "Who'll be on the radio and what will we be hearing?"

————

The CIA Learjet landed at Andrews AFB. Peter, who always traveled light, wheeled a single suitcase across the tarmac. He'd parked his car in the covered garage here. A private brought it around and helped Peter load his one piece of luggage in the trunk. Peter barely pulled out of the gates, when his cell phone rang.

"Peter." It was Baron. Peter knew another crisis brewed. Baron never wasted a phone call. "Diane and the pilots visited HSEMA. Told Director Brand everything."

Elliot had called his boss, the Homeland Security Secretary, who promised to find out more and call back, telling Elliot to hold off organizing any EMC meeting at five. The HSS—who was part of the EXCOMM—had called Baron in a panic.

"Hmm," said Peter, thought for a moment, and outlined the course of action. "Ask the HSS to congratulate Director Brand for being conscientious, then say calls to you and others in the Cabinet revealed nothing exists with the name Thunder Strike."

"You think Brand will buy it?" asked Baron.

"I doubt it. The HSS should tell Brand to go ahead and call the emergency meeting at five since this falls under Homeland Security and they should cover their asses, just in case. The Secretary should attend."

"What will happen at five?" asked Baron.

"Nothing."

———

The heat and humidity bore down upon the Avian Atoll like an oppressive force. Quince woke up and showered. When he walked into the mess hall Ranger and Knoll were already there. A few minutes later, Pfifer and Schultz showed up with orders for the next AWR.

"We take off in an hour and head to Miami from Meg," said Pfifer.

"What about Sam?" asked Quince.

Their leader still hadn't returned. Ranger, Knoll and he had discussed Sam's abrupt departure and couldn't figure out why he was flown out, where he was, or what the hell was going on.

Pfifer shrugged. "We leave without him."

"We need a second pilot."

"I can fill in," replied Pfifer. "I used to fly C-130s. Military cargo."

Knoll shook his head and stood up. "No. I need clearance from Keesler."

"Colonel Tucker?" asked Pfifer.

Knoll stopped. "You know him?"

Pfifer held out his cell with a text. Knoll read it. Ranger asked, "What does it say?"

"We leave without Sam." Knoll handed Ranger the teletype.

"This is whack." Ranger passed it onto Quince, who read it quizzically.

A private approached. The Hurricane Hunters recognized him. Quince said, "Hey, wassup?"

"Sam's on the phone. He wants to talk to you."

The Hurricane Hunters got up as one. Pfifer and Schultz started to rise. Quince stopped them. "No offense, guys. Family only."

The two men sat back down. The Hunters hurried off together. Quince looked back just before he passed through the door. Pfifer and Schultz were walking away in the opposite direction. *Or hurrying away?* They looked over their shoulder. Saw Quince staring them down. .

"I smell something shitty," Quince said when he caught up with Ranger and Knoll.

The private left them alone in the office. Quince turned on the speaker phone. "Sammy? Quince. Ranger and Knoll are with me."

"Where are you?" asked Ranger.

"We are scheduled to take off in an hour," said Knoll.

"I'm, uh, I'm in DC," said Sam. "On the bus."

———

"What?" Quince exclaimed so loudly, the line crackled.

Upon leaving HSEMA office, Diane saw a bus pull up across the street. It was headed downtown and they took it. "It'll put us where we need to go next," she said, "and you two can also shop for clothes."

"Did you go AWOL on us?" asked Ranger. "Man, should we even be talking to you?"

"Listen," said Sam. "Hear me out."

"Is there something shitty going on?" interrupted Quince.

"Let him talk!" snapped Knoll.

"What's got your briefs in a bind?" Quince reacted.

"What's going on, Sam?" asked Knoll.

Sam had known Knoll the longest. They were friends outside of work too. "You can vouch for me, Knoll. Yeah, I fool around but I'm as responsible as they come. My conduct evaluation points are in the top percentile."

"Okay," said Quince. "You're a good guy. Great pilot. We know that. Fine. Just cut to the chase."

Sam looked around the bus. The bus was pretty empty. He lowered his voice nonetheless. "Meg is classified."

"What do you mean?" asked Ranger

"Officially, she does not exist. That's the shitty smell, Quincy."

"Get outta here," reacted Quince, chuckling in disbelief.

"I'm serious. God's truth. It's not on any weather map being distributed around here." Sam gave them a quick thumbnail of Thunder Strike.

"Wo, that's actually quite awesome!" said Ranger.

"Yeah," agreed Quince. "So what's the problem?"

Sam explained why he'd been flown to the *William J. Clinton.* Admiral Grant worried that if Meg got away from its makers, the DoD was unscrupulous enough to continue to hide it. So, Grant wanted him to go to DC and raise a warning. He told them about Diane.

"Isn't that a nice bonus," said Quince, "hooking up with your girl friend?"

"Divine coincidence," admitted Sam. He believed in God and destiny and this only convinced him that intelligent design was more than just Adam and Eve. Earlier, when he'd mentioned this to Diane, she just laughed. She was an agnostic.

"So what do you want us to do?" asked Knoll. If Sam called, there had to be a reason.

"Before you answer that, what's in it for us?" asked Quince.

"You'll be heroes."

There was a long silence. Sam could picture Quince and Ranger looking at each other and he pretty much knew who'd take the bait. Quince said, "We could go for that."

"Radio me Meg's coordinates and strength from the eye at exactly five o'clock eastern time."

"That's it? That'll make us heroes?" asked Ranger.

"If Meg comes ashore."

"I knew there was a catch," grumbled Quince.

Sam laughed and hung up. He grinned over to Diane and Gene. "They're gonna do it."

———

Diane led them off the bus at the stop on 13th and F Streets. Sam and Gene were not fastidious shoppers. Gene got himself khaki pants and a white shirt. Sam bought a pair of Relaxed-Fit jeans and a T-shirt. Diane then took them to a stretch of Hispanic-owned businesses. Low priced stereos, clothes, shoes, everything. She fluently talked to a street vendor, who pointed to an electronics store down the street.

"I didn't know you spoke Spanish," said Sam.

"How could you," said Diane, "We've known each other, for what, couple of days?"

"But I feel like I've known you all my life."

"Oh, God," groaned Gene. "That's so daytime soap."

Diane nodded. "Worse."

"Well," sniffed Sam. "I thought it was quite sweet."

"If there's more like that from you," said Gene, "I'm begging the next guy who wants to kill us to take me out first."

"Good," said Sam. "Diane, we have a human shield."

They went into the store and emerged five minutes later and fifty bucks lighter. Diane picked up what she needed.

A burner phone.

"I don't know if and when we are going to get to eat again," she said. "Stuff up." They decided to splurge and went into CrustAsian, a fancy Pan-Pacific Bistro. While they waited for their order, Gene asked, "Where are we going from here?"

"Onto step three."

"Which is?"

"Warning the public."

To do so in a manner that would not cause panic, the NHC had removed competition with an electronic media pool. All branches of the media received the same advisory at the same time. This eliminated embellishment, interpretation, and rumors like those associated with Hurricane Babe in 1977. A New Orleans meteorologist, monitoring an Air Force reconnaissance aircraft, went on the air to be the first to label Babe a hurricane. This contradicted NHC advisories and caused unnecessary panic among Louisiana and New Orleans residents. In September, 1988, when Hurricane Gilbert entered the Gulf of Mexico, a private meteorological firm caused the controversial evacuation of Galveston, Texas, by forecasting a northward turn before it actually occurred. When the NHC issued a conflicting prediction of landfall farther south, it disrupted emergency procedures. Inland shelters were not open, traffic was in disarray, and pandemonium prevailed. In 1992, with the advent of the pool system, there were less than a dozen fatalities from Hurricane Andrew, which struck Miami.

Even if the pool system worked perfectly, Diane worried, there just wasn't enough lead time. Sam's crew would not be radioing Meg's position and strength until five this evening. Assuming landfall around four A.M. tomorrow, that left eleven hours in which to raise public awareness.

"I have convince the last person on earth who'd listen to me."

"Who's that?" asked Sam.

"My ex. Network TV weatherman. Jerk extraordinaire."

———

Hands on his hips, Dr. Mclaurin stared up proudly at the giant HD screens.

Meg now stood eight hundred miles east of the Delmarva Peninsula. She'd come up against the High Pressure Ridge he had created. She would remain there for the next six hours, bumping and pushing the HPR, trying to bull her way through it and continue north with the Southerlies. But the HPR held firm. HAARP emissions bombarded the upper atmosphere continuously to maintain the ridge, while they waited for the Greenland current, which would carry her down south, to materialize.

Meg tightened another fifty miles, now three hundred miles across and sixty-two thousand feet tall. Her weakest winds clocked in at three hundred and fifty miles an hour. The ocean around her undulated like shaggy hills, seventy feet high. Her eye shrank to a diameter of forty miles. With over two thousand miles of warm Atlantic Ocean to traverse on her way back to Cuba, she couldn't help but feed upon the unlimited moisture. Her spirals would tighten more. Dr.

Mclaurin planned to heavily seed her weaker updrafts. Keep the eye open, distinct, and cloud free. Otherwise, pressure in her eye would inevitably drop and cause the eyewall clouds to close in completely, suffocate her, and kill her.

These were critical hours. There could be no respite in the seeding. Even the minutest let up could prove disastrous. Right now, Meg was naturally inclined to travel with the Southerlies. At her current strength, her storm surge could waste neighborhoods as far inland as twenty miles.

Dr. Mclaurin looked at his watch, hurried into his office, shut the door, and locked it. He turned on the flatscreen and eavesdropped on Hank's final report from the NHC. He had been secretly listening in on every video teleconference relating to Thunder Strike, even EXCOMM meetings in the Situation Room at the White House. When it came to technical expertise, Dr. Mclaurin's team were in a different league. It had been child's play for them to hack in without leaving any prints.

"My department heads and I are leaving for the day now," said Hank to Baron and Peter, who were in their respective offices. The director looked wiped out. Hank asked the defense secretary if he could send the others home. "They've put in more than thirty hours, some with little or no sleep at all. A skeletal crew will work the night shift."

Baron and Peter could care less, Dr. Mclaurin knew. They just wanted Hank to make the official call. He finally did.

"Meg is done for," said Hank.

"You will leave her classified, then?" asked Baron.

"Sure," dismissed Hank and added acidly, "she never existed."

Dr. Mclaurin snorted spitefully.

———

As soon as Hank left, Peter ordered in the Agency crew of tekkies, who'd bugged the NHC. Disguised as janitors, they came in, cleaned out the wiretaps, and caused a power failure—

main and backup—which took down all the computers. When power was restored, every trace of Meg was erased from the NHC's hard drives.

———

Ned Cahill waited to make an entrance into the outsized conference room on the third floor of the network's headquarters across from Union Station, where the production crew gathered for their final meeting before the channel's flagship evening news broadcast.

"Fresh lineup everybody," said the lean and peppery Executive Producer. He presided over a news team of anchorman, anchorwoman, directors, editors, and ranking aides. "AP just in with the first pictures of the USN Hornet crash this morning on the Beltway." He nodded to the anchorman. "You'll start with a tell story."

"My source inside the Pentagon says they still haven't found the pilots," said the senior producer.

Ned had his opening. He deepened his voice and mocked, "Did they just vanish? Or were they abducted by aliens?" He strode in whistling the Twilight Zone theme. Sharply dressed as usual, he wore that smile which made him a factor in the Nielsens, the measure of a TV show's popularity.

"You're late, Ned," the EP snapped irritably and turned to the senior producer, "Can you confirm this from another source?"

"I tried, but nobody's talking."

"Go with the rumor," taunted Ned. He disliked the EP. "It's more interesting."

"I've held this job for nine years because I have a rule of thumb with regard to news," said the EP. "If there isn't enough to rest my ass in case I've to lay it on the line, it does not go on the air!"

"The news or your ass?" Ned came back at once. He never missed an opportunity to bait the guy. Chuckles broke out, bringing murder into the EP's eyes.

The speaker phone crackled, "Two minutes to air time! Where the hell is everybody?"

"Whenever you folks can tear yourselves away from Ned's stand-up," snapped the EP, turned on his heel, and stormed out of the room.

"You sure know how to piss him off every time," smiled the anchorwoman as they trooped into the elevator.

She backed into his hand and he cupped her ass. She squirmed in tighter. Ned winked. She smiled. He noticed everyone consciously avert their eyes. They all knew he was banging her and hated him for it. She was smoking hot. But then, so was he. He checked himself out in the shiny stainless steel door of the elevator as it started down.

"It's not my fault I got a face for TV and he doesn't." There was more laughter. Ned did not care that none of it was sincere.

When they got off on the studio level, a production assistant hurried up. "Mr. Ned, the guard at the gate called. Your wife would like to see you?"

The anchorwoman's eyes blazed toward him. The others hurried off.

"My wife?" laughed Ned nervously. "I'm not married."

"She gave her name as Diane Wood."

"Di," said Ned, slapped his forehead, and turned confidently to the anchorwoman. "Ex-wife." She relaxed. "How soon we forget? Send her up." He slapped her ass. "Catch you on the set."

Ned trotted over to the booth overlooking the studio, where a soundproof, clear glass separated the anchors from the staff. On TV, the glass was not apparent, making it seem like the newscasters broadcasted directly from the news room. Ned entered in time to see the EP nod curtly, directing Diane's attention toward Ned.

She waved and he noticed two strangers in crew cuts flanking her. Diane introduced them. "Sam Winger. Gene

Fellow. Ned Cahill. I need to speak with you. Alone."

"Let's go outside," said Ned.

The EP snapped his head around. "Not now. You're on after the next break."

"I'll wait," offered Diane.

"So, call me when you go to commercial," Ned retorted impatiently and gestured them out of the booth. He closed the door when they gathered in the hallway, "So, what's up. You sound serious. Not that I'm not happy to see you. You look good."

"I need your help," said Diane.

He guffawed. Her independent streak had killed their marriage. That, and his indiscretions. Like he told her, when they tried to reconcile, he never came close to marrying any of those other bimbos. That was just meaningless sex. "But heck, I thought enough of you to tie the knot. That should count for something. Actually, everything." She still walked out on him. Diane being Diane, did not claim half of his stuff. She just took what was hers. "If it's money, I can recommend a good loan shark."

Diane held her tongue. Just smiled back. *This must be important.* He quit joking. "Go on."

The overhead speaker interrupted them. "Ned, we are in commercial."

"Excuse me," said Ned and strode away. He looked over his shoulder. Diane looked back, her manner tight and tense. She was still hot—a different kind of hot, the kind that was just not about physical perfection, but a prettiness that was enhanced by bright eyes, thoughtful expressions, and intelligence. *Oh, yeah, intelligence.* That double edged sword. A boon, a bane.

————

"You were married to a celebrity," said Sam, impressed.

"He's a jerk," Diane spat.

"He plays such cool guys on TV. Wasn't he in that funny

slasher movie, Sewerman?"

"Uh-huh," Diane nodded. "I especially loved the part where he gets smothered in his own shit."

"So, is he like an accredited meteorologist, like you?" asked Gene

"Yeah, but he only got a Bachelors degree."

"Oh, excuse me, Doctor Wood."

"Besides, how hard is it to point to a map and read off a script?" ventured Sam.

"His arrogance, state college education, and lack of a post-graduate degree notwithstanding," said Diane, "it is a little more complicated."

She explained that these three-minute broadcasts were preceded by painstaking team effort. Ned came in five hours before his first bulletin. He received numbers, NEXRAD images, and satellite pictures from the WFO. A team of graphic artists assimilated the data into eye-catching weather maps with animated cloud systems, Doppler images pinpointing rainfall, the outlook for the rest of the week called trends, and local temperature, pressure, and humidity around different parts of the city and country. An hour before the newscast, Ned began to 'stack' the show—-deciding what would appear on the screen behind him. A weather phone-in line kept him updated of any sudden changes.

Diane nudged Sam and Gene back into the studio. Ned was standing in front of a blank, green screen. Using a process called chroma-key, technicians in the booth replaced the green screen with the images that the graphic artists had drawn, like city views, moving clouds, the weather map, bar charts, and forecasts. Since there was nothing behind him, Ned watched a TV set on either side of him to figure out where to point on the blank, green screen.

"Good evening, folks," said Ned with an easy charm. "It was a scorcher today, wasn't it? The temperature climbed higher, if you can believe it, from the mid-eighties to ninety-two degrees around Capitol Hill. This is unprecedented heat for October. But we did have a clear blue sky, if that's any consolation."

The remark triggered a brain flash in Diane. Air pumping out of the top of a cyclone cleared the sky around it. Satellite pictures showed this as a blue ring around the storm called a 'moat.'

Ned continued, "I'll have the forecast a little bit later."

The anchorwoman interrupted him. "Excuse me, Ned, this just in!" Her close-up replaced Ned. "There's been a coup in Cuba!"

FIFTEEN

President Avery Walker looked and felt jubilant as he stared down the horseshoe at a euphoric cabinet. News reports from different networks played in the background on the multiple TV screens. Aides with headsets took notes since the sound was muted so Avery could have the floor. "Elian Santos, the Minister of the Interior, is in control," he announced. "Juan and Carlos Castro are under arrest."

"What happened?" asked the Secretary of State. "How did Elian pull it off? Where the hell has he been?"

"It seems he was lying low, working behind the scenes on the Politburo," said Avery. He looked apologetically at the Baron. "I'm sorry, Secretary, I had to keep you out of the loop."

"I don't understand." The defense secretary, who always exuded composure and control, looked shocked and puzzled for the first time that the president had known him. Avery couldn't fault him. He'd kept Baron completely in the dark.

On the request of John Ulysses VI.

An hour after Avery had taken the NHC out of the loop and handed complete control of Thunder Strike over to Baron and the AFWA, the president had returned to his residence to rest briefly. His day had begun with that two A.M. teleconference this morning. He'd been physically exhausted. He'd barely stretched out on the couch when Whacko, the White House Communications Office below the Oval Office, interrupted him with an urgent call from a Cuban leader living in exile in Miami. The leader had advised the EXCOMM early in the crisis. He surprised Avery by conferencing in John Ulysses VI and Elian Santos!

Avery was only distantly acquainted with John. Like every president, upon taking office, he found out about the Ulysses's stature in diplomatic circles. John had offered to broker peace early on. As time went by and the standoff turned acrimonious, their contact became infrequent, and finally ceased altogether. John was in Havana. Risking his personal safety and freedom, he'd flown in under the cover of darkness unbeknownst to the Castros.

Avery did not know Elian at all. In fact, the president hadn't even heard of the interior minister's name until this crisis. Intelligence reports on the Cuban were all positive—a idealistic freedom fighter with the political savvy to lead Cuba. Listening John and Elian speak, Avery was struck by their similar temperament—honest, aware, knowledgeable, peace loving, thoughtful, and dignified.

Diplomats.

John revealed that he had been working secretly with Elian since the start. They'd targeted Castro's cronies who were part of the dictator's inner circle—corrupt men without morals—and offered them money to leave Cuba. John and Elian did not get into the numbers, but Avery guessed it was obscene. However, there was a condition to getting the money. Elian would determine when the deal would go down, but when it did, the cronies would have to agree to get on a plane within the hour. Once aboard, they would receive hard cash and safe passage to the country of their choice.

The CIA director tried to eke out some credit. "Our rumor campaign of a D-Day style attack must have also worried the Castros—that they'd be destroyed if they launched even a single nuke."

"Yeah," growled Jack, smirking.

"Hardly," said Avery, deflating their egos.

Listening to John, Avery learned why the Ulysses were the masters of diplomacy. With the cronies in his pocket and a third of the Politburo supporting him, Elian approached Juan and Carlos with an offer of a hundred million dollars each in hard cash to relinquish power. Even though it was Ulysses's money, Elian made it sound like the money was being offered by Washington, but it had to be kept secret. The US, he lied to them, did not want to be seen being brought to it knees and buying peace.

The Castros' eyes, Elian said, lit up with greed. They demanded the cash up front. Elian countered, "Hand over control of the nukes." They refused. At least, not until they saw the cash. Elian suggested they put the nukes in the custody of a man that the Castros trusted.

General Roberto Melchor.

Elian knew they would go for it, especially when he threw in, "Authorize him to launch without your approval."

Avery made a revelation that astonished the entire EXCOMM, even Baron. "You guys missed a vital childhood connection. You see, General Roberto Melchor had Elian's back all along because both were born and raised in the same village. They went to the same school and were in secret contact all along. But neither could make a move as long as the Castros controlled the nukes.

"While John orchestrated the deal with the Castros through Elian, Roberto prepared his forces for a bloodless takeover," explained Avery. "As soon as he got the nukes, Roberto moved into all of the old regime's strongholds and choked off any resistance within hours."

The horseshoe was silent. Avery allowed it all to sink in.

"John made one request of me." It only ratcheted Avery's respect another notch. "He does not want any public acknowledgement of the Ulysses's role."

"You must take credit, sir," John had told Avery. "The world needs to know that the US presidency is still the most influential office on earth, that America is not a war mongering nation that imposes her military will. Rather, we want freedom brokered peacefully, and more importantly, brokered from within."

The intercom buzzed. "Sir, the press is waiting for a statement."

Sabrina Worth, his speech writer, stepped forward and handed him a sheet of paper with double-spaced typing on it.

Avery perused it, nodded his approval, and headed out, pausing beside the defense secretary so briefly that nobody in the room noticed. He whispered for the Baron's ears only, "Terminate Thunder Strike and secure it."

———

Dr. Mclaurin was dumbstruck. He stared down at the message that Grant just handed him. They stood on the upper walkway above the Thunder Strike ops center. The fourteen meteorologists were immersed at their stations. Meg needed their attention and concentration.

Dr. Mclaurin read the message again in disbelief.

PBP/11 TOP TOP SECRET
TO USS RONALD REAGAN
FOR ADMIRAL GRANT'S EYES ONLY
XH23 65 FDMN001357 TS 18101627
ABORT THUNDER STRIKE.

"This is so shortsighted," whispered Dr. Mclaurin.

"What if she makes landfall?" said Grant.

"She won't. I can control her."

"What if, doctor?"

Dr. Mclaurin blinked. *What if, indeed.* His eyes dawned with a diabolic realization. Destiny had fashioned a payback. Meg did not officially exist, dismissed as 'done for' by the National Hurricane Center.

By Hank Rotas.

The man responsible for his humiliation and disgrace after the Vietnam rainmaking project. The man who had single-handedly exiled him to three decades of disgrace and ignominy.

"It's over," Dr. Mclaurin heard Grant say. "We have orders to stand down. Destroy Meg."

Dr. Mclaurin looked away. Leaned on the handrail. It was as if he was being asked to give up a child. But, in fact, he was playing the potential consequences of his plan in his head. If Meg dissipated, Thunder Strike would remain a theoretical option. There may never have another crisis large enough to use it. How many countries could credibly threaten the United States with Armageddon? On the other hand, if he demonstrated the destructive power of a hurricane making landfall with little or no warning against the best Emergency Management in the world, he'd prove the potency and effectiveness of weather as a weapon of war.

The price would steep. Human lives. Tragic, yes, but it wouldn't be the first time Americans had been sacrificed by their own government. From the 1960s through 80s, hundreds of experiments had been conducted on men, women, and children in US hospitals to test their reaction to different levels of radiation anticipated in a nuclear winter, the effects of various toxins during a chemical fallout, and the contagiousness of disease from viruses and bacteria inherent in a biological attack. Meg's death toll, even at tens of thousands, was a worthwhile and acceptable price to pay for owning the ultimate Weapon of Mass Destruction. There was little doubt in Dr. Mclaurin's mind that he would be forgiven.

"Fine," he said, looking straight at Admiral Grant. He turned to his meteorologists and clapped loudly like some august senator. They looked up. Silence swept across the ops center.

"You have been with me through thick and thin," said Dr. Mclaurin. "So, please do not question what I want you to do."

He paused, gazing over them. After so many letdowns and betrayals, a code of silence had evolved between Dr. Mclaurin and the fourteen men who had followed him from Vietnam to the OAR to South Dakota to here. He knew they would not dissent or say anything, at least not in front of the admiral.

"Cease all seeding and HAARP transmissions at once!"

Weather went off the broadcast schedule as the network began to gather reactions around the White House and analyze the sudden developments in Cuba.

"Can we talk in your office?" Diane asked, when Ned joined her Sam, and Gene in the booth..

"Sure," he shrugged. Sam shut the door. Ned noticed. "What's up?"

Diane told him about Meg. He checked his laughter to a snort, raised his eyebrows, and shook his head. "Okay, come on. That's extreme even for a conspiracy nut like you, Di."

Diane tilted her head and smiled sarcastically. Sam held up the Jayspid. "This is the military document outlining it." Ned took it and perused it. Sam continued, "My crew is going to radio in from Meg."

Ned handed back the Jayspid. "Okay, let's say I run with you. How can you forecast landfall when you haven't seen a report in the last twelve hours?"

"We should at least be on watch," said Diane, "don't you think?"

"When did you say your crew going to radio in?" asked Ned.

"Five o'clock."

Ned looked at his watch. "It's quarter to. We have a ham radio down in Weather. Let's go." He led them to a mid-sized room. A couple of artists worked on the graphics for the next broadcast. In the far corner was the NOAAPORT terminal along with a radio, microphone, and headsets. "This is big, all caps big. I'll need to bring in the news producer. He'll want to take it upstairs."

Diane looked at the two pilots. Off their nods, she nodded.

"I'll be back." Ned left.

"And you said he was a jerk," scolded Sam after Ned left. "Shame on you."

Diane looked up at the wall clock. Four-fifty. The minutes ticked by.

Ned returned. "Before I talked to anyone, I want to be sure this is real."

The top of the hour drew closer. Their anticipation mounted. Gene tensely fiddled with dials, checking and rechecking his frequency and volume.

Conversation came to a standstill.

Elliot walked the Secretary of Homeland Security into the Emergency Operations Center two levels below Ronald Reagan Building, an address that was once home to brothels and saloons and called the 'plague spot of Washington.' After turning briefly residential, Congress purchased the land. Today, it was home to the first federal building designed for both government and private use. The EOC moved here from Elliot's HSEMA office because the department heads hated driving over the river. They could walk here. It was hooked into the underground network of tunnels connecting all the federal buildings. The Mayor and twelve department heads shot to their feet and fawned all over the Secretary, who added to the prevailing air of skepticism.

"But," the Secretary joked, "we've mobilized for less."

Everyone responded with smiles and nods.

Chatter subsided with each minute forward the clock inched to five P.M.

Ranger occupied Sam's seat. It was his first stint ever as a pilot. The C-130 was inside Meg. Inside unbelievable turbulence. Fierce crosswinds and an endless series of powerful updrafts and downdrafts sent the Hercules sunfishing like a wild horse. Rain lashed in torrents. Dark, almost black, nimbostratus clouds glowed continuously with lightning. Visibility reduced to zero and the turbulence turned demonlike.

"That's impossible!" Schultz's voice crackled over their headsets from his station in the rear of the plane. "Check out the gust probe numbers."

Ranger did a double take. "The winds are in excess of three hundred and eighty miles an hour!"

"Are you sure it's not a malfunction?" asked Pfifer. He sat beside Ranger, doing double duty as copilot and ARWO.

"Why are we entering her at five thousand feet?" Ranger observed. That didn't give them much altitude to work with if Meg took a swing at the plane.

"Orders," shrugged Pfifer.

Meg swiped at the Hercules. The crew fell forward. She reversed herself and backhanded them. The men slammed back into their seats again.

"Four-ten!" gasped Schultz.

"No shit," said Ranger, reading it as well. His fingers gripped the shuddering wheel.

"Quince!" Knoll yelled. "Are you all right?"

Ranger swiveled. Blood drenched the comedic navigator's skull and maps. Dripped off the edge. "What happened?"

Quince shouted back, "I'm all right. My fault. I left a slack in my harness. It's not as bad as it looks."

A vicious snap! Ranger's eyes snapped forward. "The gust probe!"

The long rod that projected beyond the nose of the aircraft broke clean off. *Bang!* Hit the windshield, and disappeared end over end into the swirling clouds behind them. Knoll's eyes went wide. "That's never happened."

"Hell with your orders, Pfif," said Ranger. "I'm climbing to ten thousand feet."

Pfifer just nodded, still reeling from the gust probe breaking off and slamming the windshield in front of him. They entered the eyewall.

"Four-fifty!" shouted Schultz.

"These are tornado numbers." Ranger shouted back.

BOOOM! Engine No. 4 exploded.

The cockpit crew exclaimed together. The Hercules wobbled dangerously.

"That was a detonation," said Ranger after a moment of distinct, startled silence.

"Yeah, so?" asked Quince.

"A bomb" said Ranger quietly, immediately connecting the dots with an innocuous incident just before they took off.

A mechanic had been working on Engine No. 4. Friendly guy. He'd waved a maintenance report at Ranger and said, "There was a requisition for a coupling for engine number four. It wasn't replaced. Oversight. Outer casing. Shouldn't take more than fifteen minutes, tops."

The right wing sheered off.

The Hercules dropped like stone.

———

Five P.M. arrived and passed at the EOC. They waited another fifteen minutes. The Secretary looked visibly annoyed. "A bloody hoax."

Elliot apologized. They all left.

———

At the network, Ned just shook his head and exited, leaving Diane, Sam, and Gene alone. The trio waited another thirty minutes. Sam said, "I know those guys. Something happened to them."

Diane believed him. Only, she suspected the worst. Then she heard Ned, "In here."

"Thanks Ned," said James, walking in.

"James!" reacted Diane.

"I called him," said Ned. "I wanted to check if he knew anything."

"I'm sorry, Diane," James said and stepped aside.

The four suits from the WFO walked in, guns drawn.

TODAY

Diane glanced at her watch. It was half past three. The sun dipped fast. The sky darkened. Liz and she had spent the last hour looking for a vehicle. They were losing hope and just about ready to give up. They'd lived here long enough to know that, on foot, in the dark, they'd be taking their lives into their hands. Even before Meg's onslaught, the nation's capital had never been safe at night.

During their search, Diane had been pleasantly surprised by the depth of Liz's knowledge. She had read almost every urban demographic article that Diane had for a story about the uniqueness of DC and its residents. For one, the city had the biggest transient population in the world. Most people were temporary transplants, here for the duration of the government in power. So, they tended to mind their own business more than any other US city. Measurements of fear ran high. Seventy-one percent of respondents of a survey answered that they rarely, if ever, went out alone at night. Two thirds of the people called DC 'a place to live' rather than their 'home.' So they invested little or nothing in the city's well being.

Liz told Diane about other reports the government never included at the NOAA seminars. Graffiti, derelicts, broken windows, littered sidewalks, congested housing, smog, traffic, crime, and other signs of decay were dismissed as natural symptoms of urban growth. The deep and long recession following the mortgage crisis of 2008 left little money to address the dissatisfaction among the working poor and lower middle class, who made up more than eighty percent of the city's native population. They were also black, Hispanic, and historically discriminated. Lack of communality between the white, predominantly wealthy transient political operators and the locals exploded as intolerance and a breakdown in the rule of law on an unprecedented scale.

"At night," Diane said, "the worst predators from both

sides of the law crawl out."

"I can believe it," said Liz. "Hold up."

She pointed to an abandoned moving company rental compound. It looked more like a scrap yard. At first glance, nothing seemed salvageable. Probably why it was deserted.

"Come on," said Liz, ducking and squeezing between a couple of overturned vehicles to reach a midsize truck wedged between a pickup on its side and the office building, which now looked like a giant vase holding an eighty-year old tree. Meg had uprooted it out of the back and dropped it through the roof. The giant roots had crushed everything inside and the trunk leaned precariously against the wall. Liz opened the driverside door. She wriggled in, ducked under the steering, and ripped out the ignition wires.

"Where did you learn to do that?" asked Diane, fascinated.

"I took a month-long survival course with an undercover cop when I did the Jarvis Johnson exposé."

Tssss.

Something gave way. Both women reacted. A crack in the wall of the office holding up the tree dribbled dust, indicating the collapse wasn't complete. The wall was slowly giving way under the weight of the tree. Liz urgently chafed the wires. They sparked. The engine turned. A couple of tries later, it fired with a rough drawl.

"Yay," Diane pumped her fist.

Liz checked the fuel gauge. The needle inched up to half a tank. She slid along the single seat to the passenger side. "You know where we are going. You drive."

Diane hoisted herself up and into the truck. She settled behind the wheel, checked out the controls. Snapping on the seat belt, she released the parking brake.

"Jerk it out," suggested Liz.

Diane slid the automatic shift to its lowest gear and took her foot off the brake sharply. The truck hopped forward violently. Metal scraped, screamed, and scrawled, a sound that tore the air apart. *Thud!* The pickup on its side turned over into the spot where the truck was parked, knocking over a chunk of office wall, which shook, teetered, and started to give way as the tree began to push down, threatening to trap and crush the women.

"Pull out! Pull out!" shouted Liz.

Diane slammed down on the gas pedal. The massive trunk came down like a sledgehammer. A second, even less, from chutneying the women! Diane swerved.

Too late? *Crash!*

The tree obliterated visibility inside an opaque mushroom of auto parts and masonry that went up like a volcanic eruption. No way we're getting out this alive. Dust closed in like an overpowering monster. Darkness shrouded them. Diane couldn't see an inch in front of her. Then! Miraculously! A sliver opened. She pressed down the accelerator that was already to the floor. The truck pulled free and raced out of the billowing cloud of demolition.

"Wo!" exclaimed Liz with a smile. "That was a rush!"

"Rush?" Diane stared at Liz. Her blood was racing too. Not out excitement, but unabated fear. She cranked the wheel and turned out of the gate into the empty street. "Keep your eyes open. There is a twenty-four curfew. Night patrols open fire on all moving vehicles that are not military."

It took a block of driving to get her heart settled.

"Believe it or not, today is only my second day back," said Liz. "I was in rehab for the last eight months. I'm telling you this because you've been honest with me and I feel I should level with you. My paper isn't exactly behind me on this story. I'm not even supposed to be here."

"What does that mean?" asked Diane, looking over at Liz.

"Nothing. Just so you know how badly I want this."

Diane nodded. Said nothing. She so desperately wanted to tell Liz. Unburden the secret of Thunder Strike to someone.

But she held herself back. She could not reveal anything until they got to Bethesda. "Are you hungry?"

"Famished," said Liz. She hadn't eaten since lunch yesterday in New York.

"I knew it would take us all day to get across town," said Diane. "That's why I packed us some food."

Liz opened the backpack and pulled out the two MRE packets. "Chicken or beef?"

"They taste the same," smiled Diane. Liz laughed.

In the past week, Diane had eaten almost all the MRE menu options. There were about twelve-hundred calories in each meal, which consisted of a starch-heavy main course, crackers, cheese or jelly spread, a dessert, a beverage, plastic utensils, and a napkin. Liz selected the chicken. Diane noticed Liz grimace after the first bite but the reporter did not complain.

Eating the beef patty as she drove, Diane finally had to ask the question she'd been dying to ask all day, "So, what happened?"

———

Liz knew given time, Diane would eventually shed her reserve. Liz seized this opening to build trust. "I got caught up in my own success."

After the Pulitzer for the Jarvis Johnson exposé, she was everywhere. On TV. On radio. On magazines covers. On the speaking circuit. She signed a book deal. Hollywood snapped up the movie rights. Declaring that her 'brains did not fall out of her ass if she took her clothes off,' she posed in Playboy and caused a sensation. Liz became a household name. A bona fide celebrity. Her name came up in gossip columns. She was seen with movie stars and musicians. She kept Billy around like an old-reliable. He didn't know where he stood with her, but remained devoted despite being on-again-off-again on her dating calendar. Liz was attracted to power and realized she was falling in love with Tim.

With the spotlight squarely on her, she began looking

for front page headlines in every story she took on. She felt that whenever people saw her name, they expected a searing exposé. The nonexistent pressure she forced upon herself grew into a preoccupation and then into a relentless obsession.

Instead, arrived a year of oblivion.

She began to suffer bouts of depression. "I never finished the book and Hollywood dumped me," Liz said. "I found out I was just another notch on Tim's bedpost. I turned to my new best friend. Booze. Who introduced me to cousin Cocaine. I got so bent, I didn't know which way was up."

Just like Tim warned her, Liz lost her perspective.

She did the unthinkable.

She fabricated a sensational story.

She implicated the next president of the United States in a sex and drug scandal. At the time the story broke, he was Candidate Avery Walker, who'd just completed a remarkable rise from a relative unknown and inexperienced governor of Indiana to the win the Republican nomination. On Labor Day, the official kickoff to the presidential campaign, an unflattering picture of Avery as a college student at Notre Dame appeared on the front page of the *Daily Post* alongside signature bold headlines, "SEXED UP, DOPED OUT."

It broke Avery's bid.

Liz had befriended a sound wiz, another coke addict. Together, they electronically spliced conversations between Avery and a dealer, who alleged that Avery was part of wild drug and sex parties in South Bend while he attended Notre Dame. Follow up stories revealed that the dealer had been shot and killed weeks before Avery had been elected Governor. This fueled conspiracy theories. Liz produced an old cassette she claimed to have found in the dealer's evidence box. Was it a police misstep that it was never logged? Or a favor by a friendly cop?

The scandal swirled and deepened.

Liz held the nation enthralled day after day. She landed

right back into the spotlight. Basked in the attention. Avery vehemently denied the story that began to take a life of its own. Republicans distanced themselves. His poll numbers plummeted. Just when Liz was ready to dance on the carcass of another presidential hopeful, the FBI appeared. They launched a vigorous inquiry that caught Liz and even the Democrats by surprise.

Liz's story began to unravel.

South Bend was a small university town, where the usual six degrees of separation shrank to three at the most. The agents easily located eye witnesses and unearthed records. In an unexpected move, Avery offered fifty thousand dollars to anyone with exonerating evidence.

The sound wiz and Liz had started fighting. He was unhappy that she was hogging all the attention and glory. He got greedy. Took the money. Sold out Liz. He revealed that the dealer's voice on tape was an electronically manipulated and aged version of his own.

A firestorm of reprisal threatened to destroy Liz. Her parents intervened. Elisa Lovell's sterling reputation and high standing combined with Kenneth's acumen to make a deal saved Liz from doing hard time in prison. Tim printed a retraction. The *Post* ate crow for weeks. So did the national media, which had run with Liz's story without verifying it. In a clever ploy to garner the outpouring of sympathy, Avery's brain trust asked him to graciously drop the charges. He supported a story that Liz had been misled to the authenticity of the tape. Behind the scenes, Avery's camp played hardball.

"But someone," said Liz, "more powerful and influential than Avery was calling the shots."

She never found out. Maybe it was the entire Republican attack machine. It could've been retribution for taking down Senator Jarvis Johnson. A calculated a series of leaks exposed Liz's alcohol and drug abuse. Hints and innuendos that she masterminded the fabrication never left the media cycle. Of course, Avery neither confirmed nor denied it, and the public convicted her. Trailing by double digits two weeks before elections, the sympathy wave moved Avery into a slender lead the day before Americans went to the polls.

Liz smirked. "Tim hung me out to dry." She could not keep down the rancor and spite. "Called it Club Rules. When the shit hits fan in DC, ducking isn't reflex. It's the law." Liz's jaw clenched. "Bastard." She looked at Diane. "I should have taken the sonofabitch down." Liz caught Diane's stare and explained, "He could have stopped me."

Diane nodded. "Why didn't he?"

"Circulation of the *Post* outsold every major newspaper two to one during the scandal. Tim wasn't about kill a cash cow." In a single blink, Liz replaced the hate in her eyes with hurt. Her tone changed, soft, innocent, "I was still in love, I guess. I was twenty-seven, the age when your heart overrules your head." Liz felt Diane's empathy. "You've been in a bad marriage, you know."

"Oh, yeah," agreed Diane.

"It's a year later, now. I feel like I have the life experience of a forty-year old."

Diane chuckled with her.

Liz's eyes leapt. "Stop! Pull over! Now!"

A Blackhawk helicopter climbed into view over the frayed rooftops. Its searchlight bgan to swing toward the rental truck. The sun had gone down, pulling a blanket of darkness over DC. Diane peeled off to the side! Driving the truck up the sloping side of a mountain of rubble so that it looked abandoned rather than parked. A cloud of dust flew into air. The truck rocked. Liz looked at Diane and they turned their eyes outward with the same thought. There was no way the dust or the truck would settle before the light swung over.

The truck did. The dust did not.

A blinding circle lit up the descending dust.

Tatatatatat!!! The under-mounted machine gun swung

and opened fire! The bullets stitched toward the truck. The women shrieked and ducked between the dash and seat! Their cry did not carry above the roaring rotors of the descending chopper. They waited for the bullets to blast in and take them out.

Nothing happened.

The bullets whipped right alongside the passenger side door. Liz raised her head. The bullets chased a couple of dogs the truck had displaced. The dogs escaped. But the chopper did not leave. Kept the truck spotlighted for what seemed like an eternity. Liz held up a finger. Signaling Diane not to move. *Were the dogs just target practice? Jesus!* Finally, the light swung away and the copter banked off, joining scores of others patrolling the capital.

Liz and Diane sat up carefully.

They looked to each side and behind them. Headlights of moving patrols outlined ragged streets. Flashes of gunfire appeared first, then the stutter of bullets became audible. Gas station fires arced in distinct ropes across the starlit sky. Helicopters shot down cones of light, scouring for targets. Every now and then, a chopper banked off sharply, machine-guns blazing, chasing after hapless victims running or driving for their lives. The sense of doom and hopelessness magnified tenfold at night.

Diane reversed the truck off the mound. She turned on her headlights for brief intervals to navigate the treacherous streets. The twin shafts jabbed ahead with alarming brightness. They saw silhouettes huddled around fires within dark alleys, niches, and other temporary shelters.

"How far away are we?" asked Liz.

"Half an hour?"

———

Andrew felt relaxed, thanks to the release he'd found with those two hookers. The MILSATCOM rang with the call he was waiting for.

"Take down this address," said Peter. "It belongs to Diane's ex-husband."

"Bethesda?" repeated Andrew when Peter finished.

"How quickly can you get there?"

———

The president retired upstairs. Baron hurried back down to the Situation Room. Jack was a bundle of nerves. "What did he want?"

Baron nodded the JCS Chairman into a chair. "In a minute."

He dialed the videophone. Peter answered his call, appearing on the CIA screen. Baron revealed that Avery not only planned to step down tomorrow but tell the nation all about Thunder Strike. "So, we have to wrap this up tonight."

"Shit," blanched Jack. "Can it be done?

"I don't see why not?" said Peter with quiet confidence. "Everything's in place."

———

Peter left Langley for the White House as soon as he hung up because Baron had ended the call saying, "I want you here when the dominoes start falling."

Which, Peter did not reveal to Baron and Jack, depended on his hunch and experience of playing in the shadows for thirty years. He was gambling that the Jayspid was at Diane's ex-husband's address, that the two women were headed there, and that Andrew would not fail him.

———

Andrew slowed as he approached a checkpoint. After dark, the army had divided DC into sectors and controlled movement from one to another. It tightened security and discouraged looters from roaming freely. National Guards swung their lights on him. Seeing that it was a military Humvee, they moved the jeeps out of way and let him through.

———

Diane and Liz were not so lucky. Soldiers stepped in

front suddenly. Diane braked hard. The wheels skidded and the rental truck halted noisily. Four guns, two on each side, descended against their windows with an intimidating crash. Diane swallowed hard, color draining from her face.

"Stay cool," whispered Liz, rolled down the glass, and flashed her press badge. "Press. *New York Post*."

The soldier had Sergeant stripes. He looked at her credentials and lowered his head to look at Diane. "And you?"

"She's my local contact," Liz answered for Diane. Then she chuckled, "Making sure I don't get lost."

None of the solders cracked a smile. "Why are you in a moving truck?"

"Only rental my paper could find," shrugged Liz.

"Open the back!" barked the Sergeant. The solider beside him and another from Diane's side walked to the back, slammed the latches back noisily and rolled up the door. It grated with a rusty shriek. There were a couple of two-by-fours and a moving blanket.

"Empty, sergeant!" shouted one of them.

"What's your destination?"

"Bethesda," replied Liz.

"Reason?"

"Following a story."

The Sergeant stared at them one more time. He nodded. The door rolled down and the soldiers stepped back. He said, "You're taking a huge risk driving at night."

"We know that."

The Sergeant just tilted his head. Nodded them through.

————

Andrew cut his headlights and engine before he turned into Lancaster Drive to cloak his arrival. Meg had romped through this quiet residential street of extremely affluent homes, picking up roofs, dropping walls, ripping out the pavement, and decimating the concrete driveways. The entire street was dark and deserted.

The Humvee's tires crunched to a standstill. Andrew got out. The stench of death wafted across powerfully. He closed the door without clicking it shut. His dark clothes rendered him invisible in the opaque darkness. The moon hid behind a cloud. Ned's house was the first on the block. He loped over quickly. His shoes made no sound.

He slipped the gun into his hand. Strode noiselessly up the drive. A fire flickered within the house, the only inhabited one on the street. He reached the door. Applied just enough pressure to crack it ajar. Meg's wind had warped the frame. It could not be bolted. The door gave with a tiny creak, which was lost in a night full of distant gunfire, sirens, helicopters, and natural night sounds.

Andrew placed his eye up to the slender gap between the frame and the door. He could not see the flames, but saw a shadow sway wildly in the unsteady orange-red light. The person was sitting down, rocking back and forth. Andrew took a step back, and in one, fluid, swift move, he kicked open the door! Stepped in, gun leveled.

"Don't move," Andrew said quietly.

Headlights turned into the street. The women, he guessed. Andrew retreated so that there was only one shadow when the truck's high beams came up the driveway.

———

Diane killed the engine and the lights

"Wait here," said Diane, climbed out.

Liz sat back. Diane headed up the drive. Entered the house.

"Hello!" Diane called out, entering the house. "You're not going to believe this. Liz chartered a plane—-" She broke off abruptly, catching her a breath audibly.

Andrew stepped into view. Diane caught her breath sharply. Andrew gestured, gathering the last two loose ends of Thunder Strike in front of his gun. Diane saw movement through the window. Glanced over. Liz was getting out of the car. The assassin looked out the window.

Liz stared back at him. Diane noticed that their eyes met dead on.

As accomplices?

LAST WEEK

SEVENTEEN

Historically, there had been nothing like her.

Ever.

Her spiral continued to tighten, now less than two hundred and fifty miles across. The more she shrank, the more power she packed. She boasted statistics meteorologists only associated with the most devastating tornadoes. Her sustained gusts blew around at a record four hundred miles an hour and her radius of maximum winds, an unprecedented, mindboggling four hundred and seventy! In her eye, she sucked the water five feet higher than the rest of the ocean. On landfall, this mound translated into a surge sixty feet high and more.

She moved half a billion tons of air per hour. In the hours she had remained stationary, she released energy equivalent to fifteen thousand times the power generated in all of the United States of America, or the daily explosion of two billion twenty-kiloton atomic bombs like those dropped over Hiroshima and Nagasaki. She was like a predator on a leash, struggling to break away from the artificial forces that kept her captive. She growled and snarled with explosive blasts of thunder and lightning, and ferociously kicked up tides that rose out of the ocean into mountainous waves hundred feet tall.

For hours, she violently, rammed the high pressure ridge that blocked her way, insistently seeking to break through. Instead, she was being restrained, with heavy seeding of her weaker updrafts.

During this critical period, the seeding ceased.

Abruptly.

The high pressure ridge dissipated without warning.

The asymmetric distribution of energy which had been successfully edging her into the Greenland current shifted suddenly. The resulting effect was similar to an immovable object collapsing without warning in front of the irresistible force. She catapulted forward! Gleefully rode the Southerlies at sixty miles an hour into the corridor created by the two stubborn, prototype HPRs Dr. Mclaurin had created over Delaware, Maryland, and Virginia.

Toward the Delmarva Peninsula

Difficult to start, hard to sustain, but once mature and in motion, she became a vast heat engine, the most powerful dynamic system on earth. A hurricane was the greatest storm on earth. An awesome natural event. Oh, but she was more than that.

She was the planet's first superhurricane.

A hellacious bitch.

––––––––

Off the east coast of Delmarva Peninsula, about halfway down, was Wallops Island, about six square miles in area. Home to several military installations, it also housed NOAA's downlink station for all Atlantic satellite weather data. In the compound stood an unattended tower topped off by the radome of the WSR-88XD Next Generation Radar. NEXRAD. Every six minutes, the NEXRAD routinely scanned nine different elevations of the atmosphere in a two hundred mile radius and acquired high resolution reflectivity, Doppler velocity, and spectrum width. Reflectivity measured moisture content even in the absence of clouds, Doppler velocity provided wind direction and its radial intensity, and spectral width confirmed the accuracy of the velocity data.

A microwave run carried the nine cuts of information to a receiver and signal processor inside a tightly controlled air-conditioned shelter. A generator assured there was never a break in power. The processed signal then traveled fiber optically to a Radar Product Generator located in the WFO at Silver Springs. The RPG fed into the AWIPS, which displayed the nine elevation angles as a three-dimensional color-coded image. An advanced algorithm recognized this latest NEXRAD scan as a disturbance that exceeded the parameters of a normal disturbance.

The AWIPS triggered off an automatic alert.

A bell, mounted on the wall of the WFO, started to ring shrilly.

There was nobody to hear it.

The four P.M. to midnight shift, always a skeletal one, consisted of a lead and junior forecaster, a Hydro Meteorological Technician, and two maintenance persons. The JF and HMT had gone across the street to the convenience store together. Vick's death had convinced them not to go out alone after dark. Ivory Adams, who'd picked up the slack as lead after Vick had died, was in the restroom. He zipped up and hurried in.

"What's going on?" asked a maintenance guy, sauntering in from the back to investigate the ruckus.

Ivory settled in front of the AWIPS. The disturbance was blood red and looked like a storm cell. Isolated turbulence, he dismissed, and lazily extended NEXRAD's next scan to four hundred miles. He stretched, rubbed his eyes, yawned, and turned paler than a ghost.

The bell continued to ring.

The maintenance man asked irritably, "Can't you shut it off?"

Ivory did not even hear him. As stunned as he was and his mind raced with what he must do next, another part of his brain clicked with clarity.

Diane and Vick hadn stumbled upon this yesterday.

It all made sense now. Vick's brush off when Ivory walked in on them after Diane showed up from Miami. Diane's jumpy reaction when he chanced upon her screen a few minutes later. And last night, Ivory forgot his cell phone in the office. Came back. Vick couldn't erase the screen quickly enough. He looked nervous and surprised, quickly slamming the drawer of his desk shut, like he was hiding somethng. Ivory went home, curious and unsettled. A few hours later, James called and dropped a bombshell: Vick was dead. Mugged and murdered.

James asked Ivory to cover Diane's day shift. Ivory returned to the WFO this morning at nine. Diane had already left for the day. One of the guys told him she'd received a phone call and split in a hurry. With the AWIPS to himself, Ivory looked for the storm he'd seen on their screens. Nothing came up. He decided to take an early lunch. As he was getting into his car, Diane arrived with two guys in Air Force jumpsuits. Ivory called out to her to offer his condolences. He knew Vick and Diane were best friends. Suddenly, two suits burst outside. Two more showed themselves from a van. They opened fire!

Shocked beyond disbelief, Ivory got back into his car and gripped the steering with white knuckles even though he was a marine who was no stranger to firearms. But gunshots outside a weather office? That just did not make sense. James came outside and tried to stop the suits from shooting any more. Diane sped away. The suits got into the van and left. Nobody in the office was even aware what had happened outside because the suits had used silenced guns and everything had unfolded and ended in mere moments.

Ivory tried to talk to James, who waved him off. "I can't say anything."

James appeared distracted and distant all afternoon. Then, around five, James raced out of the office, looking distressed. He asked Ivory to cover the night shift too. Ivory had trained at the AFWA. He'd seen first hand clandestine programs involving acid rain, fog enhancement, lightning, and other weird stuff. *But concealing this?* He looked again at what NEXRAD displayed on the AWIPS. It went beyond even his wildest imagination.

The JF and HMT walked in.

Phones were ringing off the hook.

Ivory turned toward them and barked, "Find James! Find Diane! Reach as many of the day shift as you can and tell them to haul ass!" The two guys just stood there, nonplused. Ivory shouted, "There's a hurricane headed our way!"

––––––––

Calls flooded in from downrange stations from Baltimore to Norfolk. Operated by the National Data Buoy Center, they manned a network of moored buoys and automated weather observing systems. Private meteorologists and Doppler radar operators of the local TV networks picked up Meg too, now that she had come within four hundred miles of the coast. Alarm quickly turned to panic. Other agencies critical to providing warnings, like the National Meteorological Center in Suitland, the National Severe Storms Forecast Center in Kansas, and the National River Forecast Offices in Delaware, Virginia, and Maryland, rushed in off-shift meteorologists.

There was little anyone could do.

––––––––

Hank was dead asleep when he felt a violent shaking. His wife of thirty years wore an expression that he'd never seen. She held out the phone. He hadn't even heard it ring. He'd been so tired when he got home, all remembered was laying his head on the pillow last night.

"Honey, you have to take this," she said. "I'll make you a flask of coffee for the road."

Hank grabbed the receiver. He had to calm down the young meteorologist at the other end. The NHC at Coral Gables, Florida, were being inundated with phone calls, but the skeletal night shift had no idea what was going on. There was no power. The generators were dead. Their computers were down. Hank arrived on the run as did Gerardo, Ray, and Clyde within minutes of each other. They brought their laptops in, using them one at a time to stretch battery power.

They went speechless as one.

"She could not have strengthened to that since we left her," said Gerardo.

Meg was now a hundred and fifty mile-wide spiral with sustained winds around four hundred and fifty miles an hour.

Eyewall gusts reached five-twenty. She tore north and west at sixty miles an hour.

Reconfigured storm data!

Hank realized he'd been a damn fool not to have recognized Meg's sudden weakening, especially after he'd given Baron and Peter an ultimatum. He could not prove any of this and remembered Gerardo's words, "Who do you think will be sent up shit creek without a paddle?"

Baron and Peter would blame him and the National Hurricane Center. Hank's last forecast, officially declaring Meg dead, would stand.

———

Peter sat down to eat dinner. He was feeling relaxed. Diane and the pilots were in custody. When Sam's crew did not call in at five, it worked better than denying a storm existed. It also completely debunked the existence of an operation called Thunder Strike. His phone rang.

The caller ID displayed, 'Gary, AFWA.'

Frowning, Peter answered. Gary quickly and efficiently briefed Peter.

At the AFWA, a single meteorologist had been working the night shift. The others had been allowed to go home for the first time since Monday, when Thunder Strike had been initiated. The meteorologist saw the hours go by without any reduction in Meg's intensity. Then, she suddenly shot forward! He called his boss, who took one look at Meg's size and power and knew something had gone terribly wrong. The boss reached Gary, who made the five minute drive over to the AFWA, where he was privy to the panic stricken calls between the agencies of the National Weather Service in Maryland, Delaware, and Virginia.

"Do nothing," Peter told Gary and reached Baron.

They stayed on the phone with each other as they drove to the Pentagon and continued their discussion in person in the defense secretary's office. Neither man worried about the impending catastrophe.

They were more concerned about keeping Thunder Strike secret.

"Dr. Mclaurin gambled big time," said Peter, conjecturing correctly what had happened. "He figured if he shows how effective his invention is, we'll find a way of explaining away Meg. Destroying Hank was just icing."

"We need a cover story," said Baron, who was still smarting from John Ulysses defusing the crisis and diluting the Hawkes's hold on the dark shadows.

"I'll think of something," said Peter. "Satellite malfunction, whatever."

"What is the forecast?"

"She's less than two hundred miles out. Delmarva will feel her outer spirals in three hours. Gary says Dr. Mclaurin's experimental High Pressure Ridges have lined up to thread her into and up the Potomac toward DC. We are looking at a major disaster."

A lesser politician would have exploded with profanity. Peter did not expect even a trace of alarm from Baron. The defense secretary did not disappoint. "How long do we have?"

"Five hours. Give or take. Landfall here in DC is estimated around four A.M."

The two took on a clinical efficiency. "We need to get the president out."

Peter nodded. "I will call Marine One."

"Is there time to reach everyone in Congress?" Almost the entire House and Senate were in town to get through the legislative agenda before the winter break.

"Nobody can blame us if we don't," said Peter.

Baron squinted quizzically.

Peter smiled thinly, "We can reclaim the majority in the House and Senate by identifying vulnerable seats...should those seats fall vacant."

Baron lips curled coldly. He pointed a finger. Good thinking.

Peter continued, "I'm worried about guilty consciences in the EXCOMM loosening lips in the aftermath."

"As also all the low level brass at HSEMA," said Baron. "Those that went home thinking there was no storm and Thunder Strike's a hoax."

"And Dr. Mclaurin?" asked Peter carefully.

Baron and Dr. Mclaurin went a long way back. So, it had to be Baron's call. Dr. Mclaurin had kept a tight lid on Thunder Strike since its inception, but Peter knew that Baron understood what the brilliant scientist had pulled was a serious lapse in judgment. Also, he was getting old, and age made for unreliable confidants. Watergate's Deep Throat, who'd laid low all his life, couldn't resist blabbing on this death bed.

Peter added, "We recorded every step of Thunder Strike. We can replicate it without him."

Baron thought for a long moment. Then moved his head. In a nod. "Use your judgment. Make a Beta list and run with it."

"Yes, sir," said Peter, who had already summoned Andrew Burke from Paris. In fact, Peter was so confident Baron would be on the same page, he'd made the call to the assassin immediately upon hearing Diane had spilled Thunder Strike to the HSEMA director.

Six hours ago.

Baron turned at the door, "Oh, don't forget to recover Grant's Jayspid."

———

The third and final Jayspid was in Diane's backpack, which sat on the table of a deserted office along Virginia Avenue in a building just two blocks from the Watergate Hotel. Following 9/11, the CIA had created a dummy trading company and rented this entire floor as a halfway house for suspected terrorists, who were brought here first, processed, and shipped to military prisons around the US.

Two suits played cards around the backpack. The third

snored, feet up on the table. The fourth watched a primetime police drama on TV, which hung from the ceiling. Diane, Sam, and Gene sat on the floor, their hands cuffed behind their backs. The trio had been led out the side door of the network. James waited outside. He apologized again. Diane glared at him and walked by without saying a word. Much to everyone's astonishment, the suits grabbed James, roughly cuffed him too, and shoved him into the car with them. On the ride over, James told Diane they'd threatened his job and his pension. A suit pistol whipped him. Cut his lip badly. Told him to shut up. James now sat aside from the trio, scared. Blood clotted untidily on his swollen lip.

It was coming up on eleven P.M. They'd been captive for about five hours. Diane wondered what was keeping the suits from killing them. Almost on cue, the cell phone belonging to the sleeping suit rang. He stirred awake.

"Yeah," he answered. Listened. Swung his feet off the table and straightened up in the swivel chair. "Let me check." He reached over and pulled the backpack toward him. Zipped it open. "Yup. There's a thick black binder." Listened again. "Consider it done."

He flipped the phone shut. Nodded toward the two card-playing suits, who reached inside their jackets and raised their eyes toward captives.

Then their weapons.

———

Aboard *USS William J. Clinton*, Admiral Grant prepared to turn in. He started to unbutton his tunic. *Knock!* Knuckles rapped softly and politely once on the door. He opened it. His Executive Officer stood outside with a printout of an encoded. 'Eyes Only' message.

"Thank you," said Grant and closed the door.

He walked over to his desk and slid the message into the scanner. He tapped the keyboard of his computer and the screen asked him for his password. He typed it in and drew the mouse over to the icon of a Pentagon-patented cryptography software on the desktop. The seal of the Department of Defense bloomed and asked him for another login password. He typed it in, activating a woman's voice, "Ready for eye scan."

Grant leaned in toward the small dot on the top frame of the screen. A webcam. The match was successful. A square box appeared with the outline of a right hand. He lined his up to it, and moved it closer slowly, carefully. He did not touch the surface so that light from the rest of the screen could wrap halfway around his fingers for a three-dimensional handprint ID. This match automatically initiated the scanner. Its light bar whined across the glass. When the printer did not chatter, Grant slow blinked. His stomach tightened. He knew what was coming. The seemingly random numbers and letters unscrambled for a one-time read-only order on the screen.

PBP/11 TOP TOP SECRET
TO USS RONALD REAGAN
FOR ADMIRAL GRANT'S EYES ONLY
XH23 65 FDMN001362 TS 18102108
THUNDER STRIKE PERSONNEL ON BETA LIST.

Grant exited the program. He picked up the intercom. "Dr. Mclaurin, please." When he came on the line, "A plane will take you all home."

Grant was aware of the Beta list. It was an integral to classified missions. Part of the duties at his level of responsibility was to be able to obey it when it was issued. But he had never been asked to execute one. Even though he disliked Dr. Mclaurin, Grant did not realize the order would sicken him the way it did. He quickly stepped inside the attached lavatory and threw up.

———

Diane stood frozen in fear. *This is it. We are all going to die.* James looked just as scared as her. Sam remained expressionless. Gene looked sullen. Just as the two suits leveled their guns, the volume on the TV jumped with dramatic music and a deep voice announced, "This is Breaking News."

Ned came on the air. Diane distracted toward the set. It threw the two suits off. Their guns wavered. Ned looked grim. "Good evening. There is an emergency weather situation developing. A fast moving hurricane called Meg is heading toward the Delmarva Peninsula in an unprecedented storm track that will bring her up the Potomac to Washington DC."

The suit watching TV turned around. "Did you hear that?"

Ned continued, "Meg is what we call a superhurricane. Think of that as a hurricane times ten, maybe more."

"Guys," said Sam, seizing on the fact that even the gunmen started to look away, "that's all we were trying to do. Warn DC. But the government wants to cover it up."

"Why?" asked the suit who'd been sleeping.

"Meg was headed toward Cuba," explained Diane eagerly. "They kept her secret, hoping to launch an invasion behind her."

"Great plan," Sam interrupted quickly. "But she took a wrong turn."

"Gene and I both lost our families to hurricanes," said Sam. "Neither packed even a quarter of Meg's power. If you want to save yours, get them out of DC."

Ned said the same thing on TV. "People, pack up and leave now! Drive north or west. You have about four hours!"

"Shit," said one the suits with a gun.

James jumped in. "None of us here are criminals. Diane and I are meteorologists. We have to get to the office and warn the rest of DC. Let us go. Please."

The suits looked at each other uncertainly. On TV, Ned said, "We are going to our sister station in Wallops Island, Virginia, halfway up the Delmarva Peninsula."

A meteorologist appeared. He was nervous and stumbled on his words. The sound of wind and rain outside was loud enough to be audible in the broadcast. "We are beginning to experience Meg's outer spirals. The wind velocity's been dramatically jumping higher and—"

Crash! The anchor desk flew across the screen! The grid of intersecting pipes from which the studio lights hung came smashing down! The picture broke up violently into static, then settled into the steady buzz of TV snow, but not before a brief but vivid and bloodcurdling image of the meteorologist being crushed to death.

If the suits had any second thoughts, they evaporated. The sleeping suit grabbed his coat, "Let's get outta here."

One of suits uncuffed Diane and tossed her the keys to release the others. Ned continued with grave urgency. "The president is expected to go on the air in a few minutes and order everyone out of DC. The Mayor and all essential department heads are in the Emergency Operations Center."

Diane uncuffed Sam. The suit, who'd been watching the police drama, tossed a key off the wall, "Office car. A brown Intrepid. License plate number is on the chain. Take it."

Diane said, "Head toward Baltimore."

"Thanks." The suits left on a run.

Sam uncuffed Gene and James. The anchorwoman continued from where Ned left off, "We know it's past people's bed time. But if you are watching, call your friends, wake up your neighbors, pass on the warning. We are going to stay with you on the air as long as we are able."

"I have to call my wife," said James, pulling out his cell phone.

"Who's lead tonight?" asked Diane.

"Ivory," said James. His wife answered. "Honey, get into the car and drive north...Just do it! I'll be okay."

"Charlie," said Diane when got through to the WFO and recognized the voice as a junior forecaster, "this is Diane. Is Ivory there?"

"Jesus, Diane, where have you been? It's a madhouse

here."

"I can imagine."

"Hold on. Ivory! Diane's on the phone."

Diane pointed to the backpack. Sam grabbed it. Slung it over his shoulder. She turned on the speaker phone as they hurried out into the hallway.

"You knew all along, didn't you?" Ivory came on the line and exploded. "Why the hell did you not tell me? I'm the WCM!" Warning Coordination Meteorologist.

"I'm sorry," said Diane. "I thought you were part of the cover-up."

James moved up next to her and said, "Blame me if you have to blame anybody."

"Ninety percent of DC is not going to hear the warning, James," said Ivory.

"What do you want us do?" asked Diane. "Where do you want us to go?"

"Elliot needs more bodies at the EOC."

"We can be there in less than ten minutes," said Diane.

"What's the latest on the storm?" asked James.

"She's only a hundred and twenty miles across, so her swath of destruction will be limited. But her eyewall gusts are five hundred and twenty miles an hour. Sustained gusts at four-fifty. Weakest gusts are four hundred."

"Jesus," breathed James.

"What's her forward speed?"

"Around fifty miles an hour."

"How far away is she?"

"Two hundred miles. Four hours away."

James simply said, "We are screwed."

"Tell me about it," replied Ivory.

They arrived in the deserted, basement parking lot and easily found the brown Intrepid. Diane took the wheel. Sam and Gene climbed in the back. James rode shotgun. Emerging outside, they instinctively looked up at the skies and found it blanketed with high clouds.

"Muggy," observed James.

"Meg is sucking the environment around her," Diane explained. Otherwise, the night was calm. Almost serene. But she knew the weather would change rapidly and dramatically.

The bottom would literally fall out.

EIGHTEEN

HSEMA Director Elliot Brand stood aside, savoring a moment to himself. It would be his last, he knew. Elliot had just spoken with his wife. She was on her way out of DC with their two teenage daughters. Now, he faced the task of waking and evacuating the entire capital. He stood unobtrusively in a corner of the Emergency Operations Center under the Ronald Reagan Building.

The large space looked, felt, and was high-tech. It crackled with urgency. Everyone wore headsets that were handed out at the door. TV monitors hung from the ceiling for unobstructed visibility. Workstations came equipped with a telephone, computer, and 'in' and 'out' pouches to hold reports and updates in front of the operator. Half a dozen photocopiers, fax machines, and a six-channel radio set stood against the walls around the room. In case of power failure, a generator kicked in. The fully stocked kitchen could sustain the staff for three days. A pair of curtains on the wall had been parted to reveal a large street and contour map of DC, marking low lying areas, hills, location of police and fire stations, shelters, bus stops, and other emergency services.

Landfall targets in Maryland and Virginia were being handled by emergency management teams in Baltimore and Norfolk respectively. In the absence of a hurricane-specific response plan for the capital, Elliot followed the Emergency Operations Simulation Exercise for a large scale terror attack published in DC's Emergency Operations Master Plan and Procedures. The EOMPP was a thick, comprehensive manual of Command Structure and Responsibilities and Functions, Operational Procedures, Control Tactics, and Emergency Operations. It listed a checklist of evacuation procedures, communications, and operations that encompassed Hazard Analysis, Vulnerability Analysis, Population Data Analysis, Behavioral Analysis, Shelter Resource and Duration Analysis,

Utilities and Essential Services Analysis, and Public Evacuation Time Routes.

Following a checklist laid out in EOMPP, Elliot had already put the staff on twelve-hour A & B shifts. He'd called in off duty personnel, mobilized reserves, and contacted registered volunteers. There was no time to recruit unregistered volunteers. He'd issued orders to activate Field Task Forces, which were local cops, firemen, and neighborhood watches organizing themselves into emergency response teams. They conducted exercises every quarter, mostly large scale terror attacks. FTF communicated over the EOC's overlapping network of radios, telephones, teletype, closed circuit TV, and the Emergency Broadcast System. An Intelligence Control Center in the EOC coordinated, analyzed, and disseminated FTF reports.

Elliot saw Diane, James, Sam, and Gene stride in. He left the corner, greeting them, "Diane, James!" The two picked up a headset each. Elliot clapped, "Everybody! To the table!"

The department heads from earlier were all back and they hurried to the long, mahogany, oval table. A couple of DCPD deputies escorted in the reporters and news crews from the media room and they formed a standing-room only ring around the seated brass.

Elliot began, "This is James Vaughn, MIC from Silver Springs, and Diane Wood, who warned us about Meg."

The Mayor went on the defensive right away, looking from Diane to Elliot, "You must understand, when radio transmission did not come through—"

Elliot let it pass with a dismissive wave. He'd dealt with this wishy-washy politician before. "All the designated shelters like covered arenas and school halls will be open but, considering Meg's strength, they are just as vulnerable as homes. So let's use loud speakers, bullhorns, whatever public address systems we can muster up between all the agencies here and ask people to leave town. There's no time to go door to door and enforce mandatory evacuations. Repeat the warning three times per street and move on."

"We still won't cover the whole city," said the Police Chief. Elliot just tilted his head. There was nothing more they could do.

The Chief nodded and left the table, calling out instructions.

Elliot turned to the Transportation Director and School Superintendent, "Those who don't have cars need buses. Have them at regular and school bus stops. Re-route and reschedule trains and flights to take people out of the city."

They left the table, dialing.

Elliot looked at Diane and James. "Diane, you keep in contact with Ivory. Update James in the media room every five minutes."

Diane and James hurried off.

"Mayor, we'll need Red Cross, Salvation Army, and military help in the aftermath."

The Mayor got on his headset phone immediately.

Elliot continued assigning tasks to the remaining department heads and dispatching them from the table. Finally, he was alone again in his chair. The last of the media had left. Most would return to their newsrooms despite his admonition that there would be no papers printed or delivered tomorrow. A few, he hoped, would heed the warning and leave with their families. He continuously switched channels on his headset, which came with multi-band-multi-frequency versatility, and monitored every individual department. A Park Service woman saw birds taking flight in the dark. Dogs stopped howling. Strays disappeared. Rodents scurried off the streets. Even insects vanished. The air emptied of all natural night time sounds.

All across DC, police cars, motorcycles, and foot patrols of cops and neighborhood watch volunteers blared storm warnings, some with personal Karaoke machines and Jerry-rigged sound systems. Helicopters took to the air and blasted their bull horns. Elliot kept a wary ear on the worsening weather stats. Wind rose steadily to fill the silence. A curtain of steady drizzle started down from the overcast sky, easing the relentless heat. Water along the Potomac and Anacostia took on an unclean color. Above-normal swells moved in. The tide ran farther and farther up the shores.

Radio and TV updates continued ceaselessly. The Emergency Broadcast System went into an automatic cycle of repetition. Red Hurricane Flags were raised atop the Capitol, the White House, all government buildings, schools, hospitals, fire stations, and police stations.

Elliot shut the bulky EOMPP, after reading one more time—his umpteenth—that six hours were necessary for the EOC to become fully operational and twenty-four to elicit public response.

That added up to thirty hours of lead time.

DC had three, with much of the capital dead asleep.

Baron and Jack entered the Oval Office.

"How's it going?" asked Avery, looking up hopefully. He was sitting on the couch, tired and haggard and completely detached from the furor of aides and assistants clearing the Oval Office and the West Wing. Other crews dismantled the White House of art, artifacts, important papers, and other valuables. He'd also signed an Executive Order authorizing the removal of vital documents from the Pentagon, FBI, CIA, Capitol Hill, and other sensitive government buildings.

"Not good," said Baron gravely. "Public response so far's been negligible." He took the chair across from the president. Jack prowled impatiently on his feet.

Avery just shook his head. He'd been briefed that Meg was hundred and fifty percent stronger than the worst tornadoes, and tornadoes only lasted a few seconds. A minute, at the most. Meg was expected to lay DC under siege for three hours. Casualties were going to be unprecedented and the damage unimaginable.

"It's time to leave, sir," said Baron.

Marine One waited on the South Lawn to take the Avery to Andrews Air Force Base, where he would board, not Air Force One, but the National Emergency Airborne Command Post, or Kneecap—the Doomsday Plane. It was designed to serve as an alternative White House should the nation come under siege.

"We are following the Doomsday drill," said Jack. "Baron, Peter, and I will go up with you. The Pentagon, CIA, NSA, FBI, and vital law enforcement are at Site R." An underground facility in Gettysburg. "The EXCOMM are on their way to High Point." A bunker under Mount Weather at Berryville. "The VP—we put his family on the first plane to New York. He and select members of Congress are already in Greenbrier." A nuclear shelter deep inside a mountain in Virginia, it contained a scaled down replica of the Senate amphitheater. Splitting up the politicians and bureaucrats ensured one of the three locations could continue government in a worst case scenario.

"What about the rest of Congress?"

"Two planes have already left," replied Baron. "Operators are working down the list." Then he added carefully, "We probably won't get to them all."

Avery took a deep breath and looked up, setting his jaw. "I'm not leaving."

"Sir?" Baron and Jack exclaimed together sharply.

"I cannot leave," said Avery. "It would be wrong. I caused this and I cannot be the first to save myself." His address to DC residents had been brief. He did not explain why a hurricane was bearing down on them without any warning. He just spelled out her statistics and concluded with a blunt declaration, "You will not survive if you remain in your homes." Before Baron or Jack could speak, Avery held up his hand and took an iron tone, "Nothing you say is going to change my mind. So don't even try."

Baron sat back. "Sir, in that case, we have to implement TREETOP 4." The presidential Succession Plan as laid out in the Twenty-fifth Amendment of the Constitution. "I have to take your place of authority on Kneecap."

Avery nodded. "You have it. Jack will attest I'm of sound mind when I ceded it."

Jack nodded. "Yes, sir."

"Agent Connor and your Secret Service detail were going to ride out the storm in the Situation Room with the other aides and their families. I'll tell him you'll be there with them."

Avery nodded. "Where is Meg now?"

———

Diane rushed over to the Delmarva workstation. The Division Commander of the Operations Control Dispatch at Wallops was reporting an unprecedented phenomenon. "Are you sure?" she asked.

There was no answer.

"OCD Wallops, come in!"

"Try the others," said Elliot.

"OCD Bloxom, come in!" called Diane. "OCD Salisbury, come in! OCD Melfa, come in!"

Nobody answered. Not one.

———

Nearly a hundred and thirty people lived per square mile of the Delmarva Peninsula. Chesapeake Ferries and US Navy boats took away the few hundred men, women, and children who showed up in response to the evacuation order. Most residents never heard the warning, or if they did, they dismissed it. They all came awake as one when it went abruptly from steady downpour and sporadic gusts to berserk rain and wind.

At that point, there was no place to run or hide.

Thunder detonated like a million bombs. In a region which experienced a little more than ninety bolts of lightning, six hundred and fifty-eight were recorded in the first half hour. They illuminated something deadlier. Ghostly serpents. Blacker than the night. Descending through the devastating wind and rain. A sight so eerie, even in their ugliness lay a menacing beauty.

Tornadoes!

The intense heat during the day had saturated the air with water vapor, producing a squall line, or front of strong winds. Moving shoreward, a tropical storm sometimes interacted with this instability in the upper atmosphere to drop twisters in the outer fringes of the right-front quadrant of a tropical storm. Never out of the deep bowels.

The tornadoes packed three hundred mile-an-hour gusts inside a storm already blowing at four hundred miles an hour. They coiled earthward stealthily, cloaked by the blinding wind and rain. Once they touched ground, they moved with the ear rending rattle of a hundred locomotives, snatching up cars, homes, the ground itself. People were lying in bed one moment and hurled out of it the next. The floor kicked up under them, spun wildly, and tossed them around like dice in a cup.

The most violent spawned subsidiary vortexes, called suction vortexes, which moved within the parent vortex. They attacked with twice the power, stripped paint, and drove blades of grass clean through walls. Inside these twisters, the pressure dropped precipitously, sometimes as much as a hundred millibars.

Turning buildings inside out.

Then, Meg spit the pieces every which way.

The Barrier Islands within the hurricane's one hundred and twenty-mile swath of destruction disappeared beneath the ocean. Swallowed whole. Route 13, the main north-south artery, was never without traffic. Meg plucked cars and trucks off the road and threw them miles in every direction. Anchored boats flipped over, ran aground, and drowned in the rabid waters. From Salisbury in the north to Melfa in the South, Meg leveled the Peninsula. Then she replenished the moisture she'd expended with warm water in Pocomoke Sound and stomped every tiny island from Tangier to Fishing Bay underwater.

———

Diane returned to her station where her phone rang. It was Ivory. "This is probably our final transmission, We should be feeling her first spirals in thirty minutes. I've just fed you Meg's final stats. The numbers are not typos."

Diane's printer came alive. She read it and blanched. Meg was a hundred and eighteen miles in diameter. Her forward speed slowed to thirty-eight miles an hour. Her eye was small, sixteen miles across. Her fiercest winds gusted in the eyewall at five hundred and twenty miles an hour, tapering off to just four-fifty in her outermost spiral. So, her weakest gusts were stronger than the fiercest tornado ever recorded in recent memory.

"Oh, my God," James said, shaking his head. He stood beside Diane.

"Any more gate-to-gates?" asked Diane. Conflicting air flows right next to each other that had dropped those devastating tornadoes onto Delmarva.

"I have no idea. Meg took out all the frontline radars. So these are AWIPS's projections. But does it matter? Meg's way past F-5 herself." He was referring to the Fujita Wind Damage Scale for tornadoes, which measured severity of damage from F-0 or 'light' to F-5 or 'incredible'. "We do know that the HPRs have lined up her eye into the mouth of Potomac. From there it's a straight line to hit DC dead on. One consolation, if it is one, is that she'll be with us only three hours.

"Yeah," nodded Diane. "But three hours of tornado like conditions across a hundred and eighteen mile diameter? It's a first."

"Good luck and take care," said Ivory.

"You too. Ivory, I'm sorry."

"Water under the bridge."

Diane laughed. It was the first time she'd ever laughed

at anything he'd said. Diane looked up at James. He nodded to Elliot. There was no need for words.

"Order all FTF to take off," Elliot announced to the subdued room. "If people haven't evacuated by now, it's too late. Time to batten down the hatches and hope for the best."

Something in her subconscious caused her eyes to take notice of a man with a limp entering the EOC. She saw him turn the lock, turn around, and sweep his gaze around the room. There was a slow, deliberate thoroughness about him. Elliot, walking by him, stopped. Diane read his lips, "Can I help you?"

The man nodded. His hand appeared from his pocket with an unusual looking…gun!

Before Diane's mind could even register alarm—*bang!* Loud, clear, distinct. He shot Elliot between the eyes. Most of the back of Elliot's head broke loose, carried almost ten feet by the bullet. Diane screamed. The assassin looked toward her. She noticed recognition cross his eyes like a shadow.

Who is he and how does he know me?

Bang! He fired, but she was already overbalancing in fright. She fell backward. The bullet whizzed past her ear into James. As her back of her head hit the floor, she saw his skull split open. Blood, brain, and bone sprayed. She screamed again, bringing Sam and Gene, who'd nodded off in chairs beside Diane, awake. By now panic stricken cries erupted all across the EOC. The pilots hit the ground at once and hustled to Diane's side under a desk.

"What the hell?" exclaimed Gene.

"Shh!" said Sam. "Play dead!"

Diane stared at James's body on the floor. Aghast. Blood spread in a pool around his head. *Bang!* Diane looked off. The Police Chief, the only armed man in the room, dropped next. *Bang!* Then, the Mayor. People started running helter-skelter. *BangBangBangBangBang!* The assassin stayed by the door so that nobody could leave and picked off his victims one by one.

Clatter. Her face pressed the floor, Diane glimpsed the spent clip bounce off the floor, but he inserted a new one so quickly, there seemed no pause in the shooting.

Crash! Someone took down the contents of a workstation. Death cries repeated with chilling regularity. The volume of the uproar faded. The staccato of his gun came audible louder and louder, indicating more people were dead than alive.

Diane saw a woman, who had tripped and fallen, scramble to her feet hysterically, trying to make a dash for the door. The assassin caught her in midstride with a bullet. She swiveled. Diane knew the woman was dead from the stillness of her eyes, and Diane saw her eyes because the woman crumpled face down on top of her.

"Don't move!" whispered Sam. "Stay under her!"

The gunfire continued for another minute and then silence fell. Persisted.

Diane did not hear the door open.

———

Andrew could not leave. Not until everyone in this room was dead. They had all heard two words they shouldn't have— Thunder Strike. Of the eighteen primary targets, whose pictures were imprinted in his mind's eye, he'd counted sixteen as dead. Actually, fifteen. He wasn't certain he hit the forecaster, Diane Wood. He had to be certain. Peter specifically identified her as was one of the three 'must die' targets. The other two were USAF pilots, Sam Winger and Gene Fellow. He was troubled that he didn't see the two men. One of the three possessed the Jayspid—another 'must recover' directive from Peter.

Andrew took a deep, dispassionate breath and stood still. If someone was alive, they'd move. First. So he waited. And waited. And waited.

A picture of predatory patience.

———

Diane contacted Sam and Gene with her eyes. Sam rotated his head around soundlessly. He started to brace the weight of his body on his palms to raise himself.

Scrape. A heel brushed the floor.

The killer! He moved first. Sam froze.

That was close, Diane flashed with her eyes. Footfalls tread softly, carefully. *Is the assassin leaving?* Sam, Gene, and she craned their necks around with the same thought.

No.

Diane almost gave herself away with a gasp of terror. She managed to swallow it. He was going from body to body, pumping a bullet into every corpse. The gun got louder. He was getting closer. She started to wriggle out from under the dead woman.

Stop! Sam mouthed furiously. Diane went still.

She peered through the cascading hair of the dead woman atop her. A pair of shoes stepped into view. She muffled another whimper of fear. The assassin advanced. She felt bile rise into her throat. Clenched her teeth, locked her lips, and stopped breathing altogether. The barrel lowered. A pale finger tightened around the trigger to discharge a bullet into the back of the skull of the woman atop Diane.

That was as much as she could take. Unabated terror overcame restraint. She heaved with all her strength. The woman was lighter than Diane anticipated.

The assassin recoiled! Startled. He wasn't expecting a corpse to rise backward. Diane kicked out. Caught his shoe. He tripped backward.

Sam, reacting quickly, sprang to his feet. Put a shoulder into the assassin, cracking the back of his head against the edge of a workstation. The gun flew. The bastard crumpled. Diane saw his lids ebb shut, but as they did, she noticed his eyeballs stutter from her to Sam to Gene.

He's counting us off as still alive.

"Dead?" Diane squeaked, barely finding her voice.

"No, out cold," said Gene, feeling Andrew neck.

"We should kill him before he kills us," said Gene.

"Not one of us is capable of doing it," Sam chided. "So let's get the hell out of here."

"Where's the Jayspid?" asked Gene.

"In my backpack," said Diane.

None of them had it. Panic overtook them. Gene growled, "Oh, great."

Diane found it under the chairs that Sam and Gene had been occupying. She slung it over her shoulder and they fled.

The killer had been the elevator's last passenger. So it was still on their level. They rode it up to the lobby. The cops they'd seen milling about the lobby when they came in were gone. Diane, Sam, and Gene raced toward the glass doors, and for the first time, became aware of the deterioration in the weather outside. The wind whistled. Lightning bolts drew complex patterns across the overcast sky and thunder rumbled progressively louder and lower inside the low, dense, and black clouds. Emerging outside, they were instantly knocked off their feet. They grabbed each other and pulled themselves back into the lobby.

Just in time.

A blinding blue flash of lightning came alive and stayed alive. A roaring clap triggered an unending roll of thunder. The clouds exploded. Millions of tons of water came hurtling down with apocalyptic fury.

Meg was here.

NINETEEN

She swept into Point Lookout State Park, annihilated the tourists and the attractions, and roared across Scotland Beach. Diehard surfers, who'd foolishly rushed over to ride her waves, vanished without a trace. Hotels, quaint B & Bs, and million dollar homes, which overlooked the bay, had been targeted early in the warning process. Less than a tenth of the occupants evacuated. Awakened by the lightning and thunder, many just wandered through their homes and rooms, securing the doors and windows. A few glanced outside and, without exception, went catatonic. A sheet of water—they all thought it was a tidal wave, but actually it was a near solid curtain of rain—bulleted toward them. Before they could react, giant droplets hammered against the panes, walls, and roof. Building codes had been set to withstand a pressure of three tons—that exerted by a seventy-four mile-an-hour wind. Meg's weakest gusts measured four hundred and fifty. The structures and the occupants didn't stand a chance.

At piers along the Potomac, the river had been getting progressively choppier. Houseboats had received early warnings too. Most residents just dropped heavier anchors. Meg picked them up and threw them inland. Leaving a wasteland behind her, she marched into DC and announced herself with the loudest cloudburst yet.

One that sent Diane, Sam, and Gene racing back into the lobby of the Ronald Reagan Building.

———

Diane looked over her shoulder and stumbled. "Jesus! Look!" The wind stretched and bent the vast sheet glass window inward. It remained bubbled like that for a second.

"Get away!" yelled Sam.

His warning coincided with a snarling, high pitched crack that surpassed the roar of the storm. The bubble burst, releasing a blizzard of lethal shards enveloped in a haze of wind and rain. The trio dived into the stairwell. Trying to get behind the turn in the wall.

And somehow did.

A split second ahead!

The glass at the other end of the lobby disintegrated. Meg's shriek and thunderous sounds of collisions and collapse invaded from the outside.

"Where to?' asked Gene as they started downstairs. "Our killer is going to wake up sooner than later."

"Underground tunnels connect all the federal buildings," said Diane, leading the way to the chamber where they intersected. Emergency fluorescents diffused down dimly. Meg had taken out the main power here in the first minute of her siege.

"Dead ends," dismissed Sam, doing a quick three-sixty survey of signs and arrows over the archways that diverged in all directions toward the Capitol, Treasury, and other buildings.

"Not really," said Diane. "Some lead off to the closest subway stations around those buildings."

"Do you know which do and which don't?" asked Sam.

Diane shook her head. "Nope."

"What's the plan here?" asked Gene irritably.

"We keep moving for the duration of storm," said Sam. "That way, we will always maintain our head start over the killer."

"Then let's play it safe and head for Federal Triangle," said Diane nodding to the blue and white subway station logo over an eastbound tunnel. "It's just a few blocks from here."

———

Meg tore out the Emancipation Statue and broke it into two. She used a flying truck to knock the pillars out from under the Supreme Court. Half the gable crashed in. The nine-judge Bench became airborne debris. Millions of books and loose-leaf pages flew out of the windows of the Library of Congress. The Washington Monument leaned but refused to break. Meg overturned Lincoln and decapitated him. She took out every glass pane of the Capitol and hammered a gaping hole into the dome. Once inside, her demonic wind plundered every office. Meg mercilessly pounded the classic architecture, which distinguished many federal government buildings as landmarks.

Some would survive, most would not.

There were thousands of commuters even at this early hour, some fleeing DC, but most either going to or returning from work. Drivers had time to register an opaque wall of water advancing, nothing more. Every commuter on the street this morning died. Older bridges, ramps, and overpasses came crashing down. Meg fulfilled a dire prophecy of Dr. Robert Sheets, a former Director of the National Hurricane Center, who had warned of hurricanes like her, "if we have a major loss of life…it is going to be people in their vehicles trapped on the roads..." So harshly did Meg strike, damage roads, and clog DC's traffic arteries with dismembered human remains, mangled cars, and broken buildings, she crippled investigation, identification, and relief efforts in her aftermath.

Among Meg's victims were all the members of the EXCOMM, who were on their way to High Point, a bunker under Mount Weather at Berryville. Peter had deliberately released the bus minutes before Meg arrived at DC.

He wanted them to perish and she did not fail him.

Yet another secret that would die with her.

———

Andrew came to.

He recalled what happened. Three targets got away. Diane and the two pilots.

Finding his Offensive Pistol, Andrew exited the EOC. The storm penetrated the stairwell as a dull roar broken up by sharp sounds of hard impact. He reached the mid-landing of the final flight and stopped. Wind, rain, and debris hurtled through the lobby. He felt the vicious pluck of the rain and wind. *Screech!* Andrew reflexively backed up. Meg dragged a car across the lobby floor on its hood.

Shit. Andrew had not considered stalking Diane, Sam, and Gene through a hurricane. *Where would I even begin looking for them?* He didn't panic. He never did. He thought logically. He always kept track of time. The nature of his job demanded that he did. He knew precisely when Diane had attacked him. Realized he'd been unconscious ten minutes. About as old as the storm. So they couldn't have gotten out of this building. He headed downstairs to the first sublevel and came upon the labyrinth of subterranean corridors. Sloppy footprints headed in one direction. He counted six. His quarry. Upon reading the sign, he realized he'd have figured which way they'd gone even without this tell tale trail. *Count on the mindset of amateurs.*

He reloaded his gun. Started for the Federal Triangle Station.

———

After his call to Diane, Ivory ordered everyone into the basement, a well planned, sturdy shelter with all the amenities to make it through most severe floods, snowstorms, and stormy weather that models had extrapolated based on the history of the worst natural disasters DC had seen. None came close to simulating what Meg threw at the shelter.

The last twister in her belly.

The first slam of wind cut the power. Doors and windows pulverized. The walls and roof of the superstructure collapsed outward. State-of-the-art hardware took to the air. The tornado was merely drawing breath. Its winds kept accelerating and accelerating. Some gusts merged with Meg's winds and reached a combined eight hundred miles an hour! The ceiling ripped off the basement. Snatched up the cowering people. Drowned out the bloodcurdling death cries.

Ivory came to, thudding hard into the ground. He'd escaped unscathed. And staring into the narrow core of the tornado—cloudless, bright, with vivid blue flashes of lightning.

Just as suddenly, the rope receded back into the clouds. Rain pounded down upon him.

His last thought and vision was the giant radome.

Dropping straight down toward him.

She was a living, breathing monster. Sermons seeking reasons and solace in the aftermath would call her evil and cunning because of the manner of her arrival—in the wee hours before dawn, when most residents were in stage three or stage four deep sleep, called slow wave or delta. Meg evoked initial reactions which ranged from numbness to terror. She forced atheists to pray for the first time. Others wished for death to end their fear and suffering. She awakened childhood frailties and exposed inadequacies.

Frustration mounted. Hope declined.

The Disaster Behavior Index was a device used by sociologists and psychologists to score an individual's response to a crisis, taking into account personal courage, crisis appraisal, risks taken, leadership, and use of available options. In the absence of anticipatory precepts, the DBI found eighty percent of the people non-adaptive. Such was the case in most of the city, which had little or no warning.

It wasn't Meg's fault that people in DC could be neighbors for years and never be acquainted. A disaster response, called illusion of centrality, took over. Men and women reacted with primal self-preservation—or, in this city, selfishness. They trampled others to get into elevators. Fought their way out of exits. Broadsided and even stole cars. Ran over fleeing pedestrians. The few who survived would be plagued in the aftermath by the guilt of what they had done to live.

Forewarning, on the other hand, created anticipatory precepts, which lessened the shock. Stats then swung the number the other way. Almost eighty percent became adaptive, as evidenced at Ned Cahill's network. The staff and he had gathered sufficient food, first aid, batteries, and other survival necessities and trooped down to the basement. Meg stripped the building, a glass tower, to its structural skeleton, and hammered on the exposed door with her wind and rain. Ned and the staff had barricaded it firmly.

Her only access in, it was also their only exit.

Meg kept the survivors' attention riveted to the sounds of her destruction. They were unaware that a city sewer ran alongside the south wall. She began to flood it. How long could the twenty-four inch clay pipe hold up to the rapidly mounting capacity? Could she max it out during her estimated three hour assault, crack it open, and disintegrate the wall?

———

Diane, Sam, and Gene reached Federal Triangle. The gentle arch with deep soffits was cloned into the roof of almost every subway station in DC. These terminals under and around the federal government buildings usually began buzzing with commuters around seven. So it was utterly empty at this early hour, except for about twenty people, most of them derelicts. How ironic, reflected Diane, those with the resources to flee most certainly perished in larger numbers than the homeless poor, who survived because they got off the streets when it first began to drizzle.

Diane inched toward the stairway off the street. Being so tightly coiled Meg's wind and rain likely strengthened almost a mile an hour every minute. A thin sheet of water wrapped down the steps, indicating she was driving waves from the Potomac and Anacostia deeper and deeper inland. The heavy droplets had given way to a fine rain. The clouds were active with nonstop lightning and thunder. Every now and then, Meg's roar was interrupted by a crash of debris and the violent collapse of a building.

Neither Herbert Saffir nor Robert Simpson ever envisioned anything like Meg, thought Diane. The two men had created Saffir-Simpson Damage Potential Scale in 1969 to convey the destructive power of a hurricane. Saffir was the father of the Miami building code and Simpson, then the director of National Hurricane Center. A Category 1 (winds of 74-95 mph) was designated as a hurricane with minimal damage potential, Category 2 (winds of 96-110 mph) moderate, Category 3 (winds of 111-130 mph) extensive, Category 4 (winds 131-155 mph) extreme, and Category 5 (winds more than 155 mph) catastrophic. If they'd continued their classification, mused Diane, Meg would rate as a Category 10!

She retreated toward Sam, who stood on the edge of the platform.

"What do you make of that?" he asked, pointing to electric sparks crackling sporadically along the wet tracks.

"Power comes from multiple sources into the subway system and Meg hasn't destroyed them all?"

"Yet," said Sam grimly.

"Failure from one generating station automatically triggers another," Diane explained. "There are breakers every hundred yards, which also back up and bypass each other." Redundancy ensured trains ran without interruption. But Elliot had suspended all service half hour before Meg arrived. Diane couldn't imagine that would save mass transit in the aftermath. Meg was probably ripping cars off their tracks at yards where they were parked.

"Let's keep moving," said Sam.

"Through the tunnel?" asked Diane. and

"Unless you want to make like debris and fly through the storm," remarked Gene dourly.

Diane smiled. "Good one."

"I was not trying to be funny," said Gene dourly.

"What's with you?" asked Diane.

"Nothing," replied Gene resentfully. "I'm living my dream."

"We signed up for this," said Sam. "Nobody twisted our arms. So get over it."

"I will," Gene grumbled, hopping down. "Once I get out of this alive."

Sam waved off Gene's sullen attitude and helped Diane down. "Walk on the ties and be careful not touch the rails."

"Which way?" asked Gene.

Diane pointed south. "Better to come out behind Meg once she passes. Also, it puts us closer to Vick's house."

"Where do you live?" asked Sam.

"We don't want to go there," jumped in Gene. "That's the first place they'd look."

"I'm just making conversation," Sam replied, shaking his head.

"Berwyn Heights," said Diane. "It's east of College Park. A long way east of here."

Water seeped over the edge of the platform and soaked the ground. Diane noticed a few saturated sections began to fill out into puddles. Eventually, the puddles would overflow into rivulets. When Meg blew over, most of these tunnels and subway stations would be completely underwater. Halfway into the tunnel, the overhead emergency lights flickered and died completely, dropping down a blackness so thick, they could not see their own hands. *Static!Static!* Blue and white electrical flashes jumped along the tracks.

"Train power's still on," noted Diane. The periodic sparks afforded the trio just enough visibility to get used to the spacing of the rail ties, helping them find wood sure-footedly during the long spasms of total blackness inside the tunnel.

———

Andrew limped into Federal Triangle. He had not stopped walking when the backup power failed, fishing out a penlight he always carried. He'd turned it on for a moment to find the wall so that he could keep it at arm's length, and used it to guide his feet. Once he reached the station, Andrew went over to a homeless man who was stretched out in a way that suggested he hadn't moved in a while. He did not waste time. Put a gun to his head.

"Two guys and a girl, which way did they go?"

Taken aback by the suddenness and the directness of the threat from both gun and tone, the homeless man jerked his thumb toward the southbound tunnel.

Andrew dropped down between the tracks

———

The trio's pace flagged. They were running out of the adrenaline that had kept them up and going without sleep for two days. Each took turns with the backpack containing the heavy Jayspid. Sam wore it now. Ahead, a smidgeon of gloom appeared.

"Ooh, look," Sam quipped tiredly. "Light at the end of the tunnel." Nobody laughed. "Tough room."

"Bad joke," said Diane. When they got to the platform, she asked, "Can we rest?"

"Yeah," agreed Gene. His knees throbbed.

"No," said Sam. "It's too risky."

"We don't even know if he's following us," grumbled Gene.

"Do we want to gamble that he is not?"

Gene and Diane straggled behind Sam. Trudged past the Smithsonian Station, which, like Federal Triangle, was littered with more of DC's poor. About a dozen. With no homes around the area, there were zero commuters. Water sputtered in off the street with increased intensity. The trio stayed between the tracks and entered the tunnel to L'Enfant Plaza.

———

Andrew reached Smithsonian eight minutes later. He quickly surveyed the faces on the platform. He did not expect to find his quarry, though he knew he was gaining on them, and knew also that Diane, Sam, and Gene were unaware that he was. The tunnel worked like a conduit, carrying their voices a mile and a half either way. He heard them get perceptibly louder. They talked incessantly to keep their mind off the pursuit, fear, weariness, and everything else that preoccupied virgin runners.

Andrew paused with his hands on his hips. Scurrying

like fugitive rodents along the rails, electric flashes illuminated a single set of railway tracks out of this station. He started forward. Eighteen minutes later, he arrived at L'Enfant, where the Orange, Blue, Yellow, and Green Lines met. A busy intersection during working hours, it was eerily and completely deserted. He realized why he lost their voices. The top of the station had sheared off. Uneven walls circled the hole in the roof, which acted like pursed lips to create a high pitched whistle of the wind. Water poured off the steps and swept across the entire platform. It was ankle deep.

Andrew stopped. *Shit.*

Four tunnels diverged away in four directions.

––––––

At that moment, a mile north of Andrew, an updraft elevated a crowd of fifteen streamers—positive charges—above the Verizon Center, a state-of-the-art, two hundred million-dollar sports and entertainment arena. The Wizards, DC's professional basketball team, called it home. Meg had demolished the contemporary facade, and now clawed away at the sturdy roof and walls of the court inside to get to the thousand-plus refugees. The structure would survive, so too the people. The updraft collided with a stepped leader—-negative charged raindrops. Fifteen separate circuits completed. Electric current flowed along each return stroke for fifteen fiery bolts of lightning—the second most prolific killer in the US behind floods.

Meg had been unleashing more than than two hundred bolts a minute. They invaded buildings through electrical, telephone, and plumbing lines. Set off broken gas lines. Started electrical fires that incinerated internal walls, furniture, carpeting, paperwork, and people. Elevator shafts attracted lightning bolts to travel down the cables, weakening them and dropping cars crammed with fleeing residents.

What made these fifteen bolts singularly devastating was the fact that they discharged in the span of a single second! A searing white blaze radiated out and infiltrated every nook and corner in a two mile circle around the Verizon Center. Spilled down the devastated stairwells onto the subway platforms. Penetrated as deep as fifty yards into every tunnel.

Lighting up Diane, Sam, and Gene, who were almost at Waterfront. Enveloped in a blinding halo himself, Andrew saw them.

———

Diane, Sam, and Gene, like everyone inside the diameter of illumination, stopped and stared up and around. Jaws hanging. Dazzled.

The air, heated to 40,000°F by each return stroke, expanded, and collided for fifteen separate but rapid detonations, each trailing into the next in a seemingly never ending crash of thunder. The tunnels shook, dislodging dust. Rails rattled. A barrage of sparks erupted along the tracks. Breakers overloaded and the boxes went off like bombs one after the other. This awesome electrical event killed all the power, main and emergency. Diane would remember this as the moment in time when the heart of government went dark. It was also the reason electricity could not be restored in the immediate aftermath.

Meg fried every circuit serving the DC grid.

Diane looked over her shoulder. Light from the final breaker blast faded. Plunging the tunnel to black,. She couldn't see a thing except the luminous dial of her watch.

Meg was forty-five minutes old.

Her worst was yet to come.

TWENTY

President Avery Walker sat at the head of the horseshoe with his aides, working. Agent Connor and his detail of a dozen secret service agents and their families sat at the other end of the horseshoe, quietly playing cards, reading, or dozing. The adjacent meeting room was turned into a nursery for the kids, who laughed and played innocently. The giant screens had been turned off.

Born out of the Bay of Pigs invasion that failed due to a breakdown in communications, the Situation Room had been modified and updated by almost every president since JFK. Following 9/11, it was expanded to five thousand square feet and given a futuristic look with flatscreens and other high tech electronics. Contrary to popular belief, the Situation Room had never been a bunker until Avery's predecessor made it so with a twelve-inch reinforced concrete envelope and heavy steel doors. A 24/7 alert center since its inception, now it was set up to handle control, command, and communications for the National Security Council at ground zero during a nuclear strike while the president took to the air and others disbursed to alternative locations. Powered by its own emergency generator located within the concrete envelope, electricity wasn't interrupted. They barely felt Meg down here, though they could hear her through the concrete and steel. It wasn't not be hard to piece together what happened, when Avery went upstairs after the storm passed.

Meg blew out the double-paned bullet proof Kevlar windows of the Oval Office. The first slap of wind and rain smashed the president's historic and irreplaceable 'Resolute desk,' named for the source of its construction, the timbers of the *HMS Resolute.* Nothing remained but dismembered pieces of this gift from Queen Victoria to President Hayes in 1880. Disintegrating in that whirlwind was the traditional potted Swedish Ivy. Its roots traced back to JFK, who'd made it a fixture on the north mantel. She victimized the couch and high backed chairs, a familiar backdrop for thousands of photo-ops with leaders around the world. Ripped out the presidential seals sculptured on the ceiling and embroidered into the carpet. Spent the rest of her assault gouging out the walnut floor.

Meg atomized the four doors leading out of the Oval Office, plundering the offices and the cubicles of the West Wing, which had been emptied of important papers. She roared through the corridors of power into banquet halls and conference rooms. In the president's quarters, Meg tossed out the furniture, emptied his closet, and took all that was personal and dear to him.

Nobody in the Situation Room suspected Avery's turmoil behind the poker face and calm demeanor of a leader. He was utterly devastated, distressed, and distraught. His mind conjured up images of the death and destruction Meg was meting out. He did not know this depression would never alleviate. His sorrow would never pass.

He would never recover.

———

"Doesn't sound too safe in here, does it?" Diane shouted to be heard when the trio entered Waterfront Station to a slam of storm and tide. There wasn't a soul. Debris from the streets washed in and across the platform. Enough slivers of the outside were visible for her to discern that not a trace of land or building remained around the confluence of the Tidal Basin, channel, Potomac, and Anacostia.

Floods were America's number one killer. Structural flood management in DC, Maryland, and Virginia had evolved from past experience with Hurricanes Agnes in 1972, Fran in 1996, and Isabel in 2003. Each had been severe enough to cause Chesapeake Bay and its tributaries to overflow. Diane had a list in her desk drawer at the WFO. About fifty thousand structures had been identified as vulnerable to damage. With two times the combined the strength of all three storms, Meg surely surpassed the number in just the first hour. Diane would discover she was right and then some.

The Tidal Basin, between the Potomac and Washington Channel, was designed to release two hundred and fifty gallons at high tide twice a day. Meg rode in with fifty-foot high waves that spanned the width of the Potomac and beyond. The Basin, which was ten feet at its deepest point, overflowed instantly and submerged Potomac Park, East and West. Breakers clobbered the Jefferson and FDR Memorials, collaborating with the wind and rain to obliterate the pier side. Boats moored in the Washington Channel would be found fifteen blocks in.

"Jesus," gagged Gene, seeing a human cadaver thump down the steps.

"Let's get out of here," said Sam.

Fear pumped enough of a rush to hasten Diane's pace. Only the Green Line went through this station. They headed east to Navy Yard. Already running on fumes, the ankle deep water made them exert more for every step.

"I could use caffeine," said Diane.

"Me too," said Gene.

"And where do you propose we find some?" asked Sam.

"Starbucks?" Diane pointed to an open counter attached to the newsstand on the Navy Yard Station platform. There was even a light on.

"I don't believe it," laughed Sam.

Climbing onto the platform, Diane immediately recognized a change for the worse outside.

"Are we already in the eyewall?" asked Sam.

Diane checked her watch. Meg was seventy minutes old. Nodded. "Just entering it."

"The eyewall's where Gene and I met and became the couple we are today," said Sam, smiling over sweetly at Gene, who came up alongside. Gene made an unfriendly face. Sam told Diane about that first AWR flight when the Hercules stalled and fell, leading to the harrowing close call with Gene's

Hornet.

Navy Station was devoid of people too, except for the woman behind the counter. She fit the twenty-wannabe-something Starbucks stereotype. They all ordered coffee. Then, she made the understatement of the year, "Rough weather, huh?"

"Can't believe you're open," said Sam. He was so personable and outgoing, Diane was convinced he could seduce an unfriendly pitbull.

"My boss runs an all-night store," she replied and went on to tell Sam her life story without much coaxing. Being on the graveyard shift had saved her life. She knew it, thankful she did not have a family. They would be dead. She lived in an apartment ghetto close by with a roommate, who she had not been able to reach since the deafening cloudburst more than an hour ago. She assumed the worst and was beginning to realize she might be right. So severe were the casualties in DC's depressed neighborhoods of ramshackle homes and overcrowded tenements, the smell of death would pervade over the entire capital in the aftermath. \

"How do you have power?" Diane asked her.

"We are Starbucks," she almost sniffed haughtily.

"Excuse me," Sam shot back.

"Damn right," she grinned. "Can't never run out of coffee, rain or shine." Then she revealed, "We got our own generator after that cold snap couple of winters ago when almost two feet of snow fell on DC for five nights in a row, causing citywide power outages. Same thing happened last year."

"Climatologists have warned that hotter summers and colder winters were here to stay," interrupted Diane.

"Exactly why corporate figured they were blowing a goldmine of profits—if you figure how much hot coffee they can sell in winter."

The caffeine injected the trio with the energy boost they desperately needed. Diane took her cup, walked near the entrance, and peered outside carefully. Meg's intensity had ratcheted up to a demonic intensity. Diane's ears hurt. The cumulative decibels of the thunder, wind, rain, and waves measured twenty times the safe limit.

Crash! A huge wave tumbled over the entrance, which was now just a devastated hole with stairs. Diane raced backward, pursued by water roaring in. The Anacostia flowed less than a mile to the south. *Bam!* Another wave! This one dropped a police car riding its foaming crest fifty feet above the ground. Blowing at five hundred miles an hour, Meg did pretty much what she pleased.

"We have to leave," shouted Sam. Retreating away from the maniacal violence, Diane wondered if Meg would surpass half a million, the record for fatalities set in 1970 by the worst killing cyclone to date in Bangladesh.

"What the hell?" went Gene, stopping dead in his tracks, the instant they entered the tunnel toward the Anacostia Station.

Hairline cracks spider-webbed over the concrete shell. Tremors displaced tiles off the roof and walls

"It runs under the river," said Diane. She could picture giant waves combining with mammoth undersea currents hammering the outer wall of the Anacostia Tunnel.

"How long will it hold, you think?" asked Sam.

Diane shrugged. There was no way to know.

"So, why the hell did you bring us this way?" demanded Gene.

"I didn't realize it, okay?" Diane snapped back.

"I'm not going in there," declared Gene.

"It's the only way out of this station," argued Sam. "Unless you want to backtrack."

"I want to backtrack," retorted Gene. Turned at once.

It saved his life. Because the moment he did, the tile beside his face chipped off violently! *Bang!* The unmistakable sound of a gunshot and the explosive eruption of masonry superseded Meg's shriek.

"That's him!" yelled Diane. The coffee break had evaporated their lead over the assassin, who'd kept plugging forward. *Of course.* He was a professional hunter.

Sam grabbed Gene's arm with one hand, and shoved Diane with the other. "Run!"

Andrew limped out of the tunnel at other end of the tracks. *BangBangBang!* Three quick shots. Three star patterns that dissolved into one. All three bullets would have counted had Diane, Sam, and Gene not disappeared into the pitch black archway.

The coffee girl yelped in fright and dived under the counter. Andrew did not even spare her a glance, hurrying between the tracks. He reached the mouth of the Anacostia Tunnel. Heard his victims splashing away loudly. Andrew had the night sight on and waded forward. They slipped out of his range. He did not worry. Diane, Sam, and Gene would not sprint away from him. They were moving against a brisk current and it flowed ankle deep.

Diane's knowledge of hurricanes came entirely from accounts, books, and papers. So far, Meg did not refute anything she'd read—if anything, she was a hurricane on steroids, and more. Meg was strengthening exponentially by the minute because her stormy turbulence spun faster and faster closer to her eye, which Diane estimated was ten miles away and pillaging its way to the heart of DC at thirty miles an hour.

Outside, she could vision the Anacostia swirling like a giant Jacuzzi with contrary phenomena—waves routinely climbing sixty feet high and depthless holes opening all the way down to the river bottom. It created tremendous crashes of water that pervaded inside the tunnel as a terrible, reverberating roar. Tiles and masonry rained down with accelerating frequency.

"That's not good," screamed Sam.

"You think?" retorted Gene.

Crack! A huge tearing sound! *Whoosh!* A slice of water!

The first fracture opened in the roof of the tunnel and the Anacostia knifed down with a razor of water. Panic and terror seized the trio. Cracks followed the spiderweb of previous hairlines. Water slashed through, widening the cuts in the shell, and rose hip high quickly. The current only strengthened, slowing their pace further.

———

Andrew had never been afraid of anything. Until now. He picked up Diane, Sam, and Gene on his night vision. Fired. The bullets ricocheted off the trembling walls, chiseling out a hunk of concrete. Well short. They were out of range. But they didn't know that.

The trio dived. Disappeared under water.

Andrew did not. He couldn't swim. Breathing hard, he struggled forward, finding himself unable keep pace with his rising fear and the tunnel's race toward collapse.

———

Water flowed chest high. Diane looked behind instinctively, ignoring the huge noises of rending masonry. She couldn't see the assassin. Gene and Sam sandwiched her between them as they scissored in a single file through opaque black waters, unavoidably bumping into debris that included bloated corpses.

"We're there!" panted Diane, nodding to the gray end to the tunnel.

Diane, Sam, and Gene burst out of the tunnel. Blindly rolled onto the platform awash with near continuous waves pummeling through the entrance. Diane could not hear herself think. They stood on the platform. Panting. Bent over. Hands on their knees.

"Go, go, go!" she hollered, straightening abruptly.

Andrew appeared at the mouth of the tunnel and found

himself with a clean shot.

He quickly raised his gun.

———

Meg embraced all of DC inside her eyewall. She blocked out the sun entirely, preventing dawn from breaking over the capital. All she permitted was a deep, dull, grayness to brighten across. Her bowels revealed a sight to behold: airborne cars, buildings, furniture, trees, bodies, and body parts swirling through the rain and wind beneath clouds afire with lightning and thunder. Underfoot, she imposed her will with the combined of authority wind, rain, and waves, flattening anything and everything with casual ferocity.

A pocket of conflicting pressure momentarily sucked the Anacostia dry. Exposing the tunnel. Meg threw the flying debris at it. *WhabamWhabamWhabam!* A barrage of bomb-intensity impacts bombarded the tunnel. Rocking it!

———

Andrew snapped his neck around.

The far end of the tunnel atomized. The Anacostia burst inside. Corkscrewed forward as a furious, foamy cataract. The water was upon Andrew in a flash! He had time to turn away. No more. He felt a slam of water, then the slam of concrete, and nothing in between. The torrent picked him up and flung him on the platform. Quick reflexes made Andrew the elite assassin that he was, and he didn't wait to find his feet. He opened fire, still sliding.

BangBang! Two gunshots.

But Diane, Sam, and Gene were already sprinting toward the exit across the platform. The bullets zinged back at Andrew off the closing doors behind them. A cross current from the entrance steps carried him powerfully all the way. Smashed him through the doors! He hit a wall and stopped. Stairs ascended.

He stared up. Dazed for a second.

———

Diane saw the assassin tumble in. She was on the landing three flights up. It had exits on either edge. She didn't stop, didn't even think. Turned blindly into the exit marked, 'ANACOSTIA PLAZA.' Sam and Gene followed her into a hallway built out of concrete blocks, lined with ads, and ending in another set of double doors.

"Wo!" gasped Diane, opening them.

The Anacostia Plaza was a highly publicized pilot development that enclosed the subway station within a Vegas-like covered citywalk of stores, restaurants, and movie theaters. The giant skylight above the main level atrium was gone, the ring of shops wrecked, their contents ransacked by Meg. Debris from miles around, which included corpses, littered the long walkways. Balconies hung precariously.

Sam grabbed Diane before Meg did. They pulled back inside. The doors closed, abruptly cutting out Meg's howl.

"Dire circumstances be damned, you women can't get shopping out of your minds, can you?" quipped Sam.

"I figured it won't be crowded this morning," she came right back. "I know how you men hate long lines."

"Both of you, shuddap!" Gene snapped. "Neither of you is funny."

They took a side door. It opened into a fire escape that rose eight floors. The windowless tower seemed to have held up against the storm so far. About thirty-five survivors squatted on the steps. Diane wondered if all over DC, people were chancing upon pockets of refuge like this to survive. The trio loped up as fast as they could. They were five flights up. Diane looked down. Andrew stepped inside.

The moment she locked eyes with him, the stairwell shuddered.

Everyone froze.

"Did you feel it?" asked Diane pausing halfway up the next flight.

"You bet," responded Gene, bumping into her.

"Keep moving," urged Sam.

Diane took another step. The mysterious rattling returned. Stopped. She moved again. The shaft shook again. Only, this time it did not stop. Intensifying swiftly. Vibrating like a plucked guitar string! Shrill screams erupted. One of them belonged to Diane. The evacuees clambered to their feet. Diane looked ahead. She was a couple of steps away from the next landing. Lifted her foot on to the next tread. That was as far as she got.

The steps fell away from underneath her.

With a shriek, she grabbed the railing. Someone fell past her. A man. So close, she felt his terrorized cry shatter her eardrum. She urgently looked for Sam and was relieved he'd found the edge of a step. Gene, right behind her and in front of Sam, could not.

"Sam!" Gene yelled. He fell past Sam.

Diane watched Sam react without thinking. He found Gene's wrist. Gripped it at once! Gene locked his fingers quickly and stopped dropping abruptly. Sam jerked, almost losing his thin hold on the stair. But he managed to hang on.

The vibrating continued relentlessly. Stairs ripped out of the wall. People went tumbling down in a barrage of masonry. Some fell right down the shaft, their cries terminating in a sickening splat. The structure disintegrated. A chunk of wall glanced off Diane's knuckles, but she clung tight. Looked down to glimpse Andrew press himself into the niche of the doorway. It offered just enough protection. Bodies and building pieces exploded on the landing in front of him which held. Blood, bone, and dust splattered up and around.

"What's going on?" screamed Sam.

"Earthquake?" shouted someone.

"Shit," said Gene. "That's all we need."

"It's not a quake," said Diane. Actually, it was a rare phenomenon, reported only once before during Typhoon Muroto in Japan. Gusty winds, combined with a suitable period of vibration, had a dynamic influence, causing destructive resonance in the structure.

All went still again just as suddenly.

The ear-rending staccato of breakup ended abruptly. Momentarily, Meg's stormy violence registered as silence. Gasping for breath out of fear and the effort to cling on for dear life, Diane found a foothold and hoisted herself up onto the twisted landing. She reached down to Sam. "Come on."

Sam looked below toward Gene, who found his own foothold and released Sam's life-saving grip on his wrist.

"Go," said Gene. He started up after Sam joined Diane on the landing.

A jagged gash extended from the ground up. The walls on either side of the crack had moved by at least six inches. Meg spit a fine, powerful spray of rain through. Debris and metal pieces of the stairway continued to fall. Sobs and groans of agony sounded over the settling debris. Someone down below found her companion dead and started to wail. Sam leaned over to give Gene a hand. Andrew stepped out of the doorway. He could not climb up. The stairway was severed above and below him.

So, he raised his gun. Diane yelled, "He's going to shoot!"

"Quick!" said Sam. "Gene, up, up!"

Gene looked down instinctively. Andrew's gun flashed. The bullet plucked the flesh out from in Gene's lower back. Diane gasped. She followed the bullet's lethal journey. His vertebrae popped like buttons off a shirt as it traveled up his spine, ripped open his throat, and tore into his brain. Gushing blood, Gene's head lolled. He died instantly and dangled limply at the end of Sam's arm.

"No!" gasped Sam.

"Let go!" Diane cried, seeing Andrew fire again.

She violently tugged Sam by the sleeve. Saving his life. His head jerked out of the bullet's trajectory centered between the eyes. It buried into the plaster behind them. As he fell backward, Sam let go of Gene.

Bang!Bang! Andrew fired two more shots.

———

The last two shots missed because of the accuracy of the one that killed Gene. As Andrew pulled the trigger, his natural reflexes kicked in involuntarily, yanking him out of the way of Gene's body descending straight down toward him. Andrew leaned back into the doorway for the split second it took for Gene's body to sail by and leaned out at once.

The evacuees in the stairwell cringed in fear. Many were trapped with no place to run on steps that hung like precarious ledges on the strength of a bolt or two. He ignored the terrified screams he elicited, craning his neck to find Sam and Diane.

He couldn't see them.

Andrew retreated into the hallway and hurried into the main access stairwell from the station. Conditions were like night and day in the few minutes since he'd tumbled into it from the platform. The Anacostia barraged in through the doors from the station, colliding with sheets coming down off the main level of the mall, which was under six inches of water.

Andrew clenched his jaw and sat down on the steps to wait out Meg.

———

Diane and Sam had put themselves out of Andrew's line of sight and fire by pressing up against the wall. Sam's face contorted with rage. Before he did something foolish, Diane said, "Go, go, go!"

She shoved him toward the door off the edge of landing.

They emerged outside carelessly. Meg said hello and goodbye all in one screaming gust.

TWENTY-ONE

The strategy behind building a mall around the subway station was to attract shoppers who could just take the train in and out and not hassle with driving and paying for expensive parking. But the developers still dedicated three levels of parking atop the Anacostia Plaza.

Diane and Sam had burst onto the second level.

Fortunately, the low floor-to-ceiling clearances cut Meg's wind speed in half: too weak to carry them airborne, but strong enough knock them off their feet. They hit the concrete floor face down, watersliding head first along the exit ramp toward a death-drop of seven stories because Meg had crumbled the three-foot high walls around the edge of the structure. She drowned out their yells entirely. On a hope and prayer, they locked arms and leaned hard to hairpin into the center ramp. And succeeded!

Wind speed dropped to a quarter in the middle of the structure. That was still a hundred and twenty-five miles an hour. Slewing uncontrollably and unable to brake with their feet because the water flowed hard and fast, they steered into a second hairpin. Got lucky again!

The wind speed doubled back up on the edge of the structure. Accelerating them into a third hairpin and out of the parking structure down the narrow, one-lane, one-way exit ramp descending in a spiral. They slammed back and forth between the concrete walls on either side. Rain water raced in a two-inch thick current. They zoomed down four floors of the mall. At the bottom, the single lane broke off into two. Only a pair of stumps remained of the parking attendant booths.

Splash! They hit water coming off the inundated streets. It slowed them dramatically and veered them off sharply

"Watch out!" yelled Sam.

"Aaaoww!" yowled Diane, taking the brunt of the collision with a massive pillar. They bounced into a pocket of dead space, an alcove that sheltered them from Meg's insane fury.

Which peaked at almost the exact moment!

The winds reached maximum speed. Five hundred and twenty-one miles an hour, Diane recalled from Ivory's last fax that confirmed Meg's 'superhurricane' classification. Lightning and thunder turned continuous. The rain became a solid sheet. They watched waves march through the street outside. Crests rose like hooded serpents, lashing out foaming, venomous tongues of water.

While the eyewall of the hurricane brought maximum carnage, it afforded Diane and Sam their first rest. This irony, forged by incredible physics, wasn't lost on Diane, who hugged Sam tightly. They slid down to squat in an inch of water. For the first time in two days, they got a chance to catch there breath and composure.

Even if it was for only ten minutes.

Then, Meg's eye came ashore.

———

The eye was a unique atmospheric entity representing order in the midst of chaos. Here, Meg's wind, rain, thunder, and lightning dissipated to absolute calm suddenly and without warning. Located near the center and echoless to radar, this near circular dynamic core bestowed a narrow, eight-mile radius of tranquility on either side of the Potomac. Beyond her eye, the rest of DC, Maryland, and Virginia saw no respite. Meg's wind and rain continued unabated, gradually changing direction.

But the calm of the eye was a misnomer because it contained the storm surge.

A circle of devastating waves.

Meg's surge had birthed over the warm and deep ocean, where the peripheral spiraling winds swirled the water to the center. The low pressure in her eye raised it into a dome five feet higher than the surrounding ocean. Much of the water, though, descended in a powerful whirlpool beneath the surface. When Meg moved up the Potomac, these giant undercurrents came upon the rising riverbed. Unable to discharge anywhere else, the water climbed dramatically. The storm surge was proportional to the strength of the hurricane.

Meg was the strongest ever.

She lifted a tidal wave over one hundred feet tall!

Survivors in its path were caught unawares. They emerged outside, lulled into complacency by the clear blue skies and the relief of just being alive. They were shredded. Water weighed sixty-four pounds per cubic foot. The ten-story high surge superimposed upon the high wind driven waves into a battering ram that smashed anything to nothing. It overwhelmed the reservoirs, which reduced peak flood flows by storing water for later release. Levees and channel modifications, which confined flood waters to definite areas and increased flow capacity, collapsed entirely. Shoreside communities drowned. From Fort Washington to Alexandria and Arlington, neighborhoods submerged. Roosevelt Island vanished. The entire first floor of the Pentagon went under.

The tidal wave easily twisted and broke the massive, seemingly invincible bridges from Arland Williams to Theodore Roosevelt. The leaning obelisk of the Washington Monument succumbed and toppled. The sheer amount of water overpowered the storm drains and sewers with pressure two hundred and fifty times the design limit. Cracks raced inland along pipes and ruptured them.

The twenty-four inch clay pipe outside the network basement, where Diane's ex, Ned Cahill, and the TV staff sought refuge from Meg, gaped open. They'd just heard the storm abate. The first smiles began to crease their faces, unaware the corrosive sewer effluents were cracking the wall faster than the eye could see. Meg dissolved the wall and entered as a black, viscous, fecal-ridden fluid. Laughter turned to horror. Ned and the TV staff screamed. They rushed toward the only way out and tore at the barricade. They opened the door to discover Meg had piled debris outside. They could not clear a path, even with the strength of half a dozen men. Sewage filled the basement within seconds.

The surge took them all.

————

"There is not much movement," said the analyst gravely, pointing to magnified satellite returns of DC on the big screens inside the Strategy Room of the Doomsday Plane, a scaled down version of the Situation Room.

Baron, Peter, and Jack sat strapped into seats around a conference table.

The E-4B National Airborne Ops Center was a technological marvel, with one hundred and fourteen personnel on 24/7 six-hour shifts. They manned a command center located on Baker Deck, the middle of the modified Boeing 747-200's three decks. Adam Deck contained crew quarters, where the off-duty shift resided and rested. Charlie Deck was crammed with spares and supplies to stay airborne for a week.

Also called Nightwatch, or TCAMO—Take Charge And Move Out—every aspect of the Doomsday Plane's design ensured that US command capabilities survived in the aftermath of a debilitating nuclear attack. It was constantly updated with the latest command, control, and communication tools, state-of-the-art combat countermeasures, and an electromagnetic pulse shield. In the event of the plane's demise, an additional belly flap opened to discharge an 'ejectile,' which was a hybrid, Mini Cooper-size military vehicle with a dashboard full of essential electronics, a full gas tank, and a day's rations. The ejectile parachuted down and could be driven away, once on the ground. It was big enough for three: the president, defense secretary, and Chairman of the Joint Chiefs. In August 1994, the Doomsday Plane's deployment had been expanded to serve as a communications platform for FEMA in times of major natural disasters.

It circled over Meg's eye. Her spiral of clouds lacked tight integrity, indicating she was deteriorating fast. Still, she threw up tremendous updrafts of turbulence that bumped, jostled, and jolted the Jumbo jet. The analyst flashed another next photograph.

Baron, Jack, and Peter straightened simultaneously.

The tail of an Airbus jutted out of the Potomac. It had been dragged off the tarmac of Ronald Reagan Airport. Save for the roof, the terminal and hangars were underwater. Layover passengers and evacuees who'd shown up had been flown out before Meg's arrival. She slid the Airbus powerfully around with her initial onslaught, but her annulus of maximum winds and the hundred foot-high storm surge easily tossed it into the river.

"What's that?" asked Baron, pointing to a line slashing across a part of the eye. "It's erasing everything in its wake."

The analyst's fingers flew. Extrapolating a three dimensional image. "Damn. That's a tidal wave, sir." A couple of more keystrokes. "It scales to about a hundred feet high and half a mile long."

Just as they were talking, it peeled away the runway at Dulles, where Meg had overturned planes into the terminal and knocked down the Air Traffic Control tower.

"What about the White House?" asked Baron. "Is the President safe?"

———

"Good lord," breathed Avery, looking around dumbstruck with guilt and grief.

The White House fell within the radius of the eye but outside the reach of the surge. The president stood on the roof under the golden glow of daybreak refracting over the turbulent clouds circling hungrily around the edge of the eye a mere seven miles away. He heard the roar and briefly saw slices of the mammoth tide. At ground zero, it did not seem to worsen the devastation, which in every direction, was simply apocalyptic.

Avery couldn't believe they were only halfway through.

————

Hearing the wind and rain decrease sharply, Andrew stood up and entered the atrium to a rapidly reducing drizzle. He hurried across in a foot of water. Meg had demolished the internal partitions between the stores, opening the mall into one large, ransacked space. Above the shattered glass roof of the atrium, daybreak gilded the clearing sky. Andrew cared about the brightening conditions only in as much as it afforded better visibility. Reaching the edge, he looked outside. Rarely astonished, he caught his breath audibly, when he saw a towering wall of water—the tidal wave—sweep by in the distance. In the blink of an eye, it transformed roads into rivers and neighborhoods into lakes. A roof top showed here and there. A Kawasaki sign sailed by.

Andrew limped quickly along the outer periphery, Offensive Pistol in hand. Safety off. Ready to fire. Shell-shocked survivors emerged outside like wary rodents. He searched the faces. Didn't find Sam and Diane.

Vrooom! A motor fired alive. Andrew swiveled sharply.

A jet ski skidded around the corner.

Diane hugged Sam tightly.

————

Diane and Sam had no idea there was a Kawasaki showroom on this level, until one, pushed by the outward ripples of the surge, careened into the alcove where they cowered. As a Miami native and diehard weekend water sportsman, he immediately recognized it as the latest, top of the line model. "Fourteen ninety-eight cc, four cylinders."

"Great," said Diane, unimpressed. "Does it run?"

"One way to find out." Sam straddled it eagerly. "Did you know the Japanese coined the name 'jet ski?'"

"Save that for Trivial Pursuit. Don't you need a key?"

"Floor model, girl. It's in the ignition." He turned it.

Vroom! The motor came alive on the first try. Diane grinned, hopped on, and wrapped her arms around him. They roared out, turned left, and passed the shattered glass of the showroom. A few watercraft had somehow withstood Meg's brutality and still remained chained down to hooks on the floor, but they'd been knocked around and wrecked beyond recognition. Theirs belonged to three that Diane saw which had broken loose and survived almost intact.

"Oh, shit," breathed Sam.

Diane snapped her eyes. *The assassin!* He was on the terrace above the showroom. His gun flashed. The report of the shot followed a split second later.

Sam swerved. He could not outmaneuver a bullet.

"Aaahhh!" he cried, convulsing backward. A crimson flower bloomed rapidly above his heart. Hit! The .45 exited high out of his shoulder, tearing flesh and spraying blood on Diane's face as it missed her cheek by an inch, even less.

"Sam!" she yelled.

His left hand came off the handle. The jet ski slewed wildly.

Bang! Andrew fired again.

This .45 punched Diane between the shoulder blades! Knocked her forward. She shrieked!

"Aaah!" Sam yelled again in pain as she gripped his bad shoulder to stay in her seat.

They zoomed toward a floating rooftop. Its gable acted like a ramp, shooting the jet ski skyward into a long arc.

"Hang on!" shouted Sam, bracing for the excruciating jolt when the watercraft came down. The hard splash and his agonized scream became one. Diane clung on, her arms wrapped around his belly. Sam throttled. The jet ski surged out of Andrew's range.

"Are you all right?" asked Diane.

"I'm okay," Sam wheezed. "You?"

"I'm fine," said Diane. "But my research took a hit." The

Jayspid in her backpack stopped the bullet.

Sam tried to laugh and grimaced instead. Driving with one hand, "Can we make it to Vick's?"

"We're gonna."

Sam was losing blood and needed medical attention. They ran aground two miles later and had one more to cover in about ten minutes. Sam stumbled. Diane put his arm around her shoulder and kissed him. "Baby, be strong."

"Maybe with a little tongue," he winked, grinning in agony

"You make it to Vick's and you can have it all," said Diane, helping him forward.

"And live I shall, then!"

Death and destruction screamed everywhere they looked. Meg's eye presented survivors with a 'terrible silence.' Sounds of the city like traffic, birds, and animals were conspicuously absent. This magnified the tragedy, evoking a sense of anxiety and dread as men, women, and children searched for loved ones dragged away from them during the storm. Some found them, most never would. Diane observed reactions from hysteria to catatonia. Grown men and women were crying—one couple was laughing through tears. A rare reunion. The more common sight was that of people squatting beside death, cradling corpses, and mourning alone. There were those who put aside their losses and plunged themselves into rescue work. But there was also no dearth of corpses and buildings to rob.

As with any catastrophe, Meg brought out the best and worst in people.

––––––

Andrew knew Diane had escaped unhurt. The .45 ACP cartridge that he used was custom made for him. It weighed two hundred and thirty grains and traveled at eight hundred and eighty five feet per second, but not enough to penetrate the Jayspid in her backpack. He'd hit Sam, of that he was certain. Not fatally, though. He'd fired at Sam's heart without compensating for the watercraft's undulation. The bullet struck when the craft dipped down. Angry with himself for squandering the opportunity to scratch the final two names off his Beta list, Andrew returned to the main stairwell at Anacostia Plaza to sit out the rest of the storm.

––––––

Clouds circled closer and closer. The vicious pluck returned to the wind, now coming from the opposite direction. Usually, the second half of the storm was never as severe. But Meg had exploded every theory in the book. *No reason she should stop now.* Sporadic lightning and thunder resumed. The first hefty drop of water fell. Sam looked up and when he did, Diane noticed that he clenched his fists and screwed his face in terrible agony.

Diane felt helpless, whispered into his ear, "It'll pass. The pain will pass, sweetie."

His stride had weakened considerably. "Save yourself, hon. Just go"

"No!" reacted Diane, outraged. The proximity of the next clap of thunder startled them. A low discharge of lightning wagged a warning finger in their faces.

"If we die," Sam said, "Thunder Strike dies with us."

"Keep walking and don't fade on me."

"One of us must survive," persisted Sam.

"We both will."

The rain-soaked ground was soft. Their feet sank. Slop gripped their shoes, caked them with mud, added weight. Forcing them to work harder for every step. It affected Sam more than it did Diane. She knew pangs twisted up his body like a blade with serrated edges. The front of his shirt was drenched in red. Diane had used her sleeve to bandage the bullet hole but the walking kept the wound open, fresh, and bleeding.

"I'm not going to make it," he said, barely able to get the words out between clenched teeth.

"Yes, you are," replied Diane. The wind tried to grab

them and the occasional rain drops escalated into a barrage of needle points.

"Diane, come on," pleaded Sam. "We don't have much time. So don't be stubborn."

"I am not going to leave you to die," Diane said firmly.

"You must!"

"No!" Tears wanted to flow out, but she held them up behind determined eyes. They started uphill. Diane said, "We are almost there."

"Don't lie." His skin had no pallor left.

Lighting raced in like a tightening noose to a drum roll of thunder. The rain became a flat, heavy downpour from one moment to the next.

"Run, honey, go, go!" He pulled free and the effort left him gasping in anguish.

Diane grabbed his hand back. "It's on the other side of the hill. We'll make it! Come on!"

Without warning! Out of nowhere! An opaque sheet of rain, pushed by a demon wind, swooped down upon them! Meg abruptly picked up where she left off before the eye. Sweeping Sam and Diane upslope at breakneck speed. They cart-wheeled through the air. Once over the crest, Meg lost them.

They hit the asphalt. Sam yelled out in agony! The slick mud did the rest. Sledded them downhill. Diane saw still-standing homes blur by. She had headed here to Vick's and Philippe's home because she knew this neighborhood would survive. Shielded by two hillsides, the leeward slopes offered the best protection against a storm, one that even Meg could not overcome. She could only top-swipe the homes, unable deliver direct annihilating blows. But Meg was still able to puncture roofs, blow out windows, and smash everything around inside.

Diane collected at the bottom of the slope. Sam slid within arm's reach. She grabbed him. They were right outside the driveway to Vick's house. "Sam!" Diane shouted with a huge smile. "We made it!"

Sam didn't move.

Her smile evaporated. "Sam!" She turned him over. His eyes were closed and he was not moving. "Sam, wake up. Stay with me. Sam! Sam? Nooo!"

Debris began to fly dangerously close. The wind strengthened, trying to pluck Diane off the ground. She fought Meg and held on to Sam, shouting toward the house, "Philippe! Help! Help! Philippe!"

Her voice carried through the gaping hole that used to be the living room window. Philippe appeared and his eyes widened. "Diane!"

He rushed outside. Diane said, "He took a bullet."

They slung a hand each of Sam's over their shoulders and dragged him indoors in the nick of time! Barely did they pass through the door when Meg announced that intermission was over with a blast of lighting and thunder so violent, the ground shook and walls moved. As loud as that was, it quickly became inaudible in the loudening shriek of her wind and rain.

Inside, they laid Sam in the tub, where Philippe had made himself comfortable with a quilt and pillows. He'd stocked food and water in the corner.

"Why didn't you leave?" Diane asked as he pulled out a First-Aid kit with bandages and antiseptic cream from the medicine cabinet. "I called you and left three messages."

"I'm sorry, I haven't checked."

"I'm glad you didn't."

They talked softly while Diane carefully cleaned blood around the bullet hole. After Vick's death, Philippe said, he returned home from the WFO, turned off the ringer on his phone, and spent the entire day indoors. He grieved for Vick by pulling out old scrap books and remembering their time together. He went to bed early. The cloudburst jolted him awake. The storm! It was here! Diane had been right. Philippe remembered seeing a Mississippi couple explain on TV that they had survived a hurricane last year by locking themselves in the bathroom and curling up in the tub. He did the same.

Diane finished dressing the wound front and back.

Sam remained unconscious, unmoving.

———

Admiral Grant entered the Combat Information Center of the USS *William J. Clinton* and nodded. Then he moved to the window. An amphibious transport plane belonging to the United States Air Force bobbed in the waters—it looked miniscule next to this city-on-the-sea that was the aircraft carrier.

"Seven-one-oh, you're cleared for take off," said the air traffic controller behind Grant.

"Say wind again?" the overhead speaker crackled with voice of the pilot.

"About eighteen knots, gusting twenty-eight, two hundred degrees."

"Roger. Seven-one-oh rolling," copied the pilot.

The plane moved. It's turbines roared loader, propelling the plane faster across water. The skis created a fine spray that sparkled in the brilliant sunshine.

"One-five-five," reported the pilot, indicating he'd reached take off speed. "VR."

The nose rose. USAF Seven-one-oh cleared the ocean and climbed into a picture perfect sky. Admiral Grant stayed staring out until the plane reduced to an indiscernible speck in the sky. Then he returned to his quarters, pressed the intercom, "I don't want to be disturbed."

He opened the drawer and removed a Bible. Dropping to his knees, he clutched the book to his heart and lowered his head. When he saw Meg's Armageddonesque destruction on the monitors of the Thunder Strike ops center, he was glad to put the scientists aboard that plane. Dr. Mclaurin had lied about the consequences of halting the seeding abruptly. His scientists had conspired with him by remaining silent. Grant's guilt about the Beta list evaporated.

They deserved to die. When they did, in a fiery crash over the Atlantic, he prayed again and asked God to forgive them.

———

Three hours after she came ashore, Meg's winds blended with a strong Arctic system. She sucked in the cooler air, which sharply depleted her rainfall. Her circulation deteriorated and unraveled. Friction over land accelerated her spin-down.

She died as swiftly and suddenly as she was born.

———

Sam never regained consciousness, though he twitched every now and then. In the past few minutes, he stopped moving altogether. Diane met Philippe's eyes and knew what he was thinking. She felt for a pulse on his wrist and couldn't find one. Placed a finger under his nose. The sporadic blasts of air through the broken window made it hard confirm if he was breathing or not. She pressed two fingers lightly to his neck.

"Nothing," she said, her dread mounting. With grief stricken panic, urgency, and disbelief, she pressed her head to his chest. Frantically moved her ear around. Desperately searched for a heart beat.

"Is he alive?" asked Philippe.

Diane shook her head.

TODAY

TWENTY-TWO

"Liz is hunting with the hounds, not running with the foxes," said Baron Hawke and heard John Ulysses VI catch his breath sharply. Baron chuckled, "You never saw her treachery coming, did you, John?"

Admiral Grant's suite was bugged. So, when Liz called him, Baron found out. He instantly recognized John's hand. *He's using her again?* Baron recalled almost laughing out loud at this piece of luck, or was it John's weakness? Trying to be honorable, John wanted to help resurrect Liz because she'd helped him take down Jarvis Johnson and felt she deserved a second chance. Baron brought Peter in. Without mentioning the battle for the dark shadows, Baron asked the most cunning man he'd ever met how they could recruit Liz and use her subversively. Peter sought a half hour to study Liz's profile. He called back in less than twenty minutes and said, "Liz looks out for Liz." He had a plan for just such a chameleon, though he warned, "We can never trust her."

"The dark shadows are still mine, John," said Baron. He'd stepped out of the Situation Room to make the call, a tradition that John Ulysses II began, to twist the knife of victory one last time before retiring Zachariah into exile, after George Washington signed the Proclamation of Neutrality.

"Goodnight," laughed Baron, whose demeanor as a Hawke was starkly different from his defense secretary persona. The family war was a sport and he shed his formality. John and he were peers in wealth and stature. In the company of Peter and Jack, however, he carried himself with decorum, even when they played golf. Baron hung up and returned to the chair at the head of the horseshoe and resumed the wait for Andrew to topple the first domino.

So her gut had been right! Being a conspiracy freak had paid off, Diane realized. She had never been able to shake off the suspicion that Liz was brought in to flush them out. An outsider with something to prove.

Liz's boyfriend didn't die because he'd heard the name Thunder Strike. He died because Liz agreed to become the breadcrumbs of the cover-up. He was the first one she threw under the bus after he gave her Admiral Grant's name. Probably to prove she didn't care about the body count and was willing to pay a blood price for a fresh start. Then she visited Grant. He pointed her to DC and died. Murdered. Philippe met her at the airport. She picked up the next lead. He became expendable. The assassin could have killed Diane at The Gourd but neither he nor Liz had a clue where to find the Jayspid. So he was forced to let them go. Liz bared her soul about the scandal and her rehab as a calculated ploy to win Diane's sympathy and trust.

To spring this trap.

The bitch worked me, but so did I. Thanks to a knot of uneasiness which had stayed with her all day, Diane had resisted the temptation to reveal anything meaningful on their long trek across DC. Liz and the assassin still did not have the Jayspid and Diane got to where she wanted to be.

Ned's.

Now, she was not afraid anymore. She felt secure and at peace. Ready to face whatever came next. She was with the only person she trusted and the man she'd fallen in love at first sight.

Sam.

He had not died. In fact, he'd regained consciousness an hour after Meg had passed and the skies had cleared. Soon afterwards, they'd begun to discuss what to do next.

"We have to expose Thunder Strike," said Philippe angrily upon learning that Vick had been murdered for it. "We have to expose the bastards responsible, even if it goes all the way to the president.

"Baby steps," cautioned Sam. "Let's first get out of DC

alive." Philippe's Jeep Cherokee had survived intact in the garage.

"But," said Diane, "Meg's wiped out most of the roads."

Also, they did not know if enough bridges had survived to guarantee a way out of the capital. "Regardless, the ride'll be rough and bumpy and keep your wound from healing." Sam could lose more blood, thinning his chances of survival. It was too early to move him.

"I'll be fine," said Sam like a brave trooper.

"I'm not risking your life," said Diane firmly. She never wanted to be as afraid and concerned as she'd been for him after he'd been shot.

"I agree," said Philippe.

"Look outside," said Diane. "The catastrophe is Katrina plus Sandy times a hundred. There's not going to be any organized search for a while."

Philippe nodded. "The killer will think the obvious. That you left."

"So staying put could be safer, don't you think?" said Diane.

"I gave up on my plan at 'but,'" smiled Sam, his humor returning.

Diane kissed him and grinned, "Good."

The rest helped Sam recover. The bleeding stopped and he started to regain his strength. Sam figured the only man who could help them was the man who'd sent him here.

Admiral Grant.

After a direct request from the president, who was being hailed as a hero for braving Meg in the White House, the phone companies strengthened roaming capabilities of towers outside Meg's swath of destruction in Baltimore, Delaware, Maryland, and Virginia. Within forty-eight hours, cell phone traffic was restored. Sam called Admiral Grant, who had given him his mobile number, and left a message. Two days later, when he returned from sea, Grant called back and was genuinely grief stricken to learn that Gene had been killed. He was also stunned that a manhunt was on. He told them he was in New York, waiting to go to DC. He would try and speak with the president immediately. A day later he called back. He thought he was being quarantined from Avery by Baron. But he promised to find a way out for them.

When he texted them that Liz was coming and didn't return their call back to confirm if what they were reading was true, they decided to be cautious. They agreed one of them must go into hiding with the Jayspid. Diane suggested Ned's place as a safe house. It was clear across town and she'd been married to him so briefly, few people knew. Philippe and she ganged up for the mother of all arguments, telling Sam that he was not strong enough to make a run for it when he insisted on meeting Liz. They wore him down. Then Philippe quashed Diane's insistence to go to the airport. Both Sam and Diane, he said, were too valuable.

Philippe dropped Sam off at Ned's house and went to the airport to meet Liz.

———

Sam had been worried sick all day. The battery on his cell phone was dead. Being completely cut off, added to his misery and frustration. He started a fire to keep a light on for her and Philippe and was stoking it with a burning log when the door crashed open! The assassin stepped in. Then the rental truck pulled in.

"Make a sound and I will put you down," warned Andrew. "You will be dead and it'll be up to Diane to tell me where that Jayspid is. I will torture every part of her body, maybe fuck her as she is bleeding and begging to die." He snapped, "You want that?"

Sam's jaw tightened with rage. He helplessly watched Diane climb out and walk right into the trap. Andrew shoved Diane to Sam's side.

"Where is the Jayspid?" he asked.

The couple backed up against the wall. Neither spoke. Diane glanced over toward Liz in the truck. Andrew followed her gaze. Sam still held the burning log. He seized on Andrew's momentary distraction. Swatted down hard! Struck Andrew's wrist. Knocked the gun out and burned the skin.

Andrew grunted sharply. Turned angrily. Sam viciously swung the fiery log across Andrew's face. *Bam!* Nailed him square on the side of the head. Singed the assassin's hair and ears. Andrew sprawled, a gasp of pain wrenching out of his throat. Sam's fury took over. He clobbered Andrew with log. The assassin threw up a forearm to take the brunt of the next swing. His sleeve caught fire.

Sam noticed Liz slide behind the wheel.

Snap! Headlights lit them up. The engine fired. Liz had climbed back into the truck.

"Enough!" shouted Diane, pulling him away.

Sam spiked the log at Andrew, who curled away at the last minute. Sam took Diane's arm, directing her through a doorway. Liz reversed hard and fast. The back wheels of the rental truck missed the apron and thumped down off the six-inch high curb.

"What she doing?" asked Sam

"I don't know," replied Diane.

Sam led the way, sprinting down a dark hallway into the kitchen. Meg had collapsed one side of the house. Diane weaved and ducked behind him, threading between and under beams that slanted every which way in disarray. Not a piece of furniture remained.

"The Jayspid's in the oven," said Sam, veering through a ripped up doorway into the kitchen.

The oven had been built into the cabinetry, which had been ripped out, broken up, and shoved to a corner. Sam opened the lopsided door. Diane grabbed the dark brown leather satchel. The Jayspid fit snugly inside it. She bent her head under the long shoulder strap and adjusted it diagonally across her body. They raced out the disfigured French window. Meg had shattered the glass, leaving jagged triangles protruding into the frame.

"What's the plan?" Diane asked, as they emerged outside.

"Whatever works," replied Sam.

"And what's that?"

"Running like hell."

———

Andrew swatted his arm on the carpet and doused the flames. Smarting with the burns and bruises that Sam had inflicted, he picked himself up and the gun in one motion. His eyes glinted with hate and fury. Liz's headlights receded. His leg precluded him from getting into a foot chase. So, he scaled the fallen beams to a standing section of the second floor.

———

Diane took the lead. She'd lived here when she was married to Ned. The Columbia Country Club was their backyard. The exclusive golf course had been a tree-lined enclosure of picturesque green before Meg's arrival. When her fury finally abated, all the trees had been uprooted and the fairways eroded. They bolted past fallen trees. The moonlight revealed carcasses—animal and human—entangled in the branches. Even after a week being of exposed to the sights and smells of death, they recoiled with disgust. But kept their legs pumping. Used the protruding branches and death for cover.

Staying low, they skipped across wrought iron double gates that had been ripped out of their stone posts and carried clear across the course. Once a regal entrance to the club, they now collected in a rusting, mangled heap.

"We are going to lose cover," shouted Sam.

Diane looked ahead. He was right. There were no trees for the span of the green around the hole ahead. Meg had turned over the topsoil with the depth and power of a crisscrossing backhoe. Neither slowing down nor breaking stride, they instinctively reached out, held hands, and broke into the open.

———

Andrew straightened to his feet on the second floor. Immediately, he saw Sam and Diane as silhouettes darker than the night bolt across the green. Open targets. But they were out of range for his Offensive Pistol. He swiftly reached into the first of his many trouser pockets to turn the pistol into a rifle.

He removed a night vision attachment. Snapped it on. Sam and Diane got half way across the green. They needed to get on the other side of an uneven pile of debris that had collected up against still standing hedges along the entire the edge of the country club to form an untidy wall that separated the course from Jones Bridge Road. Andrew's fingers moved quickly, surely. Without a fumble or wasted movement, he screwed customized add-ons to his gun.

The couple cleared the green. They were within three strides of the debris and hedge.

Slap! Andrew slotted in a barrel extension. The transformation of his weapon was complete. His Offensive Pistol was now a powerful sniper's rifle. He looked up. Sam and Diane were two strides away from safety.

They took the first.

Andrew raised the weapon to his shoulder. Pressed his eyes into the night vision sight. Centered the crosshairs to the back of Diane's head as the fugitives came abreast of the debris pile. Began to go around it.

He heard the rental truck as he tightened his finger on the trigger. Liz hit the corner and her headlights struck the couple dead on.

White out!

His night vision burned up! Going opaque!

Andrew pulled the trigger blindly. But his hand jerked, moving his rifle up a fraction. Was it before or after the bullet left his gun? He wasn't sure. Then he was.

A fistful of soggy mud erupted beyond Sam and Diane, who hit the ground belly down. Andrew switched to normal sight. It took a second. He pressed his eyes to the sight. He knew it was all the time Sam and Diane needed. They were gone.

———

"Stay down!" ordered Sam.

They crawled out of view over splinters of wood, glass, cans, and other litter. The skin over their elbows and knees cracked bloodily. Sam jabbed his shoulder against something sharp. Emitted a sharp cry. His wound reopened.

"Are you okay?" asked Diane, immediately concerned.

"Yeah, yeah." He did not stop gator walking.

Behind the safety of the debris pile and hedges, Diane urgently helped up Sam. Both had ripped their clothes and were covered with cuts. Diane saw that Sam was oozing blood from the bullet hole.

"You're bleeding again," she panted.

Sam nodded. "I'm okay."

They straightened and resumed running. His shoulder barked and bled profusely. Each time Sam's foot came down, it sent a burning spasm radiating from the wound. He pushed the pain to the back of his mind. They looked back to see the truck angling toward them at an insane speed! Rocking the rental over the curb, she straightened out directly behind them.

Headlights centered back on them.

"She's trying to run us down!" screamed Diane.

Sam blinked. *What else can we do? Where can we run?* They'd be easy targets for Andrew if they ventured back onto the course. He had lost a lot of blood and noticed his legs began to fail him. A week of half rations affected Diane too. Her breath came in short, asthmatic gasps. Even healthy, it was impossible to outrun a speeding truck.

"Turn around!" gasped Sam, U-ing off the sidewalk onto the road.

Diane didn't expect it. Her arm stretched abruptly. Popping her shoulder at the joint as she instinctively tightened her grip on his hand to keep her balance. Sam howled! His deltoids stretched and transferred the strain to the raw nerve endings around the open bullet hole. A devastating, knifing white hout pain seared from head to toe. He screamed. Stumbled. Almost fell.

"Oh, god," Diane apologized. Released his hand. "I'm so sorry."

"I'm fine," he gasped and grabbed her hand back.

They were in the middle of the street, running right past Liz. They heard the jam of brakes. The truck skidded. Rubber squealed as the tires turned. Sam glanced over his shoulder. Liz was spinning the rental around. The passenger side wheels lost traction as they bumped off the curb. The top heavy truck tilted dangerously.

Overturning!

Sam saw Liz through the windshield crank the steering the other way. Hoping to find counterbalance. The truck teetered for an agonizing second. *Thud!* It fell with a hard, resound crash. Violently returning onto all four wheels. He anticipated Liz would floor the gas pedal. She did. The engines revved.

Sam grabbed Diane's hand. "She's behind us!"

———

Andrew smiled coldly.

Sam and Diane were racing along the far side of Jones Bridge Road. They didn't realize he could see them over the top of the hedges and debris around the course. He raised his rifle. Didn't turn on the night vision, instead waiting for Liz to complete her U-turn.

Her headlights picked them up. Andrew took the first available shot.

To Sam's temple.

———

Crack! Bang!

A sickening mix of tearing flesh, breaking bone, and the delayed report of the assassin's gun. Sam dropped instantly.

Diane felt his hand slip. Whirled! Saw his forehead peel away, spraying her with gory shrapnel.

She went down with him, screaming, "No! Sam! Oh, god, no!"

Bang! Andrew's second shot passed over her head and blasted into the asphalt as she fell forward face down. Her skull cracked into the muddy road. Dazing her for a few seconds. She lay beside Sam's lifeless body, the blood pouring out from his head and soaking the blacktop toward her.

———

Andrew did not anticipate Diane and Sam to be holding hands. So he'd fired the bullet meant for her into a spot where he anticipated her head would have been sprinting fully upright. But she fell, taken down by Sam. Now, Andrew could not even see her. She was flat on the ground. Sam lay half twisted on his side, blocking a clear view of her fatal points. He caught enough of the hair on her head and guesstimated where her neck was. He took aim for a difficult, shallow angle shot that had to be perfectly placed to kill.

He steadied the cross-hairs.

———

Roar! Diane stirred to a growl of engine. The grinning grill between the blazing headlights of the rental truck loomed. Closed in a flash! Enough time for Diane to shake off the spiderwebs. Reconstruct what happened. Liz had lit them up for the assassin. He'd taken out Sam. Now she was coming back to run them over. Finish them off. Caught between anger, terror, grief, and survival, Diane froze. Resigned herself.

Bang! The assassin fired again. This was the end.

In the moment it took the second bullet to reach Diane, Liz brought the rental truck between the bullet and Diane! *Zing!* The bullet crashed into the body work. Liz dropped her head below the window and threw open the passenger side door, and ordered, "Diane. Come on! Get in!"

Diane looked up blankly. Her eyes were wide, moist,

and overcome with sadness. Liz saw the horrific shot Sam had taken. His brain lay exposed.

"Oh, my God. That's awful. I'm so sorry," she said "But it's no use. Come on!"

Diane stared from her to Sam, her shoulder ready to heave and wrack with sobs.

"He's dead and we will be too if we don't get out of here."

Two bullets shattered the driverside window, missed Liz's skull my millimeters, and tore into the cushions of the passenger side seat. The double report came a moment later.

Liz hardened her voice and barked like a drill sergeant, "Get in! NOW!"

Diane touched Sam's face with pure love. Then, reluctantly but quickly, she scrambled into the truck.

———

Andrew switched to night vision. The women's heads lined up. He could take them both out with one shot! Gleefully, he squeezed the trigger. The rifle recoiled into his shoulder. *Zing!* As soon as the metallic sound of impact reached him, he knew he'd missed. Liz had throttled down an instant before, jerking the truck forward before Diane even closed the door The bullet hammered into the side of the back shell.

Andrew did not waste time on any more shots. He slid down a beam and hurried to his Humvee. He picked up the MILSATCOM. Peter answered at once from the Situation Room.

"Liz has switched sides," said Andrew.

Jack's head and eyes snapped. "I told you we could not trust her."

"We never did, general," said Peter quietly.

"I need chopper support to locate them."

"Use this priority call sign with DC Dispatch," said Peter. "HS-four-oh." HS stood for Homeland Security, and the four-series indicated 'superseding emergency.'

When Andrew called it in, John Ulysses VI found out.

———

The Ulysses had spies in all branches of government too. John realized that Baron had jumped the gun and called him before he'd secured the Jayspid.

"Fire up my helicopter," John snapped into the intercom. He called his wife, who was still in DC somewhere, volunteering. "I won't be home when you get back."

She knew better than to ask him why.

Five minutes later, he was airborne in the family's McDonnel Douglas luxury helicopter.

In the Situation Room, Baron looked at his watch. "It's time to go upstairs."

"Wait," Jack nervously tapped his pencil on the table. "What about the wiretaps?"

"They'll activate automatically and come up on our speakers here," said Peter. CIA techs had been working all week to set up the Situation Room for this night.

Baron opened his palms, silently asking, 'anything else?'

Jack sat back. The defense secretary swiveled his chair around, picked up his briefcase, and stood up. Jack passed a nervous tongue over his parched lips. Baron could read the Joint Chiefs Chairman's mind like an open book. *I did not sign up for this, but I'm neck deep in seditious shit.* There was no way out for Jack. Not any more.

Not alive, at least.

Baron took the steps up from the Situation Room.

The White House was a complex comprised of three buildings. The main residence was the familiar façade the universe knew as the symbol of freedom. On one side of it, connected by an enclosed gallery, was the East Wing, and on the other stood the renowned West Wing, reached by an open colonnade. Baron emerged outside into the colonnade and walked across cracked cement. Meg had dismantled the stately columns, leaning them every which way. Some, she'd shredded.

Baron dismissed the distant searchlights, fires, flashes, choppers, sirens, and gunshots as a natural part of the new nightscape of DC. None approached within a mile of the White House, a no-traffic radius that was strictly enforced by the ring of military around the outer edge of the grounds. He entered the desolate Center Hall of the main residence. Candles provided the only illumination. A secret service agent glanced over lazily, then stiffened when he recognized Baron, who took the narrow private steps that the president and staff used. The next level up was the State Floor. He circled the landing, passed the empty office of the Chief Usher, and climbed the final two flights briskly to the third floor.

Agent Connor straightened. "Good evening, sir."

Baron nodded, knocked on the door that the construction crews had reinstalled early on to give the president some privacy, and entered the West Sitting Hall. Half a dozen candles burned. Avery ate alone.

"Mr. President," apologized Baron, "I didn't mean to disturb your dinner."

"Sit down," said Avery, dismissing the apology with a wave.

Baron opened his briefcase to reveal a 9mm Browning automatic!

"Admiral Grant's dead," said Avery gravely. He couldn't see the gun. "Did you know?"

Baron's hand froze over the gun. He feigned shock and concern. "No. What happened?"

"I was trying to reach him all day. I wanted him at my side tomorrow. A couple of hours ago, they discovered his body. He's been dead since last night. Shot and killed. The police think it looked like he walked into the middle of a burglary."

"I am so sorry, sir," Baron said gently, tightening his hand over the gun. "He was a good man."

"It's been one thing after another, all bad. When will God stop punishing me?"

Baron lifted the automatic, his finger curling over the trigger.

He removed a stack of Bills underneath it with his other hand. Withdrew his finger, dropped the weapon, and closed the briefcase. "Congress couriered these emergency appropriations to continue disaster relief. These are the other Executive Orders relating to the impending transfer of power you requested."

"I know it was an imposition, but I did not want anyone else to know."

"I understand, sir."

"Still, thank you." Avery accepted Baron's pen, briefly perused the first Bill, then signed it.

"Can I use your bathroom, sir?" asked Baron as Avery flipped to the next document.

Avery nodded. "You know where it is."

Baron returned a few minutes later. Avery was reading the final document. He signed it. Baron carefully opened his briefcase, gripped the 9mm again.

"Radio and TV will be here early tomorrow for my nine A.M. address to the nation," said Avery, leaning back in his chair. "The VP, Cabinet, Chief Justice, and House and Senate leaders are flying in. They don't know why."

Baron slid the papers underneath the automatic and snapped the locks shut. "Tomorrow is going to be hectic day, sir. I may not get the chance to thank you for everything."

"No. Thank you."

Then, Avery grasped Baron in a tight embrace and held him for a quiet moment.

––––––––

An angry conversation heated up between Diane and Liz as they sped away. They were on Connecticut Avenue, heading south.

"Whose side are you on?" Diane demanded. Liz's first instinct was denial, but Diane's eyes blazed. "And don't BS me."

"Okay," said Liz. "I'm on your side."

"You're lying!"

"Let me finish. Please. Billy, my boyfriend, ex, whatever, got a call to see if I was interested in a bombshell. I said, shit, yes. He give me a lead. Admiral Grant. I go back to the office and set up an interview with him for the next day after work. Just before quitting time, I get another call. A guy called Peter Wilkins. He wants to recruit me"

"For what?"

"The Agency. CIA. He told me he knew about my meeting with Admiral Grant. He said Grant was being investigated as an enemy of the state. He would send what they had on the admiral. I got an envelope of fragments. He said I could resurrect my career as an operative working under the cover of a reporter. The Agency would allow me to break some of my assignments as exclusives and I could gradually rebuild my credentials again. This was my first assignment."

"Helping bury Thunder Strike," said Diane.

Liz nodded. "I said yes. I had to. I had no choice. I figured they'd take out Grant before I got to him if I didn't take the offer."

"I don't believe you!"

Liz packed all the sincerity she had, "No. I swear."

"Your boyfriend, Admiral Grant, Philippe, now Sam, they are dead because of you!"

Peter warned Liz that she could not look back because the Agency would be covering her tracks. Liz knew exactly what that meant. The only death she had to rationalize was Billy's. But he'd jumped ship like everyone else and wouldn't have reached out to her if he hadn't received the tip that sought her out specifically by name.

"Look," said Liz defensively, "we can argue about the morals of what I did——"

"Your hands are covered in their blood!"

"If I was working for them, why would I save you?"

Diane blinked. Then shook her head. No. "How do I know you're not hedging your bets?"

"What do you mean?"

"You're ruthless. If there's a chance you can break the story, you will. If you can't, you cross back, I lose."

"Look around." Liz gestured around at the moonlit devastation that looked worse at night. "Do you think they are going let anyone who can expose what really happened here live? I knew the moment I landed this morning that my recruitment was bullshit. As soon as I recovered the Jayspid from you, they were going to kill me. And when I saved you, I became a target just like you."

"It's not that simple, is it?" retorted Diane, who didn't know where she getting this harsh, blunt, and aggressive manner.

"What are you getting at?"

"I'm sorry. In the short time I've known you, one thing's clear. You don't do anything without an ulterior motive."

"That's not true."

"Cut the crap, Liz. Why did you do it?"

"I'm playing them, just like they were using me." Liz met Diane's stare evenly. "It's just you and me now. If we don't tell the world, nobody will because nobody can. Thunder Strike dies with us." Liz saw Diane's anger recede and pounced. "Look. I've been strategizing all day how I'm going to get the story out."

"How?" asked Diane.

"Tim. My editor," said Liz at once.

"I thought you said he wasn't behind you or this story."

"He may be an asshole, but he's not stupid." She rifled through her purse. "Let's use Admiral Grant's phone. It's prepaid. Untraceable. "

"No," said Diane. "You used it to call me this morning and we barely got away."

"Fine," said Liz curtly. "Let's use yours." Diane pulled

out her prepaid cell. Liz said, "You dial and put it on speaker so you can listen in too." Having spent many a night at Tim's, Liz knew he muted the ringer on his cell. But he had a land line with an old fashioned answering machine. She knew the number by heart. His phone started to ring.

"He may not be home," worried Diane, then snapped, "Lights! Cut your Lights!"

Liz quickly did. Their eyes rushed around to find a helicopter they could hear but not see.

———

"Got 'em," said the pilot, matter-of-fact, a heartbeat before Liz went dark. He was responding to Andrew's call for chopper support.

"Cloak you approach," Andrew had ordered.

With a flick of one switch, the chopper melted into the night. The pilot turned on his heat seeker and spotted the rental truck passing Chevy Chase Village, an exclusive neighborhood of about two thousand residents with a median income of a quarter of a million dollars. Meg had left neither buildings nor survivors. There wasn't a single tree standing either. "Heading south on Wisconsin."

"Pull back and stand by," said Andrew. "Do not approach."

"Roger," said the pilot. Bored. A jaded eighteen-year veteran on loan from the Los Angeles Police Department, he'd been part of so many police pursuits, none interested him any more. He slowed down.

———

The sound receded. The women relaxed. Liz's attention returned to the ring tone on the cell phone speaker.

"Tim's not answering," said Diane anxiously.

"He never does," replied Liz. "Tim always screens his calls."

"Maybe he's not home."

"He's home," said Liz. Tim never worked late. He told her he didn't have to anymore.

———

Tim checked the caller ID: *Unknown.* He recalled Liz's cell came up with a similar ID last night. *Probablly her.* With a dismissive smirk and irritated head shake, he answered the front door. Sabrina Worth, Avery's speech writer, stood outside. She smiled, "Sorry I'm late."

Tim kissed her. Her hand curled around his neck as his lips held hers for a long moment. He said, "You can make it up to me in the Jacuzzi."

"You're taking a lot for granted," said Sabrina. Tim drew her inside. Closed the door. Sabrina flashed her teeth mischievously, "I like it." She felt his hand slip down. "Aren't you going to answer the phone?"

"Would any man at this moment?"

She laughed. His phone reached its fourth ring. His answering machine picked up. Tim circled her wait and led her toward the stairs. "What kept you?"

The instant Tim's answering machine picked up, the wiretap activated and his voice played on the speakers in the Situation Room. "You've reached Tim O'Flaherty. Leave only your name and number."

Baron, Peter, and Jack sharpened when they heard, "Tim, this is Liz. If you're home, pick up."

"Oh, this is just great!" exploded Jack.

Liz knew Tim hated listening to messages and allowed only thirty seconds after the beep. She began to mentally tick off time. "Tim, if you're there, pick up. Please!"

Diane caught lights in her side mirror. Straightened sharply. "We have company."

Liz glanced into her side mirror. Recognized Andrew's Humvee. "It's him."

"Tim! For Chrissakes, it's urgent!" Liz's voice ratcheted up with intensity into the phone. She counted she was six seconds into Tim's allotted thirty. *Seven...eight...*Crumbling shells that were once bustling stores whipped by.

"He's gaining," said Diane.

The Humvee's headlights bounced over the treacherous road. Definitely closer.

"Hold the phone," said Liz. Diane took it. *Eleven... twelve...*

Liz wrenched the steering around as far as it would go and stood on her brakes. The front wheels snapped left and locked. The axle strained and crackled loudly. The rear wheels froze, pulled around, scorching the cracked blacktop with plumes of burning rubber, dust, and smoke. The truck snapped around ninety degrees into O Street NW. Diane rocked away and rocked back toward Liz, who accelerated at once, pressing both women back into their seats.

"Tim," said Liz breathlessly. Diane shoved the phone closer. "Pick up!" Liz whipped right onto 28th Street.

Eighteen...nineteen...twenty seconds.

Liz checked her rear view. Her quick turns did it. They lost the assassin.

She turned again, making a hard right into the next cross street, then a quick left onto 29th Street. Meg had wreaked the most severe damage in these central neighborhoods. Close to the Potomac, the eyewall and the storm surge had delivered a double whammy, obliterating anything and everything standing. Three inches of water still stood in these streets and butterflied out on either side of the truck.

"Tim," Liz continued to plead, "Goddamnit, our lives are in danger!"

Twenty-five...

———

"I had to write up a condolence that broke the president's spirit," said Sabrina. "He could barely speak. A dear friend of his and personal advisor, Admiral Grant, was shot and killed last night."

Tim's eyes froze. *Twenty-seven....*

"What's the matter?" she asked. *Twenty-eight...*

"I better get this. There's wine by the Jacuzzi." Tim hurried back to the phone. He knew how much time he allowed callers to leave ther message. I twas probably too late. *Twenty-nine...*

"Don't be long." Sabrina slunk away.

"I won't." *Thirty!* Tim picked up the phone.

———

Click. Liz clenched her teeth. Turned onto Pennsylvania Ave. Diane dejectedly lowered the phone.

"Liz?"

"Tim?" Liz's head snapped up and Diane jerked the phone higher. "I'm in DC."

"I figured." He did not sound curt or hostile. "Thunder Strike is Meg," said Liz at once. "A manmade hurricane meant for Cuba. I have the original Jayspid but no way out."

There was a beat of silence. Liz knew she had him hooked. Maybe it was over between them, maybe he'd already fired her, but Tim was a glutton for a good story—especially one that he could break before the big papers. He did not let on that he loved her for it, which she knew he did, but just said, "Let me think. Give me your number."

"No! Don't get off the phone. I don't know if you can get through. I'll hold."

Diane jumped in. "Admiral Grant was sure the president didn't order this cover-up."

"Tim," said Liz. "This is Diane. A meteorologist who uncovered Thunder Strike. She tried to raise a storm warning and became a target. She's been running and hiding for the past week. She has a point. Avery can call off the dogs."

"Head for the White House," Tim said at once.

"We are on Pennsylvania," said Liz.

"Avery's niece and speechwriter, Sabrina Worth, is here with me tonight, having dinner."

Liz felt a spark of jealousy. She caught Diane look over. Liz switched emotions in the span of a slow blink. Feigning a happy smile, "Oh, perfect!"

———

In the Situation Room, Baron, Peter and Jack looked at each other, surprised.

"Son of a bitch!" exclaimed Jack.

"Sabrina Worth," said Baron. "She came on board a couple of weeks ago. I've seen her once, but I cannot put a face to the name."

Peter looked perturbed. "It gives Tim direct access to the president."

"They cannot talk!" said Jack.

"They won't," said Peter confidently and dialed out on his cell phone.

Baron punched up the intercom. "Agent Connor. Where is the president?"

"Just a minute, sir."

While Baron waited, Peter's call was answered on the second ring and he uttered one word, "Go."

Connor came back on the radio, "He's blowing out the candles. Calling it a night."

"What about the women?" asked Jack.

Baron nodded. Peter called Andrew on the MILSATCOM. "The women are on Pennsylvania heading toward the White House."

———

When Andrew raised him on the radio, the jaded LAPD pilot responded, "That airspace doesn't allow cloaked flights. I have to turn on my lights."

"Do it," said Andrew.

The pilot snapped on the under-mounted searchlights and located Pennsylvania Ave.

———

"Pull over!" said Diane, seeing approaching beams.

"Forget it," said Liz and put pedal to the metal. "We are less than half a mile from the White House."

———

Tim burst into the bathroom. "Sabrina! Sabrina! Can you reach the president?"

She was in the Jacuzzi, naked. She stared back blankly.

"It's important!" Tim raised his voice. "My reporter—" He broke off, seeing blood dribble out of her mouth. She slumped forward and splashed into the swirling water, which he noticed was corkscrewing into a deeper shade of red with every spiral from a bullet wound through her heart. "Oh, Jesus!"

"What's going on?" asked Liz.

"Sabrina, she's—" Tim broke off, hearing a footfall behind him.

He whirled around. The shower door, misted up by the steam from the Jacuzzi, opened. Two big, rough looking men stepped out. They didn't waste time or words. Tim's mind raced.

Thunk!Thunk!Thunk!Thunk!

In that moment between the flash of their guns and the impact of the bullets, Tim made the connection. These had to be the killers who murdered Admiral Grant and Billy. When Liz took off to Washington, they were probably assigned to stake him out. It was the only way they could have moved in so quickly.

Tim felt a slam of fiery pain. Four bullets, two from each man, ripped into his chest. The ground receded. His last thought was flight. He was in the air, flinging backward! Unable to release a sound from his throat.

———

Liz and Diane heard loud popping and crackling noises of Tim's phone clattering across the floor. They knew at once what was happening. Static exploding out of the speaker—the phone being destroyed—coincided with a roar!

A helicopter thundered in low between stormed out buildings. *Zap!* Blazing cones from its three searchlights converged and exposed the rental truck.

"Shit!" exclaimed Liz.

Diane dropped the phone. Her suspicions flooded back. Her editor dies within moments of Liz getting him on the phone. Yet another victim. "Oh, spare me the surprise."

"Don't start," snapped Liz. "We are completely on our own now and we have to get to the White House!"

It became a shouting match.

"We can't go there any more!"

"Avery's our only hope!"

"Every gun and badge will be waiting for us!"

"We just have to find a way in!"

"How? There's a wall of marines guarding the compound!"

"They crossed 19th Street," reported the LAPD pilot, cross-checking visual with his GPS. "They are a just a few blocks from the White House."

"Sound an alert," said Andrew.

The pilot clicked over to the open frequency, "All units! All units!"

In his luxury helicopter, John Ulysses VI, picked up the APB. He raised the commander on the ground encircling the White House. The three-star general owed the life of his son, who had a rare form eye cancer, to the Ulysses, who flew the family from DC to Los Angeles every month for treatment. "Sullivan, this is John. I'm flying into the White House on classified business. Clear me to land on the South Lawn."

Around the rental truck, sirens quickly gathered in loudness and numbers. Diane listened to Liz's plan and said, "For that to work, we need to lose the chopper."

Liz threw her weight behind a sudden turn. Diane's side of the truck lifted off the ground. The chopper and its searchlights continued straight ahead. Liz executed the two-wheel turn left onto 18th Street. A riot of flashing red, white, and blue appeared in the distance. Approached fast!

"Turn, turn!" said Diane desperately.

Liz skidded the truck onto H Street. Roared past 17th. More lightbands appeared in the distance, both in front and behind them. Liz cranked the wheel again.

Rocked the truck into Lafayette Park.

"There it is!" Diane pointed ahead.

The White House.

Their sanctuary. If they could get to it.

Even if they did, how are we going to penetrate the teeth of the military deployment? Liz was counting on everyone looking up and down the streets for the truck. *Will they?*

Sirens, by their sheer numbers, got to deafening decibels as squad cars poured in from all sides in a spectacular rush of flashing lights. So nobody heard or saw the dark truck roar across the famous park, torn up by Meg and cleared in her aftermath to situate tents and toilets for the marines around the mansion. Liz bisected the walkways without touching a single temp structure.

She looked at Diane, "Ready!"

Diane clutched the door handle and nodded. "Let's do it!"

The truck came out of nowhere and plunged across the closed-to-traffic portion of Pennsylvania Ave NW! The chopper lit it up as it did. The marines turned and saw the truck smash over the mangled iron fence around the White House that Meg had flattened.

"They are going to crash the North Portico!" hollered the LAPD pilot over open channel.

Every radio around the White House picked up his warning. Marines, EPB officers, and secret service agents abandoned their posts. The pursuing squad cars pulled up hard and cops leapt out. As one, uniforms broke into a run toward the White House, guns blazing.

Bullets riddled the truck! It did not stop. Plowed across

the North Lawn.

Crash! The rental truck slammed through the scaffolding, noisily bringing down yards of tubing, work platforms, everything! *Whabam!* It pummeled into the Library window beside the North Portico. Stopped cold by the stone masonry in a blinding storm of dust!

The reverberations reached the president's apartment. Avery awoke sharply. His eyes darted. He heard voices. Loud. Urgent. Overlapping. The ghosts of the dead storming the White House! It was a nightmare he'd had before. Avery stayed under the covers, muttering furiously, "God, please forgive me. What's done is done, what's done is done."

The voices belonged to the marines, EPB officers, SSA, and cops swarming forward. The flashlights over their gun barrels stabbed bright, unsteady cones. They circled in on the truck, yelling at the same time, "You're surrounded! Show your hands! Open the door! Out! Out! Throw out any weapons! Show your hands! Come on out! Get out! Now!"

The rental truck was empty.

Andrew knew it would be. That's why he did not follow the crazy circus. He angled the Humvee away from the pursuing commotion. He drove past the tanks, whose turrets, without exception, were pointed toward the North Portico. A helicopter appeared out of the circling Blackhawks and put down on the South Lawn. He dismissed it as part of the chaotic response. His Humvee looked like another military vehicle in a mob of many racing across the grounds toward the unidentified truck.

Sure enough, behind and away from the converging army of uniforms, he saw Diane and Liz sprint toward the East Wing. He knew exactly what they had done. *Clever bitches.* They'd probably jammed a two-by-four—or something like that—into gas pedal, stuck it to the floor, then leapt out just before the truck left Lafayette Park and crossed Pennsylvania Ave onto the North Lawn.

The misdirection worked to perfection.

"They are on foot," Andrew said calmly into the MILSATCOM, "headed for the East Wing."

In the Situation Room, Baron looked at Jack. "You have your sidearm with you?"

Jack nodded.

"Go!" Jack rose to his feet. Baron opened his briefcase, removed the 9mm Browning automatic inside, and slid it toward Peter. "Back up the general."

Jack's eyes glinted, angry and insulted. "I'm a decorated Ranger, Baron. I know how to hunt and kill."

Baron ignored the Joint Chiefs Chairman. Jack turned on his heel, unholstering his military issue. Behind his back, Baron exchanged a conspiratorial nod with Peter, who followed Jack. Baron waited for the door to the Situation Room to close behind the two men. He waited a few seconds, then walked over and locked the door.

Everyone was converging in the main residence. He allowed himself a smile. *Perfect.*

Returning to the horseshoe, Baron picked up the intercom and tapped the button marked, 'SSA'—Secret Service Agents—and said urgently, "Armed intruders in the Residence! Armed intruders in the Residence! Shoot to kill. I repeat, shoot to kill."

The defense secretary's voice crackled into the earpieces of Agent Connor and the secret service agents around the rental truck. Agent Connor took charge. "Let's break up into two forces! SSA, inside! EPB and DCPD, outside! Military, secure the fence! Let's go!"

The secret service agents followed Connor into the Entrance Hall, weaving between scaffolding, timber, cement sacks, and other construction materials. He grabbed a young agent. "Charlie. The president's in his apartment. Go upstairs. Guard the door."

Charlie veered off. Raced upstairs.

———

Diane and Liz burst into the East Wing. Added in 1942 to conceal the construction of the underground Presidential Emergency Operations Center, it became known for hosting the offices of the First Lady. Under Avery, it served as the White House Social Office. Meg had marched through, opening huge holes in the walls and the roof by turning the heavy, ornate furniture into sledgehammers.

Between huge gulps of air, Liz whispered fiercely. "Give me the Jayspid."

Diane looked flustered. Confused. "Why?"

Liz didn't answer. She was a natural survivor but Diane was a liability. Naïve. Completely out of her league. Chances were Diane would get herself killed sooner than later. So, Liz needed that Jayspid. Diane had been right. If Liz couldn't break the story, she was going to cross back over and buy her way out of this alive. Liz decided to intimidate the meteorologist and angrily bore down, "Just trust me for once, will you?"

Headlights blazed through!

Liz whirled. Andrew advanced in his Humvee. Liz turned back and barked, "Give me the Jays—"

Diane was gone.

Liz's darted her eyes around, whispering, "Diane?" She retreated quickly. Clenched her teeth. Furious. "Diane!"

Liz passed through the gaping frame that opened into the gallery connecting the East Wing to the main Residence. Meg had broken every one of the large windows along the gallery, emptying the debris on the Jacqueline Kennedy Garden, which now looked like a landfill. Reconstruction crews had propped up the roof where it leaned precariously.

Liz saw a silhouette solidify and disappear in the

darkness ahead. *Diane.* Liz took off in pursuit

Andrew did not pull up. He drove alongside the gallery. His headlights bounced erratically over the grounds furrowed by Meg's claws, illuminating Diane running behind pillars. Liz was several yards behind. Chasing. *What the hell?*

Peter spotted Diane at the loosely hanging ceremonial doors in a momentary wash of light that spilled onto her when Andrew's Humvee slewed to a stop. Peter was following Jack off the main steps and yelled, "There's one of them!"

Peter and Jack both fired, but Diane was already diving out of sight. The shots echoed and served to energize Connor and the agents. Peter heard Connor shout, "There they are! I count two."

"Agent Connor," said Baron, throwing the SSA switch. "I'm in SSA ears only. That's them. One in a suit, one in fatigues."

Peter and Jack.

Baron had dispatched the two men, intending them to die. Thunder Strike worked and could be replicated. The prudent next step was to mothball it for now and leave no trace it even existed. The decision to kill Jack was easy. The general was unraveling. As for Peter, lately Baron had been getting an unsettling vibe that the master of deceit was beginning to figure out the dark shadows. That could never happen, even if Peter was brilliant. But nobody was indispensable. Not even Peter.

Peter and Jack walked into a slash of moonlight. Connor and the agents opened fire together in a near continuous staccato of gun blasts. Jack and Peter, caught by surprise, hit the floor.

"Hold your fire!" Jack shouted. "Hold your fire!"

His voice did not register above the berserk guns.

————

The explosion of gunfire carried as a series of surreal echoes to the president's bedroom. Avery squeezed his eyes shut and rocked under the sheets, chanting, "What's done is done. What's done is done."

————

Diane cowered. Hands over her ears. Terrified! Shaking with fear. Meg had taken down the grand chandelier and stripped it of most of the expensive crystals. Restoration crews had swept what they could find into a box in the corner. Moonlight, sparkling off multifaceted surfaces, suddenly darkened.

The shadow of a man crossed simultaneously on the scores of angled glass faces.

The assassin.

He was just around the corner.

Diane clutched her satchel, trembling. Then, swung it with all her strength! Distracted by the violent and deafening gunfire, Andrew never saw the blow coming. The heavy Jayspid in the satchel cracked into his bad knee. He grunted loudly and sprawled. Diane swung again. This time catching the back of his head as he fell. Andrew went down, losing his gun.

Diane fled.

————

Andrew recovered quickly. He couldn't find his weapon and didn't waste time looking for it. He reached down and removed a small caliber gun out of his ankle holster.

————

The gunfire continued ceaselessly. Flashlights intersected in the raucous darkness of crisscrossing bullets. Liz charged in from the East Wing gallery. Braked. Pressed herself against the wall. They must have Diane! She inched into a corner and found herself with a unique vantage of Jack and Peter. She recognized the JCS Chairman. *They're the targets. Holy shit!*

Peter and Jack saw her at the same time.

Peter pointed and shouted, "That's her!"

Peter fired. Jack pulled the trigger a moment later. Liz reacted out of reflex. Dropped to the floor. EPB officers and cops, responding to the sound of shots, raced in firing nonstop.

Liz crawled away, her mind racing. This was more than a cover-up. It was a complete erasure and total obliteration of everyone and everything associated with Thunder Strike.

A burial without a memorial service.

Peter and Jack and didn't stand a chance, scissored and shredded in the explosive crossfire! Jack twisted, bullets tearing into his chest and back.

"Stop shooting! Stop shooting!" Peter screamed. He took multiple volleys that punched him forward. He fell to the floor. Remained alive. Even had the strength to crawl through the doorway of the Library, where he collapsed and died.

Right at Diane's feet.

Diane shrieked! Recoiled! Scurried away in first reflex. Then she froze and looked back at Peter's body, focusing her eyes on the green White House pass hanging around his neck. She'd noticed that only the secret service agents wore it and deciphered it must allow unlimited access through out the White House because the uniformed EPB had orange badges, limiting where they could go. Diane tightened her jaw distastefully as she lifted and eased the strap off Peter's lifeless head. She got some of his blood on her hands and quickly wiped it off.

Footsteps pounded toward her. Agents converging. Diane raced up the stairs.

Agent Connor and an EPB Officer came together from opposite sides around Jack's body and blanched simultaneously.

"This is the Chairman!" exclaimed Connor. "Hold your fire!"

"Hold your fire!" echoed the EPB officer into his radio. "Hold your fire! Hold your fire!"

The order echoed down the line.

Gunfire abated rapidly.

"Sir," Agent Connor reported to Baron in the Situation Room, "The Chairman and Mr. Wilkins went down in friendly fire. I'm so sorry."

The radio remained silent for a long time. Finally, Baron responded. His voice was without accusation or outrage. "It happens."

A class act, thought Connor. Remarkable man, the defense secretary. Never blew his top. A true leader who understood sometimes it's not perfect or pretty.

"So the intruders are still at large," said Baron. "Keep looking."

———

Diane turned the corner and saw a young secret service agent pacing in a tight circle, head bowed, intently listening to the chaotic chatter in his earpiece. Even as a teen, Diane had lacked the nerve to fake her way into a club. She'd waited till she was twenty-one before buying her first drink. Yet now, she was going to risk arrest, and likely her life, trying to bluff her way in.

She kept the Jayspid but dumped satchel because it looked tattered. Posturing the bulky binder officiously at the end of her arm, she took a deep breath, mustered every ounce of courage inside her, and hurried forward. Feigning breathlessness. She needed to justify why she looked such a mess. The agent turned, his weapon ready.

"Hi," panted Diane, read his name off the badge. "Charles? The agents downstairs told me I'd be safe up here."

"And you are?" he asked sternly, looking at her badge. Diane had turned it around, but the 'all access' green showed around the edges.

"Sabrina Worth? The president's speechwriter."

"Sorry, ma'am," he said flatly. "Never seen you."

"I was working late in the West Wing when all the shooting began." She pointed to her dusty clothes and scrapes. "I had to crawl out of my office and I barely got out. "

Charlie stared at her inscrutably. With a staff of fifty in the West Wing alone, Diane was counting on the fact that the agent did not know Sabrina well enough to recognize her.

"I don't remember you being here during Meg." He had sat out the storm in the Situation Room with the president, his aides, and other agents.

"I evacuated to New York. The president called me back this morning." Diane stared, trying desperately not to give herself away. He wasn't buying. "They told me to come up, stay out of the way, and sit with the president. You know, I'm also his niece, right?"

Hearing that, Charlie relaxed instantly. It made sense Agent Connor would send his niece up. Charlie stepped aside, nodded her through.

Diane hurried into West Sitting Hall.

———

"Everyone!" Charlie's earpiece crackled with Agent Connor's voice. "The intruders are still at large." He turned his head around and watched Diane close the door behind her. Nodded to himself. Satisfied the president and his niece were safe.

His head never returned forward.

Snap! Two strong hands grabbed and twisted it another ten degrees. Too far for his spine to hold. *Crack!* Charlie felt white hot knifing agony, hearing only the first break at the neck and then fading instantly.

———

The agent dropped like stone. Eyes wide open, a snapshot of momentary shock and pain. Andrew stepped over his body and proceeded unhurriedly forward. He glanced cursorily into the Yellow Oval Room that opened into the Truman Balcony over the South Portico. He crossed the hall. The East and West bedrooms turned up empty too.

————

Avery's eyes snapped open when he heard Diane's voice. Plaintive. Whispered. Ghostly. "Mr. President? Mr. President?"

Soft footsteps approached. He got out of bed like he always did—with darting, scared, and guilty eyes. A shadow, almost demonlike, lengthened into the doorway.

"Nooo!" gasped Avery.

Diane showed herself into the edge of the moonlight.

Avery figured she was another angry apparition and begged, "I'm sorry. Please forgive me."

"Mr. President. My name is Diane Wood."

Avery bumped his hip against the sink. Still afraid. He went from a whisper to a soft plea, "What do you want?

Diane took a small step forward. "Admiral Grant was going to speak with you, sir."

Avery blinked, his fears quelled by the mention of his friend's name. "Admiral Grant? But he's dead."

"Yes, sir. He was murdered for this." Diane raised the Jayspid.

Avery recognized it. "Thunder Strike?"

————

Andrew advanced with measured and soundless steps. As he passed a doorway on his left, he heard voices strengthen sharply. He paused. Entered stealthily. It opened into a hallway that widened into a Private Sitting Room. At the far end of the wall, he saw the rectangular blackness of another doorway. Andrew approached it quietly, quickly. He stood at the edge of the door, raised his gun against his face, muzzle facing up. He assumed he was outside a second exit from the president's bedroom.

"Don't worry," he heard Avery say. "You are safe with me."

————

Avery listened to Diane's quick thumbnail of what she'd been through. Anger made him forget his nighttime fears. His voice crackled with a resolve he hadn't felt in days, "Just give me a minute."

Diane stepped away from the bathroom into the hallway. Avery cupped his hands and dipped them into the clear glass bowl. He splashed water to his face. Wiped down with his palm. He flicked his tongue over his lips and reached for the hand towel to dry himself.

Suddenly!

A searing pain started in his belly, scorched through his heart, and tore into his brain

"Ahhh!" Avery gasped with a cry and went into massive convulsions.

Diane straightened sharply. "Mr. President!"

The agony would not cease. It reached his eyes and blinded him! He screamed.

"Sir! Are you all right?" Diane rushed forward.

Avery opened his mouth to speak. As he did so, he felt his stomach turn and erupt. His neck snapped his head forward. His hip jerked. Everything in his guts shot out of both ends. He vomited and excreted violently and without any self control.

Diane gasped, "Oh, my god! Mr. President!"

Avery's hand swatted around powerfully just as she reached the bathroom door. *Crash!* He knocked the glass bowl off the sink. Diane covered her mouth horrified, scared, and disgusted, all at the same time. Now, blood gushed out with the vomit and feces. Avery fell to the floor. With a final spasm that ejected a stream of foamy snot from his nostrils, he went still.

––––––

Andrew peered in. Avery's eyes glassed up. The president was dead. A student of death and killing, he recognized the symptoms. Nicotine. Virtually undetectable and extremely toxic. He guessed the water in the bowl had been laced with it.

The murderer had to be familiar with the president's habits and also needed to physically visit the bathroom. Only one man had such intimate knowledge and extraordinary access.

Defense Secretary Baron Hawke.

Andrew filled the doorway.

Diane retreated, her back to him. She muttered, "Oh, god, oh god, oh no."

She stopped yard in front of Andrew, oblivious that he was behind her. She turned to flee, saw him and pulled up dead in her tracks.

"It's over, Diane."

"The president!" she blurted. "He's dead!"

"Pity," said Andrew and squeezed the trigger.

———

Without warning! Liz filled the doorway from the West Sitting Hall. She'd plucked the gun out of the secret service agent Andrew had killed. Then she'd crept forward and heard the president's agony. On her way up, she realized Thunder Strike was bigger than the President. The only way to survive this and remain alive was to possess the Jayspid.

As quick as Liz was, Andrew was faster.

Boom!Boom!Boom!Boom!Boom!Boom!

Both their guns exploded with the loudness of bombs in the confined space.

———

Diane couldn't think, let alone move. *So, this is how it feels to die. Why am I not in pain? I feel nothing at all.*

It took Diane a moment, then she realized she was…

The last one standing.

I'm still alive!

Liz and the assassin were crumpling to the floor, riddled.

Diane continued to stand still. Frozen in a surreal state of fear and relief. Even as her brain tried to cope with the maelstrom of witnessing violent deaths over the span of less than a minute, nagging questions sought clarity. Did two killers accidentally eliminate each other? Or, was the assassin going to kill them all? Liz was armed. It made sense for the assassin to kill Liz first, then turn the gun on Diane. Could it be that Liz planned to just save herself and the Jayspid?

Or, did Liz die protecting me?

Diane realized she would never know.

———

Agent Connor was in the State Level, one floor below, emerging from the Chief Usher's office. The private stairway, which Baron had used earlier to visit Avery, coiled up all six floors of the White House. The shots rang down. He barked into his cuff mike, "Charlie! What's going on?" No answer. "Charlie! Come in!" Nothing. "Everyone! Shots fired in the president's quarters! Go, go, go!"

Agents, EPB officers, and cops crammed the stairs.

———

Diane looked left! Right! Around! There was no escape. She darted across the Family Kitchen. Saw an open dumbwaiter. Scrunched in. She hoped she had time to go down one floor. Punched the button. The dumbwaiter whined. Then she heard pounding footsteps. The car lowered noisily.

It's loud! They'll hear me.

Diane could hardly breathe. Her chest tightened. Tense. Terrified. She was trapped.

———

Agent Connor took the steps two at a time, leading about ten armed men. More bounded up the main stairs. He reached the top of the steps. SSA, EPB, and cops pounded out of the main stairwell through the Center Hall, overwhelming the whine of the dumbwaiter, which was two feet away from stopping. Agent Connor blasted through the doorway. The others converged at the entrance to the West Sitting Hall.

"Wait!" said Agent Connor.

The stampede froze.

———

At that same moment, so did the dumbwaiter. It was on the State Floor. Diane slid open the door. Crawled out. She burst into the Center Hall on the State Floor. She immediately recognized it as the scene of that wild and crazy shootout. Jack's body remained where he'd died.

———

"That's the president's bedroom," said Agent Connor. Protocol mandated access to no one but his personal protection detail. "Let me go in first!"

"Mr. President!" he called out, entering the West Sitting Room. "Mr. President!"

Agent Connor stepped into the West Sitting Room. Saw Liz's body in the bedroom doorway. He rushed forward, his eyes racing inside. At the far end was Andrew's body. He stopped dead in his tracks when he reached the bathroom door, gagging. "Holy mother Mary."

Avery lay in a pool of blood, piss, vomit, and shit.

He barked into his cuff mike. "We have bodies!"

———

The loudness of his excited voice came over the speaker of the Situation Room intercom distorted and enveloped in static. Baron listened. Cold. Emotionless. Calm. He asked, "How many and who?"

"Sir, the president! He's dead! And we got two more unidentified bodies."

"Describe them."

"One male, middle-aged, one female, twenties, blonde."

Andrew and Liz. "Seal the White House," said Baron and quickly stood up. "Nobody without an ID tag enters or leaves. We are looking for another woman. Dark hair. Similar build."

How could Diane have escaped the President's quarters?

He slapped the table. Opened the radio again, "The dumbwaiter."

Following the discovery of Avery's breakdown, Baron

made the president's quarters out of bounds for everyone except the secret service. To avoid the kitchen staff walking in on an 'episode,' he'd ordered all meals be delivered via the dumbwaiter. Since the president did not want to enjoy electricity beyond the West Wing before other DC residents, Baron told Avery it would greatly help the short handed domestic staff if the dumbwaiter was restored. Avery agreed. It was the only working appliance with power in the residential wing.

"It's on the main level, sir," reported Connor.

———

Diane exited the Center Hall and found herself in the open colonnade that led to the West Wing. She started across the lawn briskly. Suddenly headlights and flashlights came alive amongst the marines guarding the perimeter. More commotion erupted behind her in the main residence.

Oh, no.

She turned and ran blindly into the West Wing. A maze of cubicles and offices were interlocked around short, narrow, and dark hallways that started and ended abruptly. Night lights plugged into outlets emitted a fog of yellow gloom. Several partitions still lay on the floor. Damaged desks were shoved to the corner to make room for the scaffolding and material belonging to the construction and restoration crews. Diane quickly became lost and disoriented.

The carpet was damp and her feet squelched loudly. She walked on tiptoes to minimize the sound. Yet another hallway. Ahead, it turned in an 'L.'

She approached a blind corner.

———

With the marines on alert outside, the SSA and the EPB and the cops closing off the north, south and east exits, Diane was trapped in the West Wing somewhere. She had no escape. Like generations of Hawkes before him, Baron knew the West Wing well. He'd find her sooner rather than later. He strode powerfully between the half-rebuilt cubicles, making no attempt to mask his wet footfalls.

————

Diane heard his squelching shoes but couldn't figure out the direction they were coming from. She stood still, looking back and forth, scared to make the wrong move and be captured.The footsteps advanced. Loud. Close!

There was nothing she could do but guess. She ducked into the doorway with the brass plaque engraved: *Roosevelt Room.* Meg had stripped it of everything memorable. Diane scurried out the door at the far end and found herself in the West Wing lobby, now stacked with document-laden boxes that the staff was beginning to reorganize. She couldn't hear Baron's shoes anymore. Her eyes and attention focused down the hallway ahead.

A threadbare doorway stood at the end it. Framed in it was the welcome sight of the grounds outside. She barely took a step forward, when a voice, soft and firm, stopped her. "Dr. Wood?"

Diane stopped in her tracks and turned fearfully.

The outline of a man formed but never emerged out of the shadows. "You have something I need."

"You have to kill me for it," said Diane, defiantly tightening her fingers around the Jayspid."

"Don't be foolish. Haven't enough people died already? Please. Hand it over."

"I have lost everything, everyone," said Diane, making no move to obey. "I have nothing to live for."

"Yes, you do. The job at the National Hurricane Center is yours if you want it."

Diane's eyes widened in surprise. "How do you know?"

"There is nothing I don't know about you. Please hand it over and nobody will come after you. I promise."

"I don't believe you."

"You have my word." There was something about the way he said it. "Just lay it down."

After a long moment, she laid the Jayspid down.

"Turn around and walk out into the South Lawn. A helicopter is waiting. You will be taken to Dulles, where a chartered flight will take you to New York. Liz has already paid for it."

"How did you know that?"

The man went on without answering. "The pilot's name is Savage. He knows you will be taking her place. When you arrive in New York, another private jet will fly you to Miami. All I ask of you have is to forget—forget Thunder Strike even existed. If you change your mind, be warned you will never be able to prove it ever did."

Diane's jaw clenched angrily.

"I know. You lost friends. I'm sorry. But that's how it has to be. Will be."

Her shoulders drooped. She knew he was right.

"Good night and good luck."

Diane turned around and left.

———

Baron entered the Oval Office. He circled the president's makeshift desk with a smile curling up the corners of his lips. He caressed the chair. Swiveled it around. About to sit down.

A voice he recognized well spoke up from a dark corner, "We never take the oath of this office."

Baron straightened sharply without sitting down.

John Ulysses VI stepped out of the dark shadows.

Baron smiled. "The rules are about to change, John."

Absolute power absolutely.

"No, Baron."

John raised the Jayspid. Baron's eyes went still.

THE END